Kensington books by Annie Rains

Through the Snow Globe

The Charmed Friends of Trove Isle

Summer in a Bottle

Summer in a Bottle

ANNIE RAINS

KENSINGTON
PUBLISHING CORP.

kensingtonbooks.com

KENSINGTON BOOKS are published by

Kensington Publishing Corp.
900 Third Avenue
New York, NY 10022

ISBN: 978-1-4967-4090-8 (ebook)

ISBN: 978-1-4967-4089-2

First Kensington Trade Paperback Printing: May 2025

10 9 8 7 6 5 4 3 2 1

Printed in the United States of America

The authorized representative in the EU for product safety and compliance is eucomply OU, Parnu mnt 139b-14, Apt 123 Tallinn, Berlin 11317, hello@eucompliancepartner.com

To one of my favorite elementary teachers, Cathie Batchelor. Thank you for watering the seeds of storytelling in my young mind. As the quiet kid in the back of the class, having one person believe and notice me was enough to nurture a lifelong passion.

To all the teachers who pour into their students; you are heroes.

Chapter 1

Opinion: When your parents are having more fun
than you, it's time to start rethinking your life.
—Delilah Dune, opinion writer

Lyla Dune turned in to her parents' driveway and parked, her gaze moving to the FOR SALE sign on the front lawn. A mixture of emotions rose inside her as she stepped out of her car and headed toward her childhood home, which soon would belong to some other family.

When her parents had broken the news that they were selling their house a couple of weeks before, Lyla had been in the throes of two different deadlines. She hadn't had time to process what they were asking her to do. They were finally going to take the trip around the world that they'd been dreaming of forever, and they wanted to get started ASAP.

"You work remotely, right?" her mom had asked. "That means you can work from anywhere?"

"Mm-hmm." Lyla had a copywriting job that was flexible about where and when she worked. She was also the featured writer for "Delilah's Delusions," a nationally popular opinion column. In fact, she was kind of a household name, even though few knew Lyla Dune was the brains behind the name.

Combined, both jobs paid the bills, but they didn't feed her creativity, which lately seemed to be funneling out of her like sand into the lower portion of an hourglass. "I can work anywhere and anytime. Why do you ask?"

"Well . . ." Her mom fumbled over a few unintelligible sounds. "It's just . . . your father and I would like to leave for our trip a little earlier than planned. We were wondering . . ." There was another long silence on the other end of the line.

Lyla envisioned her mom wringing her hands the way she did when she got nervous. What was her mom anxious about? "Just spit it out, Mom."

"Okay." Her mom sucked in an audible breath. "Your father and I were hoping—wondering—do you think you could stay at the house until it sells? There are still boxes that need to be donated, and we thought we'd let you pack up your old room. I didn't want to throw out anything that was special to you."

Lyla found that statement laughable. At one point in her life, she'd considered herself a sentimental person. Her parents used to teasingly call her a hoarder. Not anymore. Over the last decade, she'd focused on success, relishing her status as a well-known writer, even though she wasn't the best-selling author of novels that she'd once dreamed of being.

"Me? You want me to stay at the house?" Lyla had been stunned by her mother's request. First off, her parents never asked her for favors—ever. Her parents were working-class people who had penny-pinched and saved all of Lyla's childhood just to ensure she was able to attend college the way they hadn't been. Unlike a lot of her friends, Lyla hadn't taken out school loans and worked nightshifts in order to pay tuition and rent, even though she'd offered to. In her parents' minds, they took care of her, not vice versa. That was still the case even now.

Second, Lyla's parents never trusted her for important things—not since she had clogged the bathroom sink with blue hair gel and flooded the whole downstairs when she was eighteen. Maybe, the fact that they were making such a monumental request meant they now saw her, at thirty years of age, as a responsible adult.

"If it's too much to ask, just say so," her mom went on. This was how her mom operated. On the rare occasion she did ask for a favor, her mother immediately started talking a person out of agreeing. "Your father and I can just wait until we find a buyer. It's not a big deal."

"I'll do it," Lyla said, not letting her mom walk back the request.

"You will?"

"Of course. If I can help make your and dad's dreams come true any faster, my answer is yes." In fact, her mother's request was kind of a godsend. Lyla's lease on her apartment in Bloomberg was finally up, and she was about to be homeless. She'd dragged her feet in locating a new place to live because she wasn't sure if she wanted to stay in the town where she'd spent the last several years with her ex. Bloomberg was Joe's town, and now that they had broken up, maybe Lyla wanted to break up with Bloomberg as well.

Also, signing a lease was a financial commitment, and her nationally famous opinion column was tanking these days. When she'd last spoken with Bob, her editor, his exact words had been: *No one cares what Delilah has to say these days. Find something fresh or we'll find a younger, wittier Delilah with more controversial opinions.*

Lyla knew Bob was just that heartless. He'd have no problem finding a new voice for "Delilah's Delusions," even though Lyla was Delilah. She was just one blasé opinion away from losing the job that paid a majority of her bills.

Shaking away her worries about the future, Lyla's mind filled with new concerns as she headed up her parents' porch steps. *What am I getting myself into?* Packing up and selling this house was a big job that she didn't have the time or the experience to do on her own. What if she messed up? What if no one put in an offer? What if . . . ?

A dog's bark got her attention. All her senses suddenly went on alert. When she was growing up, the neighbor had a little Yorkshire terrier who was half devil-dog, half diary with four legs. When he wasn't chasing Lyla on her bike, he was finding her on the front porch when she needed someone to talk to. There were a lot of secrets she had confided to Sonny during tear-filled moments. That little dog had taken those secrets to his grave, however, the last summer Lyla was in Echo Cove. God rest his tiny terrorizing, salty-tear-licking soul.

Lyla spun in a circle looking for a dog who might be lurking in the bushes, but all she saw was flowers and trees, vibrant with color after a mild spring that had transitioned into a typical Echo Cove summer. Hot, but also breezy, which meant sunburns snuck up on you like the possibility of that dog out there in the azalea bushes.

Turning her focus back to the house, Lyla noticed that the front porch was bare. No wreath on the door. No wooden rocking chairs and no welcome mat—*Uh-oh.* That's where her parents had told her to look for the key to get inside the house. There was nothing there, though, not even an old flower pot. Pulling out her phone, she tapped out a text.

Lyla: *Hey, Mom! Where's the key to get in?*

After waiting a long moment, she remembered her parents' itinerary. Her parents were on a flight to Florida right now. They wouldn't respond before she melted in this sweltering heat.

Surely, they'd placed the key somewhere, she thought, as her gaze ping-ponged along the porch railing. There was nothing. "Guess I'll be breaking in," she mumbled, descending the steps and heading around to the back fence.

Woof!

Lyla's body tensed and prepared to run. Then she spotted

the gray-and-brown ball of fluff, and for a moment, her heart burst with this unexpected joy. "Sonny?"

The little dog padded up to her and barked again, his tail wagging like a windshield wiper on high speed. Kneeling, she held out her hand for the little dog to sniff, her mind catching up to the present moment. Of course this wasn't her neighbor's little Yorkie. Sonny had tragically met his fate that last summer before Lyla had gone off to college. He'd gone out a hero, though, saving a teenage boy who was only one year younger than Lyla and who was now Echo Cove's mayor. "You look just like him," Lyla whispered as the dog sniffed her fingers and then backed away with another bark. He kept his eye on her as she returned to a standing position and continued through the back fence. When her back was turned, she half expected the little dog to pounce, but instead, he disappeared, no doubt realizing she wasn't a threat.

Good, because fighting off a dog while breaking in to her parents' home was a recipe for disaster. It wouldn't be the first time she'd broken into this house. She'd been locked out her last summer here when she was supposed to be housewatching while her parents took their first vacation in ages. And then her father ate eel sushi rolls that had spoiled along about the same time Lyla accidentally spilled blue hair gel down the bathroom drain, clogging the pipes and flooding the downstairs. That last summer in Echo Cove had been one low, then lower low. Everything that could have possibly gone wrong had.

Lyla headed over to the kitchen window where the latch had broken the last time she'd forced her way into this house. Hopefully, her father never fixed it. Securing her fingers under the lip of the window, she grunted as she pushed the window up. It wasn't as easy as she would have thought. She tried again and this time the window budged in an upward direction.

When it was three quarters of the way open, Lyla looked

around for something to stand on. Nothing. Then she attempted to pull herself up. Not happening in this lifetime. Giving herself a running start, she ran and leapt toward the window's opening. This was where her overactive imagination sometimes failed her. She wasn't a flying ninja—far from it.

"Excuse me!" a tinny voice called out.

Lyla let go of the window and whirled to face an older woman who was standing just inside the fence.

The woman had long, white hair and light green eyes. She pointed a knobby finger in Lyla's direction. "Neighborhood watch! You stop right there, missy! I want you to know I've called the *po*-lice and they'll be here in a flat second."

Opinion: If someone overpronounces the PO in police, they're probably on a do-not-respond list somewhere.

Lyla held up her hands. "This isn't how it looks."

"Looks like you're breaking into my neighbor's house. Just because it has a FOR SALE sign out front doesn't mean it's open for looters to go snooping and stealing."

Lyla realized she knew this woman. "Ms. Hadley?" Ms. Hadley was her parents' neighbor who'd been living next door since Lyla was born. She was the owner of the little Yorkie who Lyla had just been remembering. Ms. Hadley must have gotten a new dog to keep her company. "Hi, Ms. Hadley. It's me, Lyla. This is my house. Or it was."

Ms. Hadley slowly lowered her finger, but she didn't look any less threatening. "Oh, no. Please tell me you're not taking over the place."

Nice to see you too. "No. I'm helping my parents sell, actually."

Ms. Hadley looked skeptical.

"So you can just call off the police," Lyla said, pronouncing that last word the correct way. "Everything's fine."

Ms. Hadley fluttered a hand on the air. "Oh, they aren't coming anyway. They stopped responding to me a long time ago. Said I made too many baseless reports."

Lyla never thought she'd miss this crotchety grouch of a woman, but she had. Everyone needed a crotchety grouch in their life to make them feel better about their own outlook.

"The key to the house is under the mat, you moron."

Moron. Lovely. Anywhere beyond Echo Cove, Lyla was a household name. Granted, most people in the country didn't know who the real person behind "Delilah's Delusions" was, despite the opinion column being featured on *Good Morning, America* and mentioned in just about every notable magazine over the years. "Delilah's Delusions" was even used as a satire in a *Saturday Night Live* episode once.

Across the country, Lyla was just the faceless wizard behind the curtain—the one who wrote the words that weren't even her true opinions these days. Here in her hometown, though, the curtain was down. She wasn't witty or thoughtful, controversial or anything that attracted national attention. Instead, she was that strange girl who only seemed to have one friend, an even stranger boy who was the preacher's son. Lyla had been his accomplice for dozens of childish pranks that said preacher had used as the hook for many a Sunday sermon.

Ms. Hadley pointed at the rectangular black mat in front of Lyla's parents' back door. "Even an amateur crook would try the mat before busting through the window."

Lyla followed the direction of where Ms. Hadley had pointed and sure enough, there was the welcome mat. "Thank you! Good to see you, Ms. Hadley!" She turned back to her neighbor, but the old woman was already back in her own yard.

Lyla lifted the mat and picked up the silver-toned key, grateful because she hadn't wanted to get stuck in that kitchen window. She didn't know anyone in Echo Cove anymore. She would have had to call the *po*-lice and convince them she belonged here when she herself wasn't even sure that was true. The door opened freely as she slid the key into the lock and turned. The smell inside the house hit her first. Lemon zest cleaner. Judging by the overwhelming scent, her mom must have used gallons to clean this place prior to leaving. There was also the pungent smell of fresh paint. The walls were bare and spotless. The granite countertops cleared. "Wow," she uttered under her breath. The room was familiar, but also foreign. This place didn't smell like her mother's cooking or sound like her father's favorite reruns on TV. In a short amount of time, the place that had always been Lyla's home had changed.

Lyla wandered through the bare kitchen and peeked into the living room. It was full of boxes, but nothing else. No television. No couch. No reason to spend any amount of time anywhere other than inside her childhood bedroom.

A sense of dread bubbled up as she headed in that direction. Her mom said she'd left the room for Lyla to pack up, but what if she hadn't? What if Lyla's old room was also a hollowed-out soulless space?

Lyla held her breath as she stepped in front of her open bedroom door. A movie poster for Nicholas Sparks's movie *Message in a Bottle* was still affixed with Scotch tape to the faux wood panels. Back then, Lyla had dreamed of being Nicholas Sparks. The idea of writing books that ripped people's hearts out and handed them back to them in a gooey mess was all she thought about. Writing a book that anyone might read and love was the fuel behind scores of notebooks filled to the brim with handwritten stories.

The room was exactly the way Lyla had left it. It had been a few years since she'd come home. Instead of driving to Echo Cove, her parents had visited her in Bloomberg on weekends and holidays. Lyla's ex, Joe, had thought that best. Joe hadn't wanted to "waste" his vacation time traveling to a small nowhere town. That should have been the first red flag for their relationship.

Why did I stay so long with a man who would consider coming home with me a waste of time?

Deep down, she knew the answer. She'd stayed because she was afraid of never finding someone better. Someone who would love her, flaws and all. There was a time when she'd feared falling in love—because that would keep her from chasing and achieving her dreams. When her writing career took off, however, that fear shifted to never having real love. The kind in romantic comedies, where the guy held a radio and serenaded you outside your bedroom window. The kind in those Nicholas Sparks-esque love stories that she had wanted to write so badly.

With a sigh, she looked around her room and assessed the job ahead. The space was neat, but chock-full of stuff. She'd kept every album from school, every yearbook, every trophy, every memento—it was all here in boxes stacked on top of each other in her closet. She even had her old clothes, which might still fit. Well, maybe the socks.

The bed was still in the middle of the room. Her mom had gotten rid of all the furniture except for what was in Lyla's room. Most grown women had their own furniture by this point. Lyla's furniture, however, was back in Bloomberg, and Joe was sleeping on it. By now, he'd probably moved his collection of old T-shirts into the solid oak dresser she'd picked out. He'd paid for it, so he'd kept it—which meant Lyla would keep her twin-size bed that she'd grown up sleeping on. It beat the air mattress she'd used since the breakup.

Plopping onto her childhood bed, she released another long sigh. Then, without even thinking, she slid her hand along the underside of the mattress until she touched the hard spine of a book. A small squeal erupted as she pulled her old diary to her lap. The cover was decorated in dark blue sequins with three sparkly golden fireflies on its center. She didn't open the diary immediately. Doing so almost felt like an invasion of her younger self's privacy. She and the Lyla of old were strangers these days.

Holding her breath, she lifted the hard cover of the diary, spying the looping cursive handwriting that she had taken such pride in. Before she could even read the first line, the doorbell rang. Who would be visiting? Please don't let it be Ms. Hadley again—or worse, the *po*-lice finally deciding to follow up on one of her neighbor's calls.

She set the diary down and hurried to the front of the house. When she looked through the peephole, all she saw was a blurry image of a female she didn't recognize. The woman was younger than Ms. Hadley, though, with reddish-brown hair.

Lyla opened the door just a crack and peeked out. "Yes?"

"Hi, Lyla!" The woman, who was about Lyla's age, waved excitedly. There was something familiar about her unnatural level of enthusiasm.

Lyla didn't open the door any wider. Hometown or not, she didn't know this person. "Do I know you?"

"You don't remember me?" A giggle tumbled off the woman's lips. Something about the high-pitched sound erupting from the woman's fuchsia-colored lips struck a chord.

"Wait. Allison Wilkerson? You were a cheerleader at our high school."

"Ding-ding-ding!" The woman giggled again. "Good job. Hopefully that means the years have been kind and I look exactly like I did when we got our diplomas."

There was an awkward silence when Lyla didn't immediately agree. It wasn't that the woman looked worse for wear. Just that Lyla was stumped as to why the school's head cheerleader would be standing on her parents' porch. "You look great."

Allison's smile brightened. "Thanks. You too. So can I come in?"

Lyla's internal response was a hard no. All she really wanted to do was lie down and breathe for a moment. Mindless scrolling on her phone sounded like a good idea too, seeing that there was no TV inside the house. "Not to be rude, but why?"

A hint of nervousness played in Allison's expression as the corners of her lips subtly twitched. "Well, your mom told me you were all alone here and that you'd need a friend once you arrived."

Allison wanted to be Lyla's friend? That certainly hadn't been the case in high school. Lyla wasn't even sure Allison had known who she was back then, though their graduating class had been less than a hundred people. "Umm . . ."

"I brought dinner." Allison held up a casserole carrying case. "Made it myself."

"For me?"

"Of course, it's for you, silly. Well, I made it as a favor to your mom. I owe Mama Dune a lot."

Mama Dune? What was happening right now?

Allison bopped back and forth, shifting her weight from one foot to the other. "So can I come in?"

Lyla didn't feel like socializing, but her stomach growled as she considered making an excuse to turn Allison away. "Sure. Come on in."

"This house is so adorbs!" Allison's voice rose an octave on the last word.

Lyla tried not to roll her eyes. She was probably going to have to stomach a lot of annoying verbiage tonight in exchange for a hot meal.

"If I didn't already have my own place, I'd buy this place."

Allison walked through the house, seeming to know the place well. She set the casserole carrying bag on the countertop and looked around. "Bare bones in here, huh?"

Lyla nodded. "Most everything is packed. Somebody is coming to pick up the donations next week."

"Mm." Allison unzipped the casserole bag, revealing a rectangular glass dish. "Hope you like lasagna."

Lyla's spirits lifted. "That's my favorite, actually."

"Your mom told me." Allison let out another high-pitched giggle.

"I've got paper plates and plasticware for us. Is that okay?"

"Sure. Hope you have cups too," Allison said. "Otherwise we'll be drinking straight from the bottle."

Lyla turned back on her way to retrieve the plates. "Bottle?"

Something akin to mischief flashed in Allison's eyes. "I brought wine from The Sippy Cup."

The Sippy Cup was a popular place in town where you could purchase fine wines. At least as fine as Echo Cove could muster.

"You're not sober, are you?" Allison suddenly looked concerned. "Because a woman in your condition really shouldn't be."

"My condition?" Lyla grabbed the plates and placed them on the counter beside Allison. Did Allison think she was pregnant? No, because if Lyla was pregnant, she certainly wouldn't be drinking.

"The newly dumped condition," Allison explained. "You're single. All alone and back at your parents' house." She grimaced, an undeniable look of pity in her eyes.

Lyla's lips parted. "I . . . Well, that's not exactly painting the right picture. I'm not back at my parents' home. I'm here because I'm helping them sell their house. And I'm getting my things."

Allison held up a large spoon that she'd brought with her. She carved out a huge serving and expertly placed it on one of the paper plates. Then she did the same with the next plate. "I've been in your shoes. Two years ago, matter of fact." She took a seat on one of the barstools and grabbed one of the plastic forks that Lyla had set on the counter. "I think that's why your mom chose me to be your guardian angel while you're in Echo Cove."

Lyla took a seat on the second stool to keep from falling over. "From cheerleader to guardian angel," she said sarcastically.

"Pom-poms to wings." Allison spooned some of her lasagna into her mouth. "Mmm. Not to mention chef." She gestured at Lyla's plate. "Taste it already. That pasta is sure to heal whatever ails you."

Lyla seriously doubted that. Sadly, Allison's description of Lyla's current "situation" wasn't too far off. She was newly dumped and technically, yeah, she was back home with her tail between her legs.

"And if my lasagna doesn't heal you," Allison said, "the wine I brought will."

Chapter 2

Opinion: A person without skeletons in their closet is a person who can't be trusted. Under any circumstance.
—Delilah Dune, opinion writer

The world felt too bright the next morning, and a small headache thrummed at Lyla's temples. Had she really gotten drunk with her high school's former head cheerleader last night? What kind of alternate universe had she landed in?

In high school, Lyla hadn't seemed to be on Allison's radar. But for the most part, Lyla was grateful to be invisible to the popular kids at Echo Cove High. And yet, now that they were grown, Allison seemed so approachable. Either Lyla was still under the influence of those bottles of red Cabernet from The Sippy Cup, or she'd actually enjoyed Allison's company.

Weird.

Lyla lifted her head off the pillow and glanced around her bedroom for a moment. The only packing left was still stuffed into this room. This was going to take forever. Not to mention, Lyla had a copyediting job to do as well as an opinion article deadline looming over her head. She should get started right away. But first, coffee.

As Lyla stood, the diary on her nightstand caught her eye. She'd forgotten about finding it. The iridescent fireflies on the cover were made from sequins and glitter. She picked the little journal up, recalling the tiny thrill she'd gotten every time she'd opened it all those years ago. The air had been thick with anticipation that summer. For years, she'd been dreaming of going off to college. One of her biggest fears was getting stuck in Echo Cove like her mother. Her mom had fallen in love with Lyla's dad instead of chasing dreams and had anchored herself to this town. That was why their current trip around the globe was so important.

Lyla didn't want that to happen to her too. For all four years of high school, she'd dreamt of nothing other than which university she'd attend. The farther, the better. Then, in her senior year of high school, when the time finally came to decide where she'd enroll, she was nervous. More than that, she was terrified.

Hugging the diary to her midsection, Lyla headed toward the kitchen, praying there'd be a coffeemaker. If she remembered correctly, the counters had been bare when she came in yesterday. She stepped into the kitchen and her hopes dissipated. The coffee machine was probably packed away in one of the dozens of boxes waiting to be picked up by the local thrift store. She couldn't rip off the packing tape and search through them. Not without making a ton more work for herself. Coffee was a necessity, though. A day without coffee wasn't a day at all.

Hmm, that might make a good opinion piece. Reaching for her phone, she tapped the idea into one of her digital notebooks. After a second, her shoulders rolled forward with a defeated sigh. While most folks were passionate about their morning coffees, they wouldn't be passionate enough to write into "Delilah's Delusions" to defend their stance on its level of priority. If Lyla wanted to save her job, she needed opinions that hooked readers and sparked debate at breakfast tables across the country. Bob's threats were a lot of pressure heaped on top of a recent breakup and an empty house to sell for her parents.

Lyla set her phone on the counter where the diary with sequin fireflies sparkled up from where she'd laid it. Grabbing it, she plopped down on the kitchen floor, leaned against the cabinets, and opened the book to the first page.

June 9

Dear Diary,
Nothing has ever happened to me. I've never traveled anywhere, unless you count our class trip to D.C. last year. I've never won an award or starred in a school play—although I'd much rather write the script.
When I leave for college next month, I feel like my life will finally begin. But what if nothing happens? What if I don't write a bestselling book or experience new and wonderful things? What if I don't meet the love of my life? Or worse, what if I've already met him and he holds me back here in Echo Cove?

Lyla knew exactly what her teenage self was talking about. Travis Painter. The preacher's son and world's greatest prankster. The boy who'd made her question everything she wanted in life when she was eighteen.

Lyla was only two paragraphs in and she was already regretting her decision to read this diary.

Ms. Davis suggested we create a time capsule to commemorate who we are now for our future selves. In case we forget. Or something like that.

Ms. Davis had been Lyla's twelfth-grade language arts teacher. She was always trying to inspire the students in some way or another, most of her ideas and suggestions falling on deaf ears. Except Lyla always listened.

"Time capsule," she whispered, climbing to her feet. She turned toward the window and stared out at the old cypress tree in the backyard. She'd buried her time capsule right beside it. She couldn't sell this house and leave that bottle and all its memories—her memories—buried there.

Now she had two reasons to delay packing up her room this morning. A trip to town was in order. She needed coffee. And a shovel.

Fifteen minutes later, Lyla pulled into the parking lot for Bean Time Coffee, the only coffee shop in town. She paused before entering because she was sure to run into half a dozen people from her past. The only other options were gas station coffee or caffeine withdrawal, though. No thanks.

Opinion: The truest risk-takers are those who ingest anything purchased from a gas station.

Stepping inside the coffee shop, she looked around. Each wall was a different color and showed off eye-catching abstract designs. The lighting was dim, but bright enough for the customers to read their books or newspapers.

Lyla inhaled deeply, already energized just by the store's rich coffee bean aroma.

"Ly-la-lalalaaa? Is that you?" a loud voice asked as soon as Lyla reached the short line in front of the counter.

What were the odds? She'd just been reading about Ms. Davis in her diary and now the much older version of the language arts teacher was standing right in front of her. *Ly-la-lalalaaa.* Ms. Davis was the sum of all things creative.

She wrote poems, painted, and sang opera as a hobby, and Lyla was the only student in class whose name Ms. Davis belted out in full operatic voice whenever she called on her.

Lyla stared back at her former teacher. "Hi, Ms. Davis. Yes, it's me."

The Betty White look-alike shook her head, her white curls bouncing at her ears. "Oh, I'm not Ms. Davis anymore. I'm divorced, and good riddance. Call me Louise. We're both adults, after all."

Lyla guessed the woman in front of her was around seventy years old these days. Time had wrinkled her skin and shrunk her height by a couple inches. "Yes, I guess we are."

The woman beamed. "Thank goodness for that. Hopefully, you've matured as well." She lifted a pale-colored brow. "I always thought you'd make something of yourself if you could just separate yourself from that boyfriend of yours." Before Lyla could contradict her, Louise fluttered a hand. "Oh, I know you two weren't going steady, but a boy and a girl are never just friends. It's not natural. And I admit I worried that boy would hold you back."

The consensus around Echo Cove was that Travis was a bad influence. Because he was the preacher's son, expectations on him were higher. All he'd really ever done was pull a few pranks that no one would have talked about had Pastor Painter not made an example of his son every Sunday morning.

Louise reached up and patted Lyla's shoulder. "You know where I live, right?"

"I think so." Lyla used to ride her bike past Louise's house with Ms. Hadley's Yorkie chasing her wheels. Sonny was small, but he had the energy to chase her all the way from her house to the town square.

"Drop in to visit while you're here. I love to see my old students. Some of them. Allison Wilkerson comes by often."

Lyla found that interesting. Allison was not the person

Lyla had assumed she was. "I'll try. It was great seeing you, Ms. Davis . . . Louise."

"You too, dear. Take care."

The customer in front of Lyla moved and it was Lyla's turn to order. When Lyla met eyes with the person behind the counter, her heart fell into her stomach.

"Lyla Dune." Bernadette Myer didn't look as happy to see her as Louise had been.

Lyla took the lead in the conversation. "Bernie. Hi. You work here?"

Bernie's eyelids subtly dropped, giving them a bored, hooded appearance. "I'm the owner." She lifted her chin and folded her arms over her chest. The Bernie standing in front of Lyla had matured and grown into her lips and nose, which had both been a little big for her face when they were younger. Bernie looked good. Great, actually.

"You own your own coffee shop? Wow. That's so amazing." Lyla glanced around the shop with a new appreciation.

"What do you want?" Bernie asked, all business.

Bernie didn't like Lyla, and for good reason. What happened to Bernie was an accident, though. Travis was the prankster, not Lyla. And Travis's pranks were always harmless. Plastic spiders. Rubber snakes. Fake dog poo in odd places. But after the Sloppy Joe incident, Lyla had been guilty by association.

Sloppy joes were the only choice on the cafeteria's menu that fateful day, and sloppy joes had always made Lyla gag. She'd missed breakfast, though, and her stomach had been roaring embarrassingly in algebra class. So she'd closed her eyes and had tried to imagine she was biting into a hamburger. Even her oversized imagination couldn't make that sloppy joe go down, though.

The texture. The tangy taste. The smell. She couldn't handle it. Feeling like she might vomit, Lyla suppressed a gag and spat the bite of food into the seat next to hers. She didn't have time to think. One more second in her mouth and it would have been like a scene from *The Exorcist*.

That's when Bernie pulled out the chair next to Lyla. Bernie usually sat with her boyfriend, TJ. Bernie had been crazy about that boy. Until TJ, Lyla had never seen Bernie smile— the real kind that radiated from within. The kind of smile that never left a person's face completely while they were in the throes of first love.

Bernie hadn't chosen to sit with TJ that day. Instead, she'd stomped over with her lunch tray, yanked out the chair next to Lyla's, and plopped down with a miserable sigh. Lyla was too frozen to speak. She and Bernie had never been real friends, but Lyla had always wanted to be. They shared a love of writing, and Bernie was good at it. Lyla equally admired and was jealous of Bernie.

"What are you staring at?" Bernie had asked, using both hands to pick up her own sloppy joe and hold it in front of her face as she glared at Lyla. Her eyes were red-rimmed, and there was evidence that Bernie had been crying. If not for Lyla's nausea, she would have asked Bernie what was wrong. Instead, she had suppressed another gag, quickly got up, and ran to the bathroom, not realizing that she'd turned an already traumatic day for Bernie into something far worse.

"Are you going to order or not?" Bernie asked now, pulling Lyla back to the present moment.

"Yes. I am." Lyla looked at the menu on the wall, pushing down the memories and regrets of the past. "I'll have a blonde coffee. With two raw sugars. Please."

Bernie disappeared to prepare the drink. When she returned, Lyla slid her debit card across the counter. "It's good to see you, Bernie."

"I go by Bernadette now," Bernie said, her hooded eyes narrowing as she looked up. "We aren't in high school anymore."

"Right. Sorry. I still go by Lyla, even though we're no longer in high school." Lyla didn't intend it to sound sarcastic, but it apparently had. "Listen, maybe we can grab lunch and catch up sometime." Lyla suddenly felt vulnerable like her teenaged self. She didn't want Bernie to think she'd intended for her to sit on sloppy joe vomit and return to class with brown stains on her backside, just in time for oral presentations that afternoon.

Lyla remembered how proud Bernie was of her presentation. When it was Bernie's turn, she walked to the front of the class, holding her head up high, even though TJ had shattered her heart not even an hour before. That former smile had dulled, but it wasn't wiped out completely, because she was still holding onto a paper that meant something to her.

The snickers from other classmates began before Bernie even began to speak, rolling from a quiet rumble to an all-out roar, as kids covered their faces and put their heads down on the desks in failed attempts to hide their laughter.

Bernie pretended not to notice as she read her report, but her eyes gradually took on a thick sheen of tears that splashed on her paper as she tried to blink them away. Lyla imagined Bernie thought the hysteria had to do with TJ, who was seated in the back row and already spreading his own narrative about their breakup. It wasn't until later that Bernie discovered what everyone was laughing about. She'd sat in Lyla's spat-up sloppy joe mess. TJ and his crew used the incident to their advantage, of course, giving Bernie the cruel nickname of "Brownie." It was no wonder Bernie went by Bernadette these days.

And no wonder she hated Lyla still.

"I have customers waiting behind you," Bernadette said, ignoring Lyla's suggestion that they catch up.

"Right." Lyla returned her debit card to her purse and grabbed her beverage. "Thanks for this." She started to turn away, but didn't want to leave on a bad note. "Hey, I know we weren't the best of friends in school, but . . . I always admired you."

Bernie's mouth tightened as if she was holding back a slew of not-so-nice things. "It was a long time ago, but I remember how it felt to be Bernie. It was miserable. Maybe that incident was an accident, like you claimed, but even you signed my senior yearbook to Brownie."

Had Lyla done that? She couldn't recall, but she knew she'd joined in the laughter when other kids whispered and gossiped about Bernie. Lyla could have stood up in class that day and admitted that it was sloppy joe, and it was all her fault. In high school, though, things that should have been trivial had seemed monumental.

High school was one big mission of trying to fit in while desperately wanting to also stand out for your good qualities, like being the prettiest, the smartest, the best writer. Maybe some part of Lyla had been secretly glad when classmates stopped talking about how great Bernie was at writing and instead spoke more about the brown stains on the back of her pants that one time.

"I wasn't fooled by you then," Bernie said. "Everyone thought you were so nice, but nice people don't do what you did."

Lyla wanted to defend herself, but she couldn't. "I—I'm sorry if I ever hurt you, Bernie."

"If?" Bernadette rolled her eyes. "If you have to question whether you were wrong, then you are the same girl. You haven't changed a bit. Besides, it's kind of late for an apology, don't you think?"

Opinion: It's never too late for an apology if the apology is sincere.

Lyla clutched her cup of coffee shakily. "I'll see you later, Bernadette." Or not. Turning, she headed out of the shop, walking quickly and hoping she didn't burst into tears or get stopped by any other ghosts from her past. When she got into her car, she exhaled.

Next Opinion: Gas station coffee goes down easier than humble pie.

After purchasing a shovel from the hardware store, Lyla returned to her parents' home as thunder rumbled outside. She just needed the next summer storm to hold off long enough for her to finish treasure hunting. Grabbing the shovel, she made her way to the backyard.

Please don't rain. Not yet.

She couldn't even remember what she'd put inside that time capsule. The old cypress tree towered over her as she approached, making her feel small, like a child again. Smoothing her hands over the tree's bark, she searched for the markings where she had used a pocketknife to carve a hand-sized X. There. Her fingers traced the shallow groove. Then she turned and took ten steps toward the gate of the fence that separated her and Ms. Hadley's yards. "One. Two. Three." She counted all the way to ten and stared at the unassuming patch of grass.

Woof!

Lyla looked up to see the little dog from yesterday, watching her intently. "How did you get inside the fence?" No doubt he had dug a hole the way Sonny used to, which had always infuriated Lyla's father. "I won't tell on you, but the next owners might install that electric fence my father always threatened you with."

The dog barked and then a flash of light lit up just above his head. A firefly? In the daytime? It twinkled again, confirming exactly what she'd thought she'd seen. Either she was imagining things or Bernie had poisoned her coffee.

Note to self: Never drink a beverage prepared by a person scorned.

Thunder drove Lyla back to the task at hand. She pushed the shovel's blade into the dirt, pressing her full weight into it. Then she pulled the shovel's blade up and tried again. She made slow progress, discarding the unearthed dirt into a pile off to the side and continuing for what felt like half an hour, as the sky rumbled softly and the little dog observed.

She wiped the sweat that ran down her forehead away with the back of her hand, putting more effort behind the blade. The clouds were growing darker at an alarming rate, leaving no doubt that it was about to downpour, which— ugh. That would leave this hole a muddy mess. Not ideal for a home that was scheduled to be shown to potential buyers in the coming week.

From the corner of Lyla's eye, she saw the spark of a fire-fly's light again. *What is this little guy doing out here?* And why was Ms. Hadley's dog out here? Shouldn't she be calling him back in?

With one more determined jab into the ground, the shovel's blade hit something solid. *Bingo!*

Dropping to her knees, she used her fingers to pry the pale green 7-Up bottle from the ground just as the first raindrop splashed the back of her hand. As Lyla pulled it free, thunder cracked loudly overhead. Where there was thunder, there was lightning. She'd learned that lesson once already. Actually, she'd learned it when she had buried this time capsule.

It'd been storming that day too and—even if no one be-lieved her—she'd been struck by lightning. She'd just finished covering the hole and was turning to run inside as God rolled his giant bowling bowl in the sky. Travis's allusion, not hers. Then *boom!* The ground shook and a pulse of electricity shot through her from her head to her toes.

Next thing she knew, she awoke on her parents' couch, watching her mom and dad debate whether to call the paramedics or a family friend who was a retired EMT. Once Lyla opened her eyes, they'd decided to do neither. They were nineties parents, after all, and if you were walking and talking, you were probably fine.

"If you'd been struck, the soles of your feet would be burned to a crisp, Ly-lac," her father had told her.

That was possibly true, but Lyla didn't want history to repeat itself today. Pulling the bottle free, she let out a happy whoop and hugged it against her body as the sky broke open and a flood of water poured down. Thunder clapped, this time shortly after an unmistakable flash of lightning. Maybe it was her overactive imagination, but it seemed to be aiming straight for her. With the bottle in her arms, she jumped to her feet and raced toward the back of the house.

Suddenly, the little dog from next door dashed under her feet. Lyla stumbled, feeling like she'd been tossed around in a wave, not knowing which way was up. Then, in that scenario, it felt like she'd fallen into a nest of jellyfish, all stinging her from the inside out. In reality, she was pretty sure she'd just been struck by lightning—for a second time in her life.

Chapter 3

*Opinion: If you tempt death, make sure you're
prayed-up and wearing clean undies.*
—Delilah Dune, opinion writer

Lyla cracked open an eye and sat up stiffly, and scanned her
surroundings, which were far short of Heaven. Presumably
that meant she was alive. The green 7-Up bottle caught her
eye, resting on the deck, masking tape side up. Ignoring the
pain and the surreal suspicion that she'd survived a second
lightning strike, she reached until her fingers touched the
cap. Then she rolled the bottle to her, steadied it between her
thighs, and began to peel away the old masking tape.

"Hey!" a voice came out of nowhere.

Lyla startled and turned to see Allison stepping through
the fence's gate. "Oh, hi."

Allison didn't wait to be invited. She continued toward
Lyla, talking cheerily as she walked. "You didn't answer the
doorbell, so I thought I'd walk around back. I hope that's
okay." She finally stopped and furrowed her brows as she
seemed to see Lyla for the first time.

"Are you okay? Why are you lying on the deck steps? And—
oh my heavens, you're soaking wet? What happened?"

Lyla didn't want to set off Allison's alarm bells by telling the truth. "I guess I fell." She shifted stiffly, her body protesting any movement. Something told her that she'd have a few dark bruises tomorrow and maybe some exit wounds on the soles of her feet. "The neighbor's dog must have tripped me as I ran away from the storm." Lyla lifted a hand to cradle her suddenly aching chin, wondering if she'd knocked it on the deck step in her fall.

Allison's expression pinched with worry as she sat beside her on the steps. "Believe it or not, I understand exactly what you're going through right now, friend."

Since when were she and Allison Wilkerson friends?

"I get it," Allison said.

Lyla blinked. "You do?"

"I didn't know which way was up or which was down when Ernie and I parted ways."

"Oh." Lyla shook her head. Allison had this situation all wrong. "That's not what's going on at all."

"It's okay. If anyone understands, it's me." Allison patted Lyla's thigh. "Do you want to talk about it?"

Lyla really didn't. *She* wasn't even sure what was going on right now. Her breakup with Joe had been rough, but that was three months ago. Her unstable job and home life were more the issue, but she didn't even want to admit to herself how bad things were right now.

"What's that?" Allison pointed at the soda bottle in Lyla's hand.

"This? It's just a time capsule. Do you remember how Ms. Davis suggested we all make one? At the end of our senior year."

Allison shook her head. "Honestly, I didn't pay much attention in her class. I was too busy making eyes at the football players." The way Allison made that remark sounded almost self-deprecating, like she wasn't proud of who she'd been. "I only had eyes for football players—with one exception. Travis Painter." Allison laughed quietly. "Wow, I haven't thought about him in years." There was a touch of nostalgia in her voice. She tipped her face up to the sun, closing her eyes momentarily. "I probably would have done better marrying him than Ernie."

"Ernie Maddox?" Ernie had been the star football player at Echo Cove High, and he'd been a first-class jerk in Lyla's unpopular opinion. Lyla and Ernie sat next to each other in algebra class one year, and Lyla swore he dropped his pencil ten times a class just to check out all the girls' legs. She'd always made sure to wear jeans that semester, not that he would ever be interested in her. She hadn't been unpopular with the guys necessarily, just not popular enough for the likes of Ernie.

Allison rolled her eyes. "I thought I was so lucky snagging the most popular guy in school, but it turns out, he was the worst decision of my life." She blew out a breath. The look on her face raised a lot of questions, but they weren't friendly enough for Lyla to pry. And Lyla wouldn't be sticking around in Echo Cove long enough to remedy that. Still, the writer in her wanted to know the story. Ernie probably dropped too many pencils and checked out too many legs that didn't belong to Allison.

Whatever Ernie had done, Allison hadn't deserved it. Yes, she was the stereotypical cheerleader in the popular crowd, but she'd always been nice. Allison wasn't one of the mean girls who gossiped or picked on the kids with dirty or off-brand clothes. Instead, she always made a point of talking to those kids. Lyla was in the journalism club, so it was her job to watch the goings-on in school, and every time she watched Allison, admittedly looking for something to hate about the cheerleader, all she'd ever seen was sweetness. "Sorry about your marriage," Lyla said quietly, meaning it.

Allison put on a smile that reminded Lyla of their high school days. It was bright and perfect. And one hundred percent fake. Lyla now recognized that Allison's cheery expression was just a shield to hide whatever storm was brewing on the inside. For the first time, maybe ever, Lyla could relate to Allison Wilkerson.

"So, what's Travis up to these days?" Allison asked. "He moved away not long after you." She scratched the side of her face absently. "His sister, Bailey, had that scandal, if you recall."

It wasn't much of a scandal in Lyla's opinion. Bailey had gotten pregnant out of wedlock and Pastor Painter had an adult version of a temper tantrum. The pregnancy was supposed to be a secret, but everyone knew. It was Echo Cove, after all. He'd demanded that Bailey marry the baby's father, and the wedding had been the talk to the town. Then Bailey pulled a runaway bride. She didn't stay gone long enough for anyone to worry, though. Just long enough for folks to talk.

Lyla shrugged. "I haven't seen or heard from Travis since I went away to college."

Allison seemed surprised by this. "You two were so close." She shook her head. "It's such a shame when people lose touch."

"Yeah." Lyla hugged the 7-Up bottle closer to her.

"I was surprised that Travis was the one to leave instead of Bailey. After all that drama. I guess all families have their drama though, don't they?" Allison looked over, something sad flashing in her gaze. There and gone.

"You never told me what brought you over this morning," Lyla said.

"Right." Allison folded her hands in her lap. "Well, I wanted to see if you would like to come to my house on Friday night for a little Dinnerware Party."

"Dinnerware?"

"Mm-hmm. I sell it. It's my side hustle." She let out a high-pitched giggle. "A lot of the old crowd from high school will be there," she said, as if that was a sure sell on the invitation.

Allison's old crowd was not made up of Lyla's former friends, though.

Lyla grimaced slightly. "I'm afraid I'm not much of a cook."

"Well, I'll have free food, even if you don't buy anything. And more wine from The Sippy Cup."

Something vulnerable flashed in Allison's eyes as she looked at Lyla eagerly. It made Lyla hesitate to turn her down, even though that's exactly what she wanted to do. "I'll think about it."

"Perfect." Allison stood. "Well, I'm on my way to the grocery store to buy snacks and such for Friday night. Need anything?"

"No, thanks. And thank you for the invitation. It's nice of you to consider me."

"Of course. I wouldn't dream of not inviting you. Everyone will be so happy to catch up. If you come," she added, vulnerability creeping into her expression again. That was something Lyla never thought she'd see on Allison Wilkerson's face.

"I'll try." And some part of Lyla believed she actually might. *Who knows? Maybe boy-obsessed teenagers turned into interesting adults.* People did change after all, and not always for the worse. Lyla had penned that opinion article about two years ago, and her readers had been divided right down the middle on whether they agreed.

"Great. I'll call you." Allison headed back toward the fence's gate. "It's so great catching up with you. Seems just like old times."

If by old times, she meant times that had never happened.

Once Allison had gone, Lyla took the 7-Up bottle inside and placed it on the kitchen counter. Then she used her nails to peel the masking tape that closed the flap that Lyla had once cut into the bottle. What was she going to find inside? She could barely remember the girl she'd been when she'd sealed this thing, full of hope and nerves and a million dreams that had yet to come true.

Here goes nothing. She reached inside until her fingers hit something hard and pulled it out. A green-colored whistle. She had no idea where it had come from and what its significance was. Well, that's disappointing. She reached into the bottle again and pulled out a brightly colored hair scrunchie. This she remembered! Before college, she'd gone to a salon with a picture of what she wanted. The stylist had an Edward Scissorhands technique, though, and Lyla had left her appointment with hair too short to even pull back into a ponytail. That was the day Lyla learned you can't just go to any old place for a cut and style—not if you wanted to keep the hair on your head.

Lyla moved the silk scrunchie around with her fingers, admiring the purple-and-yellow zebra print, far from any fashion statement she'd want to make these days.

Reaching inside the bottle again, her fingers brushed against a thin piece of paper, and she felt a subtle ache in her chest. The memory of what was written on this paper blew around like a tumbleweed in her mind. The list.

Her hands shook as she unfolded the paper and took in her once neat handwriting. The paper was one of her and Travis's summer bucket lists. They created one every year, checking off things they wanted to do. It was bad luck not to have completed all the things come August, when school started back. At least, that was Travis's superstition.

Lyla focused her eyes and began to read.

*Summer Bucket List for Lyla and Travis's
Last Summer Together*

She ran her gaze over the items, bullet-pointed with hand-drawn flowers. She and Travis had nearly completed all of them, but there were still a few items unchecked. The summer had wound down unexpectedly fast, and it was time for Lyla to leave for college. She was supposed to stay two more weeks, but she'd sped up that timeline herself, feeling a sudden urgency to get out of Echo Cove, afraid that if she didn't, the ground would turn to quicksand, sucking her in and refusing to let her leave.

"The list," Travis had insisted, watching her pack up the back of her car. "It's bad luck not to check all the items off by August."

"I'll be back next weekend," she'd promised, knowing full well she wouldn't. It was the first time she'd ever lied to Travis. He was her best friend. She told him everything—until pesky little feelings started to evolve, making her want more than friendship. Quicksand.

Lyla didn't reach inside the bottle again. Instead, she set the bottle down, grabbed the zebra-print scrunchie, and pulled her hair back into a quick ponytail. As she draped the plastic whistle around her neck, the story of it came back to her. She used to wear it when she rode her bike through town. It was her version of a horn to get someone's attention or blow off steam when someone rode her off the road.

I wonder if my old bike is still in the garage . . .

The thought had Lyla walking toward the garage, mostly empty—except for her beloved bicycle. Her parents must have wanted Lyla to decide what to do with it, as well. She wasn't sure about the long run, but she knew exactly what she wanted to do with it now.

She pressed the automatic garage door opener and then rolled her light purple beach cruiser, complete with lavender handlebar tassels and a wire basket with plastic daisies attached, toward the end of the driveway. When she was younger, she used to ride this thing all over town.

Swinging a leg over the middle bar of the old bike, Lyla sat on the worn leather seat, practically feeling the springs pressing up into her backside. She tossed her cell phone in the wire basket and pushed the front pedal forward, coasting down the driveway and racing into the wind.

The feeling of freedom was familiar. And also distant. When she'd been younger, her bike was the only way to get space from her parents. She remembered how much she'd loved this bicycle. In a town like Echo Cove, her bike was enough to get her anywhere she needed to go.

Woof! Woof!

The little dog from next door darted toward her bike, yapping with his front teeth bared. Lyla pedaled harder, remembering how Sonny used to do the same. He had two different personalities, and a person on a bike didn't want to be caught by one of them. If he could catch a bike, he could set his teeth into a back tire.

"Not you too!"

Lyla's thighs burned as she raced, the little dog barking after her. He finally dropped off halfway across town, and she slowed down as her adrenaline plummeted. Now that the tiny crisis was out of the way, she realized it was becoming harder to propel the wheels. *Maybe I should have checked the air pressure in these tires.* The last summer she'd ridden this bike, she'd blown the back one. Right in the midst of a torrential downpour.

Thank God Travis pulled up in his dad's old pickup to rescue me.

Lyla slowed her bike almost to a stop to swipe a bead of sweat from her brow, realizing she was at the old movie theater. She looked up at the yellowed marquee to read the current offerings written in black block letters. SLEEPLESS IN SEATTLE.

Her brain short-circuited and she stopped. *No way. No freaking way the same movie from her last summer here was playing now.*

Something sparkled in her peripheral—*Another firefly? Seriously, what was in Bernadette's coffee this morning?*

As she stood there in wonder, something wet hit her shoulder. She assumed it was sweat, but then another drop hit her cheek. *Another storm? Seriously?*

Centering her body over the bike's middle bar, she pushed one foot forward on the pedal in a mad dash back to her parents' home. She wasn't trying to get struck by lightning a third time in her life. Drops of rain blurred her vision, making it difficult to see the road ahead as she raced. She needed to at least find shelter between here and home, which was still three miles away.

Then the bike seemed to jump as a jagged rock passed underneath her front tire. The front tire took the hit, but the back tire popped and skidded across the pavement, the sudden motion tossing Lyla into a shallow ditch on her right.

Okay, Echo Cove. Two strikes of lightning and two falls. Maybe the universe was trying to tell her to get out while she still could. She had always learned her lessons the hard way, though, needing a third strike to get the point across.

She stood up, making sure nothing was broken, and collected her bike as the rain pelted her skin. No other choice in sight, she started rolling the bike forward. If she had Allison's number, she could ask for a lift. Then again, Allison probably didn't have the kind of vehicle that would fit a huge beach cruiser.

Opinion: If a car can't fit a person's bike, it's useless.

Her opinions these days were falling as flat as her back tire. A horn honked behind her, and she stepped off the edge of the road as a blue pickup truck passed. Its brake lights lit up and the truck slowed to a stop in front of her, presumably to offer a ride. Was it safer to let a stranger drive her home or risk being struck by lightning again?

Opinion: Trusting the kindness of strangers is only foolish when the sun is shining.

Finally, a valid opinion.

Lyla blinked through the rain, watching as a man stepped out of the truck. He wore a dark raincoat with the hood pulled over his face, making him look mysterious and intimidating. Perhaps trusting the kindness of strangers was also foolish in a thunderstorm.

"It's okay!" Lyla called to him, feeling more uneasy the closer he got. Being raised in a small town, she was hardwired to think everyone had good intentions, but she watched the nightly news. Even small towns weren't immune. "I'm fine! I don't need help!" She was cold and wet, and she didn't think she could run fast enough to get away.

The man didn't stop walking. He didn't even slow his pace as she protested not needing help. Instead, he continued forward until he was standing only a couple feet away.

Fight, flight, or freeze? She already knew she was the latter. She'd had her "freeze" moment on the Pirate's Plank at Memory Lake when she was fifteen, and it hadn't ended well.

She stood there, her feet cemented to the road. Was he going to force her into his truck? What should she do? Even if she knew the appropriate action to take, she felt paralyzed by her sudden fear. She should have taken those self-defense classes her college roommate had attempted to drag her to. Lyla had been too focused on her journalism classes, though. Too bad for her. Learning proper grammar wouldn't get her out of a potential kidnapping.

The man pulled off his raincoat and wrapped it around her shoulders, pulling the hood up to shelter her head. "Hey, Ly."

She blinked past her wet lashes and then blinked again, because this was more unbelievable than fireflies in the daytime. Was she also seeing ghosts now?

"Travis?"

Chapter 4

*Opinion: An old friend is evidence that your whole
life hasn't been a mistake.*
—Delilah Dune, opinion writer

Lyla didn't move for a second. Even though she was only
thirty, she must be having a midlife crisis of some sort. That,
or when she'd been struck by lightning, she'd hit her head.
Perhaps she had a concussion or a mild brain injury. Or she
was in a coma, and all of this was an elaborate dream.

Yep, that had to be what was happening right now. Because she and Travis had watched the movie *Sleepless in
Seattle* three times that last summer together, and now it was
playing at the local theater. And that same summer, she'd
gotten a flat tire on her bike in the middle of a rainstorm
after being chased by Sonny. And Travis had come to her rescue driving his dad's old, blue pickup truck. Just like now.

"No. This isn't happening." She clutched her handlebars
and continued pushing her bike forward, trudging through
the mud and breathing hard.

The man reached out and gently grabbed her arm. "Lyla,
it's me—Travis."

The touch zinged up her arm. That was real. She turned to

look at him, searching his face. How long had it been since she'd looked into those golden brown eyes? At least a decade. He had the same tiny mole on the upper right cheek and the scar that ran straight through his right eyebrow from a fishing trip gone wrong.

"You're really here?"

"Unfortunately, yeah. And I'm getting wet, same as you." He grinned wickedly, dimples carving out little holes in his otherwise chiseled cheeks. He looked just like he had all those summers ago. Then he picked up her bike as if it weighed nothing and carried it to the back of his truck.

Lyla looked around, wondering what she should do. She didn't have a choice either way, and if this was a dream, what did it matter? She followed him to his truck, her sneakers squishing around her feet. This dream felt so real that she could even smell the rain. She could taste it as it ran down her face and across her lips.

"Passenger seat!" he called across the truck. "Get in!"

Lyla did as he asked, sliding into the right side of the truck. The seat immediately became a pool of water beneath her. "Sorry," she said, glancing over. Was this actually happening?

"Don't worry about it." Travis ran a hand over his face, clearing the rainwater. Then he looked at her across the center console. "I wasn't sure it was really you. I was going to offer you a ride either way, but . . . Wow, it's good to see you, Ly."

Her whole body shivered, partly because of the truck's A/C hitting her damp skin, and partly because this moment felt surreal. "This is too weird to be true."

Travis furrowed his brow. "What do you mean?"

"Well, you're still driving the same truck you did when you were eighteen. It can't still be working."

"I've been working on her for the past few months now. Just got her running again. She's as good as new."

Lyla remembered that Travis had always referred to his truck with female pronouns. "But that's not the only thing that's weird. The same movie is playing from that last summer. At the old movie theater. They're playing *Sleepless in Seattle*." Lyla wiped the raindrops as they ran off her hair onto her face. Surely that proved she was in a dream right now. Even so, she didn't want to sound out of her mind by mentioning the other things that had repeated since she'd returned to Echo Cove. Or the tiny fireflies that seemed to be popping up out of nowhere in broad daylight.

Travis laughed lightly. "That's what happens in the summer. Theaters play old reruns for a couple bucks. You okay, Ly?"

She pressed a hand against her chest where her heart was beating out of control. She wasn't sure if she was okay. In fact, she didn't think she was. "If this is really happening, then what are you doing here in town? I heard you moved away."

"Bailey's getting married in a couple weeks. I'm walking her down the aisle. I kind of have to be back."

Lyla blinked. "Your sister was getting married that last summer in Echo Cove too."

He ran a hand through his dark hair, tousling it and making a few overgrown strands fall messily at the top of his head. "Totally different circumstances. She was being forced into a shotgun wedding to save my dad's reputation." He formed air quotes around the last word. "This time the wedding is Bailey's choice."

Lyla closed her eyes, willing herself to wake up. She only opened her eyes again when Travis spoke.

"Hey. This isn't a dream. I'm really here, Ly."

She opened her eyes and looked at him, taking in the angles of his face. Last she'd seen him, he'd still had a boyish softness to his jawline. Now he was a man. Was her childhood best friend truly sitting next to her right now? If so, his second first impression of her must be of a drenched rat who was maybe a little bit out of her mind.

Without second-guessing reality anymore, she leaned across

the center console and threw her arms around his neck, breathing in his woodsy scent. "I can't believe you're here. I've missed you." The truth spilled out like a secret she'd kept from even herself. She'd missed Travis Painter, more than she'd realized. Sharing the air between them made her feel like she somehow hadn't taken a full, deep breath in years.

Travis's arms closed in around her, but only for a second. "I've missed you too, Ly," he said in a quiet voice. Then he pulled back, his posture becoming suddenly stiff. There was something guarded in his eyes as he glanced away, not giving her his full attention. "You look good . . ."

"Good?" she repeated, looking down at herself. "I seriously doubt that."

He looked good, though. *Wow.* Her prankster best friend now filled up the driver's seat of his truck, making the space almost look too small for him. His shoulders spanned beyond the back of the driver's seat. His head nearly reached the truck's ceiling.

"You're staring." The corners of his lips subtly curled up.

"I can't help it. You've just . . ." Fumbling over her words, she tried to speak. "You, well, I—You're different."

When he glanced over this time, his gaze stuck for a long moment. "You look exactly the same. Although I don't recall you being so—"

Lyla felt her confidence shrivel. She was older than her eighteen-year-old self. She had more sun spots than freckles now, and there was no way she could fit into those skinny jeans she used to wear.

She waited, dreading whatever he was about to say. Her ex had a way of commenting on the less attractive parts of her body without being openly critical. It was a talent of Joe's. He could say something in a nice way, making it very clear that he was subtly judging her. *Your hair looks good—not so frizzy . . . That skirt hides those extra pounds from the holidays. It looks nice . . .* If Lyla ever called Joe out on the back-handed compliments, he'd persuade her that he was doing her a favor, claiming his honesty was an attribute.

"*A woman always says she wants an honest man, until he's honest about her.*" Joe loved to say that. He'd thought it was so clever that he once seriously pondered creating bumper stickers with that phrase. He'd even suggested Lyla use it for her column, as if any female would even share that opinion.

Lyla braced herself for what Travis would say next, remembering that he liked these long pauses in conversations. Pauses that begged for her to fill in the blank. "You don't recall me being so what?" she finally asked.

He pinched his chin between his thumb and index finger. "Wet. I don't remember that part about you."

Lifting her eyes to meet his, she broke into more laughter. Then she swatted his arm and leaned forward again. "Well, let me dry myself off on you some more."

He leaned out of reach. "I also don't remember you being so . . . grown up." He cleared his throat. "Lyla Dune had a glow-up. My best friend is a woman now. How bizarre."

"Did you think I'd still be eighteen?"

"Yeah." He nodded. "That's exactly what I pictured when I thought of you all these years."

Lyla looked down again. There was this electric buzz running through her body. That was part of what had freaked her out at eighteen. The moment her insides had started to sparkle at the very sight of him, like fireflies in her belly, things had gotten weird. She had big dreams though, and they didn't involve a small-town boy. Self-sabotaging herself by falling in love was not part of the plan.

She'd had opinions before she'd become a well-known columnist. Women should never flex their aspirations for a man. In fact, back then, she'd thought *Just Say No to Drugs* included the self-made kind manufactured by love—oxytocin.

Travis asked now, leaning slightly forward. "What's that on your chin?"

She touched her chin and flinched at the subtle ache there. "It's a dark spot, like a bruise." Concern darkened the color of his eyes. "You okay, Ly?"

"No one's hitting me, if that's what you're asking." She flinched when she pushed the spot he was referring to.

"Good, because if they were, I'd find them and give them a matching dark spot."

Her knight in shining armor.

Opinion: Women don't need rescuing. But sometimes it feels good.

"If I recall, you had a bruise there the last time I saw you too. I teased you about growing a beard."

"I remember. You called me the bearded lady." She rolled her eyes. "Such a bad joke."

"I admit it. So, how'd you get this one?" He reached out and tapped his finger to her chin. Instead of an ache, there was a zing.

"Oh, I, um, fell earlier. This little dog tripped me, and I was kind of struck by lightning, actually."

Travis lifted a brow. "You always did have wild, unbelievable stories." He pointed in her direction. "But I always believed them."

"I was the liar, and you were the prankster," she teased. She hadn't been known as a liar in a bad way. It was just her wild imagination that no one understood. Except Travis.

"It's good to see you, Ly-la-la-la-laaaa." He sang out the last syllable in a deep baritone voice.

She covered her face with one hand and peeked at him between her fingers. "I've already seen Ms. Davis. She hopes that I'm no longer hanging around you. You're a bad influence."

"Well, I hate to disappoint Ms. Davis." He squared himself off in the seat. "You staying with your parents?"

"Yes. Well, I'm staying at their place. They've left town to travel the world. It's just me until their house sells."

Travis snickered. "I'm surprised they'd leave you to watch the house again after that last time."

He was referring to the blue hair gel that led to the flooded downstairs. In all likelihood, it was mostly the bad eel rolls that had ruined her parents' vacation that summer. She'd just gotten the blame.

"Yes, well, I've grown up," Lyla said. "I've become a responsible adult since the last time you saw me."

"Unfortunate." Travis put the truck in motion, driving slowly as the rain beat against the windshield. "They're selling, huh?"

"Mm-hmm. They want to enjoy their retirement." And if anyone deserved an extended dream vacation, it was her parents. "I have to pack up my old room this week, which I think will be more work than I realized. My teenage self was a bit of a packrat."

Not her adult self though. Joe had despised clutter, and Lyla had gotten used to letting go of all the things she would have once deemed sentimental.

"Being a packrat is a sign of a creative person, you know?" Travis said.

She looked at him for a long moment. "You always had a way of doing that."

"Doing what?" he asked.

"Flipping something that I felt bad about and turning that thing into something positive. I've never known someone else who could do that."

Dimples formed in Travis's cheeks as he smiled again. Those deep pockets in his cheeks were the only boyish thing left about him. "Is that a good thing?"

"You have no idea how much of a good quality that is."

She secured a lock of her hair behind her ear. "In addition to clearing out my bedroom, I had to dig a hole in the backyard to find a certain 7-Up bottle that was buried there. It's my time capsule."

He chuckled under his breath. "I can't believe you actually did that. You adored Ms. Davis. I'm half surprised you didn't grow up to be her."

Lyla had considered going into the teaching field because of Ms. Davis, but that wasn't her calling. She was more of a writer than a teacher. "I adored her, but she didn't like me very much. Primarily your fault," she said, gently shoving his shoulder.

"Sorry about that."

Something told Lyla he wasn't sorry at all. "I haven't finished going through the contents of the bottle yet, but I found our last summer bucket list."

He looked over with interest. "Wow, I haven't made a bucket list since that summer."

"I haven't made one either." The list was a give-and-take between them, and neither had ever given the other grief for whatever they'd deemed worthy of the summer bucket list. "It just didn't feel right without you." She returned her attention out the passenger window as he drove. "So Bailey's getting married for real this time?"

Travis's older sister had nearly gone through with the shotgun wedding. If not for the hurricane that had rolled up the day before the big day, delaying the ceremony just long enough for Bailey to come to her senses, she might have made the biggest mistake of her life. It'd taken three days after the storm to find her. The whole ordeal had been scandalous in a town as small as Echo Cove. Lyla remembered the whispers in town the last week she'd lived here. Instead of making an example of his son that last Sunday service she'd attended, he'd torn down his own daughter as she sat in the front row, just barely showing in a flowy flowered dress.

"Is Bailey marrying the same guy?" Lyla asked.

"Heck, no. That guy disappeared right after she had the baby."

"Mom told me about that," Lyla remembered. Pastor Painter couldn't have been thrilled about that either. "So who is she marrying?"

Travis pulled up to a STOP sign and offered Lyla a mischievous glance. "Some guy named Jimmy Zitnik. You better believe I'm going to give her grief on that one."

"Why?" Lyla asked.

Travis continued driving. "*Zit-nik?* Come on. Maybe we're not teenagers anymore, but that's still pretty funny."

Lyla had forgotten about Travis's juvenile sense of humor, as well. "Well, I'm happy for her."

"Are you, uh, someone's wife these days?" Travis asked, his voice going quiet.

Tension buzzed in Lyla's chest. She wasn't sure why she hesitated to discuss her personal life with him, but she did. When they were younger, she'd never withheld anything from Travis. "No. You?"

"Someone's wife?" Travis shook his head, a wide grin carving out deep dimples in his cheeks. "No. No one's husband either."

"Never?" she asked, feeling the same dread she'd felt when she'd thought Travis was going to insult her a few minutes earlier.

"I've been what one might call a wanderer, a nomad of sorts. About a year after you left, I packed my bags too." He glanced over. "Most of the women I've met have wanted roots—a house, a fence, a dog."

"You don't even have a dog?" Lyla teased as he turned his truck onto her parents' road.

"I had one, but it ran away." Humor danced in his light brown eyes. "Even a dog wants a home without wheels, I guess."

It took a moment for Lyla to process that statement. "Your home has wheels?"

He grimaced slightly. "It's an RV. I'm like a turtle who takes their home with them wherever they go."

Lyla found this interesting. She wasn't exactly surprised, because Travis had always told her he wanted to see and do as much as possible. He loved adventure even when they were teenagers. His bucket list items were always more active than Lyla's. She might have put seeing a movie four times on the list, while he put things like sneaking out after dark. Skinny dipping in Memory Lake. Catching a fish, cleaning it, and cooking it over a campfire. She had, however, added skating on their last list together, knowing that skating was to Travis the equivalent of jumping off the Pirate's Plank for Lyla. Travis had broken his tailbone in a skating rink and that doughnut seat cushion probably still popped up in his nightmares the way the Pirate's Plank did for Lyla.

"RV life sounds fun," she said, her mind immediately working to turn that statement into an opinion for her column. Her mind was always twisting words and comments, trying to decipher their value for "Delilah's Delusions," or rather, their value to her editor, Bob.

Travis locked his hands behind his neck for a moment, his bent elbows stretching out as he expanded his chest and seemed to contemplate his response. "Life on the road is interesting, to say the least. You meet a lot of different types of people."

"What do you do for work?" she asked.

"Odd jobs here and there. You'd be surprised how little it takes to support yourself." He lowered his arms back down to his side. "Gotta admit, the women I've met haven't liked that aspect of my lifestyle. I guess RV life isn't considered stable, but that's a misconception. Stability is determined by me. When I look for the work, it's always there. I usually don't even have to look for it."

"Is it lonely? Being in a town full of people you don't know."
The question rolled out of Lyla's mouth before she considered it. Waving her hands, she shook her head. "I'm sorry,
don't answer that. It's none of my business."

"Nah, it's okay. It can be lonely." He pulled into her parents' driveway and parked. Rain was still tapping his windshield, coming down much more softly now. "I was lonely
before I chose the lifestyle, though. I never found another
friend quite like you, Ly." He glanced over.

Her whole body felt like there was an electric current running from her head to her toes as he watched her.

"Can I ask you something?" he finally asked.

"Sure."

"Why didn't you ever call me, Ly? Or write me back? I
emailed. Why didn't you reply?"

Guilt washed over her, covering every square inch of her
body and flooding her cells. She looked out the windshield,
searching for the right answer. The one that wouldn't hurt his
feelings. "A long-distance best friend wouldn't be as good as
the real thing."

He looked out the windshield too. "Did you even open the
emails and read them?"

It was a yes-or-no question, but the true answer would
have required full-page essays. It was complicated, so she just
gave him the easiest response, even if it was a lie. "No."

His gaze lowered to his lap. "I see. So you just left town
and erased me from your memory altogether? All of our
years of talking every day and sharing every secret."

That wasn't true. There was one secret she hadn't told him,
because it would have changed everything. She'd only told
her diary and Ms. Hadley's little ankle-biter, Sonny.

"That's what happens, Travis. After school, people go their
separate ways. They grow up. Did you think we'd still hang
out every break and pull pranks on each other and the people
in town?"

Some part of that scenario sounded wonderful to her, and that was what had scared her so much back then. Lyla had big-city dreams, and the way she'd felt about Travis threatened everything she'd always wanted.

There'd been these moments when she'd felt like he could make her laugh for the rest of her life, but Travis certainly wasn't going to end up in any big city. No. That wasn't who he was. Falling for him would have been like stepping into quicksand, just like her parents. Love wasn't just love. When feelings were at play, one thing led to another. It was inevitable—fate. Lyla's mom had wanted to chase her own dreams, but instead, she'd gotten pregnant and had a baby, Lyla. And she'd never left Echo Cove. Until now.

The muscles along Travis's jawline bunched and released. "Is that all you thought of us? A couple of pranksters."

"Don't do this. It's nice to see you again, Trav. I don't want us to fight." They'd never argued before. Why start now?

"You'd probably rather we be polite, civil, and for you to leave town again and never look back." He'd never used a harsh tone with her before now. His voice wasn't raised, but his words were pointed.

Lyla sighed. "Not you too."

"What's that supposed to mean?"

"Apparently, I'm the worst person to ever grace this stupid town." At least according to Ms. Hadley and Bernie.

"I don't think so, Ly. I got that rap a long time ago, thanks to my good ol' dad."

"See you around, Travis." Pushing his truck door open, Lyla stepped out into the rain.

"Yeah. I won't bother trying to stay in touch this time," he called after her.

She looked at him across the center console as the rain poured all around. "Me either."

"Well, at least you're consistent."

Lyla didn't need any more guilt. Slamming the door behind

her, she headed to the back to retrieve her bike, fumbling with the tailgate's latch.

"Here, let me." Travis met her around the back of the truck.

Lyla couldn't even look at him. Her face was soaked, and she was pretty sure half of the wetness was tears. She didn't feel great about what she'd done all those years ago, but at the time it'd felt like it was the right thing to do. "I can't turn back time, Travis. I wish I could. I wish I would have been a better friend."

She wasn't sure why she'd cut off all contact. She'd started having feelings for Travis that she'd never had before. Things were changing between them, and her mom's voice kept playing in her head as that summer sizzled to an end.

"I had dreams once, too, Lyla. But then I met your father and, well, sometimes it's a choice between falling in love and chasing your destiny."

Lyla was terrified the same thing would happen to her.

"I wish that too," Travis said, breaking her from her thoughts. He lifted her bike out of his truck and placed it on the pavement in front of her. "Have a nice life." Without another word, he turned his back to her and climbed back into the driver's side of his truck and slammed the door, leaving her in the rain with her bike and a million regrets.

June 20

Dear Diary,

Travis and I got into a fight. That hasn't happened in forever and I don't like it. He wanted to discuss what will happen after this summer, when I go off to college. How will we continue our friendship? He wanted to make a plan, which is so unlike Travis. Travis Painter only plans pranks. He doesn't plan out weeks ahead or even days ahead.

He told me he'd drive down to see me at college every other weekend, but I'm not sure that's what I want. What if these feelings of mine keep growing, and I end up pregnant and dropping out like my mom? What if continuing my friendship with Travis ruins my life?

It's not impossible. It's not even that unlikely.

Sincerely,

Lyla

Chapter 5

Opinion: Nice people don't have to be nice to everyone.
—Delilah Dune, opinion writer

The rain had been coming down for over an hour. After showering and eating half a bag of chips, crunching away her frustration, Lyla had opened the diary, slipping back in time and remembering things long forgotten.

Her younger self had been so excited about the future. *Sorry to tell you, past Lyla. We haven't lived up to our potential.* At least not yet.

As Lyla continued to read, a blurry water spot interrupted the next line with a hand-drawn arrow pointing to the smudged ink.

The roof is leaking. Dad is going to lose his mind. Lately, he's been calling our house the money pit because everything is breaking all at once.

After the Blue Hair Gel incident, the kitchen ceiling sprang a leak and a hurricane plowed through Echo Cove, ripping off half the roof. Then Bailey had bailed on the wedding of the summer, and Sonny, the little ankle-biter, died. God rest his tiny soul. Lyla was supposed to meet Travis to finish checking off their bucket list, but something inside her panicked. It was go-time. She'd texted Travis that she'd be back to finish the list next weekend. Then she'd tossed her bags in her car, got in, and headed off with barely a backward glance.

Travis had deserved more. They'd been best friends since third grade. She should have kept in contact, even if falling for him was a very real threat to her real-life bucket list. The one with items like moving to a big city, becoming an established writer, and making a name for herself.

Her phone buzzed from her pocket, pulling her from her memories and laundry list of regrets. Setting her diary down, Lyla pulled her phone out and read her mom's name on the screen. She didn't want to talk to her mother right now, but not answering the call could be problematic.

Tapping the screen, she answered. "Hey, Mom,"—she put on her I'm-happy-everything-is-just-fine voice—"how's the trip so far?"

Her mom's sigh was long and drawn out. "We've barely gotten started. There's not much to say just yet, except last night's takeout upset your father's stomach. He knows better than to eat eel rolls. He learned his lesson years ago, remember?"

Lyla's father protested in the background. Her mom always had a habit of oversharing. "Dad ate the eel rolls again?" Her father had spent the last decade cursing those eel rolls. His upset stomach was the very reason there was a 7-Up bottle in the house that summer. Her mom had gone to the store looking for ginger ale, and she'd returned with 7-Up, swearing it was the same thing.

Opinion: Even though it looks the same, doesn't mean it tastes the same.

"Enough about your father's bad stomach. I'd rather hear about you. Why are you digging holes in the backyard, Lyla? And where did you find a shovel?"

Lyla pulled back from the phone for a moment. "How . . . ?"

"Ms. Hadley has always been good about watching the house for your father and me."

Lyla's mouth dropped open. "You asked *me* to watch the house."

"Two is better than one. Plus, Ms. Hadley takes such pride in being part of the Neighborhood Watch. So where did you get the shovel, and why are you digging holes?"

Lyla cleared her throat. "I went to Mr. Tibbs's hardware store. I needed to dig up something I buried back there a long time ago."

"What on earth did you bury in our backyard?" her mom asked.

The past. At least she'd thought so. "It's not important."

"Important enough to go out and purchase a shovel."

Lyla leaned over the kitchen counter, resting on her elbows. "Don't worry. I covered the hole back up. And I've made some headway packing up my room."

The truth was, she'd made zilch progress with packing her room, but she had every intention of getting started as soon as she calmed down from her earlier run-in with Travis.

"I'm glad you're handling everything," her mom said. "Your father and I need the house to sell if we want to fund the rest of our trip."

"You don't have enough money for your travels?" Lyla had assumed they did. Why on earth would they leave town without enough income to cover their trip? That seemed irresponsible, and her parents had preached responsibility to Lyla every chance they got.

"We will, once the house sells. And it will sell. Why wouldn't it?" Her mom's laugh sounded nervous and unsure.

Lyla wasn't sure what to say right now. This was so unlike her parents.

"No more digging holes in the backyard, okay?" her mom asked.

"Sure. Unless you have a coffee brewer buried in the backyard. Then maybe," Lyla said sarcastically.

"Oh, honey. You should give up coffee," her mother advised. "It gave your Aunt Evie fibroids, you know. I just think—"

Lyla cut her mom off. "You're wasting your breath." Because coffee was her best friend these days. The kind she'd failed to be for Travis. The kind who never lied and promised to keep in touch, knowing it wasn't true.

Opinion: Coffee is a true writer's best friend.

"I'm glad you and Dad are doing okay," Lyla said.

"We are. Has Allison stopped by to see you yet?" her mom asked.

"Just like *you* told her to."

"She's such a nice woman. I don't know why you two weren't closer in school. Oh, I have to go. Your father's in the restroom again and he's out of TP."

TMI. "Okay. Love you. Tell Dad I love him too."

"We love you to the top of Mount Everest and back." She giggled quietly. "One day I'll say that and it'll actually be true. Assuming the house sells so we can afford to go . . ."

No pressure.

"Bye, honey."

"Bye, Mom." Lyla disconnected the call and looked around the room, which suddenly felt too quiet. If she had known her parents' trip relied solely on her ability to sell the house, she might not have agreed. What if she couldn't sell it? What if there was some freak accident? What if . . . ?

She stopped herself. The truth was, if her parents had stayed, they'd be driving her nuts and she'd be wishing for a little peace and quiet. Turning, she glanced at the old 7-Up bottle lying on the kitchen counter and the unfolded bucket list beside it. As she looked at the list, a drop of water splashed the paper. Lyla looked up where there was a dark wet spot forming on the ceiling.

"No!" She swiped the bucket list before another water drop could ruin it. Instead of landing on the paper this time, when she looked back up, the next water droplet hit her right between the eyes. "Ew." She wiped her face and tried to see past the sting of dirty water.

More drops came down in quickening speed. She needed a bucket. "Looks like I'll be taking another trip to Mr. Tibbs's hardware store," she muttered.

This day was turning out to be a complete wash. Literally.

"You're back," Mr. Tibbs mumbled thirty minutes later as she walked into his store.

Weren't independent business owners supposed to be appreciative of their customers? Lyla had tried to make nice conversation with the store owner earlier, and all she'd gotten for her effort were little jabs, the kind Joe used to put out. "I have a problem at my parents' house," Lyla said matter-of-factly. "A leak in the kitchen ceiling."

"Leak?" Mr. Tibbs repeated, showing slight interest in her now. "That's not good. It's supposed to rain all afternoon and into the night."

Lyla didn't need a forecast. "I need a bucket."

With a huff, Mr. Tibbs pointed to a space against the wall where there was a stack of gray buckets. "Grab one of those. Five dollars each."

Lyla headed in that direction and pulled one off the top. "How do I get the leak to stop? The house is for sale. I can't have showings with a leaky ceiling and a bucket full of rain-water on the counter."

"You'll need to climb onto the roof and patch the hole. Could be from a missing shingle. Shingles are on aisle two."

Lyla took a moment to pinch the bridge of her nose. What had she gotten herself into? She didn't know a thing about home repairs. "I don't have a ladder."

"Aisle seven." Mr. Tibbs pointed across the store. "But if I were you, I'd just get myself a handyman. Wouldn't want you to chip one of those pretty nails." He made a show of checking her left hand, then grunted. "Never mind."

It was something Joe would've done, an insult with barely a word. Those tiny insults from Joe had stuck to Lyla's confidence like barbs from a cactus, over time creating a callused exterior. Insults were the same as opinions, so she couldn't fault Joe for his beliefs. That's what she used to tell herself.

"A single woman like yourself should probably just call someone," Mr. Tibbs grumbled, reaching behind him to pull a business card from where it was pinned to a small bulletin board. He slid it across the counter. "This guy might be able to help. Give him a call."

Lyla read the name aloud. "The Handyman." There was a cartoon of a guy wearing a tool belt with an oversized hammer. A cell phone number was on the bottom of the card followed by instructions to call or text anytime. "Who is he?"

"A person with a ladder who can fix your roof. Beggars can't be choosers, now can they?" Mr. Tibbs and Ms. Hadley should hang out. They were perfect for each other.

"Thank you. How much do I owe you?" Lyla asked.

Mr. Tibbs tapped a few keys on his register and rang her up. "Five dollars and thirty-five cents."

Lyla paid, took the bucket and business card, and stepped back out into the pouring rain. She didn't want to think about how much water was standing on her parents' kitchen floor right now. One of the only things in the house that wasn't packed was a stack of towels her mom left in the bathroom for Lyla to use during her stay. Lyla would need all of them just to soak up the mess.

By the time she reached her car in the parking lot, she was drenched head to toe. Before setting off, she texted the number for The Handyman.

Lyla: *Hi. I got your business card from the hardware store. I have a leak in my roof that needs attention asap. Can you help me?*

A reply quickly popped on her screen.

Private: *Sure. Text me your address. I'll head your way now.*

She wasn't sure she could rely on Mr. Tibbs not to recommend some creep. For all she knew, The Handyman could be a serial killer. Echo Cove had never had one, but there was a first for everything, right? And most towns didn't have more than one serial killer if they ever had one at all.

Private: *Do you want me to come?*

Lyla looked out the front windshield as rain came down harder. She didn't have much choice, and the worst-case scenario of her overactive imagination probably wouldn't be the case.

She texted back.

Lyla: *Yes, please. My address is: 214 Briar Lilly Road.*

Private: *Be there in fifteen.*

Lyla: *Perfect. See you soon.*

Lyla was about ten minutes out. With a little luck, she'd beat The Handyman to her parents' home with five minutes to spare. She could use that time to devise an escape plan in the case that he was Echo Cove's first-ever serial killer.

Chapter 6

Opinion: Reality falls somewhere between the best- and worst-case scenarios.
—Delilah Dune, opinion writer

The puddle she'd left in the kitchen was a small lake by the time she arrived home. Grabbing the bucket she'd purchased from Mr. Tibbs, she placed it under the leak and glanced up just in time to get a second raindrop to the eye today. "Ugh!"

The doorbell rang.

Even though she could only see out of one eye, she headed in that direction and opened the door, apologizing before she'd even set eyes on the person waiting on the porch. "Sorry for the goth clown look," she said, covering a hand over one eye.

"Goth clown?" the man asked.

"Water from the leak got in my eye. Runny mascara and blush equals goth clown," she explained. "Never mind. Come on in. Thank you for getting here so quickly."

"Anytime." The man's voice was deep and gravelly. And familiar.

Narrowing her one good eye, she lowered her hand, blinking the other eye until the blur was gone. "Travis? What are you doing here?"

"You invited me."

"I'm pretty sure I didn't." She looked past him to the open front door. "Listen, I'm expecting someone right now, so your apology will have to wait."

"Apology? I'm not the one who did anything wrong."

After her breakup with Joe, Lyla had surpassed her limit for conflict and confrontation for at least the next year. "The past is the past. We can move on from it or stay stuck in it. It's your call. Either way, we'll have to do it another time. I'm kind of busy right now."

"Is that the reason you never opened my emails?" he asked. "Too busy?"

She tried to roll her eyes, but her left eye still stung. Where was this handyman? He said he'd be here in fifteen minutes. "Look, it's been years. You and I don't really know one another anymore. We're practically strangers."

"Whose fault is that?" He placed his hands on his hips, which she realized were strapped with a tool belt. "I disagree, though. We're far from strangers." He seemed to scrutinize her as he gave her a slow once-over. "Same eyes. Same crease between your brows when you're too serious. Or when I used to do something you knew would get us in trouble." He pointed at her face. "Same Ursa Major constellation on your cheek right there."

Lyla had forgotten that he'd always pointed out how the freckles made a perfect Ursa Major pattern.

"Maybe it's been years, but I still know you, Ly. And I know why you didn't stay in touch."

She didn't have the bandwidth for a trip down Memory Lane. "Travis, it's not a good time."

"Fear," he said. "When something scared you, you used to shut down or run away. You never just faced it head-on. I'm just not sure what it is you were afraid of with me."

Her throat constricted, swollen with emotion. Shutting down or running away felt like good options right now. Her gaze flicked over her shoulder at the leak, which seemed to be getting worse. She imagined the ceiling caving in at any point. One a sigh, she faced Travis again. "Travis, I'm waiting on someone. Two somebodies, actually, because a guy is also scheduled to pick up these donation boxes today."

"That's fine, because I'm not here for socializing," he said in a curt tone that she'd never heard from him. "I'm here for a job." He looked past her toward the kitchen, suddenly all business. "Where's the leak? In there?" Instead of waiting for her to respond, he started walking toward her kitchen.

"What are you doing?" She pushed the front door closed before following behind him.

He stopped in front of the bucket that she'd purchased from Mr. Tibbs's hardware store and looked up. "Yeah, I see. Is this the only one?"

Lyla's brain connected the dots. Travis had told her he supported his nomad lifestyle by doing odd jobs for a living. "*You're* The Handyman?"

He glanced over his shoulder. "I guess you have changed a little bit. You've gotten a bit slower without me to keep you on your toes."

Without thinking, Lyla swatted at his shoulder. "I am not slower." The touch zinged like static electricity.

"I'll take care of this leak. It's supposed to rain all night, so I better get started. If you need me, I'll be on the roof." He turned his back to her and started walking toward the front of the house.

"You're going on the roof now?" Panic shot through her. "That's dangerous. What if you fall?"

Travis glanced over his shoulder, pausing at the door. "Then I hope you'll be there to catch me. Oh, that's right. Out of sight, out of mind. In that case, I hope your neighbor Ms. Hadley is still heading the neighborhood watch." With a wink, he opened and closed the door behind him.

After a few minutes of trying not to worry, Lyla stepped

outside with her umbrella and looked up at Travis, who was already walking around on the rooftop. There was a ladder propped against the house. It was slick with rainwater now, just like the roof itself.

"Be careful!" she called up to him.

By the looks of it, Travis was hammering new shingles to the spot where the leak was originating. He had on a yellow rain jacket with a hood, which was good. Although his jeans were probably getting soaked through.

She watched as he shifted, placed his hammer back on his belt, and stood. Her pulse stopped. If it was her, she would have fallen by now. She'd be in the hospital or the morgue. One or the other.

He took a step in her direction. Then, in slow motion, he seemed to skid on the shingles, his arms flying out to the sides.

Lyla screamed and threw up her own arms as if she could catch him as his body lunged forward and he skidded down the roof. He came to a stop after a couple feet. He was nowhere near falling off, but her imagination had already gone there, and according to her blood pressure, Travis had hit the ground and broken every bone in his body.

"Are you okay?" she shrieked.

"No!" he called back. "I think I wet my pants."

Lyla stiffened, unsure of how to respond.

"I'm fairly sure it's only rainwater, but you never know."

She didn't mean to laugh, but she couldn't help herself. "Physically okay," she clarified, shouting loud over the sound of rain. "Are you physically okay?"

"I'm fine. There's just a little blood."

"Blood?" At the mention, Lyla went weak. This was why nursing school was never an option for her.

"Yeah. I scraped my arm up pretty good. Do you have Band-Aids?"

Her parents had boxed up the entire house. There wasn't

anything inside, but maybe there was a first aid kit in her car. "Yes, I think I have something. Come on down. But don't fall."

"Like I said, just make sure you catch me if I do."

"Ow!"

Lyla ran an alcohol wipe over Travis's abrasions as he laid his arm out on the kitchen counter. "I don't remember you being such a wimp." She paused. "Actually, I'm getting déjà vu right now. I do recall you being a big baby over a scrape you got that last summer together."

"Trying to climb in through your bedroom window. Totally worth it."

"We weren't dating, Trav. You could have rung the doorbell and come in the normal way."

"I didn't want to let my youth pass me over without climbing in through a girl's window. Even if she wasn't into me as more than a friend." He flinched slightly as she cleaned his wound. "You nursed my injury that day too."

"Yes, I did . . . I'm sorry," she said quietly. "I truly am."

"I scared you half to death out there, so I'd say we're even now."

She swiped the alcohol wipe over his wound again, pressing harder this time.

"Ow!"

His groan made her grin.

"You're tough, you know that?"

Yeah, she knew. One had to be tough to go through what she had these past couple of months. Or years, with Joe. Leaning forward, without thinking, she blew the alcohol on his skin dry. It was something her mom used to do when Lyla skinned her knee.

Her brain quickly caught up to her actions, and she felt the thick tension between them. This was a different kind of tension than the kind they'd shared in Travis's truck, when he'd been mad at her. This tension was the very kind that had frightened her at eighteen. The brewing kind from an attraction hard to ignore.

Peeling the backing off the Band-Aid, she stretched it over the long scrape along Travis's forearm.

"Thank you, Nurse Lyla."

"You're welcome." She pulled her hands back in front of her.

"If the whole writing thing doesn't work out, you'd make a good nurse."

"How did you know that the writing thing *did* work out?" she asked.

"I read your column. 'Delilah's Delusions.' "

Now she looked at him, her lips parting. "I didn't think anyone knew that was me." Her mom was proud of her, yeah, but Lyla knew her parents weren't fans of the opinions Lyla wrote. She doubted they bragged to the folks in Echo Cove about her accomplishments.

"You know there's no such thing as a secret staying a secret for long. Not here, at least. I enjoy reading the column."

"You do?" she asked.

"Mostly. I can tell you're trying to get a rise out of your readers. But I'm impressed with your success."

She looked down and away, some part of her wishing he was impressed by some other aspect of her current life. She hadn't done anything important since moving away. She hadn't changed or saved lives. "It's not that impressive."

"It is to me. But what do I know? I'm just a nomad with a hammer."

"Without you and your hammer, my parents' house would be underwater by now."

Travis noticed the 7-Up bottle nearby and reached for it. "So this is it, huh?"

Lyla grabbed the folded paper that she'd already pulled out. "Yup. And here's the bucket list we almost finished."

Travis inspected the crossed-out items, reading them off. "Spend a whole day at the lake without sunblock. Were we really this stupid?"

"My unpopular opinion is that we were geniuses. Albeit sunburned ones by the end of summer."

He chuckled as he kept reading. "Roast s'mores over a bonfire. Watch the same movie four times." He pointed at her. "I think that was your idea."

"I was trying to prove the theory that a good movie only gets better each time you watch it. We watched *Sleepless in Seattle*," she remembered.

"And what do you know? It's playing again now right here in Echo Cove."

Lyla wasn't sure why she was so nervous. She and Travis had been best friends once, and they'd shared everything with one another. Almost everything, at least. She'd never shared how her feelings had evolved, when they were eighteen, shifting from friendship to something more. Something scarier.

Travis tapped his finger on the list. "The list says four times. We only watched the movie three times, if I remember correctly." His voice dropped a note, delving deeper and reverberating through her. "Then I think we should see it again. Together."

Lyla had a big imagination. Maybe she'd just fantasized him saying that. "What?"

"Let's go to the movies tomorrow night." He held up the list. "It's bad luck not to finish. Fourth time's the charm?"

Say no, Lyla. Just say no. She didn't have a good reason to turn down the invitation though, and part of her didn't want to.

"Come on, Ly. You owe me. We've missed out on a full decade of each other's lives."

She rolled her lips together as she looked at Travis, debating her decision. Who was she kidding? It'd always been impossible to say no to Travis Painter. That's why she'd cut him off completely when she went to college. He could talk her into just about anything. "Sure. Seeing a movie sounds great."

June 30

Dear Diary,

Travis came to my window last night. It was like a scene out of a movie. I heard a tap, tap, tap and then I pulled back my curtain and there he was, holding a single flower. He'd picked it from my mom's garden, which she wouldn't be thrilled about if she knew. It was the most romantic thing that has ever happened to me. Romance and Travis do not go together, though. He wasn't being romantic. He was just being funny. My mind knows that, but my heart doesn't.

I have to listen to my mind. Otherwise, I'll end up like my mother. No offense, Mom, but I can't get stuck in Echo Cove my entire life.

Later, Diary.

Lyla

Chapter 7

Opinion: No one's opinion is ever the right one.
Least of all mine—according to my ex.
—Delilah Dune, opinion writer

When you didn't have a proper ladder at your disposal, you made do.

Lyla balanced while standing on her parents' countertop, using the tiny brush of her Wite-Out container to paint the dark spot on the ceiling. She'd briefly considered going to Mr. Tibbs's hardware store for real paint and a real brush, but the Wite-Out seemed like an acceptable hack, and it was actually working.

She could have called Travis, but he'd made it clear he wouldn't accept payment, in which case, she didn't want to take advantage of their friendship. If they were even considered friends again.

"There." Lyla lowered her Wite-Out brush. "Good as new."

Her ex, Joe, would've had something to say about the job she'd just done. He'd probably call it amateur or insufficient, feeding her endless insecurities. She'd never been insecure until him, and some part of her hated that she'd allowed a guy to affect her so deeply that she questioned her hair, her writing, the way she did anything, including covering this dark spot in the ceiling. Some part of her had thought that's just what people did when they were in love. They compromised who they were. She'd seen her mom do it a million times. Her dad too.

People in love didn't cheat, though. That was the final big red flag that had opened her eyes.

She wasn't sure if it was Joe's influence eating away at her inner voice, but the struggle to form a decent opinion was real these days. She'd started to stick to safe topics, like food and pets, instead of stirring the pot and riling up readers the way her editor, Bob, loved. Readers enjoyed dogs—who didn't?—but they loved controversy more.

Finished with one job on her to-do list, Lyla headed down the hall toward her old bedroom. She needed to box up some more stuff and either put it in the trash or the donation pile. *Where do I even start?* Her vast collection of stuffed animals seemed like a good place. She'd never once wanted to part with any of them, but what thirty-year-old had nearly one hundred stuffed animals? She couldn't keep them all. Maybe just one. She picked through them and finally settled on a brown bear that she'd gotten as a baby. It was her first stuffed animal, and it had seen her through her whole childhood.

Hugging it against her body, she sucked in a cleansing breath. The bear stayed. The rest could go.

Later in the day, Lyla angled her body from side to side, as she checked herself out in front of the mirror. Why had she agreed to going to the movie tonight with Travis? It wasn't a date. They were just friends, but that was the problem. He was right, earlier. She had been afraid of something. There was nothing worse than falling in love with your best friend and knowing it wasn't reciprocated. That it would never be reciprocated.

Correction. Worse would have been if he had reciprocated, because, according to her mother, a person had to choose between love and their dream. You could only chase one, and more than anything, Lyla had wanted to make a name for herself. And she had. She was Delilah of "Delilah's Delusions." It wasn't exactly the name she'd dreamed of. She'd wanted to be a serious author who wrote books that made people feel deep emotions. She wanted to use her words to reach inside of readers' chests and rip their hearts out.

Maybe that was a bit graphic, but it was the way those books that had served as early inspirations for her had felt when she'd first read them. Those books had done that with surgical precision and then neatly tucked her heart right back into its space, changed forever by a story that wasn't even real. She'd wanted to do that too. She'd wanted to make a name for herself by writing books that made a difference, not clickbait opinion columns.

"I should cancel, shouldn't I?" she asked, talking to herself. "I can tell Travis I have diarrhea."

She'd done an article on that topic once.

Opinion: If someone claims to have diarrhea, they're most definitely lying to get out of being with you.

Lyla pulled out her phone. "I'll tell him I have a headache." She'd done that opinion write-up as well.

Opinion: When a woman claims to have a headache, she's just not that into you.

It was a crummy excuse. Travis read her column. He would know she was lying.

As she debated, a text pinged on her phone.

Allison: *Are you still coming tonight? The Dinnerware Party* *starts at six, but you can come over early and hang out. It'll be fun!!!*

Triple exclamation points. Her editor, Bob, would cringe at the extra punctuation. She'd never actually intended on accepting Allison's invitation, but now she had a legit excuse to cancel on Travis.

Lyla: *Of course I'll be there. Wouldn't miss it!!!*

She triple-exclamation-pointed back. How bad could a Dinnerware Party be? Certainly not as bad as hanging out with your former best friend, who you almost fell in love with and ghosted for the last decade.

Pulling up her text message thread with Travis, she tapped her finger along the screen, not giving herself time to second-guess.

Lyla: *Hey. Sorry, but something came up for tonight. I can't hang out after all.*

There. Done. It was safer to spend an evening with Bernadette, a woman who undoubtedly despised her, than Travis Painter. She'd left him in her past with good reason—one that only she, her diary, and Sonny, the heel-biting, bike-chasing, good-listening dog knew.

At 6:00 p.m., Lyla pulled into Allison's driveway. The house was smaller than she remembered, but still bigger than the house where Lyla had grown up. Allison's parents had both been well off, and Allison was their only child. She had everything she could ever want, including the affection of the most popular guy at school.

Pushing open the driver's-side door, Lyla stepped out. She yawned as she headed up the driveway. Allison had a picture-perfect porch, with two white rocking chairs flanking the front door. She had hanging plants on either side and a huge wreath full of flowers and garlands at the center of her royal blue-colored door. It was like Allison had pulled her porch straight off a cover of *Martha Stewart* magazine.

Lyla pressed the doorbell and waited for what seemed like forever. She tapped the button again and finally heard footsteps inside. A moment later, the door opened and Allison stared back at her.

"You came!" Allison said as if she hadn't thought Lyla actually would.

Lyla glanced back at the driveway. Her car was the only one here so far. "I thought you said the party started at six."

Allison reached for Lyla's arm and tugged her inside the house. "You're right on time. We're going to have so much fun."

Fun was a subjective thing. Lyla's idea of a good time usually involved her laptop and solitude. "Thanks again for inviting me. Everyone can use good cooking ware."

Allison seemed to study her, as if she was trying to decipher if Lyla was being sincere.

Lyla wasn't, but the kind intent was there. In all honesty, Lyla didn't own any pots or pans. She used paper plates and got a lot of takeout.

"Dinnerware *is* something everyone needs. That's the beauty of it." Allison was practically beaming, her skepticism gone. "Would you like a cup of coffee?"

"Do you have decaf?" Lyla asked. It was too late in the day for caffeine, but never too late for coffee.

"Of course. I have muffins too. I just put them in my new Dinnerware container. They're still warm if you want one."

"Yes, please. I'm starving." Lyla followed Allison inside her house and into the kitchen area, where Allison gestured to a small farm-style dining table with a charming bouquet of wildflowers at its center.

"Have a seat. Make yourself at home."

Lyla looked around, noticing the framed pictures on her walls. There were two kids in the photographs, prominently displayed everywhere. Not a wall in the home was bare. But there was no evidence of the children in the house. No crayon marks on the walls. No toys. Were they Allison's niece and nephew? Lyla knew that Allison was divorced from Ernie. Did she and Ernie have kids together? Had Ernie gotten custody?

After a minute, Allison stepped over to the table and slid a plate in front of Lyla. "Here you are! One carrot muffin and one zucchini muffin. They're amazing. Trust me."

Lyla turned her attention to the muffins. They were picture perfect, just like this house. Like Allison. "These could be on the cover of a foodie magazine," Lyla joked as she reached for one. "They're almost too pretty to eat."

"No such thing," Allison said.

Without thinking, Lyla looked at the pictures on the wall again. She wanted to ask, but she didn't want to pry. She'd never even considered going into real journalism because she wasn't a prier. Putting her nose in other people's business had never been comfortable for her. Fiction is actually what she preferred, and her opinion column wasn't too far from that most days.

Allison followed Lyla's gaze and took an audible breath. "Ashley Grace and Ethan Mark." Her eyes instantly grew shiny, and her smile wobbled, as if she no longer had the strength to hold it up.

"Who . . . are they?" As soon as the question left Lyla's mouth, she instinctively knew she probably shouldn't have asked. Tonight was supposed to be fun for Allison. Judging by Allison's sudden tears, this wasn't a happy topic.

"You haven't kept up with the gossip around here in Echo Cove, have you?" A small laugh tumbled off her lips. Something told Lyla that Allison's laugh was more sad than humorous.

"I was never one for gossip, I guess." And Lyla's mom had never brought up what was happening with the people in the community.

Allison stepped away to prepare a mug of coffee. She returned a moment later and slid it in front of Lyla, then took the seat beside her at the table. "Two years ago, we were in an accident. Ernie was driving. I was in the front passenger seat. We both walked away without a scratch, but my two angels never woke up."

Lyla felt a wave of nausea. As a writer, she was supposed to have words for every situation, but there were none for this. "I'm so sorry, Allison. I had no idea."

The muscles of Allison's neck visibly tightened as she swallowed. "Our marriage was already suffering, but that was the straw that broke us. The kids were the glue that held us together anyway. I got pregnant with Ethan Mark before Ernie and I were married. I'm not sure we ever would have married if not for that. At the time, I thought getting pregnant was fate stepping in to ensure that Ernie and I stayed together." Regret worked its way into her expression, making subtle lines and indentations in her otherwise smooth skin. "I don't believe that anymore. Anyway, after the accident, Ernie started drinking, and I became depressed. The folks I thought were my friends around here really weren't. Those folks who I looked down on at one time are the ones who pulled me up." She blew out a breath. "I guess if there's any lesson in all this, that's it. True friends show up when times are tough, while those who aren't true disappear on you." She pointed at Lyla. "Now there's an opinion for that column of yours, although I think it's more fact than anything."

Lyla wasn't sure what to say. "I don't know how you're still functioning."

"Trust me, I still have my down days, but for the most part, I've learned to pull myself up on my own. Even when it's hard."

Lyla tore a piece off her muffin, not to eat it but because her hands needed something to do. "I'm so sorry for what you've gone through, Allison."

"Thanks." Allison looked past Lyla to the framed pictures on the wall. "Those two kids were my entire world. It's been a long road to building a new world. New friends. New job. New everything." She sighed softly.

Lyla was rebuilding her life too, although her story wasn't nearly as traumatic as Allison's. In comparison, Lyla's life had been a cakewalk. "I'm glad to count you as a friend. You're inspiring."

"Why? Because I lost my kids and my marriage?" Her tone was almost sarcastic. Lyla guessed that Allison had gotten the same comments from others before.

"No. You're inspiring because you survived what a lot of people wouldn't. If it were me, I might still be in bed."

It had been hard enough to get out of bed after Lyla's breakup with Joe. Or actually, the air mattress, seeing that Joe had kept the bed. What bothered Lyla most was that Joe had to be the one to end the relationship. After his indiscretions, *she* should have left *him*. She'd known it was time. She'd discovered the affair a week earlier. She'd wanted to leave, but the fear of being on her own was stronger than her desire to go. The fear had been like quicksand. If you stood in it for too long, it became harder and harder to step away.

"A good friend wouldn't allow you to stay in bed," Allison said. "*I* wouldn't allow it."

Lyla reached for Allison's hand and squeezed. "I wish I could have been there for you." She and Allison barely knew one another, but Lyla wouldn't have let Allison down during such a tragic time. At least she'd like to think she wouldn't.

Allison patted Lyla's hand. Then she cleared her throat, sniffled, and tipped her head at the muffins. "So? How are they? Good? Was the coffee to your liking?"

Lyla pulled her hand back from Allison's and broke another piece off her muffin. This time she popped it into her mouth and chewed. "Mm, they taste as delicious as they look."

"Thanks. I guess no one else is coming to this Dinnerware Party. We should probably just reschedule." She pushed back from the table and stood up, her movements rushed. Then the doorbell rang and Allison's whole demeanor lit up. She practically ran to her front door like an excited child.

Whoever had decided to come to this party, Lyla wanted to give them the biggest hug. After all that Allison had endured, she deserved the world on a Dinnerware platter.

"Bernadette! I'm so glad you made it!" Allison called from the front of the house.

Lyla suddenly felt like shrinking. If she gave Bernie a hug, Bernie might knock Lyla's head off her shoulders. Lyla briefly considered slipping out the back door and escaping.

"Lyla, guess who it is?" Allison called back to her.

There was no getting out of this. Resigned, Lyla headed into the living room and faced her nemesis.

Bernie didn't even attempt to hide her disgust. "You invited her?" she asked Allison. "Why?"

Allison seemed oblivious to the tension in the air. "The more the merrier," she said with a giggle that rolled easily off her lips. "Now come sit down, you two. I'll show you all the summer Dinnerware selection. You're going to love it, I promise."

Opinion: Keep your friends close and your enemies closer—but never turn your back on either.

Allison lifted a large plastic cake carrier and flashed it at Lyla and then Bernie. "Everyone needs one of these," she said dramatically, before proceeding to list all the carrier's features.

Lyla couldn't focus on anything Allison was saying. All she could think of was the tension radiating off Bernie sitting beside her on the couch. Why did Bernie hate her so much? Was it all about the sloppy joe?

"And the best part is that this cake carrier comes in several festive colors. Pink. Purple. Turquoise. Who doesn't want a turquoise cake carrier?" Allison was practically bouncing on her heels.

"I'll take one," Bernie said politely.

"Really?" Allison set the cake carrier down on the couch and gave Bernie an impulsive hug. "Thank you. You're going to love it." When Allison pulled back, she looked at Lyla expectantly.

"Oh. I . . . well . . ." Lyla had never made a cake. Ever. "I guess I'll take one too," she said, feeling peer pressure akin to the kind that had run rampant in high school. Then she braced herself for Allison's hug. Peeking over Allison's shoulder as they hugged, Lyla caught Bernie's eye. Bernie seemed to be laughing, but it didn't feel like she was laughing at Lyla. Instead, it felt like they were sharing a laugh at this experience.

Allison pulled back. "This is going to be the best night. I just know it. I have something else to show you, ladies. Just a second." Allison disappeared out of the room.

For a moment, Lyla and Bernie sat in silence.

"I can make up an excuse and leave if you want me to," Lyla finally offered. "I can tell her that I forgot that I have other plans." It wouldn't have been a complete lie because Travis had invited her out tonight too.

"Why would I want that?" Bernie asked. "If I have to endure this party for the millionth time, you should have to stay as well."

"Millionth time?" Lyla asked.

"Not literally, but that's how it feels. Do you know how many cake carriers I have?"

Lyla didn't mean to giggle, but the thought was funny. "You must be a great friend."

Bernie looked down at her lap. "To those who deserve it."

Lyla's chest ached. She wanted to deserve that kind of friendship from Bernie. She wasn't sure why, but she needed it suddenly. She hadn't had a whole lot of friends in her life and most hadn't stuck. In some cases, that was completely Lyla's fault. In other cases, it was just life. Some friends weren't meant to stay. They were only meant to drift in and out of your life, rolling in and out with the tide.

"Matching cake cutters!" Allison announced, walking back into the room. "Can you imagine having a cake cutter that matches your carrier?" she asked in disbelief.

Bernie slid an amused look toward Lyla. It felt like a glimpse into what it might be like to be actual friends with Bernie.

"Who wants one?" Allison asked.

Both Bernie and Lyla raised their hands. "Me!"

July 3

Dear Diary,

It's surreal to think that in just a month I'll be living somewhere new. I've lived in this house since the day I was born, but it's all about to change.

Also, I sent one of my stories off to a publisher today! I am crossing everything that the editor loves my work and wants to offer me a contract. Wouldn't that be awesome? All my dreams are on the brink of coming true and I am here for it.

Stay tuned, Diary!

Chapter 8

Opinion: Unless you're a baby, there is no such
thing as new beginnings and fresh starts.
—Delilah Dune, opinion writer

The next morning, Lyla shuffled down the hall toward the kitchen, desperately seeking coffee. She stopped midway into the kitchen and blinked heavily, her brain processing the empty space on the granite countertop.

Right, no coffeepot. *Ugh.* She had no desire to get dressed and venture out, but it appeared she didn't have much choice.

After dressing and pulling her hair into a ponytail, she got in her car and drove to the only coffee shop in town. Maybe after last night's Dinnerware Party, Bernie wouldn't be so cold to her. The cool air conditioning hit her skin as she stepped through the entrance. Keeping her head ducked, in case any more former teachers were hiding in the shadows, she headed straight to the counter. Instead of Bernie, a young man with black hair and an expander earring greeted her.

"Hello, what can I get you?" he asked in a much friendlier tone than Bernie used the last time Lyla stopped in.

"Um." Lyla glanced beyond the young man, looking toward the back area. "Is your boss here?"

"Boss?" He furrowed a pierced brow. Peeking out from his white T-shirt and dark brown apron, Lyla noticed a detailed tattoo that crept up his neck and down his arms. It looked like a giant gecko of some type, which she found curious. She had a tattoo of her own, and she'd researched the significance of various creatures before making her choice. She wasn't sure about this one, though.

"The owner of this coffee shop," Lyla clarified. "Is Bernadette here?"

The man cleared his throat. "Actually, Bernadette and I own it together. We're a mom-and-pop shop."

"Mom-and-pop?" Lyla repeated. The man in front of her was maybe twenty-one. She glanced at his left hand, and sure enough, there was a black onyx band on his ring finger. "You and Bernie are married?"

"In spirit, not legally. But we don't need papers to prove our commitment."

Lyla let that sink in for a moment. Bernie had her own business and a guy who was willing to wear an apron for her. Some part of her was a little envious.

Opinion: A man who wears an apron and cooks is a keeper.

"So, do you want a coffee or are you looking for Bernadette?" he asked. "She's in the back doing admin stuff. She's the brains, and I'm the pretty face who pours the brew." He winked and offered his hand to shake. "I'm Eric."

"Lyla Dune."

Something seemed to register in Eric's expression as he pulled his hand away and bounced a finger in her direction. "Hey, I've heard about you."

Whatever he'd heard probably wasn't favorable. "The whole sloppy joe thing was an accident," Lyla said. "I never, ever would have done that to Bernie on purpose. I wanted to be her friend. I thought she was cool and talented. You have to believe me."

Eric didn't appear to judge her. In fact, he seemed like the most easygoing guy in Echo Cove. "You gotta admit, that was a pretty brutal experience. Freshly dumped. Brown stains on her backside. An entire class laughing as she read an important paper."

Lyla grimaced. "Yeah."

"It took her a whole year to even divulge the story. That's how painful it was to her. It still is."

Lyla wanted nothing more than to fix that situation, if she could. "How do I go about being her friend?" she asked, feeling completely vulnerable.

Eric seemed to assess her. "Bernadette is kind of like an ice cube. Not saying she's cold. She's actually one of the warmest people I've ever known, but you have to melt off those protective layers, a little bit at a time."

"I have to melt her?" Lyla wasn't planning to be in town long enough to melt anyone.

"Eric, can you—" Bernadette walked into the front area and stopped when she saw Lyla, her features tightening. "What are you doing here?"

Lyla glanced between Eric and Bernadette. "I couldn't stay away. This place has the best coffee I've ever had."

Bernadette folded her arms over her chest. "Really?"

"Truly," Lyla said. "I was just about to order a Blondie with coconut milk."

Bernadette nodded slowly. "I'll make it." She looked at Eric. "We have a delivery out back. Can you handle it?"

"Sure, babe." Eric kissed Bernadette's temple before walking through a metal swinging door.

"Your husband is nice," Lyla offered, watching Bernadette work.

She glanced over her shoulder. "I'm sure you have an opinion on older women dating younger men with tattoos and piercings."

Lyla heard the bitterness in Bernadette's tone. "I do, as a matter of fact."

Bernadette placed Lyla's coffee on the counter and lifted her chin as if waiting for Lyla to throw a verbal punch. Lyla knew that feeling all too well from her experience with Joe. Always bracing.

"My opinion is that you're a badass and I'm happy for you. I'm also a little jealous, if you want the truth."

Something warm flickered in Bernadette's eyes. She pushed the coffee closer to Lyla. "On the house."

Lyla debated whether she should insist on paying, but something told her that would be an insult somehow, and Lyla's goal was to melt a few layers off her old classmate before leaving town. It was a summer bucket list–worthy goal. "Thanks. See you later." Grabbing her coffee cup, she turned to walk away, talking over her shoulder and not pausing to give Bernadette time to respond when she said, "Maybe you'll join me next time."

A blue pickup truck sat in the driveway as Lyla turned in and parked. She looked around, noting the ladder. Was Travis on her roof?

"Trav?" she called up as she approached and he came into view. "What are you doing?"

He looked in her direction. "Checking out the patch job to make sure it's still sufficient." He was on all fours with a hammer in hand.

"And?" she asked.

Travis slid the hammer into his belt loop and stood, taking slow, deliberate steps toward the ladder. "Of course, it is. I'm good at what I do."

Lyla placed her hands on her hips. "You need to work on that self-esteem though."

As he neared the edge of the roof, he turned his back to her and started to descend the ladder, and *whoa*—In those jeans . . .

She tore her gaze away and waited for him to reach the ground before facing him again. "So it looks good?" she asked.

Something playful flashed in those caramel-colored eyes. "You tell me."

Her face immediately got hot. "I'm sorry?"

He gestured at the roof. "Want to go up and see for yourself?"

"Oh. No"—she shook her head quickly—"I don't do well with heights."

"I remember. That's why we put height stuff on our last bucket list."

She jabbed a finger into the side of his arm, unable to ignore the firmness of his muscles. "That's why *you* put height stuff on the list. It was unusually cruel, if you ask me."

"I was trying to help. And since you're still afraid . . ." he trailed off as he grinned.

"I'm not afraid. I just don't like heights."

He wiped the sleeve of his shirt over his forehead where a bead of sweat was making its way south. "Right. Well, you need to get over that because it's still on our final bucket list. Along with watching *Sleepless in Seattle* for the fourth time and jumping off the Pirate's Plank into Memory Lake."

"The Pirate's Plank?" Ever since she was fifteen, she'd been having a recurring nightmare about the day she'd tried and failed to jump off that plank. Knees shaking, head spinning, she'd fainted as she edged herself on the end of the plank. If not for some kind Samaritan, she might never have made it past that fifteenth birthday. "I wish you hadn't put that on the list. Call me chicken, but I can't jump off the Pirate's Plank."

"Here's an opinion for that column of yours: No one likes chicken."

"That first time was a near-death experience," she said, putting her hands on her hips.

"There were at least fifty people at the lake. No one would have let you drown, Ly."

"You weren't there," she shot back.

He blew out a small breath. "And I regret that to this day. I'll go with you this time. I'm here for a couple weeks. Plenty of time to check off the rest of our list."

Just the thought of jumping off the plank again had her heart racing. "I'm very busy this summer. I have deadlines, and there's a lot to do to sell this house. Otherwise, I'll be stuck in Echo Cove longer than I bargained for." And her parents might not get the funds needed for the rest of their trip.

"I can't write, but I can help you with the house."

"What?"

"I'll help," he said, one side of his mouth quirking. "On one condition."

"I don't like conditions. They're like verbal contracts—not legally binding, but the guilt is way worse than a lawsuit."

"This condition isn't so awful. I need a date to my sister's wedding."

"Date?" she repeated.

The other side of his mouth lifted to make a full smile. "Not the kissing kind of date. Just the kind who enjoy each other's company."

It was a tempting offer. She was a little in over her head with cleaning and packing the house.

Travis waved a hand. "Forget the condition. You don't have to be my date. I'll help you anyway. That's what friends are for, right? What do you need?"

She pulled in a breath, still hung up on the date idea. "Well, someone was supposed to come pick up all the boxes in the living room for donation, but the truck never came. I need to donate all that stuff before the house starts showing."

"You're in luck. I happen to have a truck that's perfect for moving boxes. Let's get the stuff in my truck right now and haul it to the thrift store." Travis was always a "now" guy. When he got an idea, it didn't have time to burn out. The list was the only thing he took his time with.

"Now?"

"It'll be one less thing you have to do on your own."

"You've already fixed the roof. I hate to ask you to go out of your way to help me with this too."

"You didn't ask. I offered. And afterward, we'll check off one of those bucket list items. It's bad luck not to finish," he said for the hundredth time.

"I'm not superstitious."

Travis narrowed his eyes. "Delilah's unpopular opinion: People who believe in superstitions are lying to themselves."

That was one of her opinions from last year. "I can't believe you read my column."

"Of course, I read it. You're my best friend, even if I'm no longer yours."

Ouch. She actually didn't have a best friend. Since leaving for college, she'd focused on her career and success.

"You don't want me to have bad luck, do you?" he pressed.

"I'm serious. I'm not superstitious, and I don't believe in luck."

"What *do* you believe in these days, Ly?" His tone wasn't critical. It wasn't judgmental. In a way, it felt like he was pitying her.

"I'm . . . I'm not sure anymore." The question took her by surprise.

"Then we'll add that to the existing list too." He nodded resolutely. "Find something for Lyla Dune to believe in. Right after jumping off the Pirate's Plank."

"You know what else is on that old bucket list of ours?" She waited as he seemed to think on his answer, coming up blank.

"What?" he asked.

"Skating." She watched his expression drop in an almost comical way. "So, if you want to check off that list, at some point this summer, you'll have to pull on some skates." She could almost see the memories of the doughnut seat cushion he'd had to sit on flashing across his mind. "Rethinking that thought about finishing the list?"

He was no longer smiling. "Nope. We face our fears together, right? Wasn't that always how it worked? And if we go down—"

She held up a hand and stopped him right there. "I went down after falling off the plank. You didn't catch me."

"I'll catch you this time"—he pointed in her direction— "if you agree to catch me when I fall on my butt in those skates."

After loading up Travis's truck with boxes, Lyla climbed into his passenger seat.

"Why didn't your parents just have a yard sale?" he asked, as he reversed out of the driveway and headed past Ms. Hadley's house. Lyla glanced into the yard curiously, looking for her neighbor's new little dog. She hadn't seen him for a couple of days.

"Yard sales are so much effort."

"This is a lot of effort too," he pointed out.

"I know. And I appreciate your help. I could not have done all that without you." She watched her old street pass by in the side window, remembering how she'd ridden her bike up and down until the sun set and the streetlights lit up. "This street brings back so many memories. This truck too."

He curled and released his grip on the steering wheel, wrapped with silver duct tape now. "For me too. My first summer with a license. I can still taste the freedom this truck gave me."

"We had some fun times in this truck." Travis had only been a few months older, but she wasn't in a rush to get her license. She was always content to just ride shotgun with Travis. "Tell me about that first year after high school." She looked over at him. "What was it like?"

"Not great." His playful grasp and release of the steering wheel turned to a steady grip that whitened his knuckles.

"That's all you're going to tell me?"

"I don't know. You left, and I guess I felt lost without you. I watched my dad make a joke of my sister for being pregnant and not married. The last straw was one Sunday sermon where my dad tried to compare Bailey to Mary in the Bible."

Lyla nearly pulled a muscle yanking her head in Travis's direction. "Jesus' mother?"

"He was only referencing what people would have thought of Mary if they'd discovered she was pregnant before marrying Joseph. I think his exact words were: *"kind of what you all think of my own daughter."* Travis pressed his face into his palm momentarily. "It was one thing for him to do that kind of stuff to me, but watching him do it to Bailey was unbearable. I begged Bailey to come with me when I moved, but she wasn't convinced that RV life and a newborn were a good idea. She was a single mother and, regardless of how my parents treated her, she needed them."

Lyla reached out and touched Travis's arm. "Must have been hard." And she was sorry that she hadn't been there for him.

"Yeah, but every mile, every town, it got a little easier for me to breathe. I kind of understood maybe a little bit of why you never looked back."

"My parents weren't like yours."

"No, but sometimes shedding the skin of your hometown make you a whole new person."

"I'm sorry."

"I know some might not find being a handyman all that glamorous, but my life is one of freedom. I like what I do. Sometimes, when life is rough, it's paving the way for something good. That's the way I see it."

"Wow, you're like a Yoda trapped in a handsome handy-man's body."

Travis's gaze cut from the road to her. "Handsome handyman?"

She looked away. "I was going for alliteration, okay? I'm a writer. That's what I do."

"Handsome and handy. I should put that on my business cards." He chuckled quietly as he pulled into a parking lot and cut the engine off in front of the thrift store.

"It might not get you the clientele you're looking for." She pushed the passenger door open with a groan. Her arms were already sore from loading the boxes in the back of the pick-up. Now they needed to unload them too.

Travis walked around to the back of the truck. "I've got this, if you're tired."

"I'm younger than you, remember? I can handle a few boxes." She stepped up beside him and held out her arms for Travis to place the first box.

"There you go," he said.

She ignored the sensation of his skin brushing over hers. "What's in these boxes anyway? Did my parents pack bricks?"

He grabbed a box in each arm, acting like they weighed nothing. Then he led the way to the store's entrance and managed to open the door for her to walk through. It was lit-tle things like that Lyla wished Joe had done. Little things built into bigger ones, and those bigger things had certainly come.

"Delivery!" Travis called to the man behind the counter. "These are the boxes from the Dune house."

"Oh, wow. Sorry we couldn't come get these boxes our-selves. The delivery truck needs a new engine," the thrift store owner explained.

"Not a problem," Travis said. "There's more coming. And if you need someone to pick up donations around town for you, me and my truck are available for a while." Travis handed the man his business card.

"The Handyman, huh?" The thrift store owner looked at him. "That's you?"

"Yes, sir. Handsome and handy." He glanced in Lyla's direction.

Lyla watched Travis interact with the store manager. Travis was proud of his business and his reputation. He had made something of himself from the preacher's son who'd grown up stirring up mischief in Echo Cove. She was proud of him too.

"Can you fix shelves?" the store owner asked. "I have a couple that have fallen apart."

"I can help with that," Travis said.

"Great. I'll be calling you then." The man shook Travis's hand.

After unloading all the boxes and getting back into the truck, Lyla glanced across the center console. "So that's how you get your work, huh?"

"Pretty much. There's always more than enough jobs to cover my expenses."

"Sounds kind of nice."

"It's freedom. I suppose your work is similar," he said.

Lyla fidgeted with her hands. "I guess. I can work from anywhere at any time. In the past, I've been bogged down with mortgage bills and utilities, but after my breakup with my ex, I no longer have a mortgage." And her apartment lease ended right around the time her parents asked her for their paramount favor. "Maybe I should get an RV like you."

"RV life isn't for everyone. Most people like to put down roots."

Even though she'd had big-city dreams, Lyla had always envisioned a house and family one day, after building a satisfying and stable career. Now she had none of those things. "So," she said, changing the subject to one that didn't invite panic, "remind me, what else was on our final bucket list?"

"You're agreeing to finishing the list?" he asked.

She shook her head. "No, I'm exploring the idea. If we tried, we'd have to make it quick. Because neither of us are committed to staying in Echo Cove."

"We have plenty of time to check off those last items, and maybe even add a few."

Laughter bubbled out of her. "I thought I was the over-achiever in this friendship."

"That's the thing about growing up. Some things change." He pulled up to a red light and glanced over. "And thankfully, some things never do."

Chapter 9

Opinion: Writer's block just means you need
more caffeine and chocolate.
—Delilah Dune, opinion writer

Lyla stared blankly at her computer screen. The words weren't flowing like they used to. Her opinions blurred with other people's and pieced with things she knew Bob would like. Lately, those things had begun to contradict who she was at her very core. A couple of months back, when she'd tried to write about the beauty of imperfections, Bob had insisted she shift what had started as a wholesome story about a beloved chipped coffee mug into a story about ignoring a man's flaws on a first date, because picky women turned into old maids.

The opinion made her nauseous, but it had sparked debate. And Bob had been happy, at least for that month.

Lyla closed her laptop. Maybe another bike ride would get her ideas flowing. After dropping off the donations, Travis had fixed her bike's tire. He was indeed handy and handsome. Walking her purple bike out of the garage, she swung her leg over the middle bar and let gravity roll her down the driveway. She was halfway past Ms. Hadley's house when the barking started.

Fear shot through Lyla as something brown darted toward her. A dog. A loud, barking, vicious dog was chasing her bike just like Ms. Hadley's prior dog used to do. It didn't matter that the creature was small, no bigger than her purse, when it was barking as loud as a mastiff and coming at her at the speed of light. She wasn't going to take her chances that it was actually friendly. Maybe Sonny had been part devil-dog, part angel-dog, but Lyla wanted to keep her fingers today. She needed them for typing later.

She pedaled as fast as she could, but the dog was still leaping toward her back tire. If his teeth punctured the wheel, it would deflate. "Go away! Go away, devil-dog!" she yelled behind her, wondering if Ms. Hadley had put the dog out as payback for all of the pranks Lyla and Travis had pulled at her expense.

They were all Travis's ideas. And they'd been harmless. Mostly. Maybe the fake spiders in the mailbox crossed the line. Maybe Lyla would get some baked treats from Bernadette's coffee shop next time she was there. She could support Bernie's business and also get brownie points with her neighbor.

Opinion: The road to forgiveness is paved with chocolate treats.

As she rode, the dog eventually disappeared, most likely turning back to guard its territory. She slowed her speed and let herself calm down, as her mind wandered from one topic to the next. Travis. The summer bucket list. The items that were still left were unchecked for a reason.

Opinion: Life knows exactly how to cure an oversized ego—with an oversized embarrassment.

As Lyla rode back to her parents' home, her cell phone buzzed in her pocket. She pulled it out and stared at the unknown number. "Hello?"

"Is this Ms. Dune?" a man's voice asked.

"Yes, it is."

"Hello, Ms. Dune. This is Peter Blake," the man said. "I'm a real estate agent in town. I was told you were the contact for the property on Briar Lilly Road. Is that correct?"

Lyla balanced her bike with her feet on either side, squinting against the sun as it rose beyond the tree line. "Yes, that's correct."

"I'm good friends with your parents. I told them I'd do everything I can to get their house sold for them, and I already have a couple who is very interested in looking at the place."

"Okay." She was nowhere near finished cleaning out her room, and she and Travis had several more trips to make to get the donations out of the living room. A person could barely walk around the living room at this point. Or her bedroom that wasn't packed up at all. "When would your clients like to come?"

"My clients will only be in town for a couple of days. They were hoping Thursday would be doable."

Thursday. As in the day after tomorrow. "That soon?" she asked, breathlessly.

"These are serious buyers, so I think the house has a good shot at selling. It would be advantageous for you to make Thursday work."

There was no way Lyla could make that day work on her own. Not without a ton of hours and a lot of help.

"Sure. Of course." What else could she say? "I can definitely accommodate that. What time?"

"Three p.m.?" he suggested.

"Sounds good. I'll make sure I am out of the house so that you and the potential buyers can look around freely."

"Perfect. Selling your parents' house is my top priority."

"Thank you, that's good to hear." And even more reason that Lyla needed to get to work immediately. After saying goodbye, she disconnected the call and rode full speed past Ms. Hadley's house, hoping the little devil-dog wasn't still outside. She didn't stop until she was safely inside her closed garage.

Potential buyers was good news. If they liked what they saw, it meant she would be out of Echo Cove sooner and back to figuring out her real life, which wasn't in the town where she'd grown up. The old 7-Up bottle caught her eye as she walked into the kitchen for a cup of water. There were still items inside.

She gulped the water down and reached beyond the bottle's open flap, pulling out her Britney Spears fan club pin. Wow. It had been so hard to part with this token, she remembered. But a new high school grad and college woman was too mature for a fan club pin. At least that's what she'd told herself.

Reaching into the bottle again, she screamed and flung a rubber snake onto the floor at her feet. Before realizing it was fake, she danced around and continued to squeal in panic. Now she understood why this particular prank had sent poor Trudy Bellows, the local mail lady, to the ER with chest pains. That's when Lyla's mom demanded Lyla and Travis stop their shenanigans. That incident had also incited Pastor Painter's sermon on fools and their ungodly ways.

Maybe the good pastor couldn't see how it affected his children, but Lyla noticed. Travis was self-deprecating to a fault, because his father tore him down publicly, every Sunday morning.

Picking up the snake, she set it on the counter and decided to reach into the bottle one more time, hoping for something more sentimental. This time she pulled out a folded piece of paper and a formative memory surfaced, one that had shattered her confidence so thoroughly that it had perhaps changed the course of her life.

She'd wanted to be a writer since the moment she could turn words into a sentence. Every teacher since the first grade onward had raved about Lyla's stories and predicted she'd be an author someday, and she'd believed them. At least until the real world had gotten a chance to read her work.

Lyla unfolded the paper now, the raw emotion releasing from wherever she'd locked it up all those years ago.

> *Dear Ms. Dune,*
>
> *Your story has no plot. Your characters are flat and one-dimensional. Emotion is what drives a story, but I felt nothing in these pages. I often encourage hopeful authors to take classes and sharpen their skills before sending work off for professional review, but in my opinion, complete and brutal honesty is a favor. Many want to be what few actually achieve. Unless you are certain that you are the one in a million, the exception to the rule, save yourself the heartache.*

The words still stung. Folding the letter back up, Lyla placed it on the counter next to the whistle and the rubber snake. Enough reminiscing for one day. The first showing for the house was in less than forty-eight hours, and the place was far from ready. She needed to get busy, and she needed help.

She picked up her phone and tapped out a text to Allison.

Lyla: *Up for helping out a friend?*

Allison's response came quickly.

Allison: *Always. What do you need?*

Lyla: *My parents' house has its first showing on Thursday.*

Allison: *Say no more! I'll be over in twenty minutes.*

July 12

Dear Diary,

All my life, adults have preached to dream big and never give up. Yet now that I'm adult, just barely, the truth comes out. Dreams rarely come true and chasing them is a risk.

I may never write again. I wouldn't even be writing in you if Sonny was outside tonight. I sat on my porch and waited for him. I even had a piece of bacon to lure him over. Perhaps I'll change my college major and study accounting, even though I suck at math. All I know is I never want to feel the way that editor's letter made me feel again.

Lyla

Chapter 10

Opinion: When someone says, "It's nothing to worry about," start worrying.
—Delilah Dune, opinion writer

Lyla stared at the missed call on her phone. Earlier, she'd been so busy packing up her bedroom with Allison's help that she hadn't heard her mom calling. Now that Allison had gone home, Lyla tapped the screen to pull up her voicemail and held her cell phone to her ear, concern mounting as she listened.

"Lyla, your father and I made a little detour to the hospital here in Florida. Don't worry though. The doctors say your father will be back on his feet in no time. We'll just need to modify his diet a bit. It's absolutely nothing to worry about. Okay, I'll talk to you later. Bye."

The message was vague, so Lyla tried to call her mom back. The call went straight to voicemail. Her parents hadn't even gotten out of the country yet, and her dad was already in the hospital? That wasn't a good sign. Her parents had missed out on their last attempt at a vacation. This one needed to pan out.

The doorbell rang. Allison had just left thirty minutes ago, so the only other person it might be was Travis. Lyla's heart skipped at the possibility. Sure enough, when she opened the door, Travis was standing there in a pair of ripped jeans and a black T-shirt. Teenaged Lyla would have lost her mind at the sight of the man standing there. Adult Lyla resisted feeling anything. The last thing she needed were messy feelings for a self-proclaimed nomadic guy who wasn't good at romantic relationships.

Opinion: If you don't guard your heart, you risk having it stolen.

"Are you going to invite me in or just stare at me?" Travis's dimples deepened as he grinned. Seeing those two pock marks form was an addictive feeling, like the first sip of coffee in the morning. Or the first reader comment on an article.

Lyla realized that she'd been staring at him, practically drooling. There was no question that she was attracted to Travis, but she couldn't act on her feelings. She wouldn't. "What are you doing here?"

He held up a pizza box. "Hungry?"

"I've worked all day cleaning out my childhood bedroom. I'm starving."

"That's good news. So, uh, can I come in?"

"Oh. Yeah." Lyla stepped back and allowed him to walk past her. "I guess you just took me by surprise. I didn't know you were coming."

He turned to look at her. "Honestly, neither did I."

"So, I'm an impulse dinner date?"

He grinned. "Is it an impulse if I've been thinking about sharing a meal with you all day?"

Her heart bubbled up into her throat. "If that's true, why didn't you just text me?"

"Because I had odd jobs all over town, and I kind of thought I'd be too tired at dinner time. Which I am. But not tired enough to resist sharing pizza with you."

"Aw." Lyla tilted her head and pressed a hand to her chest. "With that amount of untapped charm, I am truly shocked that you can't hold down a relationship."

"That's because you haven't seen what I like on my pizzas. That might change your mind."

Lyla's curiosity was piqued. She seemed to recall that Travis had always had strange taste buds. His adventurous side definitely showed when it came to food. "You know I don't have furniture, right? We'll have to eat on the floor." She turned to look over her shoulder. "Maybe we can use one of these boxes as a makeshift table."

"Perfect. And after dinner, we can look at those unchecked items on our summer bucket list. We need to get a jump on it, since I'm leaving soon."

Reality check. His pending exit was all the reason she needed to resist his good looks and charm. Grabbing a roll of paper towels, Lyla pushed a box into the center of the room to serve as their table. "You're heading out of town after Bailey's wedding?"

"That's the plan." He sat on the floor and pointed at her across the pizza box. "You're still coming with me to the wedding, right?"

Lyla's mouth dropped open. "I never officially said yes, you know."

"You did. I'm pretty sure you agreed."

She shook her head slightly. "When?"

"The other day. I offered to help you sell your parents' place, and you agreed to be my date to Echo Cove's wedding of the summer."

"I never agreed to be your date," she protested. She would surely remember that agreement.

"But you didn't turn me down when I asked, so I took that

to mean you wanted to say yes. The Lyla of old had no problem saying no when she wanted to."

She was older, but she wasn't the "Lyla of old." Evidently, she did have difficulty saying no to things she didn't want to do. For example, opinion column subjects that Bob insisted on. When her career and paycheck were on the line, "no" wasn't as easy to say.

"I didn't pack anything appropriate to wear to a wedding," she said.

Travis pointed at her. "That's still not a no. And it's a flimsy excuse, if you ask me."

Opinion: No one really loves weddings. Least of all recently dumped single women.

"I could just add it to our bucket list," he threatened, his tone teasing. "Then you'd have to go. Or bad luck forever."

Lyla should say no. Being Travis's date was perhaps a little too risky. Being newly dumped and single, some might say she was vulnerable. Neither she or Travis were staying in town, and she was on the brink of total self-destruction, at least as far as her career went. "I still don't believe in luck," she said as her mind raced. *Say no. Say no.* "Fine, I'll go. If I remember correctly, you're a pretty great dancer."

He pulled the first slice of pizza out of the pie and handed to her. "That's still true."

She hadn't noticed the pizza's toppings until it was in her hand. "What is this?"

His laughter filled the room. The sound awakened dormant parts of her that had been asleep since long before her ex. "The best thing you'll ever put in your mouth." There was a mischievous spark in his eyes that awakened more parts.

She gave him a questioning look, but she was currently speechless.

"Pickles and bacon," he finally said.

She held the slice of pizza farther away from her face. "On a pizza? Are you pregnant?"

"It's so good, Ly. You have to try it. It's amazing, I promise." He held up a hand and reached inside his front pocket, pulling out a pen. Then he got up and walked over to the kitchen counter to grab the old bucket list from where it was laying.

She watched as he wrote something on the paper. "What are you doing?"

"Adding it to our bucket list. Try pickle-bacon pizza." He finished writing and looked up. "There. Now you have to try it."

She scrunched her nose. "In case you've forgotten, I don't even like pickles."

"But you lo-o-ove bacon," he teased, stretching out the L-word. "Almost as much as you lo-o-ove me."

He was only joking. She knew he didn't know how much she'd loved him back in the day. "Fine." She lifted the slice of pizza back to her mouth, flicked a look in his direction, and nibbled timidly.

"Well?" He watched her intently. "What do you think?"

She chewed, holding him in suspense. The taste was a weird blend of bitter and sweet flavors and at first, she honestly couldn't tell if she loved it or hated it. After she had swallowed and assessed the aftertaste, she offered a slight smile.

Travis pointed a finger in her direction. "Ah-ha. You like it!"

"I actually do kind of like it," she admitted, laughing quietly.

Travis grabbed a slice for himself. "That makes me so happy." He took his own bite, chewing and talking at the same time. "I've had dates who've turned their noses up without even trying it. That's how I knew they weren't right for me."

Lyla looked at him in disbelief. "Because they wouldn't try pickle-bacon pizza?"

"No, because they were too closed-minded to even consider something different. Life should be fun. It should be full of new and exciting things. Adventure."

Lyla let that thought sink in. "I can't remember the last time I tried something new or did something exciting. I think I've gotten boring in my late twenties."

Travis narrowed his eyes. "Even if you refused to try the pickle-bacon pizza and ate the same meal every night for dinner, you could never be boring to me, Ly."

She stared at him for a moment. There was something about hearing his opinion toward her that spread warmness from her head to her toes. "You just told me you have stopped dating women who refused your crazy pizza."

He lifted a shoulder while shaking his head. "Not solely for that reason. The pizza thing just served as a red flag. Other red flags existed too."

"Such as?"

"Such as saying we'd go out at seven and not being ready until seven forty-five," he said. "Or ordering a glass of wine and getting completely tipsy off it."

She pushed her neck forward. "That's a red flag?"

"Are you implying I have unrealistic expectations?" He seemed to be baiting her.

She tilted her head. "If you're asking for my honest opinion, I think you're looking for reasons not to be in a relationship with someone."

He took a bite of his pizza, chewing as his eyes danced. "Maybe so. I've always believed that when you know, you know. And if I meet someone and I don't know, why would I waste either of our time?"

Maybe that's what he told himself, but she knew Travis. A person couldn't help but have trust issues when their own father couldn't be trusted with their feelings. "I haven't dated anyone since my breakup. Three months ago."

"Do you want to date?" Travis asked.

She blinked across the pizza box. "Date you?"

His eyes went wide. "No, that's not what I meant. I meant are you ready to date anyone again? Three months of being single isn't that long."

"Well, the relationship was over long before I caught Joe cheating." Lyla picked off a piece of pickle on her pizza. It wasn't bad, but it wasn't good either. "I just . . . I don't want to spend my life alone, you know?"

"That won't happen, Ly. You have friends."

She held up a finger. "I have one friend. Allison."

"You also have me," he said quietly.

She'd misunderstood him a moment earlier. She didn't want to read into this statement too. "Even after I ghosted you for ten years? What's to say I won't do that again after this house is sold? History tends to repeat itself, you know? That's technically an opinion, but it should be a fact," she said. She wasn't sure why she was trying to push him away. Perhaps it was a defense mechanism, a knee-jerk response to her fear—because some part of her still got scared at the way he made her feel.

Travis lowered his half-eaten slice of pizza. "History only repeats if you didn't learn the lesson the first go-round."

"What lesson?" she finally asked. "What were we supposed to learn?"

"I don't know. Follow your heart. Chase your dreams. Face your fears." He bit into another slice of pizza, talking as he chewed. "In your case, I think it's the last one. Fear has always been your stumbling block."

She was tempted to take offense. "You know me so well." Leaning over the pizza box, she reached up to swipe a dab of sauce from his cheek, the touch surprising her as much as it seemed to surprise him. "For you, it's the first," she said, pulling her hand back away.

"You think I don't follow my heart?" he asked, amused by

the suggestion. "For your information, I follow it up and down the Eastern seaboard."

"Unh-uh." She shook her head. "I think you're following your mind and keeping your feelings bottled up in a time capsule of its own."

"Poetic." He still looked amused. "Delilah isn't nearly as poetic in her columns." He was deflecting, turning the attention back on Lyla. Even after all these years, she did know him well enough to see through his façade.

"The pizza is good," she said, allowing him to deflect.

"Yeah? I knew you'd like it. I fully expect an opinion column stating your allegiance to pickle-bacon pizza."

There was another smudge of sauce on his cheek, but she didn't wipe it away this time. "Do you want me to lose my column completely?" She shook her head. "Sorry, but my next column needs a better hook than pickles and bacon on pizza." And she needed that hook soon.

"Or you could just write that novel you always wanted to write."

Lyla rolled her eyes.

"Or obituaries. If I recall, you wrote a pretty good one for Sonny the devil-dog."

Lyla nearly choked on her bite of pizza. After pounding her own chest, she left her hand there to rest over her heart. "You remember that?" After Sonny had been hit by a car, Lyla had penned a full essay on the dog's qualities, not wanting him to be forgotten. She was pretty sure the obituary was in the 7-Up bottle time capsule.

"Of course. I've always been a big fan of everything you wrote."

She narrowed her eyes and tilted her head, unsure whether he was teasing.

Travis cleared his throat and lowered his slice of pizza. "Sonny, you were a good dog," he said, and then proceeded to recite the opening of her obituary for the dog, word for word.

Lyla's eyes welled as she listened.

"I'm sorry. Did I say something wrong?"

"No." She shook her head, waiting for the emotion to pass.

"I know Sonny's death hit you hard. I never understood why, because he was the devil-dog."

Lyla swiped a finger under her eye and sniffled, feeling silly. "Sonny only chased us because he thought we weren't supposed to be on the road. When we were growing up, we weren't allowed to be on the road. Anytime we headed in that direction, he darted in front of us and chased us back into the yard."

Travis's brow line lowered. "I didn't know that."

"My mom told me after Sonny's accident. He thought it was his job to protect the neighborhood kids." It was the day after the biggest hurricane that had ever hit the town of Echo Cove. Everyone was out assessing the damage after the storm. "He chased Kevin off the road that day to keep him from being hit by a car."

Travis put down the slice of pizza in his hand. "Wow. I kind of always thought he was a bad dog."

"I always knew he wasn't." Just like when Lyla had sat through all those church sermons of Pastor Painter's. She'd known the truth. "He was a good dog, and that's an opinion I'll pledge my allegiance to."

The rain was coming down this summer in record amounts, and the yard was a soggy mess for this afternoon's real estate showing.

Lyla still didn't have a coffeepot, so she pulled on her rain jacket and boots and left the house. She didn't feel like running into anyone she might know, so instead of going into town, she opted to drive straight to Allison's home. She pulled in to the driveway and ran through the downpour to Allison's front porch.

Lyla tapped the doorbell and huddled under the hood of her jacket, trying not to let the slanted rain get in her eyes.

After a long minute, Allison opened the door. "Oh. Lyla. Um . . . What are you doing here?"

"Hoping to have a morning cup of coffee with you. Am I being presumptive?" Lyla asked, curling deeper into her jacket. The slanted rain was coming after her, and she didn't want to get soaked.

Allison shook her head, but she didn't step aside to allow Lyla in out of the rain either. "It's just, well . . . I have company this morning," she said, lowering her voice and chewing on her lower lip.

"Company? This early?" It was only 7:00 a.m. Who stopped by at this time of day? Okay, Lyla did, but that was because early hours demanded coffee, and Allison had told Lyla to come over anytime.

"My company kind of stayed overnight." Allison's cheeks flushed at the admission and she glanced over her shoulder again.

"Oh . . . *Ohhhh*." Lyla's face erupted into a widespread smile. "Wow. That's great, Allison. I didn't realize you were dating anyone."

"I'm not." Allison shook her head quickly. "We just—We get together some of the time when we're feeling lonely."

Lyla was suddenly very curious about who the mystery person was. "Do I know him? Or her?"

Allison offered a sheepish look. "Yes, but I'd rather not say who it is. And he's still asleep. I'm sorry not to invite you in, but . . ." She grimaced as her eyes cast Lyla an apologetic look.

"Of course. Right. I should have texted or called." Lyla took a retreating step away from the door, still keeping under the awning. "I'll just go to Bean Time. And tomorrow morning you'll fill me in on this mystery man."

"Mm-hmm," Allison said, noncommittally, glancing nervously behind her once more.

"Okay. Back to bed you go. Bye." Lyla pulled the hood of her rain jacket further over her head and took the porch steps two at a time before running back into the downpour. When she got inside her car again, she pondered why there was no vehicle in the driveway to tip her off that someone had stayed over. Lyla couldn't blame Allison for wanting to keep this guy on the down-low. Echo Cove was small and people liked to talk.

Lyla reversed out of the driveway and drove toward Bean Time. She wanted Bernie to like her and she thought they were on that path. The past was a long time ago, after all, and a grudge over a sloppy joe couldn't last forever.

When Lyla walked through the coffee shop's front entrance, Bernie's husband was at the counter again.

"She's not in this morning," Eric told Lyla. "Bernadette spent a good portion of the night sitting with a neighbor. Our neighbor lost their dog," he explained with a regretful sigh. Then he turned and started preparing a coffee for Lyla without asking her what she wanted. Lyla watched as he made her drink the exact way she'd ordered it last time.

"That's sweet of Bernie," Lyla said.

He glanced over his shoulder. "Bernadette," he corrected.

"Right, sorry." Lyla drummed her fingers on the counter. "Why doesn't she go by Bernie anymore?"

Eric turned back and slid the coffee across the counter toward Lyla. "Bernadette doesn't like who she was when she was younger. Long before I knew her. But she's proud of who she is now."

The opposite was true for Lyla. "She should be proud." Lyla wrapped her fingers around the warm cup. "Although, I liked her back then too."

Eric gave Lyla a funny look. "Not the way I hear it."

Lyla released a small breath. "The sloppy joe thing was an accident, okay? When is she going to let that go?"

Eric dismissed that comment with a wave of his hand. "Yeah, the sloppy joe thing was bad, but that was a long time ago."

Lyla tilted her head. "Isn't that why she hates me? Is there something else?"

Eric lifted his hands in surrender. "You should talk to her. I don't want to misspeak."

Lyla wanted to press him, but she wasn't the type of person to press when someone had requested to be left out of something. "How much do I owe you for the coffee?"

Eric shook his head. "Bernadette said all of your drinks are on the house from now on." He lowered his hands to his sides. "So, you must be doing something to melt off those walls of ice."

Becoming Bernadette's friend felt like success right now. Lyla glanced at the glass case beside her. "What does Ms. Hadley get when she comes here?"

"Evette Hadley?" He turned his attention to the glass case. "She likes raspberry-filled bear claws."

"Okay, then, can I get two of those?" Lyla asked. "Not on the house. I'm paying."

"Sure thing." Eric wrapped up two bear claws and swiped Lyla's debit card. "You're going to be Ms. Hadley's favorite person if you bring these over."

Lyla placed her card back in her wallet and took the bag of treats for her neighbor. She wasn't sure about favorite but maybe she would no longer by Ms. Hadley's least favorite anymore. "Thank you. Tell Bernadette I said hello."

"Sure thing."

Turning, Lyla headed back out of the shop, ducking her head again, just in case anyone recognized her. She didn't have time to chat because this afternoon was the first showing for her parents' home.

She opened her car door and slid behind the steering wheel. Then she exhaled and allowed herself to take her first sip of the beverage that Eric had made her. She was about to put her car in reverse when an email alert came through on her phone. She glanced at her screen and sighed. It was from her editor, Bob. He wanted to know where next week's opinion article was. All she had at this moment were a few bad ideas, which would probably be the final nails in her column's coffin.

Her opinions were duds these days. She should just start looking for a new job now. Maybe Bernadette and Eric were hiring.

July 23

Dear Diary,

I'm still upset about the letter from the editor. I haven't let anyone else read my story. Not even Travis. He knows I'm devastated about something, but I can't bring myself to show him the awful things that awful editor told me. I'm so embarrassed. That editor said my writing was horrible. I don't think I'll ever write another story—ever. I've been crying all afternoon. I can't stop.

So, Travis brought me a pizza tonight, trying to cheer me up. It has pickle on it. Who eats pickle on their pizza? I guess Travis does and now I do too. I'm eating my feelings with pickle toppings.

Anyway, Diary, if several days go by and you haven't heard from me, you'll know it's because I drowned in my own tears. Or from bad pizza. One or the other.

Lyla

Chapter 11

Opinion: In order to be a master salesman,
you must be a good liar.
—Delilah Dune, opinion writer

Lyla looked around her parents' home and put herself in a new buyer's shoes. What would they see when they walked in the front door?

The showing was only an hour from now. Lyla was supposed to make herself scarce while the potential buyers were here with their real estate agent. Lyla would prefer to stay, but she understood. The potential buyers might want to complain about the water stain on the ceiling from last week's leak or the dent in the door that Lyla was pretty sure Travis had created when they were teenagers. So instead of being a fly on the wall, she had plans to meet Allison in town to go shopping.

Shopping was Lyla's least favorite activity, but she was Travis's date to his sister's upcoming wedding, and she couldn't very well wear jeans.

Opinion: People who claim shopping is their hobby
need better hobbies.

Lyla pressed her palm against her face. She was so fired. Her next opinion piece was going to be the end of "Delilah's Delusions." Her ideas were getting worse by the second.

The doorbell rang, and Lyla gave herself one more glance in the mirror. She was wearing a pair of black shorts with a casual white shirt.

"Hey," Lyla said when she opened the door, expecting to see Allison. Instead, Ms. Hadley stood there, holding the bag from Bean Time Coffee. No one had answered when Lyla rang her neighbor's doorbell earlier so Lyla had left the bag hanging on Ms. Hadley's doorknob. "Ms. Hadley. How are you?"

"What's this?" Ms. Hadley held up the bag from Bean Time.

"Um. Well, it's your favorite. That's what the shop owner told me, at least."

"Is this one of those pranks of yours? I hate raspberry filling." She wagged a finger in the air. "Aren't you too old for that kind of childish mess you used to pull, putting awful things in my mailbox?"

Lyla's face felt like all the blood in her body had rushed into her cheeks. "The store owner, Eric, said . . ."

Ms. Hadley pushed the bag of bear claws into Lyla's hands, forcing her to take them. "You probably put something extra in that filling too. My memory is as sharp as ever. I haven't forgotten about the snake skins in my mailbox."

"That was Travis," Lyla said quietly.

"You are who you hang out with. That's not opinion. That's fact. Add that to that silly column of yours."

Silly column? "Ms. Hadley, I sincerely apologize for whatever I did to you and even the stuff I didn't do. These bear claws were a peace offering. I thought you'd like them and maybe—I don't know. Maybe we'd have a fresh start."

Ms. Hadley looked around as if searching for some nasty response to put Lyla in her place. Then she reached out and yanked the bag of bear claws back from Lyla's hands. "You didn't put anything extra in these?"

"No." Lyla shook her head. "Of course not. I wouldn't do that."

Ms. Hadley narrowed her eyes, looking suspicious. Then she nodded. "Okay then. I do like raspberry. Eric knows me well."

Lyla didn't dare ask why her neighbor had said the opposite just moments before. "Wonderful. Well, enjoy them."

"I will." She gave Lyla a long look. "It's good of you to help your parents with this house. I know they appreciate it."

"I hope I can help, at least. They deserve this trip." Especially since the last vacation they'd tried to go on had been ruined by Lyla.

Without another word, Ms. Hadley turned and headed back across the yard with her bear claws that she may or may not hate.

Before Lyla shut the front door, Allison's sporty car turned into the driveway with a high-pitched *beep-beep*.

The driver's side door flew open and Allison got out. She was practically glowing as she walked toward the porch. Allison was always smiling. It was her mask. This current smile, however, was worlds different from the normal one. It reflected in her eyes and made her look ten years younger.

Opinion: Love is the true fountain of youth.

Lyla was a touch jealous. And curious. Who was this mystery guy that Allison was hiding? "Hey! Thanks for picking me up."

"Of course. No sense in us both burning up gas. Plus, if I drive, you can't get tired and ditch me after thirty minutes," Allison said.

Something in Allison's tone gave Lyla pause. "Has someone done that to you before?"

"Ernie." Allison rolled her eyes, but her good mood didn't budge. "Come on. A girls' shopping trip is one of my favorite pastimes."

Lyla locked up the front door and followed Allison down the driveway, rethinking her former opinion about shopping being a hobby.

New Opinion: A shopping trip between friends is good medicine.

Lyla walked around the car and slid into the passenger seat of Allison's little Jetta, releasing a long, drawn-out sigh.

Allison glanced over, concern pinching the skin between her eyes. "What's wrong?"

"Ha, where do I start?" Lyla muttered before remembering Allison's tragic past. Then she felt guilty. She had no right to feel bad about any area of her life. She hadn't been through nearly as much as Allison had, and Allison wasn't sitting here complaining.

"Stop that." Allison looked in the rearview mirror and slowly backed out of the drive.

"Stop what?"

"Stop thinking you can't be honest with me about what's bothering you just because I lost two children." She put the car in drive and glanced over. "You can be honest with me, even if you're just complaining about a broken nail. That's what friends are for."

Lyla let that thought sink in as the car picked up speed. "I'm trying to come up with my next topic for an opinion piece. My opinions have been so boring. I think I'm having a midlife crisis."

Allison shook her head. "You're only thirty."

"Maybe that's considered midlife to some."

"No. Fifties are midlife. I mean, please, with all the advances in medicine? And I'm sure your opinions aren't as boring as you think."

Lyla pressed her lips together, resisting telling anyone just how much her impressive career was tanking. "My boss told me that this next piece will determine if my column gets to continue."

Allison's eyes rounded. "You have a national column. I thought you were super successful."

"I thought I was too. Funny how success can just crumble and all your hard work can be easily forgotten."

"Kind of like a relationship. You think it's going perfectly and then, boom. You realize it wasn't as solid as you thought. A tragedy should bring two people closer, right?"

Guilt knotted Lyla's gut. Here she went again talking about things that didn't ultimately matter in comparison to Allison losing her family.

As the silence stretched between them, Allison sighed. "I brought up my sob story and made everything awkward, sorry. I didn't mean to. This is why no one likes to shop with me anymore. And why no one shows up to my Dinnerware Parties." Allison shook her head while keeping her eyes on the road. "People don't know how to act around me. Maybe they think I might break down. Or I might discuss things they're uncomfortable hearing. I guess it's just sad, coming to my home where pictures of my children are still hanging up everywhere. I mean—"

Lyla cut her off. "If those people disappear on you, then you don't need those people in your life. You should be allowed to say or do whatever you like and still have your friends by your side. You should keep your kids' photos up and not apologize for it." Lyla reached over and briefly touched Allison's arm. "There's an idea for an opinion piece. Real friends don't disappear when times get tough. Or awkward. I enjoy being at your house and your company. I promise to come to every Dinnerware Party that you invite me to."

"It's fine, honestly. Dinnerware Parties are for people who actually cook anyway."

"I cook. Just not very well," Lyla said.

They both burst into laughter. It felt good for the soul. Lyla couldn't remember the last time she'd laughed like this. Or the last time she'd had a true friend. That's what Allison was becoming.

Allison pulled her car into a parking space and cut off the engine. "Ready to shop?"

"Confession: I've never done the whole shopping-with-girlfriends kind of thing. I might not be good at it."

Allison rolled her eyes and pushed her car door open. "It's not a skill. It's just the two of us hanging out, and you bene-fiting from my amazing fashion sense."

Lyla pushed her passenger door open. "Sounds good to me." She'd take all the help she could get in that area.

An hour and a half later, Lyla had tried on nothing short of a dozen dresses.

"You look fabulous in that one," Allison said, still beaming.

"You're lying, because you're tired of watching me go in and out of the dressing room."

Allison shook her head. "Not true. I am ready for a frozen yogurt though. Here"—she stood and pointed to her chair—"you sit and I'll go pick out the perfect dress for you. What-ever I bring over, you have to try on. No ifs, ands, or buts."

"Whatever you bring over, I have to try on?" Lyla repeated as a question.

"Exactly. It'll be fun. What do you have to lose?"

"My dignity, for one." Lyla plopped down in the chair where Allison had been seated and served up her best pouty face. "Fine. Go forth and find the perfect dress that will make me look incredibly sexy for Bailey's wedding."

Allison lifted a questioning brow. "Sexy, huh? I thought you said you and Travis were just friends." She didn't wait for Lyla's rebuttal. Instead, she disappeared into the vast selection of dress clothes.

While she waited, Lyla leaned her head against the wall and closed her eyes. She'd forgotten how tiring shopping could be. It was also exhausting to care about how she looked. She'd gotten comfortable enough in her relationship with Joe, to the point where she didn't have to spend hours on hair, makeup, and finding the perfect clothing to wear. Those things were for the newly dating couples. Lyla hadn't exactly let herself go. She'd just relaxed. Maybe too much.

Opinion: Getting comfortable is a relationship's death sentence.

Now there's an opinion that would spark heated reader feedback. Maybe not the kind Bob was looking for.

"Okay, I've found some amazing dresses for you to try on," Allison said, reappearing ten minutes later.

Lyla opened her eyes and looked at the dresses that Allison held up. One for every color of the rainbow. "I'm not a colorful person. I can't wear those."

Allison shoved the dresses toward her. "You promised. Now shut up and try them on."

Lyla firmly believed in keeping her word, even if she thought it might mean losing her dignity. There'd only been one instance when she hadn't kept her word, when she'd promised to keep in touch with Travis. Lyla took the dresses and stood. "Okay, but you're not taking any pictures."

Allison took the seat and made a shooing motion toward the dressing room. "Just go."

Reluctantly, Lyla headed toward the fitting room and hooked the dresses on the back of the door, one at a time, inwardly cringing as she assessed each one. She tried on all seven dresses, saving the worst for last.

Allison pressed both hands to her mouth when Lyla stepped

out of the dressing room wearing the seventh dress. "You are a knockout in that dress!"

Lyla turned back to look in the mirror, angling her body back and forth. Then she looked down at herself. "Wow. It looks different on me than it did on the rack. I didn't think this dress would work, but I actually kind of love it." The dress was pale yellow with little white daisies in the print, so small that they looked like pin dots until you inspected the fabric at close range. The fabric tapered at the waist and at the knees, giving her an hourglass figure that she didn't think she still had. It was sweet but also sexy. Very sexy. It was a dress she never would have picked out for herself, in a color she never would have considered. She preferred monochrome colors. But now that this little yellow dress was on her, she kind of loved it.

"Travis is going to lose his mind if you go to the wedding in that dress. Now you need some strappy heels to lengthen your legs." Allison clapped her hands excitedly in front of her. "Oh, this is so much fun!"

Lyla was surprised that she agreed. This *was* fun. Much more than she'd anticipated. Who was she, and where was the real Lyla Dune?

By the time Allison dropped Lyla back off at her parents' house, Lyla had spent way more money than she'd intended, but it would all be worth it when she stepped out with Travis, feeling fantastic. After what had happened with her ex, her confidence needed the boost.

"Looks like the potential buyers have left," Allison said of the empty driveway. "I hope they loved the place."

"Me too." Although something inside Lyla also ached at the possibility. This was the home where she'd grown up. Once it sold, she could never return. Everything was changing lately, even her. Pushing the car door open, she dipped back in to look at Allison across the center console. "Do you want to have coffee tomorrow morning, or are you expecting your mystery man for another sleepover tonight?"

Allison's cheeks blushed. "Coffee tomorrow sounds great. I'll make muffins in my new Dinnerware muffin tin."

"Dinnerware sells breakfast ware?" Lyla asked.

"Of course. Haven't you ever heard of breakfast for dinner?" Allison beamed. "That was my kids' favorite."

Lyla felt slightly uncomfortable at the mention of Allison's children, but only because she didn't know what to say. Allison apparently didn't need her to say anything. "See you then, okay?"

"See you then." Lyla closed the car door and headed up her driveway, stopping in her tracks when something flashed in her peripheral vision. A firefly? She stood, waiting for another flash of light. It could have been her imagination. Or the sun glinting off the taillights of her own vehicle. Just as she was about to look away and continue up the steps, the light flashed again. It *was* a firefly.

Lyla laughed quietly to herself. There was something so magical about those little sparks of light. Since when did she believe in magic? Not since she was a kid, at least. Back then, everything had felt magical. Something about adulthood vacuumed up that unworldly sense.

Her brain chewed on that revelation, trying to twist it into some sort of opinion Bob would approve of. Lost in thought, she continued up the porch steps, unlocked the door, and started to step inside, stopping short as water squished inside her shoes. "Oh. No."

Confused, Lyla stared down at the shallow puddle of water on the living room floor. As she glanced around and assessed the situation, she realized the water was everywhere. Trudging down the hall, she headed in the direction of the closest bathroom where the water was deeper by at least an inch or more. *What in the world?*

She wasn't a plumber by any means, but she opened the

bottom cabinet of the sink and easily saw the problem. The pipe had burst and water was gushing out. *No-o-o-o-o.* Had the real estate agent and potential buyers done this? Had this happened when they were here?

Lyla rushed to grab the towels that her mom had left out for her and wrapped them around the leaky pipe. They would soak through quickly though. Then what? She needed a handyman ASAP. She needed Travis.

July 31

Dear Diary,

I ruined my mother's life—again! First, she fell in love with my dad and got pregnant with me, effectively halting Mom's plans for college and a life beyond Echo Cove. Now, my mom and dad are on the vacation of my mom's dreams and they have to come home because of my stupidity.

All I did was knock over a container of blue hair gel on my way to go off with Travis. It poured into the sink, clogged the pipes, and somehow flooded the entire house. Not the entire house, but ugh. This is turning out to be the worst summer of my life. Can I just leave for college already? Please?

Lyla

Chapter 12

Opinion: Calling in reinforcements isn't a sign of weakness. It's a sign that you're in over your head.
—Delilah Dune, opinion writer

"What happened in here?" Travis walked into Lyla's front door and looked down at his boots. "Not gonna lie. This is bad."

"I know. Can you fix it?" Lyla asked as she sat on one of the kitchen stools to keep her feet dry.

He looked around the room and gave a confident nod. "Yeah, but we have to get the water up before it damages the flooring."

"Allison is on her way. She's bringing more towels."

"Good." Travis gestured toward the bathroom. "Please tell me you've already shut off the water to the house."

Lyla furrowed her brow. "Hmm?"

Travis pressed a hand to his forehead. "What would you do without me, Ly?"

"Today? I have no idea."

He turned to go right back out the front door.

"You're leaving?"

"The water has to be turned off from the outside," he

called behind him. "Then I'll see what kind of parts I need to buy while you and Allison get this mess up. I have a shop vac in my work truck. I'll grab it."

Lyla watched him go out, thankful that he was here. Otherwise, she'd be standing in this house and wondering what in the world she was going to do. Her parents were counting on her to handle things. What were they thinking? Her own life was falling apart. How was she supposed to keep their house from doing the same before finding suitable buyers?

Her phone buzzed from inside her pocket.

She tapped the screen and connected the call. "Hello?"

"Ms. Dune?" a man's voice said. "This is Peter Blake."

"Yes, hi, Mr. Blake," Lyla said, nervously, hoping the real estate agent had better news than what she was expecting.

"Ms. Dune, I should've called you earlier, but I wanted to tell you, in case you haven't figured it out yet, your house has a busted bathroom pipe. The prospective buyers and I only got as far as the hallway when we noticed the puddle."

Puddle was actually good news. By the time Lyla had gotten home, that puddle had been a small lake.

"Needless to say, we turned around and walked out."

Lyla's hopes scattered like ash. "It's just a cracked pipe. It could happen to any house. Once we get the water cleaned up and the pipe fixed, the house will be as good as new," she told the agent, hearing the desperation seeping into her voice.

Opinion: Desperation begets the death of whatever one is hoping for. No exception.

"We viewed several other houses afterward, and my buyers found one that suited their needs perfectly. I'm sorry, Ms. Dune. I thought your parents' place was the perfect match for this couple. I know how eager your folks are to sell their house. As soon as you fix the damage, give me a call and I'll schedule more showings."

"Sure, I'll do that. Thank you, Mr. Blake." She was about to disconnect the call, but thought better. "Mr. Blake? If you don't mind, can we keep this just between us? My parents are on a trip of a lifetime. I don't want to give them any reason to come back. I can fix this. There's no reason to concern them." She waited for Mr. Blake's answer, which seemed to take longer than it should. "Please," she added.

"Sure, I can do that," Mr. Blake finally said. "Like I said, your parents are friends of mine. Technically, *they* are my clients. But I agree with you. Your parents deserve this trip, and I have faith in you, Lyla. Just like they do."

Lyla was beginning to wonder if that faith was misplaced. "Thank you." After disconnecting the call with Mr. Blake, Lyla walked back into the living room, her feet skimming across Echo Cove's newest lake. Lake Lyla.

This is just a small setback. Travis is handy and he will fix the pipe. We'll clean up the water and everything will be fine. Just fine.

"Everything okay?"

Apparently, Travis had stepped back into the house with a shop vac. She hadn't even noticed he was there. "I honestly have no idea. I appreciate your help, though. You're right. I don't know what I would do without you this summer."

"Things tend to work out the way they're supposed to."

Lyla felt an opinion article somewhere in that statement. She was too numb to even try to search it out, though. "Let's get this place cleaned up, shall we?" She pulled in a breath and pushed down her emotions. She could cry later. Right now, she needed to do damage control. As she wondered where to start, the doorbell rang. "That must be Allison."

"I'm here with towels," Allison announced, as Lyla swung open the door. Allison stepped inside and noticed Travis standing off to the side. "Oh, hi, Travis. Long time no see."

"Hey, Allison. How've you been?" Travis asked, making normal small talk.

Lyla inwardly cringed, though, because Travis probably had no idea how Allison's life was going lately. Not unless Bailey kept him filled in on the happenings and goings-on in Echo Cove.

Allison's mask was firmly in place as she responded. "Never better. You?"

"I'm good," he said with a small nod.

Lyla wondered if everyone lied when they were asked how they were. What would life be like if people told the truth?

Depressing, she decided.

Opinion: No one wants the truth when they ask how you are. Not even your family and closest friends.

Two hours later, the floor was dry and Travis had already gone to Mr. Tibbs's hardware store and returned.

"Strangely, there was a ton of hair gel blocking the pipe," he said, emerging from the bathroom.

"Hair gel?" That was exactly what had caused the pipes to burst that same summer when Travis had moved away. This was too much of a coincidence, right?

Travis headed toward the front door, carrying his tools back out to his truck. "Other than that, your pipes are working perfectly fine now."

Allison started giggling from the corner of the room as she stepped outside.

Lyla gave her a sharp look. "Are you being juvenile right now?"

"Sorry, I was a boy mom. That is exactly Ethan Mark's humor." Allison's giggling continued a second longer. "It's a positive that I can remember the good without breaking down into tears. My therapist says so."

"You see a therapist?" Lyla asked.

"Of course. Even before the accident." Allison gave her a curious look. "You don't?"

Lyla had always been one to handle problems on her own.

"Perhaps after the stress of selling this house, I'll need one."
She looked at Allison for a moment, admiring the glow that
hadn't dimmed in well over a week. "So did your mystery
man come over again last night?"

Allison locked a strand of hair behind one ear, revealing
the rosy flush of her cheeks. "Are you circling my house or
something? How'd you know?"

Lyla rolled her eyes. "Of course not. Are you two serious?"

Allison seemed to squirm where she stood. "No. I'm nowhere near ready for anything serious. We're just having fun,
that's all. Lots of fun." She waggled her brows. "You should
try it sometime."

Lyla should have known the conversation would swing
back to her. "Travis and I are just friends."

Allison nudged Lyla's arm softly. "Friends who fix each
other's piping," she said on another immature giggle.

"I'm not even sure that makes any kind of sense. And if it
does, it's gross." Even so, she burst into giggles as well. "I
had no idea you were so strange. And funny."

"I don't think I was the last time you knew me. So, now
that your pipes are working, want to grab lunch?" She asked
the question as Travis walked back into the room. "You too,
of course. All three of us should go get something to eat."

"Sure you don't want to make it four and invite your new
friend?" Lyla asked, referring to Allison's mystery guy. She
raised her brows a notch along with her tone of voice.

"Not just yet." Allison avoiding looking in Travis's direction.

He gave his head a subtle shake. "That's okay, ladies. I actually have a job to do for someone else today."

"A handyman job?" Lyla was intrigued by how easily Travis
found work, even though he no longer lived in Echo Cove.

"Someone's teenage son backed into their mailbox." Travis
began to return a few items to his toolbox. "I'm putting in a
new mailbox for them. Maybe I can catch up with you later,
though," he told Lyla.

Lyla felt Allison watching. Nothing to see here, except two old friends who happened to be the opposite sex. "I guess I owe you for helping me today."

"You can take me to dinner then," Travis suggested. "What do you say?"

From her peripheral vision, Lyla saw Allison's growing grin. "I say . . . sure."

"Great. I'll pick you up around six thirty, if that suits you."

Lyla avoided Allison's watchful gaze. "It does."

"Good." He waved at Allison. "Nice to see you again."

"You too." Allison squealed once he was gone. Even though the door was closed, Lyla guessed Travis probably heard the squeal outside. "Lyla! He's totally into you, whether you want to believe it or not."

"What? No. What makes you think that?" Lyla tried to temper her response even though she was secretly thrilled by the possibility that it might be true. Maybe Travis was into her in the way Allison was referring.

"Are you blind? It's in the way he just looked at you."

"And how was that?" Lyla wanted proof that she wasn't imagining things. She did have a huge imagination, after all.

"He was looking at you like he wished I would take a hike so that you two could be alone."

Lyla laughed out loud. "That's absurd. Let me change clothes before we head to lunch," she said, changing the subject because she was on the verge of a full-fledged hot flash.

"I have a spare outfit in my car. A mom of two can never be too prepared."

Allison's glow dimmed momentarily. Her comment must have caught her off guard. As if Allison had forgotten, just for a second, that she didn't need to pack spare clothes in her car anymore because she didn't have children to be responsible for.

Allison cleared her throat. "I'll, um, just go grab it."

"Sounds good." Lyla watched her friend leave through the front door, pondering a dozen different things all at once.

Mostly, she worried that this mystery guy would hurt Allison. Lyla also worried that Travis might hurt her. As long as she kept things platonic, that wouldn't happen. Having a fling with your former best friend was never a good idea, no matter how one sliced it.

Opinion: There are no magic erasers in love. Once friends have crossed the forbidden line, they can't uncross it.

After lunch and a lot of laughs with Allison, Lyla walked back in to her parents' home and assessed the damage. One almost wouldn't know there'd been a busted pipe earlier and a resulting flood on the living room floor. Travis and Allison were lifesavers. Maybe the potential buyers from earlier in the day had chosen to go with another home, but the next buyers were sure to love this place.

Lyla wished there was a couch to lie on, but since there wasn't, she headed down the hall to her childhood bed. Lying back, she closed her eyes, took a couple deep breaths, and before she knew it, she was fast asleep.

Her mind immediately took her to the recurring dream about the Pirate's Plank.

She was fifteen and standing on the wooden board that was suspended over Memory Lake. Her knees wobbled, and she could feel the prickle of goose bumps on her flesh, even though she wasn't cold. The sun's heat burned her bare shoulders and the back of her neck as she looked around the lake, noticing all eyes on her. At least that's how it felt.

It also felt terrifying. The fear made sweat prickle along her forehead, rolling down her face, the saltiness reaching her trembling lips. Travis had put this item on that year's bucket list, knowing that she was afraid.

"If you don't jump, it'll be bad luck," he'd said just the day before.

He was the reason she was standing up here, shivering and shaking. *Thanks a lot, Travis.*

Lyla looked around at all the people near the lake, noticing Bernie in the water. Ten minutes earlier, Lyla had watched Bernie dive like it was no big deal. Now everyone in the lake, including Bernie, was watching Lyla and wondering what was taking her so long to jump.

Lyla's mind spun as she inched forward on the plank, her vision growing blurry. She'd taken swimming classes. Swimming wasn't the issue. It was the dive and the way the water sucked you under with no promise to spit you back out.

I can do this. I don't have to be afraid.

No one had ever drowned in Memory Lake, and she wasn't going to be the first. Sucking in a deep breath, Lyla filled her lungs to capacity. She tried to take another breath, but it felt shallow and insufficient. Then her breaths came faster, and her thoughts jumbled. Her vision became blurrier, and suddenly the people in the lake looked like little blobs of color. Fainting on the Pirate's Plank would be worst-case scenario. She didn't have on a life vest, and she wasn't convinced anyone would jump in to save her. They'd probably just laugh harder than they already were.

"Jump already, freak!" somebody said from behind her.

Lyla turned to look over her shoulder at who it was, and then she looked back at the scene in front of her. The height suddenly felt too high, and the water seemed impossibly deep. Her heart rocketed up into her throat, cutting off her air supply. That's when liquid panic flooded her veins, her vision went black, and she felt herself falling.

She hadn't jumped. She felt her body plummeting toward the water, but her eyes were closed, and for the life of her, they wouldn't open.

Lyla clawed at the air and braced herself for impact. *No. No.* "No-o-o!"

Someone's hand grabbed Lyla's shoulder and shook her awake. Lyla's eyes burst open as she gasped for air.

"Ly, are you okay?"

Lyla blinked at Travis leaning over her, looking more concerned than she'd ever seen him. "What? What are you doing here?" she asked, in a breathless haze, as she tried to sit up.

"You didn't answer your door. Or lock it. Sorry to just walk in, but I could hear your screaming all the way outside." The skin between his brows formed a deep divot. "Were you having a nightmare?"

Lyla pressed a hand to her chest, attempting to calm her breathing. "I guess so."

"What were you dreaming about?"

She blinked up at him, still trying to wake up and collect her bearings. Travis hadn't been there that day when she'd nearly drowned at Memory Lake. Maybe if he had, things would've gone differently. When she'd tried to explain the life or death gravity of the situation, he'd accused her of being dramatic. "N-nothing." She climbed off the bed and stood. "Why are you here?"

"We said we'd get back together this evening, remember? You went off with Allison for lunch. We said we'd meet back up for dinner."

Lyla vaguely remembered that plan. "Right."

"We have a bucket list item to check off," he reminded her.

"Oh. Travis, I don't think I'm up for that tonight." Lyla wasn't even sure if she was up for anything he might have in mind. A slight headache thrummed at her temple, and she still felt uneasy after that nightmare.

"All the more reason we should do this."

"Do what?" Judging by the look on his face, she probably wasn't going to be thrilled about this idea. She tried to remember what was left on the bucket list, but her mind was drawing a blank.

"Camping," he finally said. "We put overnight camping on our bucket list. Remember?"

Lyla released a breath that came out as a small laugh. "Our parents' heads' practically exploded when we told them we were going to spend the night together in the woods. Even though we were already eighteen. I'm not sure if they were more scared about us being eaten by bears or being two teenagers alone in a tent." Travis placed his hands on his hips right above his tool belt. His shirt was stained with dirt, which probably shouldn't have been as sexy as it was. "Probably both, but especially that latter one, considering Bailey's out-of-wedlock pregnancy that summer."

"We couldn't check camping off then, but there's nothing stopping us from checking that item off now." He rubbed his hands together. "Nothing except you. Come on, Ly. What do you say? Spend the night with me."

August 2

Dear Diary,

I lied to Travis. I'm not a liar but, in my opinion, sometimes a lie is the only thing to do. He wanted to go camping. He even put it on the bucket list. There are so many reasons camping is a bad idea. Bad! So I told him that my parents said no. Yes, I know I'm an eighteen-year-old woman. An adult. I have full control of my actions, but I don't trust myself to be alone, under a sky full of stars with all these feelings that seem to have come out of nowhere this summer. So, I lied.

Keep my secret, Diary!
Lyla

Chapter 13

*Opinion: A bad idea will never turn into a good one,
no matter how much you drink.*
—Delilah Dune, opinion writer

Going with Travis back to his place was probably a bad idea. Not that she didn't trust him. Even after all these years, she trusted him with her life.

"That's a cute tattoo on your left ankle," he said as he opened his truck door for her. "Is that a butterfly?"

Lyla glanced toward her foot, admiring the dark black ink on her skin. "A firefly, actually. My ex hated it. He said tattoos were stupid."

Travis waited for her to step inside the truck. Then he held up a finger. "Hold that thought." He shut the truck door behind her and jogged around to the driver's side, sliding behind the steering wheel. A woodsy scent wafted into the truck along with him, awakening Lyla's senses. "The Lyla I knew would never have settled for a guy who called anything about her stupid." He placed the key in the ignition, turned, and the engine rolled, sputtering for a moment.

Lyla pulled her seatbelt across her body and buckled. "Joe,

my ex, had a way of criticizing something and then love bombing with compliments afterwards. It was a constant head game with him."

Travis backed the truck out of her driveway. "Why'd you date someone like him to begin with?"

She'd asked herself that very question a lot lately. "Hindsight is twenty-twenty. That's not an opinion, it's fact. We dated for the usual reasons, I guess." She glanced across the middle console. "At first, everything was perfect between us. Isn't that how relationships always start before they fall apart?"

"Honestly, I have no idea." Travis's lips tilted in a slight frown. "I am the last person to know anything about relationships. I stay as far from those as possible. But I'm sorry someone treated you like that, Ly."

She studied his side profile as he drove. It was no longer soft and rounded like it had once been. "I honestly think keeping your heart to yourself is even sadder than having it broken."

"Maybe so. All I know is, you deserved better. You *deserve* better, Ly."

She looked down at her hands in her lap, noticing that they were shaking. She was shaking.

"Why a firefly?" he asked, returning the focus to the tattoo. "Why not a dragonfly or a butterfly?"

The connection of her tattoo and seeing the daytime fireflies since returning to Echo Cove gobsmacked her, making her speechless for a moment. Were her tattoo and the little daytime fireflies she'd been seeing somehow related? "I was in college and I felt lost in a way. I was so sure when I moved away from Echo Cove that I would find myself, but all I found were shallow friendships, parties, and a boyfriend who made me hate myself some days."

"*Hate?* Strong word," he said as he steered the truck.

She felt a sense of shame admitting it, but it was true. "So

I went to a tattoo shop one night, slightly intoxicated, and my roommate started looking up the meanings of different tattoos. Apparently, fireflies symbolize illumination of one's self. That's exactly what I wanted, so I said yes, and I put it on one of the most painful spots I could think of." She laughed a little. "I mean, I'm sure there are more painful spots, but of the places I was willing to ink, the ankle was pretty rough."

"Self-illumination," Travis repeated.

"And guidance and inspiration. All those things sounded good to me. I needed it all."

"You could have reached out to me," Travis said quietly. He didn't wait for her to respond. "But personally, I like the firefly tattoo."

"Yeah?"

His grin stretched for maximal dimple depth. "I have a tattoo."

Lyla's eyes roamed the bare skin of his body. "Where?"

Waggling his eyebrows, he shook his head. "Wouldn't you like to know?"

She shoved a playful hand against his shoulder. "Actually, no. I don't think I would." As her laughter died, her stomach growled loudly. *How embarrassing.*

Travis's gaze jumped from the road to her midsection, confirming that he'd heard the monstrous sound. "Hungry much?" he asked before refocusing on the road.

"I guess nightmares take a lot of energy."

"All that tossing, turning, and wrestling your personal demons in your sleep." He pulled up to a STOP sign. "Good thing I have dinner simmering in a Crock-Pot at my place."

"A Crock-Pot?" Lyla asked in disbelief. Crock-Pots were something that her mom and grandma had used when she was growing up. They weren't for single, attractive men. "Is this a prank?"

Travis seemed amused by her reaction. "We're adults now, Ly. Crock-Pots are sexy."

Lyla appreciated that he had cooked dinner. "What are you cooking?"

"Steak, rice, and peppers simmering in a savory beef bone broth." He kissed the tips of his fingers. "Chef's kiss."

"I must say, I am impressed." Lyla meant it. "You've grown into a responsible adult."

Travis chuckled quietly. "I read 'Delilah's Delusions.' I happen to know that your opinion on Crock-Pots is that they are equal parts lazy and genius."

He was referencing an article from the column's first year in publication. It hadn't garnered too many reader responses, and Bob had forbidden her to write anything remotely domestic again—unless it was sexy domestic, he'd said. "I still stand by that opinion. You can create an entire meal with only fifteen minutes of prep. It's lazy, but also genius, because look at all the time saved. What you do with that time seals the deal on whether the meal is lazy or genius," she explained.

Travis slowed his truck and turned down a gravel road, turning the ride from smooth to bumpy. Lyla reached for the handle on the truck's ceiling and held on as she glanced around curiously. This was the lot that his parents' double-wide trailer used to sit on, but now the land was empty except for a small RV parked on the grassy waterfront.

"That's yours?" she asked.

"Mm-hmm." He gave her a long look, something hesitant about the way he pressed his lips together, as if holding in a thought. Or confession. "Her name is Delilah."

Everything inside Lyla went still. "You named your RV after me? You're kidding."

He shrugged. "You were my best friend, and our adventures were legendary in my mind. When I got this RV, I hoped the same would be true for us. Me and Delilah number two."

Lyla opened her mouth to speak, but no words came out for a few seconds. Finally, she said, "I'm not sure what to say."

"Naming my RV after you is a compliment." He parked

his truck in front of the RV and pushed open his driver's side door. He didn't step out just yet though. "For the record, my opinion is that the time saved with Crock-Pot cooking is never lazy, even if the chef just steps out onto their back porch and watches the sky. Spending life the way you choose is always genius." He stepped out and closed the truck door behind him, leaving Lyla sitting there speechless for a long moment. In her profession, she was always being served up others' opinions, but they usually weren't so deep and thoughtful. Most readers offered a knee-jerk opinion that they were ready to defend, tooth and nail. That's why the "Delilah's Delusions" column was so popular.

Lyla pushed her passenger door open and stepped out as well, meeting him around the front of the RV. "Have you become a philosopher since our senior year?"

"It comes with all the sitting I do while watching the sky." He turned toward his RV. "Lyla, meet Delilah."

It was an older model RV, but Lyla could tell that Travis took very good care of it. The mobile home was a soft cream color with wide horizontal baby blue stripes. "Hello, Delilah." She felt a bit silly talking to a vehicle.

Travis climbed a set of three metal steps and then opened the camper's door. He stepped in and offered his hand to help her up. She didn't need help, but letting him take her hand felt nice. That was one of the gestures her ex had stopped doing along the way, in addition to many others—too many to count. She'd written an article about that too.

Opinion: Time to buy lingerie, stat, once the hand-holding and kissing fades.

The lingerie bit was just clickbait, attracting interest by mentioning something sexy. She hadn't purchased lingerie once the hand-holding and kissing had stopped with Joe, though. In her mind, a relationship didn't need those things to survive. It needed time and nurturing, and date nights to places that weren't grocery stores. Joe had considered a trip to Harris Teeter to buy steaks a date. She didn't even like steaks.

Struggling relationships maybe even needed couples counseling. When she'd suggested that to Joe, he'd laughed her out of the room. The country loved her opinion, but her boyfriend found it amusing at best.

Travis let go of her hand and gestured around the main entrance of his RV. "These are my living quarters. As you can see, I have a couch. A TV. A coffee table." He led her toward a small kitchen. "A stove. Fridge. Sink." He gestured for her to step ahead of him. "The hall is pretty narrow. Be my guest. The bathroom and bedroom are down there. I'll stay here to give you space. Just make sure your *Oohs* and *Ahs* are loud enough for me to appreciate."

Lyla grinned over at him, intrigued by the pride radiating off him right now. Then she headed down the hall, taking her time to note the detail. "Is this your work?" She pointed to the paneled walls and crown molding.

"It is. Not many RVs have crown molding. Or a Jacuzzi bathtub," he said.

"You have a Jacuzzi tub?" She peeked into the bathroom, and sure enough, he had a fancy tub that put the one in her parents' home to shame. "Wow. This is amazing, Trav." She caught a glimpse of herself in the bathroom mirror and stopped to fix a few out-of-place hairs. Then she entered the bedroom and stopped to take it all in.

It was a man's bedroom, for sure. The bedspread was designed with dark greens, browns, and blacks. The walls were wood paneled, just like the front room. He had a small TV mounted to the wall and a couple framed pictures hanging, as well. She stepped over to inspect them closer. They were nature shots. A waterfall. A view from what appeared to be a mountain peak. She guessed that Travis had taken these photographs himself.

"I can't hear you back there," he called down the hall.

A laugh tumbled off her lips. "Ooh. Ah," she said as she headed back toward the kitchen where Travis was waiting for her, hands propped on his hips.

He suppressed a sheepish grin and looked away. Lyla thought maybe Travis's obvious pride in his RV made him feel vulnerable. She understood that feeling. It was the same feeling she got when someone was reading her writing. It felt like one critical word could break her. That's how it felt with her fiction writing, at least. She'd grown a thicker skin for her opinion articles. The fiction felt more intimate, whereas the column wasn't always her honest opinions. Sometimes she just wrote to create controversy, because that's what her editor wanted.

Maybe that was one of her problems. She hadn't written any fiction since her failed attempt at eighteen. Fiction didn't pay the bills, but it did nurture that creative part of her that seemed to be starving lately.

"She's just an RV, I know that, but I've invested a lot of time and effort in Delilah, here," Travis said.

"You really did name this place Delilah?" she asked.

"I hope you're not insulted."

"Of course not. She's beautiful." Lyla glanced around, noticing all the little details. Travis had poured his soul into this home.

When she met his gaze again, he nodded. "Yes, she is."

She was only imagining the way Travis was looking at her, right? Her and her big imagination. It always led her mind down paths that weren't entirely based in reality, like the time she could have sworn Joe was about to propose. Instead, he'd just been hiding the fact he was seeing someone else behind her back. What a mistake dating Joe had been.

Pushing away her thoughts of the past, she said, "It smells delicious in here." Focusing on the present moment was always the better idea. This present moment was quiet, and it smelled intoxicatingly wonderful, a combination of Travis' woodsy scent and rosemary and basil from the stew that was cooking. This present moment also included one of her favorite people in the whole world. How had she shut Travis Painter out of her life? That was maybe her biggest mistake—and her biggest regret.

He grabbed a wooden spoon and sidestepped to the Crock-Pot on the kitchen counter. "Well, the food is ready when you are."

"You heard my stomach earlier. I've never turned down a home-cooked meal, and I won't start tonight."

"Except for that brief time when you decided you were vegetarian," Travis reminded her. "You turned down a lot of good food during that time."

Lyla pressed a palm to her forehead. "I can't believe you remember that."

"Of course, I do. I ate nothing but meat that entire week to help change your mind."

She shook her head and turned to lean her back against his kitchen counter. "Why am I not surprised? Of course, you would do that."

"What's that supposed to mean?" he asked, looking mildly concerned.

"Nothing. You always loved to press my buttons. Not just mine, but everyone's."

He blew out a heavy breath. "Is that why no one threw me a goodbye party when I moved away?" He was teasing, but there was something sad in his expression. Lyla remembered that Travis was sometimes sensitive about his reputation for mischief, especially when folks pointed out that he was a preacher's son. People expected him to be an angel, and he was often the opposite. His sister Bailey had played the good girl role, until she'd gotten pregnant and been branded by her own father and church with an invisible scarlet letter.

"Trouble with a capital T," Travis quipped. "That's what people used to say about me." He lifted the lid off the Crock-Pot and pulled the two bowls that were already laid out closer. After dispensing their servings, he carried the bowls to a tiny rectangular shaped dining room table that folded out of the camper's wall. "What would you like to drink? Sweet tea?"

She tilted her head, feeling the flirtiness in her micromovements. She couldn't seem to help herself. "Did you make it yourself?"

"It's instant," he admitted. "But I did stir it myself. Are you still impressed with me?"

Lyla sat down at the little table in his RV. "Very much. I'd love some sweet tea."

Opinion: If your Southern host doesn't serve sweet tea, they aren't hospitable. If they do, they're hoping you'll stay a while.

Chapter 14

Opinion: Glamping is the only civilized way to camp.
—Delilah Dune, opinion writer

The cicadas blared loudly a couple hours later as Lyla sat in a chair and watched the fireflies twinkle in the distance. She looked at Travis, who looked completely at home in the scene. She, however, had fear and worry niggling around in the back of her mind about whether some creature of the night was watching her and sizing her up to be its dinner.

A noise got her attention from somewhere in the brush. "Did you hear that?" She sat up in her chair and strained her eyes trying to see in the dark.

"What is it you think you heard?" There was a healthy amount of amusement playing in Travis's tone of voice.

"I don't know. What kind of wildlife do you have around here?" She turned to look at him, noting the twinkle in his brown eyes. She knew that mischievous twinkle well. "You think this is funny?"

He shook his head. "No, I think it's adorable."

Lyla looked away and then melted back into her chair.

"I'm not used to being out in nature anymore, I guess. I spend a lot of my time inside, behind a computer screen."

"That's not healthy, Ly. Fresh air and dirt under your feet is good for the soul. Haven't you ever heard of grounding?"

She shook her head.

"Look it up. Opinion: Grounding is the earth's medicine." One corner of his mouth kicked up in a grin.

Maybe that was what was wrong with her lately. Perhaps she needed more dirt in her life. "So, you do this kind of thing regularly? Camping outside."

He chuckled as he nodded. "A couple times a week."

"What? The RV isn't enough of a camper's lifestyle for you?" She folded her arms over her chest, trying to pay attention to him and not the strange noises coming from all sides. Nature was noisy and anxiety-inducing when she didn't know what was surrounding her.

He seemed to consider his answer. "I like to be outside with nature. It's where I feel most at home." He looked at her again. "At least, until recently."

Lyla felt a fluttery feeling inside her chest. "What does that mean?"

"I don't know. I've never considered Echo Cove to be my home, at least not in my adult life. But being back and seeing you, that feels like home. You feel like home."

Lyla internally warned herself not to read deeper into that statement than Travis intended his words to mean. They had been best friends growing up. Seeing an old friend would, of course, give someone the sense of home. She felt the same way seeing him.

She sucked in a breath and looked out at the scene again. "Our parents had nothing to worry about if we would've spent the night together when we were out here at eighteen," she said, trying to convince herself as much as Travis. She'd had feelings for him, but Travis had never shown any sign that he had feelings too. Maybe that's what scared her most back then.

"You don't think so?" he asked.

Lyla's lips parted for a second. She was surprised at his question. "You do?"

His laughter came easily. "I mean, you were a teenage girl, Ly, and I was a teenage boy."

"Yeah, so?" She pretended not to have any clue what he was suggesting.

Travis reached for an open soda can on the ground beside him. He lifted it to his lips and took a long sip.

Lyla tried not to notice his mouth, his lips . . . him. It was nearly impossible not to, though.

"I try not to think about the past too much," he said, avoiding the question. "I like to think about the now. And right now, I'm glad we're doing this."

"Me too." She reached for her own soda, but didn't take a sip. She just needed something to hold onto, to keep her hands busy. Travis had never made her nervous until that last summer together, when she'd started to feel this undeniable attraction to him. She felt nervous now too.

Travis leaned up now and stared at the brush several yards in front of them. "Hey, did you hear that?" He turned to look at her over his shoulder, his expression and tone of voice suddenly serious.

Reflexively, she pulled her legs up into her chair, trying to make herself as small as possible. "What? What did you hear?"

"I don't know. Some strange kind of noise. A low growl maybe." His brows were high on his forehead, and he looked frightened. If Travis was scared, something was wrong because Travis laughed in the face of fear. He was always calling her a scaredy-cat, because she cowered.

"A growl?" Lyla's voice went shrill. "Are there wolves out here? What else growls? Wild dogs?"

"Maybe it's those wild hogs I saw out here the other day. Those things can be aggressive," he said. "I saw some wild turkeys too. They're territorial."

Lyla jumped out of her chair and began running toward his RV when she heard him burst into laughter behind her. Her fear quickly molded into anger, and she turned, marched back over to him, and whacked the back of his shoulder. "I hate you!"

He laughed harder, doubling over in his seat. "No, you don't. You love me, and you know it." He reached for her arm and pulled her back toward him. "I'm sorry. I couldn't resist, Ly. Don't hate me. Old habits die hard. You know that."

It was hard to hate him when he was smiling at her like that, all wide with dimples and all.

"Opinion," he said, continuing to hold onto her arm, "Old habits die hard and old flames never do."

She narrowed her eyes. "I never wrote that article," she said quietly. "That's not one of mine."

He released her arm. "That's my own opinion, and I think it's pretty good."

She waited for her breathing to go back to normal. "It's not bad."

"You can steal it if you want—on one condition."

She lifted a brow and waited.

"You sit back down and rest assured that whatever's out there, I'll protect you."

She relented and returned to her camping chair, plopping down beside him. "You're not forgiven."

"I forgave you for not talking to me for ten years. I think you owe me."

True.

"So what's going on in your life, Lyla?" He angled his body in his chair and looked at her with interest.

There was still adrenaline pumping through her veins from

the scare he'd just given her and from the words he'd said afterward. 'Old flames never die?' Was he talking about her? "It depends on which area of my life you're asking about."

"All of it. I want to know everything that's happened since we've been apart."

It struck her that he honestly looked like there was nowhere else he'd rather be right now and no one else he'd rather be with. When was the last time she'd felt like this? Well, Allison made her feel this way too, but before coming back to Echo Cove, it had been a long time. Too long.

She leaned back in her camper's chair and crossed her legs. "Let me just skip to the last part. I just got out of a two-year relationship. I'm thirty years old. And the next opinion piece that I turn in to my boss might be my last. I'm back in my hometown, and I have somehow befriended the school's most annoying cheerleader"—Lyla looked over at Travis—"who, it turns out, is one of the sweetest people I've ever known."

Travis lifted his brows. "Sounds to me like your life has taken a turn for the better."

She thought he was being sarcastic, but his expression seemed sincere. "For the better?"

"Heck, yeah. Any guy who can't see what he has right in front of him is probably an idiot. And a jerk. Your old friends are probably jerks too. People change, and from talking to her just once in your house, I can already tell that Allison isn't who she used to be. And your boss? If he's thinking about getting rid of you, he's an idiot and a jerk too."

Lyla laughed at the absurdity of Travis's statements. "So everyone in the whole wide world is a jerk?"

Travis dug a finger into his chest. "Except for me."

Lyla found it hard to breathe for a moment. Travis hadn't had those mounds of muscle below his T-shirt when they were eighteen. "So if I asked all the women you've dated in the last year, they would say you're not a jerk?"

Travis seemed to find this humorous. "Oh, they would probably say I'm the biggest jerk they've ever known."

"But they'd be lying?"

Travis didn't answer for a moment. "Opinion: People give you exactly what you expect."

Lyla shook her head slightly. "What do you mean by that?"

"If you expect someone to be a jerk, they will be. If you expect them to treat you with respect, there's a good shot they will."

Lyla waved a finger in the air. "I don't agree. That opinion would never fly with my editor. I expect everyone to treat me with respect, and that is not how everyone treats me."

Travis leaned forward in his seat. "You teach people how to treat you, Ly, and the way you expect them to treat you is how you teach them."

She felt her brows pinch as she tried to process his statement. "That makes no sense."

"Take us, for example. You expect me to make you laugh, and so you find a lot of what I say funny. At least, you appear to. But I'm actually not all that funny anymore, Ly."

Just hearing him say so made her laugh quietly. "Yes, you are. You're the same Travis you've always been."

"With you. Overall, I've become more introspective, though. I spend most of my time alone, outdoors, working odd jobs and camping. I'm not the same guy. I'll prove it. I haven't pulled a single prank since I was eighteen."

"I don't believe that."

"It's the truth. After you left town, I felt different inside. I didn't want to pull pranks, and the only reason I did anything so-called wrong was to take the negative attention off Bailey. I probably looked like the same old Travis on the outside, but in reality, I was just depressed. My best friend was hundreds of miles away. My sister was miserable, and my parents were fakes."

"So you left Echo Cove," Lyla said, filling in the blanks.

"Leaving Bailey was one of the hardest things I'd ever done. She pushed me to go, though. She was older than me. An adult. She said she could take care of herself in Echo Cove, but that if I stayed, I'd continue to suffocate. The only reason I hadn't yet was because of you, Ly. You were my fresh breath of air."

Lyla had already wondered but felt guilty asking the question until now. "You had a driver's license. You could have driven up to see me."

Travis looked away. "Driving what? That blue truck was my dad's. He didn't let me take it with me when I went. I caught a bus and rode my bicycle to my first jobs until I could afford my own truck. Then the RV." He turned his attention back to her. "By the time I bought that bus ticket, you'd ignored all my emails for six months. You'd even come home for Christmas and somehow snuck past me. You made it very clear that you weren't interested in being friends anymore. Believe me, I considered using that bus ticket money to go see you, but I assumed you had a boyfriend or something."

Lyla did have a boyfriend by that time. She'd met Joe. Not that Joe had swept her off her feet. That was probably why she'd let him stay in her life for so long. Joe hadn't been a threat to her dreams. Not the way Travis had.

"Have your parents forgiven you for leaving yet?" Lyla asked.

"No, they never forgave me. In fact, hearsay is that I became the topic of Dad's sermons again. At least my leaving took the focus off Bailey and the baby."

Lyla resisted reaching out and touching his hand. She wanted to, but something told her he was an inch from breaking and maybe one gentle touch would pull the tiny thread that kept his composure together. "I'm sorry. Do you still see them?"

Travis slowly rotated the soda can in his hands. "They passed away."

Lyla gasped. There was another important fact her mom had failed to mention during their weekly calls over the years. "Travis, I'm so sorry. I didn't know." She wouldn't have brought it up if she had. "What happened? You don't have to tell me if it's too painful."

He stopped rotating his soda can and glanced over, his eyes suspiciously shiny under the scattered moonlight that fell on them from the canopy of tree branches overhead. "Dad died of a sudden heart attack when he was fifty. I did come home for a little while after that happened. I helped my mom as much as I could. I even revived the old Travis pranks to see if I could cheer her up." He shook his head. "For months, she barely crawled out of bed. She said she just wanted to curl up and die. And that's what she did. She died from a major cardiac event six months after my dad, to the day."

Lyla hadn't experienced much loss or grief in her life. She could empathize but, big as her imagination was, she didn't think she could imagine just how painful it was to lose a parent, or a child, like Allison had. "I'm so sorry, Travis."

He exhaled into the night. "I believe my parents were deeply misguided people. You don't disown your own kid, regardless of what they do or don't do. Love isn't conditional. I don't agree with how they treated me. Or Bailey. I do believe my parents were good people, though. I have to believe that, because they're part of me and believing otherwise would mean I'm not a good person."

Lyla didn't resist anymore. She reached out and laid a hand on his arm. "You're a great person," she said, quietly. "One of the best."

He pointed a finger in her direction. "Now that is definitely a debatable opinion."

"I'll have you know I get paid for my opinions. I'm a professional. At least for the time being."

"Don't offer that last opinion to your editor. You'll definitely be unemployed," he said, probably not understanding just how close to the truth he was.

Lyla tucked her chin as she looked down. Then, after a moment, as gentle as the caress of a feather, his index finger lifted her chin, turning her face until she was looking directly at him.

"You won't be unemployed, Ly. You're going to come up with something amazing, and this blip of time where everything seems out of place will be over. You'll realize that these weeks or months were the best blip that could have ever happened to you."

She studied his brown eyes with golden flecks. "I'm supposed to be the one who's better with words."

His finger continued to hold her chin in place. This felt like a kissable moment, if the person sitting in front of her was anyone other than Travis. Her subconscious asked, *Why not Travis?* Her mind answered swiftly. Because she wasn't ready for dating. She wasn't ready for casual flings and definitely not for anything serious. Because if she and Travis were to become more than friends, deep down she knew she would be all in, and without a doubt, she'd get hurt when Travis left. Yeah, she'd done the leaving the first time, but he was a traveler now. He didn't put down roots. He'd told her that in not so many words. Travis Painter would leave Echo Cove, just like her.

As her thoughts raced, a firefly lit up in her peripheral vision. "Did you see that?" she asked.

"See what?"

She didn't answer. All she knew was she'd seen the flash of light and like her tattoo, it meant something. Self-illumination. This summer with its crazy déjà vu-like coincidences were all guiding her to discover something about herself.

Travis lowered his hand from her chin. "You were better with words maybe, but I was best at taking action. Together we were the dream team."

"Yes, we were."

"Imagine if we put our heads together now. We could sell your parents' place, save your job, and marry off my sister to a good guy. All in a week's work."

"Assuming nothing else goes terribly wrong with the house." She leaned back in her chair and tipped her head just in time to see a large, fuzzy blob in the sky. She gasped and pointed. "Do you see that?" she practically shouted.

"Hard to miss." Travis chuckled. "Amazing, huh?"

"It's a comet. An actual comet," she said, unable to believe her eyes.

Travis looked amused when she turned to him. "It's not like this is the first time you've seen one. We saw one"—his bemused expression turned into something serious—"that last summer together."

She watched as the comet came and went, soaking in the wonderous moment. "Most people never see a comet with their bare eyes. That's rare, right?"

"I guess," Travis agreed. "Unless you're one of those who stalk comets with a telescope."

"It's proof that things are repeating from our last summer together."

His eyes narrowed and searched her face. "What are you talking about?"

Lyla counted on her fingers. "First, I was struck by lightning. Second, the same movie was playing at the cinema. Then there was the rainstorm and my bike's tire blew out. You pulled up to save me, just like the summer we were eighteen." She'd lifted all five fingers on her left hand so she started counting with her right, holding up one finger at a time. "Then there was the leak in the roof and the busted bathroom pipe. And I found out Bailey was getting married," Lyla said excitedly. "Even my dad's upset stomach is a repeat of what happened that last summer together." She was holding up nine fingers in the air.

"An upset stomach is not so uncommon, Ly. If you want the truth, I had one after that pickle and bacon pizza." Concern etched in the lines that veered from the corners of his eyes.

"But my dad's upset stomach was from an eel roll. He swore them off after that summer, but for some reason he decided this was a good time to try them again. What are the odds he'd try eel rolls and get sick that summer and this one too?"

"Ly, you're sounding a little . . ." He trailed off. If he was only teasing, he would have completed the sentence. He would have said she sounded crazy. Insane. "Do you remember that time you got your wisdom tooth pulled and you were under the influence of laughing gas?" he asked.

Lyla blinked. "I was eighteen." And now she was suddenly worried that she'd be having a dental emergency that involved laughing gas in her future.

"You said a lot of strange things that night." His grin came back.

"Explain the comet," she said, like a lawyer making her case. The thing about being an opinion writer is that she didn't need to prove her stance. Opinions were subjective. What she was trying to tell Travis wasn't an opinion, though. This felt factual. Why couldn't anyone else see it?

"Explain the comet," Travis repeated. "Okay. Usually we can't see them with our naked eye, but sometimes the coma and the tail are illuminated by the sun as the comet passes through the inner solar system." He gestured around them. "The dust reflects sunlight while the gases glow. It's called ionization."

Lyla wanted to be irritated with Travis's cluelessness, but

she was also a little turned on by his nerdy side, something very few knew people knew about Travis Painter. "Seeing the comet makes ten. Ten things have repeated from our last summer together."

Travis took his time before responding. When he did, his tone was gentler, another clue that he was worried. "I'm an outdoorsman. I've seen lots of comets, Ly."

"Well, I haven't. I've only seen two." From her peripheral vision, she saw another flash of firefly light. She didn't dare ask Travis if he saw it too because it was clear that this experience was solely hers.

He scratched the side of his head. "Let me get this straight. You think our last summer together is repeating? You're being serious? This isn't some practical joke?"

She inhaled, filling up her lungs with fresh air. "I'm not the Lyla of Old, or whatever it is you keep saying. I don't joke around anymore."

"That's tragic," he said, a teasing tone in his voice.

He was going to make light of this, but she needed him to hear her. She needed him to believe what she was saying. "I know it sounds insane, right? The events of one summer repeating."

"A little bit, yeah." He let out a low, nervous-sounding laugh. "It sounds a little bit like you've been slipping a little extra something in your Coca-Cola. Or maybe hitting that laughing gas again."

Lyla felt herself deflate on the inside. This was no use. He couldn't see what felt so clear to her. "Well, I haven't. Although I wouldn't mind some of that laughing gas, except without the tooth extraction." She wasn't losing her mind, although she was certain she sounded that way. Backtracking, she said, "I guess I'm just tired." She added a yawn for good measure.

"You don't have to make excuses to me. You okay, Ly? I mean, really."

"Yeah. Of course. I'm fine," she said while contradicting

her words and shaking her head just slightly. "It's just been . . . a weird year, if you want the truth." Which she'd only shared in part this evening. "I'm okay." Her voice was shaky. Her hands too. Travis didn't seem to be buying the theory that moments from their last summer together were repeating, and she couldn't blame him. She wouldn't believe him if he brought this same story to her. It wasn't rational. "I'm just tired," she said again.

He gave a small nod and returned his attention to the sky. "Did you make a wish?"

"I thought that was just for shooting stars."

"In my book, wishing on comets is even more lucky. Go ahead. Try it," he said, his tone coming out as almost a challenge.

Feeling foolish, not for the first time tonight, she closed her eyes and offered up the first wish that came to mind. She wished she could do things differently with Travis. That this time, this summer, she could somehow make him stay. That she could stay, as well. Putting her feelings in a bottle, keeping them shut in all this time, hadn't done her any favors. The attraction between them was still there. She still wanted more from Travis than friendship, and it still terrified her.

Her eyes popped open, and she turned to Travis. "Did you make a wish too?"

"I've wished on a million shooting stars and half a dozen comets in my lifetime."

"And none of them came true?" she asked.

The corner of his mouth quirked softly. "One of them did." The way he was looking at her made her wonder if that wish was about her.

She cleared her throat. "So, this camping thing? Is this all it is?"

"What do you mean?"

She looked around. "We just sit around this fire and talk all night?"

"You don't know anything about camping, do you?" He reached for something off to his side. "S'mores. Not making them would be a waste of a good campfire."

"We're making s'mores?" The thought made her laugh. "I'm not sure I've ever had one before. I mean, I've had a S'mores Pop-Tart, of course."

Travis looked at her in disbelief. "How were we ever best friends and you've never had a real-life s'more?"

"You failed to put it on one of our bucket lists, I guess."

"I failed big-time. We'll fix this. Tonight, you are having the world's greatest s'more. It's going to be the best thing you've ever put into your mouth, aside from the pickle-bacon pizza." He waggled his brows, making her laugh harder, which felt amazing. Laughing with Travis felt like air right now. Like life.

"You're still a preacher's son, right?"

He side-eyed her. "You and I both know I was never any good at that role."

August 5

Dear Diary,

Travis is adamant we finish this last summer bucket list before I go, but have you seen what's written on it? He wants me to jump off the Pirate's Plank. Is he crazy? I almost died last time.

Travis says it's bad luck if we don't finish the list. I've always thought that was baloney. I'm more scared that if I tempt fate too many times, I'll die young and never leave Echo Cove and follow my dreams. Well, first I have to find a new dream because according to that editor, pursuing a career as a bestselling author is a lost cause and waste of time.

Lyla

Chapter 15

Opinion: No opinion.
—Delilah Dune, opinion writer

Lyla tossed and turned, trying to get comfortable in the small tent with Travis. "If you have an RV, why don't we use it when we camp? Technically, staying in an RV is considered camping, right?"

Travis rolled toward her in the small quarters. "Not if one lives in an RV. Delilah is my home, Ly, so it's not camping to sleep inside. Camping is staying in a tent and being uncomfortable on the ground. It's going without the convenience of a bathroom."

"And where is the glamour in that?" she mumbled.

Travis laughed into the darkness before rolling onto his back and staring up at the nylon ceiling. He put his arms behind his head, propping himself up, his elbow touching Lyla's hair as it fanned out beneath her head. "Who said anything about glamour?"

She blew out a breath. "If this was a date between me and you, I'm sure my questions would be raising all kinds of red flags, right?"

"Good thing it's not a date then, huh?" he said without answering the question.

"Good thing." She tried to close her eyes, but she thought maybe she was lying on a few pointy rocks. The ground was hard, her body was uncomfortable, and the sounds beyond the nylon enclosure were too loud. She knew that Travis was pranking her earlier, but she still wondered if there was a coyote or wolf or even a bear wandering around. She could also hear Travis breathing beside her, the sound steady and constant.

Lyla listened, subconsciously matching her breaths to his. Eventually, since neither of them was talking anymore, she began to drift off, vaguely aware of the hard earth beneath her back and the warm body that she absolutely could not cuddle up to snoring beside her.

"Do you remember that last summer?"

Lyla was about to drift away into sleep. "Hmm?" She was half alert, but barely.

"I knew you had just a couple more weeks until you went off to college, and I felt this urgency. I had this now-or-never feeling, like I was about to lose the best part of me, and I had no idea what to do."

The silence drifted between them.

"I thought I felt something between us," he said quietly. "I wanted to say something. I wanted to kiss the girl."

Lyla had felt something too. "You never said anything."

"I wanted to. There was this night that I had amped myself up to tell you. Then you said something. You made a point of telling me you thought all those people choosing love over life were crazy. A lot of our classmates were getting married straight out of school. Basing their college decisions on their boyfriends and girlfriends. Do you remember that?"

"I remember." She remembered the exact conversation, word for word. Something inside her could feel that Travis was about to tell her something that would change things, and she'd felt an urgency too. Her urgency was to stop him, though.

Travis continued. "You said love was a stumbling block that trapped people from their true purpose in life."

"I guess I was a little dramatic back then, huh?"

His elbow knocked against her. "Back then?" He chuckled quietly. "I would have stumbled and fallen for you, Ly. I didn't have those same big plans like you did, though, so stumbling wouldn't have been quite as tragic."

"Most of those couples that married straight out of high school didn't even last," she pointed out. "Look at Allison and Ernie."

"I don't know. I think we would've been different. Maybe. Who knows?" He laughed again, but the sound struck her as odd. "We had different paths, and I came to my senses that night. It wasn't like I was losing you forever, right? You'd be back for fall break, winter break. That's what I told myself, at least. Because the thought of losing my best friend forever would have killed me."

A tear slipped from the corner of her eye, crossing the bridge of her nose and dripping onto the tent's floor as she rolled to her side. "I'm sorry, Travis," she whispered. She'd apologized before, but this time she felt the regret deep within her soul.

When he didn't respond, she leaned closer, trying to catch a glimpse of him in the dark. "Trav?"

His breathing was steady and deep. Seriously? He'd just poured his heart out and now he was already asleep? How did men do that?

She lowered herself back to her side of the tent, fully awake, no thanks to Travis's confessions in the dark. What did he want her to say? Choosing love at eighteen would have been crazy. Was she supposed to have chosen him over college? Closing her eyes, she forced her thoughts away, focusing on her breathing. Focusing on Travis's breathing. Focusing on anything except what might have been.

The dream started again, almost exactly where it had left off when Travis had stirred her awake earlier in the day.

Teenage Lyla stood there on the diving board, heart pounding, blood rushing. Her vision went black, and she suddenly lost all control of her body. The world disappeared until, the next second, she hit the water with a cold splash. She felt frozen and unable to do anything except regret the decision to step on the Pirate's Plank this afternoon. She also regretted coming to Memory Lake.

Her body descended into the depths of the lake, going down, down, down, until finally buoyancy took over, and she started to rise again, her arms and legs flailing. There was no grace to her movements. If she had to guess, one leg was going right and the other was going left, while one arm was going forward and the other was reaching backward. This was not the lifesaving measures she'd learned in swim class all those summers ago.

Breaking through the surface of the water, her mouth popped open and gasped for air. Just as soon as she rose to the surface and got a mouthful of air, her body went under again and she accidentally swallowed water. She went up and down, up and down, breathing air and swallowing water as her limbs continued to flail without any rhyme or reason.

This was it. She was going to drown. Everyone who'd watched her jump off the Pirate's Plank was probably laughing at her right now. Bernie was likely laughing—while Lyla was maybe dying. At fifteen.

Her life flashed before her eyes. It was a quick flash, because she'd barely done any living to this point. If she had played it safe and had stayed in the shallow water, she would have been fine.

One risky move.

Lyla felt a hand grab her, pulling her to the surface again.

She couldn't see when she came up. There was too much water in her eyes, and she was too busy trying to breathe.

"Stupid kid." A man clutched her to his body as he waded through the water.

Lyla allowed her body to go limp in his arms. She'd exerted all her energy, and now that she was safe, presumably, she couldn't seem to move. She just allowed herself to be carried to shore, promising herself she'd never do that again. She would never again allow herself to get in over her head.

Her body was tossed onto the shore, and pain seared the side of her right knee where a rock was jutting out of the ground. "Ow," she groaned, still choking on lake water.

"Sorry, kid." The man didn't stay to make sure she was okay. He'd done his good deed.

Opening her eyes, she blinked past the sting of dirt and sun, watching the back of the man walk away from her. Then she looked down at her knee where a large gash was spurting blood. She felt lightheaded and nauseous.

Someone walked up to her and knelt. "Are you okay?"

Lyla blinked the girl into focus. Bernie. "Oh. Um, yeah," she stammered. "I'm fine. I think I just got too hot up there or something." No way was she going to admit she passed out from fear. She was never admitting that to anyone.

She was pretty sure she *had* passed out, but not because of the heat. She'd been terrified standing on that plank, and that fear had gotten the best of her. She'd gone off the diving board like she'd wanted to, but it hadn't been on her own terms.

Bernie's face contorted with concern. "You're bleeding."

"Yeah, there was a rock. It's fine." The humiliation had hurt more than the laceration.

Bernie ignored Lyla's unconvincing lie. "You should apply some pressure on that."

"Don't jump if you can't swim," someone said as they walked by.

Lyla's cheeks flared hot.

"Ignore them. You can swim, right?" Bernie asked.

"Yeah. I mean, kind of." Lyla still wasn't feeling well. She just wanted to disappear. She wanted to go home where it was safe and where no one would point or laugh. "I've got to go." She climbed to her feet and stood on wobbly legs.

"I'll see you here tomorrow?" Bernie asked.

"Yeah. Of course." But Lyla hadn't gone back for a multitude of reasons, all valid. The number-one reason being that she liked breathing. She liked living too. She didn't like being afraid.

Lyla stirred, the nylon tent rustling quietly beneath her. Her eyes opened and squinted against the sunshine peeking through the tent's tiny window. Travis was no longer lying next to her. "Travis?" She sat up and leaned her head out the tent's open flap, looking in all directions.

"Hey, sleepyhead." He was sitting in one of the chairs they'd sat in last night, drinking a cup of coffee.

"Is there more of that?" she asked before breaking into a yawn.

"Of course. Want some?"

"I would love some." She crawled out and stood stiffly, stretching her body in all directions.

"Were you having a nightmare?" he asked, glancing over.

"Was I talking in my sleep?" she asked, taking the chair next to his.

"You were flailing and gasping for air. I figured you were having some kind of dream. Were you having the one about Memory Lake again?"

"How'd you know?"

"I remember that dream always plagued you. You're still having it, huh?"

"Not until recently. I guess being in Echo Cove has made it come back." She blew out a breath, letting her eyes adjust to the morning light. "You didn't wake me up this time."

"I'm a big believer that at some point, you have to finish out the nightmare. Otherwise, your mind will keep going there. It ends well enough, right? You didn't die that day."

Lyla blew out a breath and took the cup of coffee he handed her. "Only my pride. And I injured my knee." She took a sip. "Mm, this is really good."

"Camping coffee is always better than regular coffee. It's a fact." He watched her as she took another sip. "I was going to wake you up if you went much longer. I have a job to get to this morning."

"Oh." Lyla felt disappointed. She was enjoying the morning and the unexpected peace that came with being out in the woods with no set agenda before her. "Sorry. It took me a while to get to sleep last night. The tent isn't the most comfortable place."

"Being uncomfortable isn't a bad thing." Travis tipped his mug toward his lips. "It can be positive."

Lyla let out a humorless laugh. "Well, it doesn't feel positive when a rock is poking your hip in the middle of the night." She drank more of her coffee. "I can be ready to head back as soon as possible."

"Just need to break down the tent and load it all in the back of the truck. I was thinking maybe after my jobs today, we could meet back up. Maybe hang out."

Lyla sipped her coffee. "I can't. I have plans with Allison."

Travis's brow furrowed, making deep creases along his forehead.

"What? I thought you preferred your alone time these days, anyway."

"Alone with you is nice too," he said. "What are you two doing?"

Lyla cleared her throat. "We're going to a bar to pick up guys."

"Seriously? You're choosing to go to a bar rather than hang out with me?"

She wasn't sure if his wounded expression was a tease or real. "Yeah. We're both single, although Allison has some mystery guy she sees sometimes. She says it's not serious, so we're going out for a girls' night."

"To pick up guys. I don't know, Ly. Two beautiful women getting drunk by themselves . . ."

Lyla rolled her eyes. "Since when did you become sexist?"

"I'm not sexist. I'm protective. And maybe a little bit jealous, if I'm honest."

Lyla lifted her brows over her cup of coffee. "Jealous?"

"Allison is stealing away my best friend position."

Lyla looked away. "Right."

"Were you hoping I'd be jealous of the guys you're picking up?"

She waved a hand, feeling all kinds of foolish. "I may have misunderstood."

"I'd be jealous of them too, if I didn't know which guys frequent the local bar around here."

Lyla folded her arms over her chest. "How would you even know that? You don't live in Echo Cove anymore."

"I'm not jealous, just concerned for you and Allison. Maybe I should stop in after the jobs I've lined up."

Lyla set her cup of coffee down on the ground beside her. "Unh-uh. You're not invited."

"You might need a designated driver. I have a truck."

Lyla sighed in exasperation. "We are grown women having a women's night. No men invited."

"But you just said you're going out to pick up men," Travis pointed out.

"Men. Not you. You're a man, but we're not picking you up. You're disqualified," Lyla clarified.

"Fine." He reached for his coffee cup. "I'll just go back to my RV after my jobs. Alone."

Lyla wasn't falling for his guilt trip. "Perfect."

"Perfect," he grumbled before sliding her a teasing look. "I hope you two have a great time. Without me."

August 7

Dear Diary,

As the summer fades, all I know is, some part of me wants time to stop while another part wants it to speed up. I'm nervous about the future, but also excited. I'm ready for everything except saying goodbye to Travis.

Some foolish part of me thought he was going to tell me that he had feelings for me the other day. There was this vibe between us and he seemed to be leading a conversation in that direction. Then it just stopped, and he returned to his normal, joking self. It could have been in my big imagination.

I wanted him to say something in that line of thinking, but honestly, that's the worst thing that could ever happen because then I'd have to choose. Surely, you can't have both. An out-of-state dream college and a boyfriend in the middle of Nowheresville, North Carolina.

Sonny got out again tonight, but not to ruin my mom's flowers. Instead, he came over and casually sat with me on the porch while I cried. I spilled my guts to that dog, things that only this diary and Ms. Hadley's little Yorkie knows. Maybe I'll get a dog one day. Falling in love with a person can wreck your plans, but a dog, I think that's pretty safe.

Lyla

Chapter 16

*Opinion: Girls' nights keep a woman young
at heart.*
—Delilah Dune, opinion writer

Lyla gave Allison a long hard look as she stood in Lyla's doorway. "If I was attracted to women, *I* would try to pick you up tonight."

Allison looked down at her attire, shifting nervously on her sandaled feet. "Really? I tried on at least five different outfits before settling on this one."

Lyla had a hard time believing there was an ounce of insecurity inside Allison Wilkerson. "You still look like that popular cheerleader I went to high school with. The guys are going to ignore me and buy you all the drinks. I expect you to share, by the way," she said with a wink.

Allison shook her head, her red-toned hair bouncing along her shoulders. "You were adorable in high school, you know. You just didn't flirt with the guys like I did. And look where that got me." She was referring to her status as a grieving mother and divorcee, who some might say worked for a pyramid scheme.

"Look where *not* flirting got me," Lyla pointed out. "We're in the exact same place. Kind of." Stepping onto the porch, Lyla pulled the door closed behind her and jingled her car keys. "I'll drive this time."

Allison side-eyed her. "You've been in the city for a while. Can I trust your skills behind the wheel?"

"I've been accused of being a 'grandma driver.' "

Allison snickered as she opened the passenger seat and got in Lyla's car. "That doesn't make me feel any better. My grandma has the record for most traffic citations in Echo Cove."

"Speeding?" Lyla asked as she cranked the engine and put her tiny Subaru into reverse.

"Hitting mailboxes." Allison hugged her purse against her. "There have been people in Echo who have dived into their own ditches when they saw Grandma Wilkerson coming. Her lemon-yellow Cadillac is hard to miss."

Lyla found herself laughing along with Allison. "New life goal unlocked. I want to be that old lady one day."

Allison snorted from laughing so hard. "Me too, actually. I'll probably inherit her Caddy. Let's just take turns behind the wheel and keep the tradition."

"The real-life version of Thelma and Louise." Lyla felt a momentary twinge of sadness knowing this fantasy they were musing about was just a silly pipedream. Lyla wasn't in town for long. Whatever friendship she was building with Allison wouldn't have time to deepen. "No hitting mailboxes for us tonight."

"Absolutely. I don't believe in drinking and driving, even when I'm under the legal limit."

"Travis offered to be our designated driver," Lyla offered.

"Did he now?" Allison angled her body toward Lyla. "And what did you say?"

"I said no, of course. Tonight is our girls' night, and I haven't had one of those in far too long." Lyla tapped an index finger to her chin. "Actually, I don't think I've ever had an actual girls' night." All her friends, starting with Travis, had always been guys. Lyla worked remotely, so she didn't go to an office or have female coworkers to hang out with. And when she'd dated Joe and had inherited his friends, they all went out as couples. Lyla had never had a female friend to hang out with before. It was nice.

"When your mother suggested I come over and help you out, I wasn't sure if we would hit it off," Allison confessed.

Lyla wasn't sure why her mother never mentioned knowing Allison before. "I'm glad she suggested it."

"Me too. You are a great friend to have. The rest of my so-called friends could barely be bothered to listen to me cry or complain. At first, they were there, of course. But then, I guess they grew tired of my grief. I can't say I blame them. I was a bit of a Debbie Downer. Your mom was always there, though. So when she asked me to look after you, I agreed. I had hoped we'd be friends, but even I, the eternal optimist, was skeptical."

"I'm glad we're friends," Lyla said, meaning it. She slowed the car as she came to a stop sign, looked both ways, and continued driving forward. The little bar where they were going wasn't much farther down the road. "I don't want Travis as our DD, but we do need a plan for getting home. Maybe I should limit myself to one drink, so that you can have as many as you want. I've never been that good at holding my alcohol anyway."

"Well, that's not fair," Allison said. "We should both have as much as we want."

"We both need to get home safely tonight," Lyla said. "Speaking of which, we also need a plan for what to do if we meet a guy here. Whether we like him or not, neither of us are separating and leaving with someone. You and I came together and we're leaving together. And we don't give out our personal information. We'll take theirs if we're interested."

"Yes, Mom," Allison said with a giggle. "You're pretty bossy, you know that?"

"I read an article on dating in your thirties. I thought it might be helpful."

"You haven't dated since the breakup?" Allison asked, surprise evident by the lift of her brows.

"I'm not sure I'm emotionally ready. I put a lot of energy into my relationship with my ex. I was planning a future that is suddenly just gone. I think I need to figure out my life on my own before I venture into another relationship. Casual dating might be okay though. And thanks to a recent opinion piece I did, I've done my research on going out." She held up a finger. "Never lose sight of your drink in public places and if you do, get a new drink."

"Oh, come on, Lyla. You're back in Echo Cove now."

Lyla shook her head. "Opinion: One can never be too careful when dating. You and I are playing it safe tonight, okay?"

Allison nodded. "Deal."

"Good. So about the DD . . ." Lyla continued.

"We'll call my mama to come get us. I'll text her right now to be on call."

"Your mom?" Lyla glanced over. "Did I hear that correctly?"

"She has always been my designated driver, except for the times she came out drinking with me. Then my dad was the DD."

Lyla chuckled at the thought. "Your parents are so different than mine."

"You'd be surprised," Allison argued in a singsong tone of voice. "I've been to this same bar with your mother too."

Lyla covered her ears with her hands. "No. No, I don't see my mom that way." Dropping her hands to her side, she shook her head. "That is so weird. I've never seen my mom drunk."

Allison cackled from the passenger seat. "I'd say that's probably for the best."

Lyla mentally agreed as she pulled into an open spot in the parking lot of The Drunk Skunk.

Opinion: A place of business should never have the word skunk in it.

She pushed her car door open and stepped out, briefly rethinking her choice of clothes. She was used to staying in and working from home. She wasn't the most fashionable person. Never had been. In comparison to Allison, she looked like a schoolmarm.

"Stop that." Allison put her hands on her hips. "You're being down on yourself. I can tell. You're gorgeous, and we're just here for fun, okay?"

"You're right. And we're here for drinks," Lyla said. "Fun and drinks."

Allison looped her arm in Lyla's as they stepped through the noisy bar. One might think a place called The Drunk Skunk would stink, but it was actually a nice hole-in-the-wall. A local band was playing in the back of the room. The bar was already half full, but there were still a couple of open stools. "Let's go say hi to Sam."

Lyla stopped walking. "Sam Hall?"

Allison gave her a funny look. "He's the bartender. You knew his dad owned this place, right?"

"Yeah, but I didn't know Sam worked here. He was top of our class."

"He's still a genius, trust me. No one ever said that just because you made good grades in school meant you had to go off to some fancy college and get a fancy degree." Allison continued walking toward the bar.

Lyla felt a little foolish. Allison was right.

As Allison slid onto a bar stool, she patted the one beside her. "Come on. First drink is on me."

Lyla took a seat. "I won't argue. Thank you."

"You're welcome. Here's hoping some handsome hunk buys your next drink," Allison said.

"Hunk?" Lyla laughed out loud. "Here's my unsolicited opinion. If you're calling guys hunks, then you're probably too old to be sitting around the bar."

"Never too old. Your mom came out with me a few times," she reminded Lyla.

"That one's still hard to believe. I'll need pictures."

Allison laughed loudly, signaling the bartender.

"Hey, ladies." Sam made his way to stand in front of them. "Lyla, long time no see."

"Yes, it has been. How are you, Sam?"

He shrugged broad shoulders. "Life is good. I can't complain. How about you?"

Up close, Lyla noticed that the former class valedictorian had buffed up since high school. He truly had become a hunk. "I'm good," she said, even though her relationship had failed, she was practically homeless, and she'd possibly be unemployed sometime soon. It was a total lie.

"Great. What kind of drinks would you ladies like to start with?" he asked.

"Dirty martinis," Allison interjected. "For both of us."

Lyla looked at Allison. "I've never had one of those in my life. I'm not sure I'll like it."

"You'll love it." Allison looked at Sam and held up her fingers. "Two dirty martinis."

"Coming right up." He turned his back and started preparing the drinks.

Allison elbowed Lyla and lowered her voice. "You think he's cute," she whispered.

"What?" Lyla shook her head. "No, I don't. Why would you say that?"

"The way you just acted." Allison covered a hand to her mouth. "You're totally blushing."

"Am not." Lyla lowered her face, because she could feel that Allison wasn't lying. Her cheeks were flaming hot. "He's cute, okay? I admit it. I've always thought so. But it's not an opinion, it's a fact. I'm sure every woman and a fair share of the men here think he's a hunk."

Allison pointed a finger. "You stole my word."

Sam returned with two drinks. "Two dirty martinis." He looked between them. "Everything okay?"

"Oh, everything is dandy." Allison grinned. "We're having a girls' night tonight. We're here to pick up guys. Got any suggestions for Lyla here?" She elbowed Lyla.

Lyla hadn't felt this level of embarrassment since—well, since high school probably. She felt Sam's eyes on her.

He leaned forward on his elbows. "I don't know. What's your type, Lyla?"

Was it hot in here? "Um, I'm not sure. I don't think I have a type."

"Her type is a guy who isn't a total jerk," Allison supplied.

Lyla couldn't refute that. "Yes, that is a requirement for my type these days. No more jerks."

Sam's grin spread wide through his cheeks. "I'll keep that under consideration and let you know if someone comes to mind." His voice dipped as he spoke.

"You do that." Allison nudged Lyla again.

Lyla was ready to nudge her friend right off her barstool at this point. She was getting a sore spot in her arm from all of Allison's poking.

"Let me know when you need another drink," Sam said. "I've got to get to the other patrons."

Allison saluted him and reached for her drink, waggling her brows at Lyla over her cup. "There's great potential there."

"Why don't you date him then?" Lyla reached for her own drink.

"Been there, done that."

Lyla's mouth fell open.

"Not recently. Once, right after high school, when Ernie and I were broken up. It was brief. No big deal. Me and Sam are more friends than anything else. He's all yours."

"No, he's not," Lyla objected.

"Why? Because you already have your eye on Travis?" Allison took another sip of her drink.

Lyla rolled her eyes. "He and I are just friends."

"Who spent the night together last night."

Lyla felt her eyes go round. "You truly are a spy, aren't you?"

Allison laughed wickedly. "See? This is fun. I love a good girls' night. It's been way too long since I've had one." She knocked her drink back again.

Lyla grinned and found her gaze tracking back to Sam as he worked the bar. He *was* pretty hunky. Maybe she should come here more often while she was staying at her parents' house.

"Hey, Ly," a deep voice said.

From her peripheral, Lyla saw someone plop into the stool next to her. Lyla glanced over, shocked to find Travis sitting beside her. "What are you doing here? I told you that you weren't invited."

"I don't need to be invited to come to the local bar." He looked up as Sam moved over to stand in front of them again. "Hey, bud."

"Hey, Travis. Crashing the girls' night?"

"Just getting myself a drink. I'll have whatever's on tap." Travis looked calm and relaxed—unlike Lyla right now.

"Sure thing." Sam turned his back to make Travis's drink.

"Not him, Ly. You can do better," Travis said under his breath. "Sam seems nice, but he wouldn't treat you right in the long run."

Lyla wondered how Travis knew or why he cared. "Who said I was interested? And who said anything about the long run?"

"You want a one-night stand?" Travis asked.

Lyla huffed. "What I want is a girls' night, free from over-bearing guy friends." She gave Travis's shoulder a gentle shove. "Go. Home."

"But I haven't had my beer yet."

"I'll drink it myself," Lyla said. "Go."

Allison stood and headed over to Travis's stool. "But before you go, dance with me."

Chapter 17

Opinion: Never, ever date a friend. Ever.
—Delilah Dune, opinion writer

One dance had turned into two while Lyla sat on her barstool throwing a silent pity party for herself. She knew Allison was just having fun, and Travis was just looking out for her, but right now, under the influence of alcohol, Lyla felt completely out of her element.

Sam polished a glass as he stood in front of her. "Need a listening ear?"

Lyla watched him for a moment. Travis was probably right about Sam. She remembered in high school, Sam had dated quite a few girls. He wasn't the doting type. He was nice to have as a friend, but from what Lyla had heard, he was clueless when it came to being a good boyfriend.

People changed though. Wasn't that what she was learning this summer? They changed and yet, they stayed the same. It was a fine balance.

She blew out a breath and looked around the room. She had had just enough alcohol that her ability to attempt any self-preservation was gone. "I feel like I've wasted all those years since graduation. And now I'm thirty. I've spent a full three decades on this earth, and I have no idea how to have fun. Allison and Travis are out there having a great time, and honestly, I'd rather be at home watching TV. Or camping." *Camping? Where had that thought come from?* She'd never considered herself a camping person before last night.

"Camping?" Sam set the polished glass down on the counter. "I never pegged you as a granola nature lover. You were more of the nose in a book type."

"Well, I never pegged you as the type to serve drinks to sloppy drunks."

Sam chuckled. "Just so you know, *you* are that sloppy drunk tonight." He winked when she looked up. "I'm kind of a bartender psychologist. Do you want my professional advice?"

"Okay."

"The only time wasted is time spent regretting the past and hesitating on the future."

She lifted her brows. "Wow. That's actually pretty deep."

Sam reached for another cup to polish. "So the question is, what are you hesitating on?"

Travis immediately came to Lyla's mind.

As if hearing her thoughts, Sam tipped his head. "Go on, Lyla. Get out there and dance."

She turned and looked out on the dance floor where Allison was laughing. Someone cut in to dance with her and Travis stepped away, smiling as Allison turned to dance with the new guy. Lyla didn't recognize him, but Allison seemed to know who he was.

Without another thought, Lyla began walking in Travis's direction. He'd come tonight, even though she'd practically ordered him to stay away. She should be mad—furious, even. But right now, if she were honest, she was just glad. She didn't want to dance with any of the other guys here. She didn't want to flirt or be picked up by some random stranger, who would probably turn out to be all wrong for her anyway. She didn't need hunky Sam. The only guy she wanted to flirt with, dance with, or be picked up by was Travis Painter.

A woman stepped up to Travis right before Lyla reached him. Lyla stopped walking and stared at the interaction. Travis looked past the woman and saw Lyla. She watched as he told the woman something and then walked around her, heading in Lyla's direction.

"Hey." Travis looked handsome tonight. She hadn't noticed before, but he was wearing a button-down shirt with a nice pair of jeans.

"You clean up nicely," she said.

He lifted a shoulder. "So do you. Although, I liked the version of you that woke up in my tent last night too. Your bedhead is the best I've seen."

"And you've seen a lot?" She tilted her head to one side.

"I didn't say that. Do you want to dance, Ly?" His voice dipped low, slipping past the flimsy walls she'd built up around her inner recesses, where sparks and butterflies happened.

No. The correct answer to Travis's invitation was no. Instead, she tilted her head to match his and allowed her voice to drop low. "Only if I'm dancing with you."

With a sly grin, Travis slid his hands around her waist and pulled her close.

She didn't breathe for a moment. Then she wrapped her arms around his neck and breathed in his woodsy sandalwood scent. How was it that a handyman with wanderlust smelled better than anything she'd ever breathed in? "Why did you come here tonight?"

"Isn't it obvious, Ly?"

She shook her head slowly as she searched her brain for the answer. "I honestly don't know."

"I came to see you. I had to make sure some other guy, who didn't deserve the time of day, didn't bother you."

"So you're being protective? Like my bodyguard?"

"No, I'm being a jealous idiot, because I probably don't deserve the time of day from you either."

"Why would you think that?"

He lifted a shoulder, the corresponding corner of his lips rising as well. "You tell me. You're the one who promised it wasn't goodbye and then never responded to my emails. Never answered my calls. I figure you finally realized you could do better than a nobody like me."

She sucked in a surprised breath. "Is that really what you thought?"

"All I know is that I got you into a lot of trouble when we were kids. My reputation wasn't the best. Maybe I dragged you down. I know I dragged my father down. He never let me forget that."

Lyla had hated sitting in church and watching her best friend be torn down every Sunday morning. She suspected that the man standing in front of her now still carried the weight of those Sundays strapped to the leather tool belt around his waist. "You didn't drag me down, Travis."

He watched the other couples dance around them. "You know, I never faulted you for cutting me off. I always knew you were born to fly. It was just a matter of time before you got your wings."

Lyla hated that she'd made Travis feel in any way the way his father had. "I was a horrible friend."

"You were my best friend. To this date, you're still the best friend I've ever had. The most beautiful one too."

Her lips parted.

"What?" he asked.

She shook her head, feeling like she wanted to dissolve in a puddle of tears. She wasn't sure if they'd be happy or sad. Both, probably. "I just, I wasn't expecting you to say that."

"Sorry."

"I'm not." She thought about what Sam had just told her.

She was only wasting time if she was hesitating on what she wanted. Right now, what she wanted was to be here in Travis's arms. She wanted him to keep telling her the things he'd just said and more. "I want to spend the night with you again."

"Camping?" he asked.

"Not camping." Her skin burned as he watched her.

"We are spending the night together. Here, dancing and drinking. I'll make sure you and Allison get home safely."

That's not what she meant either, and he knew it.

"Not because I don't want to spend the night with you, Ly," he whispered, leaning in to her ear so that she could hear him. "It's because you mean a lot to me, and I don't want to move things too fast."

Pulling back, she looked at him. "But you'll be leaving soon. We're running out of time."

Travis tugged her closer, leaned down and, with his gaze trained on hers, he brushed his lips over her skin, working his way from her cheek to her lips. The kiss was soft and slow. It felt like she was enveloped in a dream. During those rare times she'd allowed herself to wonder, she'd imagined Travis's kisses would be more rough. More urgent. Instead, his kisses were slow and gentle.

"We have time," he said as he pulled away. "Plenty of time."

Lyla flopped restlessly on her bed the next morning. Where was she, and how had she gotten here? The last thing she remembered was drinking, laughing, dancing, and—kissing Travis?

Lyla shot up in bed and nearly screamed at the motion on the other side of her mattress. Allison was lying there asleep with her mouth gaping open. There was a string of drool falling to the mattress below. No sign of Travis, though. Lyla remembered that he'd offered to be their DD. He must have taken them here and gotten them safely to bed.

As gently as she could, Lyla got up while trying not to

wake Allison. After a pit stop in the bathroom, she headed toward the kitchen. She wished Travis would have left her and Allison at Allison's home because then there would have been a coffeemaker.

As if on cue, the doorbell rang. Lyla looked down at herself. She was still dressed in last night's attire. Her hair was likely a mess, and she was pretty sure she didn't smell all that great.

The doorbell rang again. She didn't want the sound to disturb Allison so, reluctantly, Lyla headed to the front of the house. Allison deserved to sleep in as long as possible, because when she awoke, Lyla suspected her hangover would be miserable.

When she opened the door, she found Travis holding up a tray of coffees. The caffeinated aroma was strong and welcome.

"I bet you want one of these right about now."

All her insecurities about bedhead and bad breath melted away with his grin. "How did you know?"

"Low-key genius here. Can I come in, at least to put the coffees down? I won't stay. I have a couple jobs around town, anyway. One of which happens to be right next door, for Ms. Hadley."

Lyla opened the door wider, gesturing Travis inside. "Thank you for the coffees. They are much appreciated."

"Allison still sleeping?" he asked, talking over his shoulder.

"She is. I just woke up, myself." Lyla stepped up to the coffee cup that he'd set on her counter. Her name was written on the side of the cup. "You remembered how I like my coffee?"

"I'm a details guy, remember?"

"Well, I'm a coffee girl. Thank you." Lifting the cup to her mouth, she took a sip and tried not to compare Travis to her ex. Joe had never remembered the way she liked her coffee, even though it wasn't complicated. She was also a simple girl. Two raw sugars is all she took. Two. Raw. Sugars.

Opinion: A man who doesn't remember the little things is sure to forget the big things.

"You're in deep thought over there, Ly. Whatcha thinking about?" Travis looked amused as she sipped his own coffee. "Could it be the kiss?"

"Kiss?" she echoed back, her breath catching in her chest. The memory of what he was referring to came slamming back into the forefront of her mind. The kiss.

He looked momentarily disappointed. "You forgot?"

"No." She shook her head, which made it pound slightly. She didn't have a monster hangover, but the small thrum of a headache was there. "I wasn't that drunk. I guess part of me thought it was a dream."

"Not unless we were sharing the same dream. Last night was . . . nice."

"Yeah." Lyla continued to sip her coffee, using the moment to figure out what to say next as she stared up at him over the rim of her cup. Seeing the way Travis was looking at her convinced her that last night's kiss had been real. And, judging by his expression, he didn't have regrets. Did she?

"Drink fluids," he instructed, pointing a finger in her direction. "I need you to be in tip-top condition for tonight's bucket-list item. I hope you packed your swimsuit."

Panic flared through Lyla's body akin to the feeling of stepping on a jellyfish tossed on the shoreline. "Travis—"

"It's happening, Ly. And it'll be okay. Trust me."

"I'm not jumping off the Pirate's Plank. I can't."

"We'll start off easy. We'll just go for a swim. Me and you."

She tugged her lower lip between her teeth, nibbling softly. "I'm not jumping. I'm not."

"We'll see." He looked so confident. If she could borrow just a pinch of that confidence when it came to the things that scared her.

"Why? Why is finishing the list so important to you?" she

asked, searching for a way out of what felt inevitable. When Travis got something in his mind, he went for it. He would never pressure her into something she didn't want, but he could convince her to want it.

"Because finishing the list, that was who we were. So doing the things on that list makes me feel like we're us again. Only different."

See? That was a good answer. The kind that made her want to say yes.

"Plus, I don't care what you think, not finishing the list is bad ju-ju."

Pulling a breath into her lungs for a long moment, she began to nod as she exhaled. "Okay," she said quietly.

Travis's expression told her he never thought her answer would be anything less. "Okay." Turning, he headed out the front door, calling over his shoulder, "See you this afternoon."

"What did I just agree to?" Lyla asked herself as the door closed.

Allison cleared her throat from the hallway. "I don't know, but I'm excited for you."

Lyla turned to look at her friend. "Morning, sleepyhead."

Allison groaned. "I think you mean, painful-head. Is that other coffee cup for me?"

"Travis brought them for us. One for me and one for you."

"I love him," Allison muttered, walking over and grabbing the cup with her name on it. She eyed Lyla as she sipped. "I don't literally love him. I know he's spoken for, and you can't deny it anymore. I saw last night's kiss." She waggled her eyebrows and then winced in pain.

"It was one kiss, and we were drunk."

"Correction, you had been drinking but weren't drunk, and he was completely sober." She sighed after another sip of coffee. "This is so good. So, so good—mm . . . I have to go."

Lyla lowered her own coffee cup from her lips. "But you don't have a car."

"My mama is picking me up. I texted her while you were flirting with Mr. Wonderful."

A horn honked outside, and both women turned toward the front door.

"That's her." Allison clutched her coffee against her. "I'll call you later, bestie."

Lyla had never had a real female friend. This was nice. "Bye." Once Allison was gone, Lyla stood there, sipping her coffee and contemplating the day. The unfinished bucket list was lying on the countertop nearby. She reached for it and glanced over the items that had never been checked off that last summer. After the camping trip, there were only three more items to complete.

- Watch *Sleepless in Seattle* 4 times.
- Go skating (Travis).
- Jump off the Pirate's Plank (Lyla).

This was the list of two kids who had no idea what life was about. Doing the items on their list had amounted to conquering the world. Life wasn't that simple, though. In fact, it was exceedingly complicated, especially when it came to her relationship with Travis.

At one time, she could tell him anything. Their conversations had been unfiltered. Not these days. She wasn't even sure she would confide her hopes and fears with him anymore. If she told him what her thoughts were now, specifically the ones she had about him, things might get a little awkward. It was just physical attraction, nothing more. And as long as she kept it that way, spending time together was completely harmless.

Opinion: No strings, no rings, no messy disasters.

Lyla nearly choked as she simultaneously sipped her coffee and gasped. That was perfect! That opinion would definitely stir debate among her readers. Bob would approve too. Carrying her coffee to her bedroom, she plopped down on her bed and pulled her laptop to her thighs. When inspiration hit, one had to take advantage. And all the credit for this inspired moment went to last night's kiss with Travis.

Lyla's fingernails clicked along the keys. The opinion needed a touch more flair. As Bob liked to say, "Drama sells." With a few taps of the backspace key, she reinvented the initial opinion until it was something sure to spark debate. Then she sighed contentedly and read the opinion that would save her job.

Opinion: No strings, no rings, no ruined lives.

August 10

Dear Diary,
I've never been kissed. Unless dog kisses count.
Sonny has kissed me multiple nights, especially lately
as I pour out my heart to him on the back porch.
Devil-dog by day, angel-dog showering me with dog
kisses by night.
Here's the thing. The only person I hang around is
Travis, and kissing my best friend solves one problem
(the never been kissed one) but creates a dozen more.
Lyla

Chapter 18

*Opinion: When inspiration strikes,
drop everything else and grab on tight.*
—Delilah Dune, opinion writer

Lyla wasn't sure how long she had been sitting with her laptop. Long enough for her back to complain about not having a proper desk or an ergonomically sound setup. If her phone hadn't started buzzing, she might have sat there longer, ignoring the subtle aches and pains that had seemed to come out of nowhere after turning thirty.

Picking up her phone, she eyed the screen before eagerly answering. "Hello?"

"Lyla. It's Peter Blake. How're you doing?"

"Good. It's nice to hear from you." Lyla hoped her parents' real estate agent was calling with good news.

He cut to the chase. "I have another buyer looking for a house that fits your parents' home's description. Is the pipe fixed yet?"

Lyla sat up straighter. "It is. I was planning to contact you this afternoon and let you know." Right after she'd penned her inspired article for Bob—"No Strings, No Rings, No Mess." "You'd never know there was a burst pipe last week.

My friends and I got all the water up and, thankfully, there's no damage to the flooring."

"Great to hear. So can I take the buyer out there this afternoon?" Peter asked.

Lyla ran through her mental checklist. All the boxes for donation had been delivered to the thrift store. The leak in the roof was fixed, and she'd painted over the water spot. The floors were also polished. The house was ready to be someone's dream home. "Yeah, of course. I can find somewhere to go this afternoon." In fact, she already had quasi-plans with Travis. "What time are you hoping to come by?"

"Is four o'clock good for you?" Peter asked.

"Sounds great. I'll make myself scarce and cross all my fingers and toes. Second time's the charm, right?"

He chuckled. "Maybe so. Thanks, Lyla. Talk to you soon."

Lyla squealed softly as she disconnected the call with the real estate agent. Then she quickly reread her article for Bob, hoping it was as good as she'd thought as her fingers had flown across her keyboard. It was as if the piece had written itself. Sure enough, the article was golden. Inspired, even.

She rolled her lips together, sent up a silent prayer, and composed a brief email to her editor.

> *Bob,*
> *I think this is what you asked for.*
> *Enjoy,*
> *L*

After hitting SEND, Lyla moved to get up and stopped when she saw a tiny fleck of light. Either she'd moved too fast or she'd seen another firefly. In her bedroom, of all places. She chose to believe it was the latter and that it was a positive omen about the work she'd just completed. She looked around for the little lightning bug, but it was as if it had vanished.

Continuing toward the bathroom, she showered and dressed.

Her day was off to an amazing start, and she couldn't help wondering if it was all due to her kiss with Travis. If so, she should have kissed him a long time ago.

She finished getting herself ready for the day and, since there was nothing to do at her parents' empty house, she packed up her laptop and headed out to work at the coffee shop. Maybe, since the stars were finally aligning, Lyla would finish smoothing things over with Bernadette. Perhaps by the end of this summer, they could even be friends.

It would go over easier if she took Allison with her. She tapped Allison's contact and let the phone ring as she walked to her car. No answer. She'd just drive over there and ask Allison in person if she wanted to hang out. Allison never seemed to mind her arriving unannounced.

Lyla drove the short distance to Allison's home, slowing at the mouth of the driveway. There was a truck Lyla didn't recognize parked next to Allison's sporty little car. Did it belong to the mystery guy that Allison was trying hard to keep under wraps? After the way Allison had been teasing Lyla about Travis, it was only right Lyla tease her friend right back and give her a taste of her own medicine. Resolute, she headed up the driveway and rang the doorbell.

A tall, dark-skinned, and handsome man answered. He was wearing a ball cap and sunglasses, looking very incognito. "Oh. Hey."

Lyla wasn't sure she even knew this guy. Why would Allison care if Lyla didn't even know him, though?

"Lyla. What are you doing here?" Allison stepped up behind the mystery man, her cheeks pink and her auburn-colored hair tousled as if she'd just climbed out of bed.

"I, well . . . My parents' house has a showing this afternoon, and I wanted to go out to get coffee. I was stopping by to see if maybe you wanted to come along. But I can see you're . . . busy."

Allison pulled her robe tighter around her. "I can't this

morning, but, um, I have something for you in the kitchen."
She tugged Lyla inside, past the man.

"You can't tell anyone about this," Allison begged just as
soon as Lyla was in the kitchen. "If people found out about
me and Timothy—"

Lyla held her arms out to her side. "What would I even
say? I don't know him. Who is Timothy?"

Allison's eyes widened in surprise. "No one. Never mind.
Just give me my privacy, if you don't mind."

"We're friends, Al. We share things. You know about Travis."

Allison's eyebrows lifted high as she looked at Lyla again.
"What about Travis? Are you two a thing now?"

Lyla shook her head. "I don't know."

"See? You're not being honest with me. Why should I spill
the tea on my love life?"

"Love life? I thought you said this guy was just a fling."

"I never said *fling*." Allison waved a finger. "And keep
your voice down." She glanced over her shoulder. "I just, I
don't want to scare him off. I like him, and I haven't liked
anyone since Ernie. He makes me laugh, and that's good because I'm tired of crying."

Lyla wanted to pull her friend in for a hug, but they might
both start crying, and it was too early in the morning for
that. "I'm sorry for barging in. If you don't want me to know
who he is, I'll leave and I won't say another word."

Allison unfolded her arms. "Thank you."

Lyla blinked. "What?" She shook her head. "I was bluff-
ing. You're supposed to tell me who he is now."

Allison laughed out loud, but the sound wasn't one of amusement. "You are one big contradiction, you know that?"

"Oh, come on, Al. Who would I even tell? Bernadette?"

Allison's eyes grew wider.

That was suspicious. "Is he Bernie's old flame or something? Is he her ex?"

Allison's skin blanched. "Bernadette would hate me if she

knew. She holds grudges. I'd never get coffee in this town again."

Grudges? Lyla couldn't imagine who this Timothy guy was. Then it hit her. Bernadette's first love, TJ, who'd dumped her just before Bernie had sat on sloppy joe? The TJ who had gotten the entire school to start calling his ex "Brownie" instead of "Bernie," thus emotionally scarring Bernadette for life.

Allison avoided eye contact. "Timothy John Butler."

"TJ?" Lyla practically shouted.

"Shh." Allison glanced around as if the whole neighborhood might be listening.

"If it's such a secret, why did he park in the front of your house for everyone to notice?"

"It was quick and he delivers meat. People can just assume that's what he's doing. I love meat."

Lyla knew she should stop teasing her friend, but she couldn't help one more comment. "Oh, I'm certain he's delivering you meat."

Allison crossed her arms over her chest. "Was that supposed to be dirty?" she asked in a clipped tone. "Because my freezer is stocked with the best steaks you'll ever eat."

Lyla grinned. "Bernadette will indeed spit in your coffee for this. She still hates me for letting her sit in the sloppy joe spit-up. I think you're going to join me on her crap list."

"He's a good guy, okay? Yeah, he was a jerk back then, but weren't we all at some point? It doesn't make us bad people. Just people."

Lyla understood that perfectly. She was guilty of doing hurtful things too, especially to Travis.

"Anyway, even after all these years, TJ is still kind of scared of Bernadette, so he wants to keep our relationship under wraps. We both do, for obvious reasons."

Lyla pretended to zip her mouth. "My lips are sealed." Then, unable to resist, she leaned in and gave Allison a tight hug. "I'm so happy for you," she whispered against Allison's cheek. Of all the people she knew, Allison deserved a happy-ever-after most.

"And I'm equally happy for you," Allison said as she pulled away. "We both deserve a second chance. Oh, come on. You and Travis," she clarified.

Nervous laughter rolled off Lyla's lips. "No, it was just a kiss, and next week he'll be on his way somewhere new. And so will I, if this house sells."

Allison's shoulders seemed to slump as her energy visibly drained. "Then your parents won't live here and give you reason to come back. There'll be nothing left to anchor you to Echo Cove." Her lower lip poked out in a micro-pout. "Just when we're becoming friends."

"Stop with the sad face. You'll invite me to your Dinner-ware Parties, and I'll travel down, assuming you have a couch where I can crash."

"Always. Anytime."

Lyla gestured toward the front of the house. "I'll be leaving now. I'm going to work at the coffee shop and try to continue melting Bernadette's icy exterior. Hey TJ," Lyla said, walking past where he was still standing in the living room.

"Hey, Lyla." He shoved his hands in his pockets and avoided her gaze. "I'm just, uh, delivering meat to Allie."

Lyla worked to contain her laughter. "So I hear."

"Would you, uh, like some meat?" he asked, offering brief eye contact. He seemed so much more awkward than the guy she remembered from school.

Lyla fielded a warning look from Allison and shook her head. "No, I'm good, thanks."

A couple hours later, Lyla felt awkward standing in front of Travis wearing a bathing suit. She'd never been one to have body-image issues. She typically felt comfortable in her own skin. She always had. But standing next to Travis right now, she felt the need to tug at her shoulder strap and then at her bikini bottoms. The sun was beating down on her bare shoulders, and she could feel it burning the tips of her ears.

"Why do you look so nervous? You haven't even gotten in the water yet," Travis said.

"And I'm *only* getting in the water. I told you I wasn't going to jump off the Pirate's Plank today." She wasn't even sure if she knew how to swim anymore. She could probably back float and keep herself from drowning if she had to, but that was all.

"Stop worrying, Ly. I've got you. I'm not going to let you sink. And if you don't jump off the Pirate's Plank today, we can work our way up to it."

Lyla liked the way he said *we*. As if she and he were an *us*. She hadn't been part of an *us* since Joe. And even though she was better off without her ex, she had liked being part of an *us*. "Why do you guys get to wear shorts and nothing else in the water?"

Travis chuckled. He was wearing board shorts and a water shirt, and showing no more skin than he normally would. "You can wear shorts and a T-shirt in the water too. There's no law about swim attire. But I like what you're wearing right now." He cleared his throat. "Not that I'm checking you out or anything."

She squirmed a little, wishing she hadn't brought the focus on her body. She'd meant to put the focus on his. "Thanks." She shook out her arms and then her legs before stretching her neck from left to right. Then she rubbed her hands together and looked at Travis. "Okay. I can do this."

"Yes, you can. I believe in you, Ly. Always have."

She knew that was true. She'd cut ties with him all those years ago, fearing that he would hold her back, but all that Travis Painter had ever done was lift her up. Her chest ached when she thought of how she'd ignored Travis. He hadn't deserved that. Not wanting him to see the sheen of tears filling her eyes, she started walking, hearing his footsteps following behind her.

The closer she got to the lakeshore, the faster her pulse raced. She knew she was being silly. She was only getting in the water today and only in the shallow end. But once upon a time, her life had flashed before her eyes in this lake. She'd nearly died, or at least, that's the way it had felt. And afterward, she felt like she had died of embarrassment, as everyone around her had laughed and pointed. It was the stuff her nightmares were made of. It was also the reason Travis had decided that jumping off the Pirate's Plank had to be on their final bucket list that summer. He'd said she needed to face her fears. Otherwise, she'd always be running away from them.

Dipping her big toe into the water, she sucked in a startled breath. "Cold, cold, cold."

"No, it's not," Travis objected. "It's ninety degrees outside and the sun has been up for hours. The water is fine." He gave her a gentle nudge to plant her whole foot on the lake floor.

She turned quickly, without thinking, and found herself pressed into his chest. He wasn't cold. He was warm, and it felt good to have his arms clamp around her. He kept moving forward, deeper into the water as she faced him, back stepping so that he didn't knock her down. She held onto his forearms, appreciating the fact that he was moving slowly.

She appreciated that he had moved slow last night too. She vaguely recalled suggesting they spend the night together. *What was I thinking?* That would have been a huge mistake. She'd never had a one-night stand before. She was usually one to get emotionally attached to everyone and everything. If this reunion between her and Travis would be over in a few days, the last thing she needed was to become overly attached.

"We're only knee-deep. There's nothing to worry about."

She opened her eyes and looked at him, feeling that cliché

feeling of butterflies in her stomach. Then she saw that familiar mischievous spark flash in his brown eyes.

His movements were quick and unexpected as he scooped her up in his arms.

Clawing at him, she squealed. "What are you doing?"

Without answering, he plunged deeper into the lake's depths.

"Travis?" She tightened her hold on him and didn't plan on letting go anytime soon. "No. Please don't do this."

He stopped walking for a moment and looked down at her. "I would never do anything to hurt you. You know that, right?"

"Tossing me in this water right now would hurt me," she whispered, panic sweeping through her.

He lifted a brow. "Really?"

"Yes. Please put me down."

That mischievous spark was still in his eyes. "Okay-y-y."

Before she knew what was happening, Travis let her go. Her legs didn't get under her fully and she plopped down into the water. Travis caught her under her arms to keep her from dunking under. Then she scrambled to find her lake legs.

"I hate you!" she called out to him, only teasing.

"You love me," he objected, pulling her close.

The L-word made her feel the equivalent of standing on the Pirate's Plank. She could fall and get hurt. Or leap and swim. He didn't actually mean that he loved her romantically. She knew that, but it still affected her.

"Now that you're here, you might as well enjoy yourself. With me." He lay back on the water and started floating, his face tilted to the sun. His eyes closed.

On an impulse, Lyla lunged toward him, pressing his midsection until he sank under the water. Then she let go and swam because when he came up, she was certain there would be payback.

Chapter 19

Opinion: Sometimes less is more,
because more is left to the imagination.
—Delilah Dune, opinion writer

Lyla waved at Travis, who was still sitting in his truck as she made her way to the front door of her parents' home. Travis had wanted to walk Lyla to the door, but she'd insisted he stay put. If he'd walked her to the door, they might've ended up kissing. And if they ended up kissing, she might have invited him inside.

No, it's better this way.

She let herself inside and soaked up the cool air-conditioning. Then she glanced around to see if anything had changed since the buyer had come. There was no indication that anyone had even been there. Not one single footprint. She headed toward the kitchen for a cool bottled water out of the fridge. The day had been draining, but also wonderful. Maybe she and Travis hadn't checked off one of the items on the bucket list, but she'd swum in Memory Lake, and it had felt amazing. She'd addressed one fear, and now she felt like she could do anything. Almost, at least.

Twisting off the cap, she drank half the bottle in a single gulp. Then she set it on the counter next to the bucket list. Maybe she would jump off the Pirate's Plank before this trip was over—not that she bought into the superstition that she'd get stuck with bad luck if she didn't finish the list.

Lyla's phone dinged. She picked up her phone and saw that she had an email from her editor. Everything inside her froze momentarily as fear and excitement warred. Instead of opening the message on her phone, she headed back to her bedroom and grabbed her laptop. On an inhalation and a prayer, she opened her MacBook and pulled up the email from Bob, reading the message quickly. When she was done, she exhaled loudly and started to laugh.

He loved it! He loved her opinion article so much that it was printing on Friday.

Lyla punched a fist into the air. "Yes! Yes, yes, yes!" She laid her laptop beside her on the air mattress and stood for a mini victory dance. She wasn't fired. She had a job, at least for the time being. Grabbing her phone, she tapped out a text to the first person she wanted to share the good news with.

Lyla: *My job is saved! My editor loved the article and I still have employment. Thanks to you.*

Travis didn't respond immediately, but she knew he was probably driving. She tapped out a text to Allison next.

Lyla: *My editor loved the article! I don't have to worry about being homeless or hungry anymore.*

Allison didn't text back either. Instead, Lyla's phone started to ring.

Seeing the name that appeared on the screen, Lyla connected the call and held her phone to her ear. "Hey."

"Hey, it's me," Allison said, as if Lyla didn't have caller ID.

"Did you get my message?" Lyla asked.

"I did! And I think this calls for a celebration," Allison squealed.

Lyla laughed. "We already celebrated prematurely last night, remember? I don't think I can have a drink at least for another week. I still have a small headache."

"I'm not talking about alcohol or the bar. Let's go out for ice cream. My treat."

Lyla considered the invitation for a moment. She and Travis hadn't made plans for tonight, and she didn't want to assume that they'd get back together this evening. And staying in this empty house didn't sound like much fun at all. Allison was right. A celebration was in order. "Sure. When?"

Allison laughed. "Now, silly! There's no time like the present."

Opinion: There's no time like the present, but the present is rarely enjoyed for worrying about the past and the future.

Well, she wasn't so concerned over the future any longer. In fact, the future was suddenly looking brighter.

An hour later, Lyla wasn't drunk on alcohol, but the sugar was definitely going to her head. That and the exhilaration from the day.

"So, what's the article about?" Allison scraped the bottom of her ice cream bowl and spooned the now runny Mint Chocolate Chip into her mouth.

"Relationships, I guess. I've always been so serious about them, but my opinion has changed. You don't have to be all-in to be with someone. It doesn't have to be forever. I was dating Joe for so long and look at us now." Lyla licked her spoon clean. "No strings equals no mess. Or something like that."

"No strings, huh? Is that what you're doing with Travis?" Allison had a spot of chocolate on her lip that she seemed to sense. She poked her tongue around her lips until she got it.

"One kiss. Last night. We haven't had time to figure out

what we're doing. And we don't have time. So, yes, no strings," she said, decidedly. "No strings, no mess." That was her opinion and she was sticking to it. At least that was the plan.

Allison set her spoon down and sighed as if she'd just finished a Thanksgiving dinner. "Done."

"Me too." Lyla grabbed her purse hanging from the back of her chair and stood, noticing a sparkle of light right in front of her. "Did you see that?"

"See what?"

"The spark of light," Lyla said. "A firefly."

"Firefly? Inside the ice cream shop?" Allison started to laugh again. "What are you even talking about?"

Lyla turned to look at her friend and then somehow lost her balance. As she swung out her leg to catch herself, she kicked her big toe into the base of the table. "Ow!" she squealed, dropping her trash, her purse, and ultimately her butt on the floor.

"Oh! Are you okay?" Allison set her trash down on the table and looked down at Lyla who was clutching her foot.

"No. Not okay." Lyla breathed through the pain that splintered through her big toe. "Not okay at all."

"What was that?" Allison asked.

"I think that was me . . ." Lyla breathed some more. How could a toe hurt this bad? "It was me breaking my big toe again."

"Again?" Allison asked.

"Yes." The pain seemed to dull as Lyla realized she had indeed broken this exact same toe before. During the summer after graduation. "Oh, wow. This is so much more than a coincidence," she whispered under her breath. Maybe not finishing the list *was* bad luck after all. She'd thought that notion was silly. But maybe it wasn't.

"What is more than a coincidence?" Allison asked.

Lyla picked herself off the ground and slid back into her chair. She waited for Allison to do the same. "Something weird has been going on this summer." Her toe was throbbing, but she ignored it. Suddenly the most pressing thing on her mind was convincing someone else in her world that there was something magical and unexplainable happening. Travis hadn't bought into Lyla's claim that the summer was somehow repeating itself when she mentioned it to him the other night. But she hadn't had much evidence. And after his reaction, she'd kind of convinced herself it wasn't true. But breaking her toe just like she had that summer years ago was yet another one of those coincidences that seemed too coincidental. How many times did a person get struck by lightning in their lifetime? Never. Much less twice.

"The summer after our senior year," Lyla told Allison, "Travis and I made a bucket list. Well, we always made bucket lists, but this was our last one, and we didn't have time to finish it."

"Okay-y-y." Allison drew out the final syllable of the word, her tone suggesting she thought Lyla may have hit her head when she'd fallen. "I'm listening."

Lyla took a breath, filling her lungs and hoping she made sense when she started to talk. "Travis and I always said that it would be bad luck if we didn't finish our bucket list. But that last summer, there were still a few items we couldn't check off. I created a time capsule in an old 7-Up bottle just like Ms. Davis told us all to do. I planned to bury and dig that bottle back up in twenty years." Lyla laughed softly. "I put random things in that bottle. Yo-yos, rubber snakes."

"Rubber snakes?" Allison's brows lifted high on her forehead.

Lyla was surprised that Allison didn't remember hearing about the childish pranks. She hadn't attended the local church back then, though. Pastor Painter was usually responsible for letting everyone in town know what mischief his son had gotten into that week. "Travis and I were always joking and teasing. He loved to pull innocent pranks. One of which included a rubber snake. Anyway, I rolled the bucket list up and put it inside the bottle. Even though it wasn't finished." She shook her head. "I never believed Travis's superstition that it was bad luck not to finish the list." She took a moment to catch her breath and collect her thoughts. "When I came back to help my parents sell their home this summer, I remembered the time capsule I buried by the old cypress tree. I couldn't just leave it in the ground for the next homeowner to find one day."

Allison leaned over the table on her elbows. "Do you think the next homeowner would actually dig a hole in the exact spot that you left the time capsule?"

"I don't know. I guess I also just wanted to dig up the time capsule and see what I put inside. Anyway, ever since opening that time capsule, something strange has been happening."

"Strange how?"

"Do you remember when you walked up on me that day? I was lying on the back deck of my parents' home after the storm?"

Allison nodded.

"I swear I had just been struck by lightning."

"What?" Allison pushed her head forward. "Lyla, shouldn't you have gone to the hospital?"

"Probably, but that's not the point." There was a far bigger point than nearly dying. "Later, I took my old bicycle out for a ride around town and it started to rain again."

Allison furrowed her brows. "Doesn't sound so strange to me."

Lyla held up a hand. "That's when I noticed that the exact same movie was playing at the old theater that had played that last summer with Travis. We watched it three times that July, but our bucket list said we needed to watch it four times."

"Okay-y-y," Allison said.

"Then there was a huge downpour. I was on my bike, and

suddenly I got a flat tire," Lyla explained, talking fast. "The exact same thing happened that summer. And just like that summer, a blue pickup truck pulled to the curb and saved the day—Travis's blue pickup. That's when I realized he was back in town."

"Let me guess, Travis drove that pickup truck the first summer too?"

Lyla nodded quickly. "He put my bike in the back of the truck and brought me home that summer *and* this summer. So maybe those things could've happened coincidentally, but that's when I started to notice that time was mirroring itself. I got a leak in the roof of my parents' home. They had a leak that summer too. And then the pipes burst in the bathroom. That also happened that summer. I saw a comet in the sky with Travis and it was only the second time in my life I've ever seen one, the first time being that summer. And now this." Lyla gestured down at her foot and the toe that was quickly swelling inside her sandal. "I broke my toe that summer too! This exact toe!"

Allison still looked skeptical. "I guess all of that is kind of weird. You think all of this is happening because you re-opened the time capsule? Like you had bottled up that last summer in Echo Cove and now you've released it somehow?"

"I know it doesn't make any sense, but yeah, I kind of do believe that's what's happening." Pain suddenly shot through Lyla's toe. The excitement over another coincidence had temporarily blocked the pain, but her toe was beginning to throb in pain, almost as much as it had the first time she'd broken it.

Allison returned her attention to Lyla's injury. "We need to get you to the doctor."

"No." The last thing Lyla wanted was to spend the evening in an urgent care. "It's okay. I'll just ice it and buddy tape it to my second toe. It'll be fine. I do need to go home, though."

Allison looked at Lyla's foot as if it were something slightly grotesque. "Can you walk?"

Lyla wobbled her head back and forth, weighing her answer. "Of course, I can. It's just going to hurt."

"I don't think I can carry you. Should I call Travis?" A teasing grin spread across Allison's face.

"No. I'll hobble to the parking lot."

"Great. I'll drive. This was not what I was intending when I said we should come out and celebrate this afternoon." Allison grabbed Lyla's purse and slid it on her shoulder before disposing of their trash and opening the door to the ice cream store so that Lyla could go through first. They navigated slowly through the parking lot until they reached Allison's car. When they were both inside, Allison cranked the engine and then looked across the center console. "If you're right, and things are really repeating, what do you think it means?"

"Means?" Lyla asked.

"Well, I believe things happen for a reason. Everything—the good, the bad. Even the most insignificant thing. I believe there's meaning behind all of it. So if your summer is repeating itself, what's the reason?"

Lyla shifted around, trying to get the pressure off her toe as she thought. "Maybe it means we need to finish that bucket list. I wouldn't consider that I've been having bad luck ever since that summer, but maybe my luck could've been better." Lyla's mind raced. "Travis always put the things I was afraid of on the list, just to mess with me, but also because he believed in me. I was so confident when I was younger, and I have Travis to thank for that."

Allison reached out and squeezed Lyla's forearm. "Friends make us better, but make sure you give yourself credit too. I've always thought you were brave."

Lyla hadn't felt so brave these past few days. "What if this is why things are so bizarre this summer? I didn't finish the list, and now bad-luck events from that summer are repeating. I mean, I got struck by lightning. Twice! Then a flat tire, the house having issues, and now I've broken my toe." Fresh pain sprang up through her foot as she looked down.

"How many things are left on the bucket list?"

Lyla thought about it. "I think there are only three things left to do. One is mine and one is his. The last one is watching a movie for the fourth time. I guess I could do that on my own."

"Not on your own." Allison gave her shoulder a gentle shove. "With me. I'll watch it with you. It'll be fun. We can even invite Bernie if you want."

Lyla actually did want to. "I'm fairly certain Bernie would turn me down."

"Maybe, but not if I'm the one asking." Allison gave her steering wheel an energetic tap. "Girls' movie night with popcorn. Yay!"

"Yay . . ." Lyla said, with only half of Allison's enthusiasm. How had she gotten here, planning a movie night with the most unsuspecting friends? She wasn't sure, but it felt right.

The smell of buttery popcorn filled Allison's tiny living room. Lyla sat on one side of Allison and Bernie sat on the other. Allison was their physical buffer, although Lyla could tell that Bernie wasn't as opposed to being around her as she used to be. Bernie was melting, as Eric had called it.

"I'm so sorry we couldn't find *Sleepless in Seattle*," Allison said regretfully. "I wanted to help you check off an item on your bucket list."

"It's okay." Lyla turned her attention to the large plasma screen TV on the wall that was currently playing *You've Got Mail*. "I mean, it does have Tom Hanks in it."

"And Meg Ryan too," Allison added. "That has to count halfway for checking off the list, right?"

Lyla knew that a half-check didn't count. When she and

Travis used to check off their lists, there were no short-cuts or exceptions. The item to be checked was watching *Sleepless in Seattle* four times. *You've Got Mail* didn't count. "Sure," she said instead.

"I've never seen *Sleepless in Seattle* before," Bernadette confessed, popping a piece of popcorn into her mouth.

Both Allison and Lyla looked at her.

"You're kidding," Lyla said.

"I've seen that movie at least six times," Allison told her. "I don't know why, but my daughter, Ashley Grace, loved this movie. She liked that little girl who booked the plane ticket for the boy. The one who used all the abbreviations." Allison giggled quietly to herself before stopping abruptly and looking sheepish.

Lyla reached for her hand and squeezed. "You can talk about them as much as you want."

Bernadette grabbed Allison's other hand. "Of course you can."

Allison's eyes grew shiny. She seemed to fight her tears momentarily, visibly trying to ward them off. "If you both are holding my hand, how am I going to eat popcorn?"

Bernadette used her opposite hand to reach into the bucket, grab a piece, and bring it to Allison's lips. Lyla did the same, followed by Bernadette again. Soon they were all laughing with a few tears gracing their cheeks as well.

"Shh-shh, this is the best part," Allison finally said.

They watched the screen where Tom Hanks was walking up to meet the woman he'd been emailing back and forth with, only to realize she was his arch-enemy.

"It's so unfair," Allison whispered.

Lyla wasn't sure if she was talking about the circumstances in the movie or about her own circumstances. Either way, Lyla held onto her hand. She hadn't had friends like this in her old town. She hadn't even had friends like this when she was growing up. She and Travis were more jokesters than the type of friends who watched movies and cried together.

Opinion: Everyone should have a friend or two to cry with.

Bob would veto that idea immediately, but Lyla thought it was one of her most profound. There was so much power in friendship, a real friendship.

Allison laid her head on Lyla's shoulder and sighed. "Who would have thought that us three would be hanging out one day?"

"Not me," Bernie said, catching Lyla's eye.

"Why not though?" Lyla asked. "We were never all that different?" Especially Lyla and Bernie. They'd both been in journalism. They'd both enjoyed writing.

"Because. In high school, there are groups. Allison was in the popular group. I was in the outcast group," Bernadette said. "It's okay. I own it."

Lyla was afraid to ask what group she was in.

"You were one of those special types," Bernadette supplied without needing to be asked. "You bounced from group to group, pretending to fit in with them all when, in reality, you were judging everyone and refusing to lower yourself into settling for any one group. You thought you were better."

Lyla's mouth fell open. "What?"

"Bernadette, that's kind of mean and it's not true," Allison said, defending Lyla.

"It is true. That's why she couldn't wait to leave town. Why she rarely came back except to visit her parents. If you read her column, you'd know," Bernadette told Allison. "She looked down on us small-town lifers."

Lyla couldn't speak. It was hard to breathe. *Small-town*

lifers. An opinion article that she wrote a long time ago came to mind.

Opinion: The path to success is linear. Small-town lifers go in circles.

Bernadette was right. Some of her articles were so judgmental. They weren't her views though. They were the views of an alter ego she'd created named Delilah. She didn't believe what she wrote.

Allison slowly pulled her hand away from Lyla's.

"Those columns weren't personal," Lyla said quietly. "It's just my job."

Bernadette nodded. "Glad you're so successful at it."

They all turned to continue watching the movie, but Lyla could hardly focus. There was a reason she'd been so unhappy in her life lately. She wasn't proud of her work. She didn't enjoy writing for the opinion column and copywriting bored her. She didn't have these satisfying relationships in her life to make any of the success she'd found worthwhile.

Thirty minutes had passed, at least, before Lyla leaned forward and grabbed the remote, pushing the PAUSE button. "I'm sorry. Truly sorry for any of the hurtful words I put out into the universe. They weren't meant to be personal to you. They were more geared to myself, telling myself why I needed to keep pressing forward on this road that was making me miserable. The road to misery is straight," Lyla said, her voice shaking. "The circle isn't for small-town lifers. It's for those who want to return to their roots. Find themselves. Find their joy."

Lyla was practically shaking.

"Wow," Allison said. "You've always been so wonderful with words." She leaned forward and wrapped Lyla in a warm hug. Lyla closed her eyes so that she didn't have to look at Bernadette. Something told her that Bernadette was going to need more time to process that apology. Pulling back, Allison grinned at Lyla. "I've always liked circles myself. You should print that opinion. I like it a lot."

"My editor, Bob, would hate it though," Lyla said, without thinking.

Bernadette glanced over. "Whose opinion column is it anyway? I thought it was yours."

"It's complicated," Lyla muttered, but it really wasn't. Whatever success she'd made for herself didn't feel like it belonged to her at all. She wasn't the author of most of those opinions; she'd just penned them for somebody else.

August 20

Dear Diary,

Okay, an eighteen-year-old should not have any regrets by this point in life. That's my opinion and I'm sticking to it. But I do have regrets. I wish I had more friends. Travis is equal to a hundred friends. He's the best. I wish I had a few girlfriends, though. Not the romantic kind of girlfriends. The kind you have sleepovers with and paint each other's nails. I would have wanted to be friends with Bernie, but she hates me now because of the whole sloppy joe nickname that some of the mean kids came up with. I saw Bernie's senior yearbook. Half the entries addressed her as Brownie.

Maybe I don't deserve friends because of the sloppy joe thing. Maybe I'll make friends in college. Opinion: It's never too late for sleepovers.

Lyla

Chapter 20

Opinion: The shoes are everything.
They make or break one's fashion.
—Delilah Dune, opinion writer

There was nothing in this house to prop her foot up properly, so Lyla used her suitcase as a makeshift footrest. Her toe was now a pretty violet color, the shade one might find in a flower arrangement rather than one's body.

Lyla hadn't told Travis about her toe just yet. First off, she hadn't had the opportunity, because Travis was working some odd job in town. Second, Lyla was still in denial that she was going to have to wear some kind of ridiculous shoe with her dress to the wedding. Was this actually happening? She didn't believe in supernatural things. In her mind, they didn't exist. She'd written an entire opinion article on that topic once, and her readers had come out of the woodwork to argue differently.

Lyla had gotten emails from people detailing their paranormal, otherworldly experiences. Time travel. Worm holes. Ghosts. Lyla had heard it all, and she'd considered all the tall tales to be nonsense. No one had written about a time capsule that had caused some sort of strange alteration in time, though.

Her cell phone rang beside her. She glanced at the screen and immediately answered. "Hey, Mom. I was wondering when you and Dad were going to check in with me."

Her mom's laughter sounded light and relaxed. "Well, we're on vacation time, I guess you'd say."

"How's Dad doing? Is he feeling better yet?"

"Oh, yes," her mom said. "Much, much better. How are things with you? And the house?"

"Good. I haven't burned the place down, if that's what you're asking."

"Of course you haven't. Any news on selling?"

Lyla had already decided to spare her parents the details of the things that had gone wrong with the house so far. She'd handled them, so there was no need to concern them. "We've had two potential buyers so far. One wasn't interested, but the other one might be. I'm still waiting to hear the buyers' thoughts."

"Oh, wonderful. That's hopeful news. The sooner it sells, the sooner you can be out of there. Although, if you've already packed up your belongings and handled the donation boxes for us, there's actually no need for you to stay. The agents have keys. You can go home and get back to your normal life."

Home. Lyla didn't intend to return to her last residence. She didn't have plans at all. "I finished all the packing and donating last week. I can't leave Echo Cove just yet, though," she told her mom. "I have an obligation here this weekend."

"Oh? What kind of obligation?" her mom asked.

Lyla really didn't want to tell her mother the truth, but this was Echo Cove, and she was certain her mom would find out eventually. "Travis Painter is in town for his sister's wedding. He invited me to go with him."

"Travis? Really? That's a surprise." Her mom's tone of voice wasn't exactly thrilled. "And what a coincidence that the two of you are in Echo Cove at the same time."

There was that word again. *Coincidence.*

"Yeah. We've been hanging out a little bit. Allison and I have been spending time together too. We went out for ice cream today." Lyla's gaze fell on her broken toe. She decided not to concern her mom with that detail either.

"That's so nice. Bailey is getting married, huh? That's a shocker."

Lyla didn't know Bailey all that well. "Why would you say that?"

"Well, she's dated quite a lot over the years. I kind of figured she'd never commit to anyone. I'm happy to hear she's finally found *the one*."

"Hmm. Mom? Why didn't you tell me about Allison?"

"What about her?" her mom asked, innocently.

"You know, her story. The accident."

"Why would I tell you that?" her mom asked.

"Because I knew her. You might have considered I might want to know what she was going through."

"Oh, everyone is going through stuff, Lyla. I guess I just don't like spreading the worst news about a person. You and Allison were never close, so I figured there was no need for you to know. Just like when people ask about you, I don't immediately tell them that you're going through a breakup."

"Went through a breakup," Lyla corrected. "There's absolutely no chance Joe and I are getting back together." She considered what her mom had said. "Thanks for not spreading my dirty laundry everywhere."

"Of course. So, you and Travis, huh? Are you two spending time as friends or . . . ?" She trailed off.

"Friends, Mom. We've always been just friends."

"Oh, Lyla. You never fooled me. A girl is supposed to be excited when she's about to go away to college, but I could tell. A mother always knows. The thought of leaving your best friend behind was weighing you down in a big way. So much so that you started to distance yourself from him before you even left."

"No, I didn't," Lyla protested.

"You hardly left your room the entire week before the move."

Lyla rolled her eyes. "Maybe that's because of the huge hurricane that was barreling toward Echo Cove," she said sarcastically. The hurricane was a category three, but it was slow moving and had caused a lot of wind and water damage. "Billy. Hurricane Billy, right?" she asked her mother.

"Good memory."

Lyla hadn't thought about that storm in a long time. It had wreaked havoc on Echo Cove, flooding everything. It happened right before she moved away for college, and it felt like the final blow on a pretty crummy summer. Bailey was supposed to have a shotgun wedding and the storm had even ruined the big event—although that was probably for the best. "But maybe you're right. The thought of leaving my best friend behind was painful."

"Of course. Growing pains. I think you were more upset about leaving him than you were about your recent break up with Joe."

"That's probably true," Lyla admitted. "Where are you and Dad right now?"

"Puerto Rico, and it's so lovely here. Your dad's stomach is doing much better. See? Spreading only good news."

Lyla spoke to her mom a few minutes longer, then said goodbye. After disconnecting the call, she shifted uncomfortably on her mattress. She was tired of lying still, so she got up and headed down the hall toward the kitchen, stopping in front of the time capsule. She wasn't sure why she hadn't taken all the items out just yet. Maybe she was savoring the discoveries.

Opinion: Do it now because tomorrow isn't promised.
Never creeps up on those who hesitate.

Lyla reached inside the bottle's open flap and pulled out several items. They were mostly silly things that she couldn't remember the significance of. A painted rock. A penny. A compass. There was nothing meaningful in the last of the items, which left her feeling disappointed. She was hoping there would be something surprising left inside the bottle. *This is all?* She wasn't sure what she was expecting, but it was more than this.

Opinion: Lower your expectations and you'll never be disappointed.

That one wasn't a Delilah original. It was universal.

The doorbell rang, snapping her out of her spiraling mood. "It's open! Come in!" she called, stepping back to see who would enter.

Travis walked inside, wearing that ridiculously sexy tool belt.

Immediately, her mood lifted as if whatever she hadn't found in the bottle had materialized in her parents' living room. "What are you doing here? We don't have plans, do we?"

"We do now. I'm going to help you get this place hurricane ready."

Lyla felt the blood inside her freeze. "What?"

"There's a hurricane rolling up the shore and it's going to hit this weekend. Perfect timing for Bailey's wedding, huh?" he said sarcastically. "Anyway, I don't want you to have any damages on this house."

Lyla's brain stuck on the word hurricane. "What are you talking about? I haven't heard about any storms?"

"Because you don't have a TV," he pointed out, continuing to assess her windows. "Hurricane Bill is on its way."

"Bill?" Goosebumps fleshed on her arms. "Hurricane Bill?" she repeated.

"That's right." He gave her a strange look. "Why do you look like you've seen a ghost?"

"Because Hurricane Billy hit the last summer I lived here." She limped toward him.

Travis seemed to notice that she was injured. "Did you sprain your ankle?"

"Broken toe," she said, feeling breathless. "Again."

Concern mounted in his brown eyes. "That's weird. Maybe you're on to something with this whole summer repeating nonsense."

The fact he still referred to it as nonsense didn't go unnoticed. "There's no maybe about it. This is happening, Travis, and if this hurricane is in any way similar to the last, we have more to worry about than Bailey's wedding getting ruined."

Lyla watched as Travis stored the extra wood for boarding the windows in the garage. The storm wasn't expected for a few more days and maybe there would be more showings between now and then.

"We can board everything up on Friday afternoon before the wedding rehearsal."

"Wedding rehearsal?" Lyla shifted to take some weight off her toe.

"Well, yeah. You're my date, remember?"

"To the wedding. Not the rehearsal."

"To both." Travis looked at Lyla like she was losing her mind. "Haven't you ever been part of a wedding party before?"

"No." She'd been to plenty of weddings, but she'd never been part of the close-knit circle that orchestrated the event. "I have to go to both occasions?" she asked, truly surprised.

Travis took her head, squeezing it softly, a silent plea. "I need you, Ly. There'll be family members there that I haven't seen in ages."

"And?" She didn't see the problem.

"And I won't feel like such a loser with a beautiful woman on my arm."

"Beautiful woman? Where will you find one of those?" she asked, admittedly fishing for a compliment.

"Right here." He dropped her hand and then looped his arms around her waist. The motion took her by surprise. Yeah, they'd kissed the other night, but she wasn't sure where they stood. Did that kiss move the line to where he could hold her close anytime he wanted? He brushed a kiss on her lips that liquefied every bone in her body. Did flings include flirting like this? She wasn't sure.

"Fine. I'll be your plus-one to both. That counts as an extra favor to hold over your head."

His mouth fell open, disbelief lifting his brows. "This is how you thank me for boarding up your windows?"

The easy banter between them was so addictive. "Right. I guess we'll be even then."

Travis leaned in slowly, and kissed her again, lingering longer this time. "I don't mind being indebted to you."

"Actually, I'm indebted to you." She pulled her mouth from his, her eyes flicking up to meet Travis's. "Because of you, I wrote an inspired article that my boss just so happened to love."

"Because of me?" The corners of his lips lifted. "What's the article about?"

"Relationships." She immediately felt embarrassed as if telling him he'd inspired her article was also claiming that's what she thought she and Travis were in. "Those always do the best with my readers."

He planted tiny kisses along her jawline, his breath tickling her skin as he exhaled. "Well, I can't wait to read this new article of yours."

"You don't need to," she said.

"Why wouldn't I read it?"

"Because it's personal. It's my opinion."

Travis stopped kissing and pulled back, narrowing his eyes. "An opinion that you allow the entire country to read," he pointed out.

"But those are strangers. This is you."

"All the more reason I should read it."

There was too much tension gathering between them, and Lyla needed a break before she did something crazy, like pull Travis to her and start making out right here on the front porch for all to see. She dropped her gaze to her toe. It was a deep purple color reserved for eggplants. "Do you think I can still dive with this toe?"

Travis glanced down at her foot as well. "What?"

"If Hurricane Bill is on its way, we need to finish off our bucket list. It's bad luck to leave anything unchecked. If we don't check those other items off, that storm might wipe Echo Cove off the map. At the very least, it'll do some serious damage to my parents' house."

Travis tapped a finger to his chin. "I thought you didn't believe that not checking off the items would bring bad luck."

She hadn't. Not until now. Now she felt sure that all the bad luck of this summer and her last one here was due to her unchecked bucket list.

"But if you're feeling brave and want to go for a swim," Travis said, "I won't argue."

Lyla felt the opposite of bravery. More so, it was a feeling of panic driving her to jump off the Pirate's Plank. "Let's go. Before I change my mind."

"Even with your toe?"

"It's wrapped. It's fine. If it'll stop a hurricane and save your sister's wedding, I have to jump, right?"

Travis chuckled softly. "Are you sure you didn't hit your head when you injured your toe?"

"My head is fine," she said. She knew it sounded crazy, but she believed the next week and the town hinged on two unchecked bucket list items.

Travis cocked his head and grinned in her direction. "This is why I love you, Ly."

Lyla gasped softly. He didn't mean that he loved-her loved her, but the L-word still made her freeze. She looked away, hoping her expression didn't reveal feelings.

"Your ex was a fool if he couldn't see how wonderful you are."

Lyla's skin felt hot. She was certain if she looked in the mirror right now, her skin would be red and blotchy. "Are you still going to think that if I fall off the Pirate's Plank and sink like a rock? Again?"

"You're not drowning on my watch." He reached for her hand, the feel of it akin to a plug being pressed into an electrical socket. "Okay?"

Travis always had a way of making her want to say yes. It was never forced or coerced. It was more that his confidence in her made her feel like it was warranted. She could do anything if he was with her. "Okay."

Lyla's confidence waned as she walked toward the Pirate's Plank. Her toe began to throb harder and she felt herself begin to limp.

Travis reached for her hand and gave it a reassuring squeeze. She squeezed back, but she was too nervous to talk.

She'd been having the recurring nightmare for years. She had passed out on the plank that day, and she never wanted to feel so helpless ever again.

But here she was, feeling the familiar panic jolting through her veins. She stopped walking and closed her eyes.

"You okay?" Travis asked quietly.

"Fine. I just . . . just need . . ." She struggled to pull in a deep breath. Then she slowly started climbing the ladder, one rung at a time. "Remind me why we're doing this?" she called over her shoulder.

"If you don't want to, you don't have to, Ly. We're just having fun."

She wasn't just having fun, though. In fact, no part of this was enjoyable to her right now. She turned and looked down at him, finding something gentle in his eyes.

"I didn't realize the idea of jumping scared you so much."

She pressed her lips together, noticing that she was shaking. She wasn't just scared, she was terrified. The more she thought about it, the more her flesh seemed to tremble. Her vision was starting to fade, and she saw stars. She was pretty sure they weren't fireflies this time.

"Hey. It's okay. You don't have to do this, you know? Let's get out of here, Ly."

She wasn't going to argue with him. Not when he was suggesting the exact thing her mind was screaming at her to do, turn around and flee. She was on the verge of passing out anyway, which wouldn't check off that bucket-list item.

Descending the ladder, her legs shook harder as she lowered to each step, feeling like a complete coward. Once her feet were on the ground, she headed in Travis's direction. "Where are we going?"

"To my camper."

Anywhere was better than being here. On a nod, she followed Travis to his truck.

Chapter 21

Opinion: Saving the world is overrated.
—Delilah Dune, opinion writer

An hour or so later, Lyla sat in front of a bonfire that Travis had made on his property. She could feel the heat radiating off the bonfire's flames and it was enough to make her want to close her eyes and go to sleep. Dusk was falling and Travis had gone quiet while drinking a bottled water beside her. At least she thought it was water in that bottle. Maybe he had gone to sleep himself.

"I lied the other day," she finally said, needing to confess.

He looked over. "About what?"

"When I said I didn't read your emails. I don't know why I told you I didn't, because I did. I read them all."

He stared at her, expressionless. "You did?"

She offered a brief nod. "I kept them in a special folder in my inbox, so I wouldn't accidentally delete them. I still have it."

"You do?" he asked.

"Mm-hmm. I guess I didn't want to sound like a total loser the other day, admitting that I hung on every word you sent. Especially since I never reciprocated. It seemed almost worse if I read the emails, but didn't respond."

"It's not worse," he said quietly. "I think maybe it's better. My words weren't wasted."

"If I could go back in time, I'd email you back, Travis. I'm not sure what I'd say, but I wouldn't have lost touch with you." She ran her open palms over the soft fabric of her cotton pants.

"That's the thing about life. You can't go back, even when quasi-magical time capsules offer a little glimpse at the past."

She saw his laugh more than heard it. "Where are you going next?" she asked. "After you leave Echo Cove? Do you know?"

He turned his attention back to the fire. "I thought I'd stay in town as long as you're here, in case you need more help on the house."

"My parents gave me their blessing to leave. The agent can handle the rest of the showings—assuming this weekend's hurricane doesn't wipe the house off the earth." She was making light of it, but Hurricane Bill was still a major worry in her mind. She also still believed that checking off their bucket list would somehow change the storm's path. Or at least lessen its impact.

"If it does cause damage, you've got a handyman you can call. I'll rebuild the house from scratch if I have to."

Lyla studied his side profile, believing him. "I don't recall you being this charming when we were younger."

He offered a dry, humorless chuckle. "I definitely wasn't. I would say I was a bit of a jerk back then. A guy has to be a jerk to put fake snakes in a woman's mailbox."

"I don't think so. You may have been a prankster, but your pranks were never mean-spirited. You were always just having fun and never at anyone's expense. At least not intentionally."

"You were always good at making me feel like I was a good person," he said quietly.

"That's because you are. Anyone who made you feel less . . ."

She trailed off, knowing exactly who had made Travis feel small and insignificant.

"Where are you going after this weekend?" he asked. "Now that you're free to leave."

She'd wondered that same question. "I'm not sure. I don't have anything back in the town where I was. I'm kind of lost right now."

"What about Echo Cove? You could stay."

She breathed a laugh. "I'd feel like a total failure. Coming back home with my tail between my legs."

"You worry about others' opinions too much, Ly. Even in your column, it's more about what others think than you."

Was that true? "They're *my* opinions."

"But you write them based on what you predict other people will respond to. Who cares what others think?"

"I do, I guess. I have to in order to make a living." It was important now that she was single.

"You used to want to be an author, if I remember correctly. What happened to that?" he asked.

It was true. That had been her dream once upon a time. Then she'd written that one-hundred-page story. She'd poured her very writer's soul into that manuscript and the editor who'd responded had pulverized that soul. It wasn't easy for a person to put themselves out there for anything one cared about. Maybe that's why she hadn't responded to Travis either. "Do you know how hard it is to get your book published and shelved at an actual bookstore?"

"I doubt it's as hard as getting a national opinion column in your name," he responded.

Touché. "True . . . and also not true. I don't know. I guess I realized that writing an actual book that can be found at the library was a pipedream. No one would read it."

"I would."

She looked at him for a long moment. Her story had been good. She thought so, at least. Maybe she could rewrite it now that she was an adult. "Perhaps that's still in my future. What about your dream?"

He lifted a brow, looking surprised. "I had a dream?"

"Yeah. You wanted to be a world-famous guitarist, remember?"

"Oh, right." This made Travis chuckle. "Now that is what you call a pipedream. I still play guitar, but I have no desire or need to be famous. In fact, fame is conditional, and I grew up in a conditional household. I'm happy being free. I love what I do, and I think I'm good at it. There are things that could make me happier, but no man can have everything, right?"

The way he was looking at her made her wonder if she was one of those things that could make him happy. *There goes your overactive imagination again, Lyla.* "Right."

"So, are you going to write your great American novel?" he asked.

"Right after I jump off the Pirate's Plank," she said sarcastically.

"I'm being serious."

"So am I. I've started and stopped lots of stories. Then I convince myself they're silly or a waste of time."

"Don't listen to those voices. They're lying to you."

"Well, one of those voices was my ex's. He got a hold of one of my stories—Okay, truthfully, I left it out for him to see. I guess I wanted confirmation that it was good."

Travis looked disappointed on her behalf. "He didn't give you that confirmation?"

"Just the opposite. He confirmed that I should stick to my day job." She laughed dryly, but the memory ached inside her.

"This is the same guy who thought it was a good idea to let you go. He's an idiot. Not an opinion. Fact."

Some part of Lyla needed to hear that. Her ex was a lot of negative things, but he also had good qualities. She never would have dated him if he didn't. He was intelligent, and if he thought her work wasn't good enough, maybe he was right. "He was an idiot for sure, but I'm still guessing the book was pretty bad."

"You know what I think?"

She braced herself, even though, deep down, she knew Travis would never intentionally hurt her. "What?"

"It probably was bad. It was probably horrible."

Everything inside of Lyla stilled. *Okay.* Maybe she was wrong about Travis never hurting her.

He held up a finger. "It's like when I learn a new song on my guitar. It's rough. But I play it again, I work on the notes, I polish it. Perfect it. The first draft is crap. It's horrible. And that's okay. The music doesn't happen until the twentieth draft or the one hundredth. If I had read those chapters of yours, I would have seen the potential instead of the mistakes."

"You're a good guy, you know that?" And from her experience, most of the good guys, the kind that didn't break hearts, were spoken for. "Why are you single?"

His eyes narrowed just slightly. "You know why, Ly."

"By choice," she said.

"I live my life a certain way, so yeah, it's a choice. Just like tonight, I choose to be with you."

Without thinking, she reached for his hand. "And I choose to be with you. Obviously."

"Well, you do have a broken toe. Maybe you're just here because you can't leave." His fingers wrapped around hers.

"That's not the case." She looked away for a moment, inspecting the nature around them. "There was a bonfire that you and I made that last summer together. Kind of like this one. I remember it because I felt kind of the way I do now."

"Oh?" He leaned toward her in his chair. "How is that?"

Looking at him again, she gave herself full permission to say exactly what she was thinking. "Like I wanted to kiss you, but I didn't know how to get you to kiss me first."

"Hmm. I know how you can make that happen tonight. Just come a little closer."

She leaned his way.

Like magnets, each drawn to the other, closer, until finally, their lips touched. Lyla opened her mouth against Travis's. The kiss was slow. It evolved from something sweet to something needy as Travis tugged her toward him. Her toe didn't hurt anymore. She didn't even feel it. All she felt was a thick desire pulsing through her.

"Remember the other night when you said you wanted to spend the night with me?" He pulled back and searched her eyes.

"Yeah." He'd turned her down, feeding her a list of reasons that may or may not have been true.

"I want that tonight. If you still want it. If you don't, I'll drive you—"

She stopped his talking with another kiss before pulling back and looking at him. She'd only wanted a kiss that summer. A kiss would have been enough to make her teenage dreams come true. But tonight, she wanted more. So much more. "It's been a while since I've been with someone. I might not be . . ."

Travis narrowed his eyes. "You'll be amazing, and I would guess that just like polishing those chapters or me working on a new song, you'll only get better with practice."

"Practice, huh?" She grinned back at him.

He chuckled and kissed her lips. Then he took on a serious expression. "Are you sure about this? Because you can change your mind. We have something special, Ly. We've always had. If we do this, I don't want it to ruin how we feel about each other."

She couldn't see how it would ruin how she felt about Travis, but maybe that's because her hormones were doing the happy dance right now. "I'm sure."

Travis nodded. Then he got up and scooped her up in his arms.

"What are you doing?" she said on a nervous laugh.

"I don't want you to reinjure that toe on the way to my bed. I plan to make you feel so good that you'll never doubt yourself again."

Lyla knew it was just a line, but she felt it all the way to her core. If one kiss with Travis had inspired her to write the article for her boss, maybe sleeping together would inspire her to actually go write that great American novel after all. Anything was possible, especially on a magical summer night such as this.

Lyla's legs were jellylike as she made her way to the Pirate's Plank in her dream. Fear gripped her and she felt like one of the little fish that she and her father used to catch and release on their father-daughter fishing dates.

Her steps were slow and hesitant as she looked out upon all the people in the water. There was Bernie. She liked Bernie, and she wanted to be friends.

Lyla stepped up to the plank. There was a person behind her, waiting impatiently to jump in. Lyla was taking too long. She could feel it and with each passing second, more eyes turned in her direction.

She sucked in a breath, pulling it into the deepest recesses of her lungs.

Someone laughed. Another pointed. Lyla's breaths came out shallower. She felt hot. Perspiration rolled down her temple. As she went to swipe it away, her vision went black and the lake and the noise disappeared.

Lyla shot up in bed, her breathing labored and heavy. A hand reached for her, and Lyla screamed softly until she realized it was only Travis.

"You okay?" he asked.

Her mind rushed to process the current scene. She was in

Travis's RV and—*Oh, wow.* She and Travis had done things last night that crossed every line between two friends. "I—I, um, I was dreaming."

"Same dream as last time?"

"Yeah." She hurriedly began to collect her clothing, which was *not* on her body. Instead, it was strewn about on the floor and at the end of the bed.

Travis's hand gently caressed her back. "What are you doing?"

"Getting dressed. I have to go."

"We haven't even had coffee yet."

Lyla paused for a moment to look at him. She was in panic mode, not just because she'd been falling in her dream, but because this was Travis. She could legit fall in real life, and after a year of trying to get her feet back underneath her, that was the last thing she needed. "I need to go home. For all I know the ceiling is leaking, pipes have burst, and the living room is a swimming pool."

Travis seemed to accept this rationale. "I'll drive you."

He'd driven her here, so she couldn't refuse the ride, although she probably would have if there was any other option. She needed space and time to think. Her head was spinning.

Travis stood and collected his clothes as well.

Lyla couldn't help watching him for a moment. Yeah, she could fall for him. She could fall, hit the water, and sink like a stone. Nausea rolled through her body. *What have I done?* Travis didn't live in Echo Cove, and neither did she. He could move on tomorrow and leave her feeling broken the way she'd been after Joe's betrayal. She'd barely climbed out of bed and only when she had to. All the joy had drained out of her, and no matter how hard she tried to find a glimmer, it was gone for a long time.

Sliding her feet into her shoes, Lyla reminded herself to breathe as she headed toward the front of the RV, stopping when Travis tugged on her arm.

"About last night," he said quietly.

She shook her head quickly, bracing for impact as tears burned her eyes. "We don't have to talk about it."

"I'm not sorry." He looked at her expectantly, his brown eyes moving back and forth, searching hers as he waited for her to say the same.

Was she sorry? "I, um, well . . ."

As the seconds passed, hurt crossed over Travis's expression, dimming the light behind his eyes. He seemed to subtly deflate, his lips turning downward.

"It doesn't change anything," she said finally, thinking that was what he wanted to hear.

If anything, his look of hurt visibly deepened. "Of course, it doesn't. I'll take you home now."

The drive to Lyla's parents' house was quiet. She knew she'd said the wrong thing, but what was the right thing to say after having sex with your childhood best friend? It was usually the guy who said the wrong thing, or maybe that was a lie that all the romantic comedies she'd grown up watching fed her. Those types of movies had spoiled her into believing that love would save the day, and that once she met *the one*—another lie—her life would be perfect.

Travis pulled into her driveway and parked. He didn't move to get out and walk her to the door.

"Thanks for the drive. And, um, for last night," she said.

"Thanks?" His brows twitched as he looked at her. "Wow. Okay. You're welcome, Ly. Glad I could be of service."

She couldn't say anything right at this moment. She had no idea what he needed to hear from her. "What do you want from me?"

He looked straight ahead, staring out the windshield. "Nothing. I'm here for all your needs. Just like my business card says."

All she'd said was thank you. "That's not what I meant."

"Could have fooled me," he muttered.

"Travis, come on."

He wrapped his fingers around the steering wheel tightly. "I have a job to get to, Ly. And you have possible disasters to avert." He was talking about her house, but maybe he was referring to himself as a disaster too.

She felt like she should backtrack and apologize for how she'd acted this morning, but she wasn't sure she'd done anything wrong. What else could she have said? He didn't regret anything, but she did? Or she should. Conflicted and shell-shocked, she pushed the truck door open. "I'll text you."

"Sure." He nodded but didn't look at her.

Lyla felt like a criminal as she made her way up the porch steps and let herself inside the house, heading straight to her bedroom.

Maybe Travis had actual feelings for her too.

Unsure of what else to do, she pulled out her phone to text the only person who would understand her right now.

Lyla: *I spent the night with Travis.*

Allison immediately texted back.

Allison: *Ummm, on his couch?*

Lyla: *Nope.*

Allison: I'll be there stat. You're home?

Home? The word was foreign to Lyla right now.

Lyla: *Yeah, my parents' house. Bring caffeine and sugar.*

Allison: You got it!

Chapter 22

*Opinion: Sometimes what you don't say
matters more than what you do.*
—Delilah Dune, opinion writer

Allison sipped her coffee and sighed. "I can't believe that's what you said to him."

"Why?" Lyla asked, even though she had a pretty good idea why her friend would say that.

"You told Travis that sleeping together changed nothing. Are you kidding? It changes everything between you two."

"For me, maybe, but not him. He's a guy," Lyla said, as if that was sufficient rationale.

Allison shook her head. "That doesn't mean he's heartless. You two were close once. You're growing close again. What makes you think that having sex wouldn't mean anything to Travis?"

Lyla massaged her forehead in an attempt to get her thoughts straight. "Do you think that's why he seemed upset?"

"Uh, yeah." Allison nodded definitively. "The hit to his ego must have been massive."

Guilt pummeled Lyla's gut. "I was just trying to protect my own ego. But in hindsight, that seems kind of selfish, I guess." She blew out a breath, thankful to have a friend to talk to right now. After her breakup with Joe, she'd needed someone to vent to. "What do I do?"

"You tell him you're sorry, and that last night meant more to you than you let on," Allison said.

Was that true? It had meant more, but how much more?

"Honesty is always best." Allison offered a definitive nod.

"You're a good friend." Lyla sucked in a sharp breath, suddenly realizing something she hadn't considered. "I know you and my mom are friends too. Please don't tell her I slept with Travis." How mortifying. She didn't share details like that with her mother.

Allison waggled her brows. "How many Dinnerware purchases is it worth to you for me to keep mum?"

"I'll buy the whole lot," Lyla promised, knowing her friend was only yanking her chain.

"Deal!"

They both started giggling.

"But seriously, your mom and I are friends, but it isn't that kind of friendship. She's the kind who comes over and listens to me cry about life. And I do the same for her. She's not the kind I share other stuff with. Like sex stuff."

Lyla cringed. "My mom and I have never had that kind of relationship either."

"So," Allison lifted a brow, "was he any good in bed?"

Lyla's jaw dropped at the boldness of the question. She was still getting used to having a close friend to share these details with. Nudging Allison's arm, she said, "You first. Is TJ any good?"

"I don't kiss and tell." Allison lifted her chin, looking prim and proper, but Lyla knew she was only joking.

"Me either. Not usually. But yes, he was amazing. Not that I have much experience. Just Joe."

Allison looked surprised. "Ernie was kind of an aggressive lover. Not in a bad way, but I had bite marks sometimes."

Lyla's eyes rounded. "Bite marks?"

Allison burst into giggles. "I really am your first female friend, aren't I? You've never heard other women's stories."

"Maybe I haven't missed anything if it involves vampire lovers."

They both started laughing again, harder and longer. Aside from Travis, Lyla wasn't sure when she'd enjoyed someone's company so much. And before returning to Echo Cove, she hadn't had a good friend who made her laugh until she cried. She hadn't realized what she'd been missing. "Thanks for putting my head back on straight."

"Anytime." Allison took a loud sip of her coffee. "Now I need you to return the favor."

"Oh?" Lyla noticed Allison's whole demeanor shifted. "What's going on? Is it about TJ?"

Allison looked down at her coffee cup. Lyla realized Allison's hands were suddenly shaking. "This is decaf coffee. Mine, not yours."

"Decaf? Why on earth would you be drinking decaf?" Lyla asked.

When Allison didn't immediately answer, Lyla's brain began to piece together the only reason that made sense.

"You're pregnant? With TJ?" She slapped a hand over her mouth. "Is it true?"

Allison's face flushed. "I don't know. Maybe. I've thrown up three mornings in a row, and I never throw up. Only when I was pregnant before." Her skin paled. "Lyla, I can't be pregnant. I don't want to be pregnant."

Lyla reached for her friend's hand. "If you are, it'll be fine. It doesn't matter that you're not married or that you're not in love. Women raise babies on their own all the time."

"That's not it." Allison drew a hand to her throat as she seemed to swallow past a tightness in it, her eyes suddenly wide and shiny. "I can't have another child. I've had two, and

I lost them both. I can't go through that again. It'll destroy me, Lyla."

Lyla squeezed her hand. "Hey, that's not going to happen. You won't lose another child."

"But I could. That knowledge would hang over my head. It'll paralyze me. Just wondering if I'm pregnant and knowing that I might lose some imaginary baby is terrifying."

The Allison that was giggling until she cried just minutes ago was now about to cry for real.

"Hey, it's all right. Everything is okay. Before you panic even more, you need to take a test."

"A test?" Allison repeated.

"To know if you are or aren't. You might not be pregnant at all. You might just have a virus or something."

Allison nodded, the motion so small that it was barely noticeable. "You're right. I could be sick." Hope flashed in her eyes.

"In which case, you're getting me sick," Lyla said, trying to lighten the mood. "Thanks a lot."

"I can't buy a test," Allison said in a tinny voice. "This is Echo Cove. The cashier will see the test and tell every customer who comes in after that. Or I'll grab the test and run into everyone I know. Then everyone in town will talk about me and how irresponsible I am. I lost two kids and now I'm bringing another into the world." Tears rolled down Allison's cheeks. "How did I let this happen?"

"Can't TJ buy the test for you?" Lyla asked.

"TJ? No, he can't know. I don't want to get him involved. He's the kind of guy who'll go out and buy me a ring if he thinks I'm carrying his baby."

"He is?" Lyla was surprised.

"He's old-fashioned in that way." Allison dropped her face in her hands. "I am screwing up the little bit of happiness that I've finally found. I don't want him to propose just because he thinks he has to."

Lyla reached out and squeezed Allison's forearm. "I'll buy you a test, okay? It'll be fine."

Allison looked up, her lips parted, hope playing in her bloodshot eyes. "You'll do that for me?"

Lyla didn't want to. She didn't even like buying tampons at the store. A pregnancy test would be so much harder to purchase. But she didn't know everyone in town anymore. The probability that she'd run into someone she knew who would find her life interesting enough to gossip about was low. "Of course, I will."

Allison threw her arms around Lyla's neck. "Thank you, Lyla. Thank you so much. I'm so glad we're friends."

Later that evening, Travis wasn't answering his phone, so Lyla got into her car and drove to his RV. He couldn't ignore her forever. And he couldn't stay mad at her forever either.

She turned onto the dirt path where his RV was currently parked and followed it to his blue pickup truck. Travis was already sitting outside in his chair, as if he were waiting for her.

"Hey." Lyla walked toward him, stopping when she was a couple feet away.

"I didn't know I'd be seeing you today."

"I tried to call. You didn't answer. Are you ignoring me?" she asked, wringing her hands.

Travis didn't answer for a moment. "I guess you could say so. I just needed some space and time. To think."

"If you're thinking about what I said, then stop. I didn't mean it."

His eyes narrowed as he watched her. "Which part?"

Lyla took the seat next to his. "When I said sleeping together didn't change anything. It does. I just meant that I don't want it to change the fact that we're friends. I care about you, and I don't want to mess things up between us. I just found you again."

"Don't you mean that I found you? You were pushing a bike with a flat tire in the rain storm, if I recall."

"You found me," she agreed. "And I'm so glad. I'm not sorry about last night either. It was a great night. I just wish I hadn't messed up our morning with my big mouth. I'm sorry. Truly sorry, Travis."

Something in his eyes softened. "I guess I took what you said a little too personally. I think it's because I like you, Ly. It wasn't just a one-night stand for me."

"Me either," she said in almost a whisper.

Travis leaned toward her, and she felt her insides light up, because she knew he was coming in for a kiss, and she wanted that more than anything.

"Wait," she said right before his lips met hers.

He paused and lifted his gaze from her mouth to her eyes. "Yeah?"

"Saying that I'm not just a one-night stand implies there might be a second time."

The corner of his mouth quirked. "That's not up to me. If it were, there'd be at least a dozen more times before I go."

Before he went. Right.

She implored herself not to think about next month, next week, or even tomorrow. That was the real reason that she'd tried to make last night irrelevant. It didn't matter how much it did or didn't change things, because neither of them lived in Echo Cove anymore. There wouldn't be a relationship.

"Do you have anywhere to be right now?" Travis asked, leaning toward her and sprinkling kisses along her cheek and neck.

"No," she whispered. There was nowhere she'd rather be right now. Her brain short-circuited and her body took over. A kiss had never felt like this, especially not the closed-mouth kind.

"How about we go in the RV and make this agreement of ours to avoid the one-night stand official?"

Lyla's yearning was on a scale she'd never known. She'd thought what she was feeling was part of the fairy tale lie, yet here she was, heart hammering and body trembling like a character in a romance novel. "Yes," she said simply. She didn't need more words. At this moment, she was counting on actions speaking louder.

An hour later, Lyla got up just like she had that same morning and started reaching for her clothes.

"Already?" Travis asked.

She paused and turned to him. "I need to get home. There's still packing left to do. But know that . . ." She paused, not wanting to sound cheesy or more invested than he was.

"I know." Travis leaned in and pressed a kiss to her mouth. "See you later."

"Mm-hmm." She continued dressing and then headed out of his RV. It was convenient that he was parked in the middle of nowhere, where no one would see her coming and going. Not that she was hiding him in the way that Allison was hiding TJ.

Allison and TJ. Right.

Lyla needed to get that test for Allison like she'd promised. Poor Allison was probably freaking out right now.

What would Lyla do in her situation? She'd never been pregnant, but she'd fantasized about having a baby—one day. If she and Joe had gotten pregnant, she wouldn't have been disappointed. It would have been a shock, but she would have probably embraced motherhood.

Allison was in a completely different boat with TJ, though. She'd had children, and she'd been through an unimaginable trauma. Plus Allison and TJ weren't ready to go public with their relationship. They apparently wanted to keep their relationship under wraps. There was something romantic about that. A secret relationship. Possibly a secret baby too.

Lyla drove to the closest grocery store and parked. She

wanted to be a good friend and help Allison any way she could, which meant walking inside that store, putting a pregnancy test in her basket, and buying it as quickly as she could. That's what friends were for.

Pushing the car door open, she walked with determination. She probably looked a mess. She'd just had an hour of cardio in Travis's bed. Had she even brushed her hair? She swiped a hand over the top of her head, attempting to tame any stray strands without a mirror as she scanned the aisles and looked for one that might carry pregnancy tests. Deciding that aisle nine seemed like the right one, she headed in that direction, glancing around as if she was doing something wrong.

When Lyla got to the end of aisle nine, there was an older woman looking at other feminine products. Lyla didn't recognize her, which was a relief. Lyla redirected her attention to the tests. She spotted a pink box that looked like a good option. Glancing around to make sure no one she knew was around, she tossed the box in her basket. Then she walked quickly toward the register, holding her breath, on a mission to purchase and leave.

"Lyla! Lyla Dune, is that you?"

Lyla's usual freeze response didn't win this time. Instead, she was in full flight mode as she picked up speed, walking toward the checkout lane.

"Lyla? Oh, Lyla—it's me, Jamie McClendon!"

Jamie McClendon. A face immediately came to mind. Jamie was the school's biggest gossip. What were the odds that Jaime would be here now?

Unable to avoid her old acquaintance, Lyla stopped walking and slowly turned, because not doing so would make her rude. And Lyla didn't want that to turn into some sort of gossip. She could just hear the story now. *Guess what? Nice girl Lyla Dune has turned into a snob since becoming a nationally acclaimed writer. She thinks she's better than us.*

Clearing her throat, she faced Jamie. "Hi, there. Long time no see."

Jamie was practically glowing. She was the same age as Lyla, but she looked ten years younger. "I was just thinking about you the other day. Remember that time you nearly drowned in the lake?"

Lyla wrinkled her brow, as if stumped by the random throwback. Was that the first thing Jamie thought of when she remembered Lyla? "I'm sorry?"

"Oh, come on. You remember, don't you? Or did you hit your head when you fell in the water?" Jamie looked briefly concerned. "It was a nasty fall."

"I remember. Yes." Lyla only wished she could forget. It was a long time ago, but something about that fall had molded some deep part of her. "Why were you thinking about that?"

"Oh, well, because my son was teasing his friend for not jumping. He said that there's no way to get hurt on that plank, but I begged to differ. I told them both how you fell and nearly drowned. If not for Mr. Tibbs."

Lyla hugged her shopping basket closer. "Mr. Tibbs?"

"You know. The owner of the hardware store. He was the one who pulled you out of the water."

Lyla's mouth fell open.

"You don't remember?" Jamie asked. "He was your real-life hero."

Lyla stared at Jamie blankly. Her mind refused to categorize Mr. Tibbs in the hero column of her brain. He was an old curmudgeon. "Mr. Tibbs doesn't even like me. Why would he pull me out of the water?"

"Well, someone needed to. Was he supposed to let you sink?" Jamie cackled quietly and then noticed Lyla's basket. "Well, well. Are congratulations in order?"

Everything inside Lyla shriveled. "Oh. No." She shook her head quickly. "This test isn't for me. It's not mine."

Jamie gave her a skeptical look. "It's none of my business

anyway. I'm just glad to see you. Bernadette told me you were in town."

Lyla looked up. "She did?"

"Mm. Can't keep anything under wraps in Echo Cove, you know." Jamie glanced at the pregnancy test again. "But don't worry. I'll keep this little secret between us." She tipped her head at the pregnancy test. Before Lyla could reiterate that it wasn't for her, Jamie waved and walked away. "Hopefully, I'll see you around," she called behind her. "I've got to get going. I'm a soccer mom, and soccer moms can't be late. Bye!"

"Bye!" Lyla beelined toward the register, hoping Jamie wouldn't mention the test to anyone. Not that it mattered. Hardly anyone in Echo Cove knew Lyla anymore.

As Lyla stepped up to the register, the clerk reached into the basket and pulled out the box, staring at it for a moment. She looked at Lyla's face and then Lyla's midsection.

Seriously? If I'm showing already, then I wouldn't need a test, now, would I?

Lyla pulled out her debit card and waited impatiently.

"That'll be eight dollars and seventy-five cents," the cashier finally read out.

Lyla laid a ten-dollar bill down. After the woman made change, Lyla grabbed her bag, thanked the cashier, and practically ran through the parking lot. Once inside her car, she closed the door behind her, feeling like she'd just navigated an escape room. Then she started her engine and drove over to Allison's house. There was no meat delivery truck in the driveway. Allison was probably alone and likely biting her nails to nubs. Grabbing the plastic grocery bag, Lyla got out and walked up the driveway.

When Allison answered the door, her eyes were red-rimmed.

"Please tell me you haven't been worrying yourself over the what-ifs." Lyla held up the bag. "For you."

Allison took the bag and blew out a ragged breath.

"Thank you. I'm not ready for this just yet. TJ and I . . ." Her chin quivered and tears flooded her eyes.

Oh, no.

"We got in an argument and, well, he said maybe we should give each other some space. Apparently, according to him, I've been acting secretive and dramatic."

"Did you tell him that you might be pregnant?" Lyla asked.

"No"—Allison shook her head quickly—"of course not. And since we're kind of broken up, I'm not in a place to take this test right now. Emotionally."

Lyla was disappointed, but she understood. Allison must be so scared right now. Life as she knew it was threatening to be flipped upside down. "What do you need from me?" Lyla asked.

"You've done enough." Allison smoothed a lock of hair out of her face. "I think I just want to be alone right now."

"You're sure? I can stay."

"I'm sure. Thanks, Lyla. I'll see you tomorrow, okay?" Allison avoided Lyla's eyes.

"Okay. You can change your mind and call me back anytime. Even in the middle of the night. I'll come over whenever."

"Thanks. Who needs a boyfriend with a friend like you?" Allison took a step back, practically closing the door in Lyla's face. "Night, Lyla."

Lyla stood there until the door was fully shut, listening to the deadbolt click into place. Turning, she headed back to her car. She didn't want to leave her friend upset, but she couldn't stay when Allison had asked to be alone. Lyla remembered those days after Joe had left. She'd just wanted to be alone too, but then again, no one had asked if she'd needed them to stay. All her friends in her old town had been Joe's first, and they'd chosen him in the breakup, leaving Lyla to grieve alone.

She'd never realized the value of a good friend. Being one and having one.

Lyla got into her car and backed out of the driveway. Time to go home. *Scratch that.* It was her parents' home. At least until it sold, which would hopefully happen soon.

When she got there, she stepped onto the back porch and looked up at the dark sky. It was clear tonight. One wouldn't even know a hurricane was barreling toward the coast. One wouldn't know this wasn't the same sky of yesteryear either. This time, though, unlike that summer when she was eighteen, she hoped Hurricane Bill took mercy on the small town of Echo Cove—despite the two items still left unchecked on her and Travis's bucket list.

August 25

Dear Diary,

There's a hurricane on its way. What if it wipes us all off the planet? What if I never go to college or kiss a boy? What if I never write a novel—oh wait, yes, that's right. That dream has already been crushed. Not by mother nature, but by man. A real jerk of a man, in my opinion.

Mom and Dad are boarding the windows and fearing the worst. If I don't write in you tomorrow, you'll know it's because of Hurricane Billy. How much can a redneck hurricane actually do?

Lyla

Chapter 23

Opinion: Luck is a lie. What happens to you is related to your work ethic or karma. Nothing else.
—Delilah Dune, opinion writer

Lyla awoke to her phone ringing the next morning. She patted the area around her air mattress without opening her eyes, until her fingers clasped the phone and brought it to her ear. "Hello?"

"Lyla? This is Peter. Good news. We have a contingency offer for your parents' house."

Lyla's eyes shot open and she sat up. "What's the contingency?"

Peter chuckled dryly. "Well, I must say the condition on the sale is a little unusual. My clients have been burned in the past on an offer they put in for their previous house. They purchased their home and the day after the sale went through, a wildfire tore through their neighborhood. They lost everything."

"That's bad luck," Lyla said, even though she didn't believe in luck.

"You're telling me. These buyers want to put in a bid, but

under the contingency that this weekend's hurricane doesn't damage the house."

Lyla laughed a little because that was absurd. "I can't control the weather any more than you can, Mr. Blake."

"And I can't control whether this couple buys your parents' home. They love it, though, and as of right now, they want it. So let's just pray that Hurricane Bill cuts us all a break."

Lyla absently massaged her temple. "Right. Okay."

"So, do you want agree to their terms? It would mean no more showings. The house would be taken off the market, contingent on Hurricane Bill."

Lyla nibbled at her lower lip. "I guess so."

"I need a yes or a no, Lyla."

Lyla pulled in a breath. It wasn't as if she had buyers breaking down the door. Echo Cove was a small town that people didn't generally move to. "Okay. Yes," Lyla said, "it's a deal."

"Perfect. I'll draw up the paperwork. Talk to you soon."

Lyla disconnected the call and broke into a drawn-out yawn. Remembering Allison, she quickly pulled up her friend's contact and dialed. When Allison didn't answer, Lyla tried again. She tried three times before giving up and texting.

Lyla: *You okay? I'm checking on you.*

She waited, but Allison didn't respond. It was early still. Maybe Allison was just sleeping. She'd try again later. And even if Allison insisted that she didn't need company, Lyla would go over and bring Allison something to eat. Even when you were depressed and possibly pregnant, you needed food, right? Especially then.

Lyla headed to the bathroom to freshen up. She needed coffee. And if Allison was still sleeping, presumably, she couldn't get a cup of coffee there. So, instead, she'd go to Bernadette's place and maybe make a little more progress on building a friendship. The only problem was that relationships couldn't be built on secrets, and now Lyla had one to keep for Allison and TJ.

A lump of guilt formed in the pit of her stomach. The same stomach that begged for a steaming cup of coffee.

Opinion: Coffee was meant to be drunk hot, no matter the season.

Lyla got in line and shifted back and forth on her feet. There were three customers ahead of her. Then two. Then only one. Lyla rehearsed how she'd greet Bernie in her head, wanting desperately to keep their cordialness going. Bernadette had warmed to her a little bit the other night when they'd hung out with Allison.

The customer in line ahead of Lyla turned and walked away with her coffee and breakfast. Lyla's turn.

"Hi!" Lyla said, a bit too bubbly. She was trying too hard and she knew it.

The corners of Bernadette's lips lifted slightly upward. "Lyla. What can I get you?"

Straight to business. Lyla tried not to take it personally because that was how Bernadette had always been. Glancing up at the menu on the upper wall, Lyla pretended to make her choice even though she already knew exactly what she wanted. "Um, let's see. Can I have a . . . medium coffee with two raw sugars? And a bagel with cream cheese, please."

"Sure. Coming right up." Bernadette turned to prepare Lyla's coffee while she asked her employee to make Lyla's bagel.

"And no freebies this time," Lyla called to her back. "I don't want to take advantage of our friendship." She immediately felt foolish. Were they even friends?

Bernadette didn't respond. Instead, she took her time with the order.

A moment later, Bernadette slid the drink across the counter to Lyla. "Here you go." She tapped her finger along the register and read out the price. "Six dollars and thirty-three cents," she read out.

"Wow. Maybe I should buy my coffee at the gas station," Lyla joked. Even as the words tumbled off her lips, she knew they weren't funny. They were possibly offensive. "Just kidding. The gas station coffee would likely send me to the ER, and I don't want to spend my night that way, so . . ." She trailed off, her hands shaking just enough to make it challenging to swipe her card in the reader. "Do you, um, maybe have time to sit and have coffee with me?" she asked hopefully. "I'd love to do some more catching up. Just the two of us."

Bernadette's mouth opened, forming a little *o*. "I don't think so," she finally said, hooking one thin brow high on her forehead. "I'm working."

"Right." Lyla nodded. "Yes, I see that. It's pretty busy in here. No gas station coffee for anyone in Echo Cove," she teased. *Why do I ramble so much when I'm nervous?* That begged the next question, why was she so nervous?

"Enjoy your breakfast, Lyla," Bernadette said politely. Then she stepped to the side as the other employee slid Lyla's bagel to her.

"Thanks." Lyla grabbed her coffee and her breakfast, just wanting to slink away. This interaction had high school energy, hot and cold, love to hate, all in a blink of an eye. "See you later, Bernie. Bernadette."

It wasn't exactly a rejection though. Bernadette was working—of course she couldn't stop what she was doing to sit and catch up with Lyla. Maybe she was reading into things too much. Bernadette had never given her the warm fuzzies. She just wasn't that type of person.

As Lyla turned to leave, she considered walking out of the coffee shop, but she'd brought her laptop and she needed to finish a copywriting job. She also didn't want Bernie to think she'd been intimidated by her in any way. Bernadette had been fine with Lyla and Allison the other night, but maybe she wasn't comfortable without the buffer of Allison's over-the-top optimism.

That was fine. Just the fact that Bernadette tolerated Lyla without showing her the door or spitting in her coffee was progress from their younger years.

Instead of leaving, Lyla set her coffee and bagel down and took a seat at an open table against the wall. Sliding the breakfast items to the side, she pulled her laptop out and opened it in front of her. She'd always liked working in a public space such as a coffee shop. Inspiration was everywhere.

A blank document greeted her with its blinking cursor. When the words didn't immediately start flowing, she reached for her bagel and took a bite, looking around the shop. Bean Time Coffee was a nice place. It was impressive and something to be proud of.

Lyla took another large bite of her bagel, the cream cheese squishing into her mouth and satisfying her senses. Then she startled when someone pulled out the chair in front of her and sat down. It took a minute for Lyla to chew and realize who she was staring at.

"Hi, Lyla. How are you?"

Lyla was still chewing her large bite of bagel, so she simply nodded, her mind scrambling to put a name to the face.

"Travis told me you were back in town. I know you've come home over the years to visit with your parents, but I haven't seen you. You look great. Amazing, actually."

The woman seated across from Lyla looked so familiar. Who was she?

She seemed oblivious of the fact that Lyla couldn't figure out who she was. "Travis tells me you're going to be his date to my wedding this weekend."

Lyla finally swallowed her bite of bagel. "Bailey! Hi! Congratulations on your upcoming marriage."

Bailey laughed as she stared at Lyla. "You had no idea who I was, did you?"

"Well, it's been a minute since we've seen each other." Lyla hadn't seen Bailey since going off to college.

"Yes, it has. When I saw you sitting over here, I just had to come say hello. I read your opinion column, you know? I think your pieces are fantastic."

Compliments always made Lyla feel like hiding behind a rock. "Thank you. That means a lot to me. So, what are you up to these days? Besides getting married."

"I'm an animal groomer," Bailey said, lifting her chin and smiling proudly. "I work out of my home. Cats, dogs—I even have a ferret that I groom for a lady here in town. You'd be surprised how profitable a grooming business is. And," she said proudly, "I'm an entrepreneur. My parents told me I was ruining my future when I got pregnant and then refused to marry the guy, but I have a great life."

"I'm happy for you." Lyla was also jealous. Bailey had her act together, and Lyla's act had been falling apart at the seams this year.

"So? You and Travis? Finally?"

Lyla blinked, immediately slipping into an innocent act. "What? Us?" She lifted her brows as if she were surprised by the mere suggestion. "No, we're just friends. Why? Did he say something?"

Bailey snickered as she leaned back in her chair. "My brother had such a crush on you that summer you moved away. You know, he wrote you an email that he never sent. I saw it on his monitor one day and teased him mercilessly." She grimaced. "I wasn't the nicest sister back then."

"Brothers and sisters are allowed to be merciless to one another. I think it's a rule that they have to."

Bailey nodded. "I teased him until he almost cried."

Lyla felt her eyes widen. "Travis almost cried?"

"It was an emotional summer. On a lot of levels." The glimmer in Bailey's eyes dimmed.

"What did the email say?" Lyla asked.

"Wouldn't you like to know?" Bailey grinned. "A bunch of ooey-gooey crush kind of stuff. I think he was scared to send it to you. I felt bad for him. Mostly because I knew I couldn't be there for him. A big sister should be there for her little brother."

"You had your own things to deal with."

She lowered her eyes momentarily. "Like being a single mom with no family support. Yeah, that was hard—but I wouldn't change a thing. Sometimes you have to go through the storms to see the rainbow." She let out a dry laugh. "My dad used to preach that. He probably thought I wasn't listening, but I was."

Lyla wished she'd seen that email from Travis. Maybe if he had sent it, she would have shared her own feelings for him. "I had no idea that Travis liked me in that way."

"How could you not know?"

Lyla shook her head. "He was the same old Travis. Always."

"Well, I know my brother, and he's still just as smitten with you as ever. I'm glad you're going to my wedding together. Assuming Hurricane Bill doesn't have any objections." She pushed her chair back from the table and stood again. "I know you don't live here, and neither does he. Sometimes things work out, though."

"We're just—"

"Friends. Yeah, yeah. Right." Bailey winked. "See you Saturday, Lyla."

"See you." Lyla watched Bailey walk toward the café's exit. Then she reached for her coffee and took a sip. That's when inspiration hit. She knew exactly what her next article was going to be about, and Bob was going to love it even more than the last. She was feeling inspired. On a roll. And once again, she owed it all to Travis.

Later that night, Lyla watched as Travis pulled a board off the floor and dragged it over to the exterior window. "You're sure you don't want my help?"

"I do this for a living, Ly. I've got this."

She fidgeted with a torn piece of her nail. "So, these boards are going to ensure that this house is still standing after Hurricane Bill blows through? And that the real estate deal holds up?"

"No promises. Unfortunately, I don't have any ins with Mother Nature." He secured the board in front of the window, leaning into it with his body.

"Well, I say you need my help even if you claim you don't." She walked over and held the board against the side of the house and window.

Amusement danced in his eyes as he glanced over. "Thanks." He used his free arm to wipe the sweat off his brow, which was somehow an ultra-attractive move. "These boards will keep your windows from blowing in. If the roof blows off, then you have bigger problems."

"But I have you, so it'll all be fine." She realized how that sounded. "I mean, I have you to put the roof back on for me." She focused on holding up the board. It was heavier than it looked. "After we do this, I have a suggestion for how we spend the rest of the evening."

Travis nearly dropped the drill he was holding. There was something wild and excited in his expression, and it didn't take a detective to know where his mind had immediately gone.

"Not that." She rolled her eyes. "I want to go to Skate Nation." She kept her gaze straight, but she felt his eyes on her and imagined the deep pinch of his brow deepening. If she looked at him right now, she'd probably start laughing.

"You want to go skating?" he asked.

"Mm-hmm."

He cleared his throat. "Why?"

"Because skating is on our final bucket list, and we need to finish it before the hurricane hits." Not that skating was the final item, but the more items they checked, maybe the less bad luck there'd be. Or maybe she'd get up the nerve to jump off the Pirate's Plank between now and Hurricane Bill's landfall.

Travis licked his lips. It was a nervous tell of his. "I'm not a big fan of skating, Ly. You know that. And we'd be the oldest people there."

"Are you scared?" She couldn't contain her grin. Travis hated to be accused of being scared. Always had.

"No. Of course not." He licked his lips again. "I mean, I don't want to make a fool of myself out there. I couldn't even skate when I was a teenager."

"You'll be fine. I'll help you," she promised. She was actually looking forward to holding Travis's hand in the rink.

"When was the last time you were in a pair of skates?" he asked, still looking unsure.

"Probably when I was eighteen. But it's like riding a bike, right?" She nibbled at her lower lip. "I'm serious about finishing our list. It's important."

"I don't believe in luck, remember? I'm not superstitious."

"Well, neither am I. At least not usually. But this time . . ." She wasn't sure why, but she knew finishing the list was imperative. "This time, I guess I am."

"Because you think it'll save us from imminent disaster with this hurricane?" One corner of his mouth quirked, but there was still discomfort in his eyes. He was probably remembering that doughnut seat he had to sit on their senior year of high school.

She tilted her head. "Please. For me."

He blew out a breath. "Okay. Fine. But if I break something . . ."

"You won't," she promised. "It'll be fun."

He didn't look so sure. "For you, maybe. You always did enjoy watching me make a fool of myself."

She laughed softly, excited about their plans. Truthfully, she was mainly just excited about spending time with Travis, and yeah, maybe she would enjoy watching him take a few spills in the rink. It was the one place where he seemed vulnerable and where she excelled.

He lifted his drill again, lining it up with a screw. Then he pressed the trigger, and the sound of metal spiraling into wood silenced them. He lifted one board after another and secured one window after another. When he was done, he put away his tools and used the front of his T-shirt to wipe his face.

Lyla couldn't help noticing his abs and chest as he lifted his shirt. As he lowered his shirt, he caught her watching.

"You sure you don't want to spend the evening at my RV instead of Skate Nation?"

"Nice try, but no. I need this." Echo Cove needed this.

Chapter 24

*Opinion: The skating rink is the only acceptable
place to go around in circles.*
—Delilah Dune, opinion writer

Lyla watched as Travis struggled to get his skates on as the strobe lights danced across his complexion. "Want me to help you lace those up?" she called over the booming music that seemed to bounce off the walls along the rink.

"I haven't worn a pair of these bad boys in decades. Literal decades." He pressed back against the wall where they were sitting on wooden benches and looked at her. "Yes, I would love some help."

She squatted at his feet and proceeded to lace up his skates, pulling them snug on his foot and tying. "There," she finally said, looking up at him.

There was something indescribable in Travis's eyes. He looked like he was about to be tossed into a ring with bulls. "Thanks."

"You're welcome." She patted his knee and stood. "Are you going to be able to handle yourself out there or do you need me to hold your hand?"

He tilted his head to one side. "The problem with holding my hand is that if I wipe out, you go down with me."

"That's always been the case between us. I go, you go. You go, I go." She waited for him to get up, but he wasn't budging from the bench.

"That's not true, actually. You went when we were eighteen, and I went in the opposite direction."

She reached for his hand, wriggling her fingers. "Come on. Not this time. Step one, we go out there and get your skating legs working." Lyla skated backward, putting a couple feet of space between them so that Travis could push forward. He lost his balance a little and she braced him at the elbow. Then she began to skate backward as he skated forward, leading the way to the rink.

"Whoa, whoa, whoa," Travis said, desperately trying to maintain his balance as other skaters whizzed by.

"Relax. I got you." Skating came easy to Lyla. It always had, in the same way that jumping into a lake and swimming came easy to Travis, whereas she sank like a rock.

"Do you still come here every weekend or something?" Travis asked. "How is it that you can skate backward just as gracefully as you could when we were teens?"

"I haven't been skating since the last time I came here with you. It's not that hard."

"Says you." He stumbled again, and Lyla tightened her hold on him. After a few rounds in the rink, Travis stopped looking at his feet and glanced around. "Uh-oh."

"What?" Lyla looked around too.

"Ryan Light is here," Travis said under his breath.

Ryan had been one of the popular kids in school. Contradicting his last name, he had thick black hair that hung in his deep-set dark eyes. He'd been tall and lanky, and he'd always had a guitar strapped to his shoulder.

Lyla glanced around the rink, but there was no one in the

room that matched the mental image she had of Ryan in her mind. "Where?" she asked.

"Right there. Against the wall."

Lyla continued to search and then spotted a skate guard leaning against the rink's railing. He was tall, but much more filled out than the boy she remembered. And he was bald. Gone was the black hair hanging in his eyes. She wasn't sure she'd ever seen Ryan's face when they were younger, so he was hard to recognize.

"I think you're right. That's him," she whispered to Travis. "A thirty-year old Ryan, but Ryan nonetheless. I can't believe one of the most likely to succeed at our school is working as a skate guard."

"Success is subjective, Ly." Travis sounded like one of her opinions in her column. "Who knows. Maybe skating is his passion. Maybe he won the lottery, and this is just something he does as a hobby. Never judge a book by its cover."

Lyla narrowed her eyes at Travis. "I hate it when you're right," she teased. "You're wiser than I remember."

"And you're prettier than I remember. Though I always thought you were the prettiest girl in the room."

Lyla gave him a playful shove and then panicked when it sent Travis's feet rolling out from under him. She reached her arm forward to catch him by the shirt, but Travis was too heavy when gravity was against him. Instead, Travis clutched onto her like a drowning person, taking her down with him. Lyla fell forward, landing with a thud on top of him.

"Ow," Travis finally muttered as skaters dodged rolling over them.

Lyla lifted her head to look up at Travis, who wore a tight grimace. "Are you all right?"

"No," he bit out.

Panic shot through Lyla. "What's wrong? Where does it hurt? Show me."

"Can't do that. Not here at least. I think I broke my behind. Again," Travis muttered.

Lyla burst into laughter. Then she startled as the skate guard blew the whistle, drawing everyone in the rink's attention to Lyla and Travis.

Ryan Light skated over, blowing the whistle around his neck loudly three times. "You two okay?" he finally barked, looking down at them.

"Yes, we're fine." Lyla could see the moment he recognized them. It wasn't instant. Ten years changed a person in more ways than one.

"Only my pride is hurt," Travis moaned, rolling stiffly to one side and nearly taking out a passing skater.

Ryan reached out a hand to Lyla and pulled her up first. After Lyla, he pulled Travis to his feet, holding onto him to keep his skates from slipping out from under him again. "Don't be embarrassed. I'm impressed that you two are even out here. Most people our age stick to walking and running. Or lying on their couches."

"We're not that ancient," Lyla said, taking mild offense.

"No, but we're not teenagers anymore either." Ryan looked between them. "Wow. So you two are finally together, huh?"

Lyla pulled her lower lip between her teeth and looked at Travis. Were they? What would he say?

Travis seemed to intentionally avoid looking at Lyla. "I picked Lyla up and brought her here. So, yeah, I guess you'd call that a date."

A noncommittal answer. She wouldn't expect anything more. "I convinced Travis to give skating another try tonight," she added. "It's not really his thing."

"And he agreed?" Ryan chuckled. "He must like you a lot. A man only risks his pride when he's in love."

Travis made a choking noise beside Lyla.

She patted his back, being gentle and careful not to knock him over this time.

"I haven't forgotten that doughnut pillow thing you wore in the twelfth grade. We still laugh about it from time to time," Ryan said.

"We?" Travis echoed. Then he shook his head. "I don't want to know."

"Well, my advice is to stick closer to the guardrails," Ryan told Travis. "To catch yourself before you hit the floor next time. Your butt will thank you. Your pride too."

Travis palmed his face for a moment, but Lyla knew he was only joking. And she thought maybe he was having a good time.

"Thank you for being here," she said as Ryan skated off to blow the whistle at someone else. "I know you'd rather be at your RV."

"With you," he agreed. "I'd rather be there with you. Does this effectively check off the skating item on our bucket list?" he asked.

"I think so. But I'm not ready to leave just yet. We're just warming up." She turned to start skating backward in front of him, reaching her hands to help him roll forward. "We can go back to your RV later."

"Something to look forward to. I'd bust my butt a hundred times out here tonight just to be able to take you home later. And not because I'm eager to get you in bed. I just like being with you, Ly. I've missed it. I've missed us."

"Me too," she confessed.

"I've missed *you*."

She had to read his lips over the music, which meant she was only halfway attending to her movements. She was about to respond when she stumbled on her own skates, clutching Travis's hand.

"I've got you this time," he said.

It took a moment for her to find her balance, but she still felt like she was falling hard for the guy in front of her.

They skated quietly, finding their rhythm.

When Travis appeared more confident, Lyla cleared her throat. "Bailey said that you wrote me an email. That summer after graduation."

The tension between them seemed to pulse as they rounded the rink.

"Yeah, you already knew that. I wrote you a bunch of emails that you never responded to. Which one are you referring to?"

"There was a specific one that she found on your computer screen. One that you never sent. Bailey said she teased you mercilessly about it. She said she almost made you cry."

Travis ran his free hand over his face now. "Geez. Sisters are so brutal. Be glad you don't have one."

"I always wanted a sister." Being an only child was lonely. Having Travis's friendship was the only thing that kept her grounded growing up. It was necessary, but it also scared her once it was time to leave home. At the time, it had felt like she needed to cut the cord if she ever wanted to fly.

Opinion: Young people think they're wise, but they're really just inexperienced and a little stupid, especially when it comes to love and other lies of the heart.

They grew quiet again, skating slowly as others passed them by. Lyla could skate much faster, but she didn't want to leave Travis behind. She'd done that once before, and in hindsight, it was one of her biggest mistakes.

"How do you know I never sent that one?"

Some part of Lyla thought the past was best left behind. She had questions though. "Because Bailey told me you didn't. Why didn't you send it?"

"I wasn't sure what you'd think if I sent the email. I wasn't sure it would make any difference anyway. It would have just complicated things. I didn't want to lose you, Ly." He shrugged, something so helpless in the gesture as he looked at her. "And somehow, I still did."

"I always felt like handwritten letters were more romantic. I wrote you one."

The brown color of his eyes brightened. "Yeah? What did it say?"

She shook her head, feeling foolish and flustered. The details of that letter were intimate, and she wasn't sure she could trust Travis not to laugh. *Wow. Catching Joe cheating has really left an emotional scar—like the memory was branded on my brain.*

The morning she'd realized what was going on behind her back, she'd been standing over the stove, making scrambled eggs for breakfast. Joe's cell phone had been right beside Lyla on the counter, which was odd because he never put that thing down—ever. She remembered hearing his alert as a text message came through. Without thinking, she stepped over and glanced at the screen.

Unknown: *One day I'll get to wake up with you beside me.*

There was a winking face emoji that came through after that. Then an emoji blowing kisses.

Lyla had blinked and read the message again, trying to figure out the context. She'd reread the messages. There was only one context.

A moment later, Joe walked into the kitchen, humming as if nothing in the world was wrong. "Morning, darling," he said, with a loud, obnoxious yawn. He stepped over and wrapped an arm around her.

Lyla whirled out of his reach. "You jerk!" She picked up an egg and pitched it right at his chest. He was wearing his favorite suit that day. Egg yolk ran all down the front of his pale blue dress shirt.

Joe's arms flew out to his sides as he looked down and back up at her. "What the hell are you doing?"

"Jerk!" She grabbed another egg and threw it. This time,

he ducked. He dodged the rest of the eggs in the carton, but the initial egg remained on the front of his shirt. She hoped it had ruined it. "I know," she finally said.

He shook his head, his face flaring a hot red color. "What is it you think you know?"

"I *know-w-w-w.*"

That's when his eyes had widened. He didn't even try to lie or cover up the truth. Lyla guessed he realized it was useless. Or maybe he had wanted to be found out. Maybe that's why he'd left his phone there for her to see.

Travis squeezed her hand now, pulling her from her memories and anchoring her back in the skating rink. "Hey, you okay?"

A teenage skater zoomed past, nearly knocking her down.

She reached for the skating wall and centered herself. "I'm—I'm fine. Just lost in thought." She looked over and blinked Travis into focus. There was something about his face that calmed the noise inside her. "What about you? Feeling better on the skates?"

"I think I'm getting the hang of this. I still disagree that skating is like riding a bike." He squeezed her hand. The disco ball in the room came on and colorful lights danced around them. It felt magical and romantic. "In my email," Travis said, "I told you that you were my best friend, and that I wasn't sure I'd ever find someone quite like you again. I was right. I never have, Ly."

He was her biggest contradiction. She had been too scared to keep him and too scared to lose him as well. "I never did either."

Travis's gaze hung heavy on her. "Let's not lose each other again, okay? No matter what."

She wanted to promise, but the fear was still so strong inside her. "I changed my mind," she finally said.

Travis's brows lifted. "About what?"

"I don't want to go back to your RV."

His demeanor seemed to drop. His shoulders. His head. His eyes. "That's okay." His tone was soft and sincere. He really didn't mind putting her wants and needs before his. He was a real man. Some might say his parents had raised him right, but Lyla knew all the credit went to Travis himself.

"I don't want to return to your RV, because I want to go back to my house instead. With you." She inhaled deeply, expanding her lungs and holding her breath as she waited for Travis's response.

His answer was visible in his expression before he said a word. There was a sparkle in his eyes that said yes. "Your place it is."

Chapter 25

Opinion: Dreams do come true.
If you're willing to open your eyes.
—Delilah Dune, opinion writer

Lyla was on the edge of a sweet dream. She was half awake and half asleep, and indecisive about whether she wanted to keep snoozing or get up and face reality.

In the dream, she was with Travis. They were laughing about something. She wasn't sure what, but the vibe between them felt amazing. It felt like love, which would have terrified her if she was awake, but since this was a dream, she soaked the sensation up.

The sun came through the blinds, warming her face. She stirred and slowly started to realize she was dreaming. Then the memory that Travis was lying beside her on her childhood bed came to mind. They hadn't done anything more than kiss last night before their eyes had closed and they'd slipped off. Nothing physical had happened, but something more had.

Opening her eyes, Lyla turned to look at the space beside her. Vacant. She sat up and looked around, searching for proof that him coming home with her hadn't also been a dream. His clothes were gone. "Travis?"

The house was quiet.

Lyla sighed and got to her feet, shuffling toward the bathroom to freshen up. Afterward, she headed toward the kitchen to pour a glass of water, stopping short when the doorbell rang. Who would be on her porch this early?

She opened the door and grinned. "Hey. You weren't here when I woke?"

"I have to work today." He held up a carrier with two cups of coffee. "But first, coffee. I wanted to make sure you started your day off right."

"You are a godsend." She grabbed one of the cups, feeling the warmth soak into her skin. "Come on in."

Travis stepped inside and closed the door behind him. "I can only stay for a few minutes."

"Long enough to discuss last night," she said.

"That discussion is only for those who actually did something last night." There was a teasing element in his voice. "You were snoring before we got to first base."

Lyla laughed and lifted her cup of coffee to sip as the top popped off and hot liquid splashed the front of her sleepshirt.

"You okay?" Travis asked, following her to the kitchen sink.

She set her coffee down and pulled her damp clothing away from her body. "Yeah. Just a mess. Let me go change. Do you mind waiting?"

"Of course not." He lifted himself up onto her kitchen counter and sat there. "I've got some messages to check anyway." He pulled out his phone. "Take your time."

"Great." As Lyla pulled on a fresh shirt, her cell phone chirped from where she'd set it on her mattress. She excitedly picked it up. She knew what that sound meant. It was Friday. Her new opinion article had posted. And maybe, just maybe, this one would save her job.

"Yes!" Sure enough, there was an email in her inbox alerting her that "Delilah's Delusions" had a new article available online. All her subscribers were getting the exact same alert right now. Soon their opinions would start coming in. They would either agree or disagree with her. That was the fun part.

Lyla quickly looked over the article, reminding herself of the key points.

- The promise of forever wasn't necessary for a relationship.
- Relationships could be beneficial even if they were short-term and wouldn't amount to anything in the long run.
- Waiting on forever was a pipe dream for fools.

On one hand, she sounded bitter and resentful. On the other, she sounded like an independent woman who didn't need a man to feel whole. What would Travis think if he read this? Isn't this what guys wanted anyway? To have all the fun without the commitment? Especially a self-proclaimed nomad like Travis.

Yeah, this article would probably give him a sense of relief. It was sure to get her readers writing in. On an inhale, she left her bedroom and walked back toward the kitchen where Travis was still seated on her countertop next to the time capsule and the unfinished bucket list.

"Hey. I'm fresh, clean, and ready for company," she said brightly.

Travis looked up from his cell phone.

There was an indescribable look in his eyes. She wasn't sure she'd ever seen it before.

"Bad news? Is it the hurricane? Bailey's wedding?" Lyla hoped the weather didn't require that the wedding be postponed. Then again, that would be reason for Travis to stay in Echo Cove longer.

He looked stunned. "I was, uh, just reading the new article for 'Delilah's Delusions.' " He cleared his throat as if something was lodged there.

"Oh? What do you think?" She sensed that he hadn't liked what he'd read.

"No strings, no rings, no mess." He offered a definitive nod. "Great opinion, Ly," he said with a hint of sarcasm. He slid his phone into his front pocket. "I didn't realize what your thoughts on relationships were these days. I mean, I should have. You are the best friend who lied about keeping in touch after high school. If I was so easy to discard then, why would things be any different now? Just because we kissed doesn't mean you've transformed into someone different."

"Travis. That's just an opinion article."

"Your opinion article, Ly. They're your words and—I don't know, I guess I just needed to hear them. I needed a wake-up call, because here I was thinking that things would be different. Heck, even after we slept together you told me that nothing had changed. You told me." He laughed quietly and headed toward the front door.

"Travis, I already explained about that. I was just scared that you would get scared."

He turned back. "You were just scared. You've always been scared, Ly. That's why we started making those stupid bucket lists."

"They were for you, too," she shot back.

He shook his head. "I've always looked at fear as a challenge, and I've never regretted taking the challenge. There's only one thing I've been afraid of as an adult, and that's putting down roots. Home is not a place that represents stability for me. It's not safe." The muscles of his jaw bunched. "For the first time in my adult life, this summer, I've actually had the thought that maybe a home without wheels wouldn't be so bad."

"Travis . . ." Lyla didn't know what to say. "It's just a stupid opinion article. I'm trying to save my career."

"Why?" Travis asked.

She lowered her brows. "What do you mean, why?"

"Why are you trying to save something that isn't even you? Being some opinion writer isn't what you always dreamed of being, Ly. Why are you working so hard to be something you're not?"

"I need a job. I need to support myself financially. If my column sinks, then I'll be putting in applications at Walmart."

"At least you'd be happy. When we were young, I put items on our bucket list that I thought would push you. If I created a list for you this summer, Ly, I'd put three things on it."

Lyla folded her arms over chest. She couldn't decide if she was offended or apologetic. She needed time to process what was happening right now.

"One: Quit that 'stupid column.' Your words, not mine. Two: Write a real story. Something that makes you feel alive inside. Three: Figure out where home is. Even I know the answer to that, Ly, and I haven't stayed in one place in more than a decade."

"Travis . . ."

"I should go." He opened the door and stepped onto the porch.

She stepped out behind him. "Don't be angry."

Travis turned to look at her. "I'm not angry. I've just realized, I guess, that time changes things. It changed us. We can't go back."

Lyla's thoughts spiraled in her head, racing a hundred miles an hour.

Before she could respond, Travis jogged down the porch

steps toward his truck. He kept walking, opened the door, and stepped inside. He didn't wave. Didn't look at her. He just reversed out of her driveway and drove away.

Lyla stood there, watching the road. She considered chasing after him, but instead she stood there frozen. Her editor was happy. Her readers were inspired. Her opinion had hit a nerve with everyone, including Travis.

August 30

Dear Diary,

The hurricane has come and gone. I'm still here, but our house took a huge hit. Mom and Dad are so upset. First the busted pipes and the leak in the ceiling. Now a tree is lying in our living room.

Life is strange.

I have another disaster to look forward to as well. I'm all packed up and ready to go to college. It's almost time to say goodbye. Travis says that we won't say goodbye because we'll still see each other as much as we can. That's supposed to comfort me, but it kind of does the opposite. I'll never kiss a boy, ever, if I'm still focused on Travis. If I'm still having thoughts about him that I'm not allowed to act on.

Opinion: Sometimes goodbye is a good thing.

Lyla

Chapter 26

Opinion: All opinions are my own. I think.
—Delilah Dune, opinion writer

Lyla's phone signaled a text. She quickly snatched up her phone and read the screen, desperate for some sort of lifeline that would salvage this mess of a day.

Travis: *Tonight's wedding rehearsal is canceled due to Hurricane Bill.*

Lyla texted back quickly. She'd been trying to reach him for hours and he hadn't responded. She wanted to talk. He'd read too much into her article for "Delilah's Delusions."

Or had he? She'd meant every word. Or she'd thought she did, at least. She didn't know what to think now.

Lyla: *I hope Bailey isn't too devastated.*

She hit SEND and then waited for Travis to text something else. Maybe he would offer to get together later, or he'd apologize for getting so upset earlier. As the minutes ticked by, though, she kicked herself for texting a statement that didn't require a reply. She should have asked a question. She should have kept him talking.

She nibbled at her lower lip. Then she texted him again.

Lyla: *Are you bracing for Hurricane Bill alone?*

She didn't hit SEND. Instead, she deleted the message and waited some more, until she felt like a complete loser, hanging on a text from a guy when one obviously wasn't coming. That's exactly what she didn't want. She didn't want to need someone. Or want someone. Because then she was vulnerable.

Was Travis right? Was fear still the thing keeping her from living her life?

She set her phone down, telling herself she was done waiting for Travis. As soon as it left her hand, it chirped with a message. She practically threw out her shoulder snatching her phone back up to see what he'd said.

The text wasn't from Travis.

Allison: *Can you come over?*
Lyla: *Sure. Are you okay?*
Allison: *Not sure. I just need a friend.*

Lyla jumped to her feet, prepared to fly to Allison's house as fast as she could.

Lyla: *Be there before you know it.*

The skies were darkening as Lyla locked the front door behind her and got into her car. She sat in her driveway a moment and took in her parents' home. The windows were boarded. There was nothing to tie down because everything had been donated and carried away. Hopefully Bill wasn't the big bad hurricane everyone was expecting. If he was, Lyla's parents' dream of traveling the world would be over when it had barely gotten started.

With a sigh, Lyla reversed out of the driveway and headed toward Allison's neighborhood. When she pulled up in Allison's driveway, she noticed that nothing was tied down on her porch. The beautiful wreath was still on Allison's door. The windows weren't boarded either.

The front door opened before Lyla even had a chance to knock.

Lyla was momentarily taken aback when she saw her friend.

Allison's hair was uncombed. She wasn't wearing makeup. There were dark half-moons under her bloodshot eyes. "Hey."

A small smile fluttered on Allison's lips, but it didn't reach her eyes. It was the mask that Lyla recognized her friend always had on. Even in high school before the loss of her children, Allison had worn a mask. Maybe everyone did back then.

"Hey." Lyla stepped inside. She was afraid to ask the question on her mind. "Did you, um, did you take the test?"

The blood drained from Allison's complexion, making her even paler than normal.

Oh, no. Lyla watched as Allison visibly tried to hold herself together. Allison's chin quivered and tears welled in her eyes as she stood there hugging her arms around herself. She looked lost. Alone. Allison wasn't alone though. Lyla was here. "It's okay. Whatever it is, it'll be okay," Lyla promised, wrapping an arm around Allison's shoulders. "I'm here for you."

Allison melted in Lyla's embrace as a guttural sound erupted from her throat.

Lyla wasn't accustomed to playing the role of the caring friend. She'd spent her adult life selfishly looking after her own needs. She wasn't a bad person. She just wasn't a person who'd understood the value in letting others in.

Lyla held Allison for long minutes as Allison's body shook violently. Slowly, Allison began to settle down.

"I'm s-sorry," Allison finally whispered. She stepped back and wiped her ruddy cheeks with shaking hands. "I took the test," Allison confirmed, voice cracking.

Lyla took Allison's hands and led her over to the couch in the living room. They sat and Lyla let Allison take her time.

"I took the test," Allison said again, "and it was . . . it was negative." The tears rushed back to Allison's eyes, and her head fell forward into her hands.

"Isn't that what you wanted, though?" Lyla put a hand on

her friend's back and rubbed gently. "You said you didn't want to be pregnant right now."

"I didn't," Allison's voice squeaked out. "I didn't think I did. But some part of me . . ." She struggled to pull in a breath. "I don't know. I miss my kids so much that it hurts. It hurts so damn much."

Lyla wasn't sure she'd ever heard her friend curse.

"I don't want to be alone anymore, Lyla," Allison said, with a sniffle. "I started imagining this baby that doesn't even exist and it—I don't know, it filled this void that has been . . . been suffocating me for years." She looked at Lyla through tear-soaked eyes. "I started to fantasize that maybe there was a baby. I wanted it to be real, and now I'm even more alone than ever."

Lyla continued to rub Allison's back. "No, you're not. I'm here. You have family and friends, and people who love you."

"Thank you for saying that." Allison's lips trembled. "I'll be okay," she finally said, swiping below her nose. "I just needed someone here tonight. I thought I might go crazy for a moment."

"Want me to make you some hot tea?"

Allison nodded and wiped at her eyes. "That would be great."

Lyla stood, eager to do something, anything, to make her friend feel better. As she walked toward the kitchen, her gaze caught on the photographs of Allison's late children. It was easy to forget all that Allison had been through since high school, because she was such a cheerful person. Allison was typically smiling. She was bubbly, even. But internally, there was an invisible storm brewing, as big and monstrous as the one outside. Lyla couldn't fathom how Allison had even made it through one day since her children's passing. She was so brave. She was the strongest person Lyla had ever met.

Lyla realized that she'd frozen in place and was staring at the photographs.

Allison came up behind her. "This is why my friends have all shied away from me. It's too much for them. *I'm* too much. I try to be okay, but sometimes I just can't."

Lyla turned to look at her.

"I know they're still my friends," Allison continued, "and they want to be there for me. I just—Sometimes I just make them uncomfortable, like you are right now."

"I'm not uncomfortable, Allison." Lyla wiped at her own tearstained cheeks. "And you're not too much. You're amazing, and I owe you a tea."

"I'll make it. I'm actually feeling better." Allison walked past her into the kitchen. "Truly, I don't want to be pregnant. I gained fifty pounds with both of those children." She laughed under her breath. "I have stretch marks to prove it."

Lyla stepped up to the counter. "If I'm being honest, I don't know if I'll ever have children. I'm not sure I want to."

Allison glanced over as she grabbed two mugs from her cabinet. "Why is that?"

Lyla watched as Allison squirted honey into the mugs and added the tea bags. "Maybe I'm not cut out for being a parent. I can barely take care of myself some days."

Allison narrowed her eyes. "I'm not one of those people who ever judged a woman for not wanting children. It's her choice."

Lyla nodded. "Anyway, neither of us are expecting a child right now. Maybe we should have wine instead of tea."

Allison's eyes lit up. "You are a genius. Great idea."

The doorbell rang and both of them looked at each other.

"Are you expecting anyone?" Lyla asked.

Allison shook her head. "No. It's a weird time to visit. We're about to have a hurricane. Everyone should be tucked away inside their homes."

The doorbell rang again.

Allison swiped at her eyes again, as if trying to wipe off

imaginary mascara smudges. When she got to the door, she peeked out the peephole and gasped.

"What? Who is it?" Lyla whisper-yelled.

"It's Travis," Allison whisper-yelled back.

"Travis?" Lyla's spine stiffened. "What does he want?"

Allison rolled her eyes. "How would I know? I haven't answered the door yet. Want me to tell him you're not here?"

Lyla narrowed her eyes and then they both started laughing. "And you haven't even had wine yet. My car's right out front. And who's to say he's here for me? It's your house." Lyla wanted to run and hide, but she stayed frozen just like she had when she'd stared at the photographs of Allison's children a few minutes earlier. "Open it."

Allison nodded. Then she reached for the door knob and pulled the door open. "Travis. What a surprise."

"Hey, Al." Travis was wearing his tool belt. "I'm making a few rounds through town and helping folks get their homes ready for the hurricane. I was thinking you might need help too."

"Oh, wow. That's so nice of you." Allison turned to look at Lyla. "Isn't that sweet, Lyla?"

Travis didn't look at her. He'd been ignoring her since this morning, and he was still ignoring her.

"That's thoughtful of you," Lyla said.

"It is," Allison agreed. "Thank you, Travis. I would love your help. I should have done the work myself. I could at least turn my rocking chairs upside down. I'll go do that."

He held up a hand. "You stay in and visit with your friend."

Your friend? He wouldn't even say Lyla's name. This wasn't fair. She hadn't even done anything wrong. Not *too* wrong, at least.

"I'll handle everything. It won't take long. Do you want me to board your windows?" he asked.

"You have extra wood?" Allison asked.

"I have everything." His gaze finally flicked to Lyla.

She froze. Should she wave? Mouth a hello?

He didn't give her time. Turning his back to them, he got to work securing Allison's porch furniture.

Allison stepped outside to talk to him for a minute longer, while Lyla stayed seated on the couch. She felt an emotion she couldn't quite place. Like she'd lost Travis when she hadn't even had him. She'd always known their situation was temporary, that whatever was going on between them would be over after she left town, which was probably next week. She hadn't expected to lose him before it was time, though, and she hadn't expected that he would walk away because of something she'd done. Or written. She felt like she'd betrayed him somehow, but that didn't make sense. It also felt like she'd betrayed herself.

Allison stepped back into the house. "Want to fill me in on what happened between you two?"

Lyla wasn't even sure what had happened herself. "I guess it's like with you and TJ. Not all relationships are meant to last forever."

Allison looked down at her hands. "Maybe not, but I still believe in forever. And if I can believe, so can you." She looked back up at Lyla. "I wouldn't be a good friend if I didn't say that to you."

It took a moment for Lyla to process why that opinion rang familiar. "You read my article too?"

"Of course, I did. I'm your friend." She grimaced. "Your column had bitter-woman-who'd-recently-been-dumped written all over it."

"Maybe that's who I am now," Lyla muttered. "A bitter thirty-year-old woman whose career is washed up."

Allison walked over to the counter where Lyla was standing. "Who you are now is who you've always been. The only problem was you might have forgotten who you were for a millisecond. I realized, after quite a bit of therapy following the accident and my divorce, that I didn't know who I was anymore. Somewhere along the way, I became someone's wife and someone's mother. When I lost those roles, I realized that I had just disappeared somewhere in the mundane, everyday things. Maybe you should see the therapist that I go to. Dr. Allmer. She's amazing." Allison offered a sheepish look. "Of course, she's here and you aren't staying, so . . ."

Lyla had never been to a therapist before, but she knew her mother had and it had helped a great deal. "I could find someone wherever I go. Or maybe do something virtually."

"Perhaps."

Lyla cleared her throat, not wanting to think about this anymore tonight.

"Right now," Allison said, "all we need is wine." She crossed the room to where she had a small rack on the far counter. "Red or white?" she asked.

Lyla's mind was on other things, like the sound of a hammer tapping nails into place on the front porch. "Red," she said, not actually caring. What she really wanted was to step outside and talk to Travis, but she was so confused right now, she wasn't sure she'd make things any better.

"Red, it is. We'll have to limit it to one glass unless you plan on staying the night." Allison lifted a brow. "I have a guest room. Hurricane party tonight?"

"I've never had a hurricane party before."

"The funny thing is," Allison said, "I had originally planned another Dinnerware Party tonight. Hurricane Bill had other plans, though. Leave it to a man to ruin everything."

Lyla laughed. "Who's the bitter one now?"

Allison struggled as she attempted to pop the cork off the wine. "I said my therapist had helped. I didn't say she'd completely fixed me."

Lyla walked over to help her with the cork. "Fixing implies you're broken. If you were broken, though, you wouldn't have befriended me this summer. You would be too wrapped up in your inner storm to be here braving this real-life one with me."

"I wouldn't?" Allison asked, with a sincere tone.

The cork came loose from the bottle with a loud pop. "You're making friends, dating again, and living your life. You are an inspiration, in my opinion." Lyla gave her a long look. "And my opinion is a nationally acclaimed one. Also, I'm glad we've gotten closer this summer."

Allison grinned. "Ditto. You know, we could check off one of those bucket list items of yours. Maybe work on saving the world while we drink."

"What are you talking about?" Lyla asked.

"I found my old Blu-Ray player and my collection of Blu-Ray movies, to include *Sleepless in Seattle*. We can watch it tonight. Maybe there's still time to fully check that item off."

"Wow, Blu-Rays. I haven't heard that term in a while. Those were a big deal back in the day." Lyla took in the giddy expression on Allison's face, all because she was happy to be doing something to help Lyla. She was a true friend—the kind that Lyla wanted to be for others going forward.

"What do you say?" Allison pressed.

"I say yes. One thousand percent. I'd love to watch *Sleepless in Seattle* with you."

Allison was a lightweight. After two and a half glasses, she was drooling on the arm of her couch as *Sleepless in Seattle* played on the screen in front of them. The wind howled outside. Lyla was glad that she wasn't at her parents' house alone. There was nothing she could do to keep it from blowing away, anyway. The only thing she could have possibly done to stop this storm was finish the bucket list. Yes, she had watched *Sleepless in Seattle* a fourth time, but she still hadn't jumped off the Pirate's Plank. Would it have changed things? Maybe. Maybe not. She guessed she'd never know.

The summer of Hurricane Billy, she and her parents had huddled in the bathroom all night as the wind shook their humble home. She remembered hearing the crack of the tree in the front yard right before it came crashing through their living room ceiling. Lyla's mom had cried hysterically over the next half hour. Her father had just sat there holding Lyla with wide, frightened eyes. It was rare that Lyla had ever seen her father afraid. He was fearless. Why hadn't she inherited that trait instead of his early graying hair and propensity for talking too much when he was nervous?

The night of Hurricane Billy had been the longest night of Lyla's life. The way her parents were acting, she'd thought they'd surely die before the sun came up.

They hadn't been able to stay in their home again for two months after that night. Instead, they'd lived with Lyla's grandparents, while a construction crew repaired the roof. It had been an end to a summer that Lyla never wanted to revisit. Yet here she was feeling a wave of déjà vu, along with a small headache from the red wine that she and Allison had consumed in the night.

Lyla glanced over at Allison. It was amazing that she slept through this storm. The high winds sounded like a freight train coming down the road. The lights flickered on and off, on and off. The movie stopped streaming. It was almost over, so hopefully that was enough to check off the bucket list.

Unable to resist, Lyla picked up her cell phone and texted Travis.

Lyla: *You okay?*

He was in an RV, after all. That wasn't the ideal place to ride out a hurricane.

Travis: *Fine. Staying with Bailey. You?*
Lyla: *I'm still with Allison.*

She rolled her lips together, wondering if she should try to keep the conversation going.

Lyla: *I hope Bailey is okay. Canceling the wedding has got to be devastating.*

Travis: *Not canceled. Just postponed.*

Lyla: *Right.*

Travis: *She's okay.*

Lyla: Good. *I watched Sleepless in Seattle for the 4th time. Maybe that buys us some luck.*

She stared at her phone, willing Travis to make an effort. Her phone remained silent though.

Allison snorted and rolled over on the couch, her lips slightly parted.

Lyla was scared. She wished she had someone to talk to right now, to soothe her worries. Instead, she was left to soothe herself. She was tired of doing things on her own, though.

She pulled up her cell phone and tapped the app that took her straight to "Delilah's Delusions." Below her recent column, she hit the REPLY link and posted a response to her latest opinion. It posted in her real name.

I disagree. Without roots, any storm can come along and blow you away. Relationships keep you grounded. They're vital. Your opinion is immature and selfish. I hope you grow up one day.

Lyla blinked back tears and hit POST.

Opinion: A house divided cannot stand. Neither can a person.

Chapter 27

Opinion: Stories that begin with "It was a dark and stormy night" rarely have happy endings.
—Delilah Dune, opinion writer

When the sun came up, Lyla was still seated and wide awake on Allison's couch. The wind had died down outside as the night wore on. Now it was morning and Lyla needed to check on her parents' home and see if it had made it through nature's turmoil. What were the odds that the house would have been hit by a hurricane twice in its lifetime?

Lyla reached out and gently grabbed Allison's foot. She shook it back and forth. "Hey. Hey, Allison?"

Allison stirred and snorted before opening her eyes and blinking sleepily at Lyla. "What's going on? Is the storm over?"

"The storm is over," she confirmed.

Allison's yard had an array of sticks and pine straw, and one of the neighbor's chairs had blown over onto her property. There were no fallen trees and no major damage that Lyla could see.

She turned back to Allison, who was now sitting up on the couch and stretching her arms overhead. "I need to get back to my parents' house and see how it looks."

Allison nodded and stood. "Want me to make you a cup of coffee first? It won't take long."

Lyla waved her off. "I can make it. You stay there. Do you mind if I borrow one of your to-go cups?"

"As long as you bring it back," Allison teased.

"It's not like I have a coffeemaker to fill it back up at my parents' house, anyway." Although if she stayed in Echo Cove much longer, she was going to have to go back to that thrift store and see if they did have one she could purchase.

Lyla went through the motions of making herself a cup of coffee and pouring it into a to-go cup. "I'll call you later," she said on her way out the door. Lyla climbed into her little car and nervously drove down the streets that led to her childhood home. She had to navigate slowly because there was debris in the roads.

As she drove, she looked at all the houses. There were a few with major damage. Trees had cracked in half and one had fallen on someone's truck. *Yikes.* Someone's roof appeared to have caved in on one side. There were shingles missing and some had blown into the street.

Could she have prevented this by jumping off the Pirate's Plank? The thought sounded ridiculous in her mind, but some part of her still believed it might be true.

As Lyla turned onto Briar Lilly Road, she held her breath. She remembered all the damage that had happened to her parents' house during Hurricane Billy, when she was in high school. It had taken a lot of time and money to get her parents' home looking the way it had before the storm. Slowing the car, she turned the corner and then her eyes quickly jumped to the yellow house where she had grown up. It took a moment to process what was different.

"Oh, no." She sucked in a quick breath and pulled her hand to her chest. The garage had a giant tree lying on top of it. It was ruined. The house wouldn't sell with a tree lying on it. Tears sprang to her eyes as she pulled into the driveway and cut the engine. She opened the driver side door and got out. Then she walked around the house toward the backyard and let herself inside the fence, noticing that a couple of the wooden panels were on the ground. The tree that had fallen was the big cypress tree that she had buried the time capsule underneath. It had come completely out of the ground, roots and all.

Lyla had no idea what to do right now. Time felt like it was at a standstill.

"I think it's just the garage that got damaged," Ms. Hadley called over the fence. "It could have been much worse."

Lyla turned and looked at her neighbor, too stunned to speak.

"I heard the noise when it came down," Ms. Hadley continued. "At first, I thought it hit my own house. It'll be a lot of work to get that tree pulled off and your garage rebuilt. I hope this doesn't ruin your parents' trip."

Her parents' trip. Oh, no. "You haven't told my parents about this, have you?"

Ms. Hadley shook her head. "I figured you'd want to be the one to break it to them."

Lyla absolutely did not want to break this news to her parents. The last time they'd tried to take a vacation together had been ruined. If they came home to tend this house, they might never leave again. They might miss out on the trip they'd been planning for more than a decade. "Please don't tell my parents, Ms. Hadley. I'll handle this on my own."

Ms. Hadley seemed to inspect Lyla for a long moment. "You're a good daughter," the woman finally said. "If you need any recommendations for construction workers and roofers, I know a few. I'll help you in any way I can."

Wow. What a lot of good a bag of treats from Bean Time could do.

"Thank you." Lyla continued to walk around the house, finding that the main damage was to the garage. She could at least continue to live here while the repairs were being worked on. That was a small blessing.

Finally, she walked inside and looked around the empty home. It hadn't bothered her so much that the house was empty when she was only planning to stay a couple weeks. But now that she was looking at more like a month, possibly more, she wanted a real chair to sit in. And a coffeemaker too.

Lyla sat in the middle of the floor, tears springing to her eyes. "Okay. Okay. This has happened, and I'm going to deal with it," she said to herself.

Opinion: Things are bad when you start pep-talking yourself.

"It's okay. Everything is okay. I'll just be staying a little longer," she told herself. Because the buyer was most certainly backing out on their offer. The deal was definitely off.

The next morning, Lyla walked into Bean Time Coffee and headed straight up to the counter.

Instead of her usual coldness, Bernadette tilted her head, something warm in her eyes. "I heard about your parents' place."

Lyla forgot that everyone knew everyone's business in Echo Cove. Her parents' home wasn't the most damaged, but it was in the top five. She'd already been stopped several times by people offering to help.

"If you need anything, let me know," Bernadette said, further surprising Lyla.

"Thanks. But honestly, the best you can do for me right now is a coffee and bagel. With extra cream cheese."

"Of course." Bernadette set to preparing those two things. When Lyla offered her debit card a moment later, Bernadette waved it away. "I'm just about to go on break. Can I join you?"

Lyla was pretty sure her expression at that request was priceless.

Bernadette looked serious, though. "Do you mind?"

"Um, not at all. Please do."

Bernadette nodded. "Find yourself a seat and I'll be over after I warm up my muffin."

Lyla collected her coffee and bagel, and found the same table she'd used the other day. It was as if it was waiting for her. Her table.

Careful, Lyla. Creating a hangout with a table just for her might lead to making Echo Cove her home again. Maybe she wouldn't mind that so much, though. She had a friend here, after all. Maybe two after this breakfast with Bernadette. She'd also made friends with Ms. Hadley—kind of. She was beginning to like her own opinion more than her alter ego, Delilah's.

Opinion: True success was measured by how many friends showed up when you were down.
Opinion #2: True success is measured by how many friends you show up for in life.

A minute later, Bernadette sat down and looked at her. "Listen, I'm sorry for being so cold to you."

Lyla tried not to choke as she sipped her coffee. It was so weird that the people who hated you, who treated you poorly, felt guilty after something tragic happened. Not that a tree falling on her parent's garage fell in the tragic category. "It's okay. I'm sorry for not telling you there was sloppy joe on your pants before you got up in front of the class for your oral report."

Bernadette pulled the top of her muffin off. "That was hilarious. I wouldn't have told me either." She chuckled. "That's not why I was mean to you."

Lyla raised a brow. "It's not?"

Bernadette rolled her eyes. "That was high school nonsense, Lyla. I wouldn't hold a grudge about something so trivial. The reason I didn't like you when you came back to Echo Cove was because of the article you wrote about me."

Lyla blinked. "When did I write an article about you?"

Bernadette chewed her bite of muffin. "Not me, specifically. It was about all of us here in Echo Cove." She tilted her head and narrowed her eyes. Then she made air quotes with her fingers. "Opinion: People who never leave their small hometowns are destined to be small-minded."

The bite of bagel Lyla had just bitten off lodged in her suddenly tight throat. She pounded a hand against her chest and swallowed hard. That had been her very first opinion article for "Delilah's Delusions," and it had caused quite the reader response. It was an unpopular opinion that she'd truly believed at that time. "You took it personally?"

"It was personal. I chose to stay in my small hometown. Most of us did. The fact that you left doesn't make you any better than me."

Lyla hated that she'd hurt Bernie's feelings. "I know that now. In fact, I admire you. You've created something amazing here. I'm the one who went out looking for success. Now I'm back here with nothing to show."

"Nothing to show? You're a household name. A celebrity."

"A celebrity who is about to be unemployed, who has no home, no love life, and who had no friends to speak of until a couple weeks ago."

After a beat, Bernadette responded quietly. "I guess some part of me took what you wrote personally, because deep down, I was afraid you were right."

"I wasn't. I was the small-minded one. And I'm sorry."

Bernadette looked at her for a long moment as if weighing her thoughts and feelings.

There was nothing insincere about Bernadette. No pretenses. Lyla admired that quality.

"Apology accepted."

"Thank you." Lyla brought her cup to her mouth and took a sip of coffee. "So what else is going on in your life? Are you and Eric ever going to tie the knot for real?"

Bernadette rolled her eyes. "Not if I have a say. I'm happy where I'm at. Why change things if they're working for you?"

Lyla nodded. "I'm planning to make a whole lot of changes, I think. Maybe just one at a time though."

"Is Travis one of those changes?" Bernadette raised a brow. "A romantic relationship, maybe?"

Lyla wasn't sure she and Bernie were friendly enough to discuss romance. Not yet. "Travis and I are just friends," she said honestly. It was the truth, even if she wanted more. She was still being small-minded, but it was out of a need for self-preservation. It was out of fear. "Or maybe we're not even friends anymore. We kind of got into a fight."

Bernadette popped a piece of muffin into her mouth. "About your latest opinion?" she asked knowingly.

"He told you?"

"I haven't seen him. I read the column, though. If Eric wrote something like that, I'd probably pour castor oil in his coffee. Sloppy joe pants for real."

Lyla's mouth fell open. Then she burst into laughter. Bernie laughed too.

When the laughter died, Lyla looked at her own cup of coffee and gave Bernie a suspicious look. "Is this cup of coffee going to keep me in the bathroom all night?"

"No. I would never do that. In all seriousness, that opinion would hurt if I was the guy who was falling for you right now." She cupped a hand along one side of her mouth as if sharing a secret. "And guys are a lot more sensitive than we given them credit for."

Lyla liked the lighter side of Bernadette. "Maybe you should take over my opinion column."

"Running this coffee shop is akin to having a gossip column, as it is. I hear Allison is seeing my ex, TJ," Bernadette went on, lowering her hand back to the table and leaning back in her chair.

Lyla blinked. "I thought that was a secret."

"In this town? Please." Bernadette popped a piece of muffin into her mouth and chewed. "I just hope he doesn't do Allison the way he did me. Allison has been through enough. She deserves better. And so did I." Bernie notched up her chin. "That's why I dumped TJ and found Eric."

"Wow. The more I get to know you, the more I respect you."

"We should be friends." Bernie lifted her cup of coffee to the middle of the table. "Let's make a toast."

Lyla lifted her cup too. "To what?"

"To the small-minded losers who we're better off without."

Lyla tapped her cup against Bernadette's. "I can definitely toast to that."

When Lyla got home, she started making calls to all the nearby construction crews and handymen. There were repairs that needed handling and they needed taking care of ASAP. She was under no illusion that the house would be back to new today or tomorrow, though.

She stepped onto the back porch, a small lump growing in her throat as she looked at the old cypress tree lying on the back side of the garage. That tree had weathered so much, but this final storm had been its undoing.

Rest in peace, tree.

Her phone buzzed in her pocket. She pulled it out and saw her mom's name on the screen. Immediately she knew that someone had called her parents and let them know what had taken place. Maybe not Ms. Hadley, because she'd promised not to, but another person in Echo Cove had reached out.

"Hi, Mom." Lyla leaned against the deck's railing.

"Oh, honey. Why didn't you tell me what happened? How awful. Were you hurt in the storm?"

"No, Mom. I'm fine. I wasn't even home." *Home*. The word resonated through her. "At your house. I was staying with Allison."

"Allison? For a Dinnerware Party?" her mother asked.

"No, for fun. Or friendship." And support.

"I was told the house is bad. I'm so sorry. Your father and I have discussed this, and we've decided we're going to change our plans and turn back. We're coming home."

"No!" Lyla said automatically. "You don't need to do that."

"Well, the house has to be fixed. It won't sell with a tree in the middle of the garage." Her mother laughed quietly. It wasn't the kind of laugh that came with humor. More the inappropriate kind that happened at a wake when a loved one was lying in a box at the front of a room and people stood around chatting and laughing when the mood was solemn.

Okay, that was a morbid thought.

"I'll stay," Lyla told her mom. "I've thought it through. I'll hire the repair crew. I'll get it all done."

"You don't want to do that," her mom said. "You've already put your life on hold for the last few weeks for us. You're young. You should be out living your life."

Lyla thought about that. The funny thing was, while her life was supposedly on hold, she'd done more living than she had in years. "I want to stay, Mom."

"Is this about your friend Travis? Is that why you're trying to stay?"

"No. He's not even in the picture anymore. We had a fight."

"You broke up?" her mom asked.

"Mom, we weren't dating," Lyla said, but that was a bit of a lie. If you were kissing and spending the night together, you were dating. Then again, if she and Travis were dating, she wouldn't have written an article saying that basically it was better not get attached to someone. "Stay on your trip. I want to do this, and I'm not taking no for an answer," Lyla said.

There was silence on the other line.

"Mom?" Lyla asked finally, wondering if her mom had disconnected the call.

"You have really grown up, haven't you?"

"I don't know." Lyla watched a tiny firefly light up and go dark. It lit up again and again.

"Young people are self-involved a lot of times. That's not a bad thing. That's how it should be. That's how you need to be sometimes to make your dreams come true. You've already achieved so much, though, and now you're taking care of those around you too."

"I haven't achieved anything," Lyla said.

"You're famous. People know you around the world."

"They know Delilah. I'm Lyla," she said, watching the tiny firefly. "No one knows Lyla Dune."

"Well, maybe they should, because the Lyla Dune that is my daughter is one of the best people I know."

Lyla was surprised that her eyes suddenly stung. "Your and Dad's opinions are the only ones that matter. Thanks, Mom."

"Thank you. And let me know if there's anything I can do to help you from across the globe."

Lyla laughed. This was the real laugh. The humorous kind. The laugh that sourced itself from joy. "I will." Her phone dinged, signaling that she'd gotten an email. She glanced at the screen and saw that it was from her editor, Bob. "Mom, I need to go. I'll talk to you later, all right?"

"Sure. Love you, Lyla."

"Love you too." When Lyla disconnected the call, she opened her inbox and the email from Bob.

Lyla, Lyla, Lyla. What a hit that last article was! It's generated hundreds of responses already. You're back

to being a star. Keep it up, kid, and have your next
opinion to me by next Wednesday.
   Bob

Lyla guessed she was supposed to feel a sense of pride or happiness that her opinion had pleased Bob. That same opinion had hurt Travis, though. Maybe that was the beauty of her column. It either hurt people or resonated with them, and either way, that generated engagement.

But this time, she'd hurt someone she loved. She'd also hurt herself in the process.

Chapter 28

Opinion: The storms of life stir up
all the junk that needs getting rid of anyway.
—Lyla Dune, aspiring author

A few days later, Lyla angled from left to right in front of the bathroom mirror. She was wearing the beautiful yellow dress that Allison had picked out for her during their shopping trip. It was sleeveless and had a scalloped neckline that dipped low enough to showcase the pearl necklace she wore. The material hugged her curves perfectly. It wasn't tight, but it didn't flow either. Allison was right about this dress being sexy. Not too sexy for a wedding. It still followed the unwritten rule that a woman should never turn heads more than the bride.

Bailey was getting married today. Unlike the summer after Lyla's high school graduation, when the storm had blown through and delayed Bailey's wedding plans, this summer's wedding was still taking place. Bailey's first wedding wasn't meant to be. This one, this summer, was.

When Lyla had purchased this dress, it was to wear as Travis's date. He was barely talking to her now. Her opinion article had hit him hard, and he was shut down to any romantic possibilities or even friendship. His texts had been brief.

I'm going alone . . . I don't need a date . . . Bailey still wants you to attend . . . See you there.

Lyla worked to push down the hurt feelings that rose from her gut to her chest and made lumps in her throat. She wasn't going alone today, though. Allison was going with her. Maybe this was for the best. She didn't want to hurt Travis any more than she already had. She had no plans to stay in Echo Cove indefinitely, and neither did he. In fact, as far as she knew, Travis was leaving right after Bailey's wedding today. Lyla couldn't. She was staying to handle the repairs on the house.

The doorbell rang. Allison was right on time, as usual.

When Lyla opened the door, Allison waved and then did a spin on the front porch showing off her dress.

"Wow. You look amazing." It wasn't a lie. Allison was every bit as beautiful as she'd been in high school. Maybe more so.

"So do you." Allison gave Lyla a once over. "You're a knock-out, actually. Are you trying to snag one of the groomsmen?"

"Definitely not. I am happily single and happily attending this wedding alongside one of my best friends."

Allison's lips parted. "Me? I'm one of your best friends?"

"Of course." Lyla grabbed her purse off the table nearby the door and locked the door behind her. "Ready to go to a wedding?"

Allison nodded and took her time walking down the steps. "I'm awful in heels. You would think all those beauty pageants my mother put me in growing up would've have made me good at heels, but no."

"That's why I'm wearing flats." Lyla gestured to her own feet. "Plus, my broken toe is still on the mend."

They got into Allison's little car and pulled out of the driveway.

"I hope TJ isn't there," Allison said as she drove.

"What if he is? What if he asks you to dance?" Lyla asked.

Allison pulled her lower lip between her teeth. "I don't think I'm ready. When I thought I might be pregnant, that was a huge wake-up call for me." She glanced over. "I want love and another family one day. Maybe even a year from now. I need to do some more work on myself first."

Lyla reached over and squeezed Allison's forearm. "I need to work on myself too. Maybe I'll get the contact info for your therapist, since I'm staying in town a little longer." Maybe a lot longer, but she wasn't ready to share that yet. It wasn't written in stone. Nothing was, right now. "I'm proud of you, you know."

"For what?" Allison asked.

There were so many reasons. Lyla would be here all day if she listed them all. People changed and evolved out of what happened to them. Sometimes those changes weren't for the best, but Allison could make lemonade out of anything. Out of nearly nothing. "For being who you are, despite what's happened to you."

Allison's face lit up at the compliment. "I could say the same for you. Look at us. Who would have thought we'd turn into best friends?"

Lyla blew out a breath. "Not me. No offense, but I didn't think we had anything in common. Maybe we didn't back then, but we do now."

"We have wine in common," Allison agreed. "And we have the town of Echo Cove and a thousand disappointments. A few successes too." She drove in silence for a moment. "Our class reunion is coming up in the fall. Do you want to go with me?"

Lyla felt herself grimace at the very thought.

Opinion: Class reunions are a bunch of people wearing fake smiles and pretending they've turned out a lot better than is true.

"Oh, come on, Ly," Allison prodded. "It'll be fun. I'm trying to talk Bernadette into going too. We can be a terrific trio."

"Maybe." Lyla looked out the window. Her answer wasn't a solid no. In fact, even though it sounded like a miserable time, being with Allison and Bernadette sounded fun. Who was she these days?

"Great. We can shop for dresses again. I'll pick out yours, and you'll pick out mine," Allison said, as if Lyla had given her a definite yes.

Lyla laughed. As they pulled up to the little church on the waterfront, nerves took over once again. Travis would be inside. At some point, they'd probably have to talk.

"What if Travis asks you to dance?" Allison asked. "Would you say yes?"

Lyla looked down at her interwoven hands in her lap. "I'm not ready either." Except her reason for not being ready was different from Allison's. She wasn't ready to be so close to Travis that she could lean in and kiss him, but know that it wouldn't happen. She'd hurt him. She wasn't ready to feel the rejection that he would no doubt give her—and she deserved nothing less.

The church was filled to the brim with people and noise. Lyla and Allison slid into the back pew of the church and chatted with folks as they stepped up to give them hugs. Allison was a social butterfly as always. She was gracious, and she complimented each woman she spoke to as if she was the most beautiful woman in the room. And none of it was insincere. Allison Wilkerson didn't have a fake bone in her body.

"This is the church that we held my son and daughter's funerals at," Allison whispered as the church grew quieter in anticipation of the Wedding March.

Lyla reached for Allison's hand. "You okay?"

Allison nodded. "Better than okay. Some part of me thinks that they're watching over me. Maybe they sent me you."

Lyla narrowed her eyes. "Actually, my mom sent me you. I'll have to thank her for that."

The wedding party entered the church. First the groom's party walked down the aisle all the way to the front. Then the bride's party followed, taking their place on the other side of the podium. Finally, "Here Comes the Bride" began to play. Everyone in the pews turned to watch the bride escorted by the best man. Since Bailey's father was no longer alive, Travis was giving her away. He wore a black suit, and he looked so grown up. He was a man these days, and Lyla loved him. She'd known she was falling for him, but now she realized that she was already there. She was fully in love with her childhood friend. The one she'd done countless pranks with and on. The one she'd ridden bikes with all over town and made yearly summer bucket lists with.

"You're staring at him," Allison said, leaning over and whispering.

Lyla blinked and looked down at her lap. "I probably shouldn't have come today." This was torture.

"Or maybe you need to ask him to dance later," Allison suggested.

As soon as the wedding was over and Bailey and her new husband had said, "I do," Lyla got up and headed out of the church.

"Ly! Ly, wait up." Allison jogged over in her heels, nearly stumbling. "Aren't we staying for the reception?"

"You can if you want," Lyla said. "I can call an Uber or something. I need to go home."

"If you really want to leave, I'll drive you." Allison folded her arms over her chest and glanced toward the large metal building beside the church where everyone was going to celebrate the new marriage. "But I think you'll regret leaving without seeing him."

All in a rush, Lyla said, "He's upset with me. He's barely

responding to my texts, and he's not answering my calls. He doesn't want to see me."

"So, if you go now, he'll know it's because of him. He'll know that you gave up and—like it or not, true or false—it'll be on you."

Lyla blinked her friend into focus. "Me?" She thought about it for a moment.

"You messed up. It's your mess to fix, not his."

"Well, he's not making it very easy," Lyla said. "Or even possible."

Allison tipped her head toward the venue. "Let's go in there, have some finger foods and congratulate Bailey. You can say hi to Travis and be finished. The ball is then in his court to snatch or drop."

Lyla twisted her mouth to one side as she debated. "Fine. Fine. But I know you're only vying for us to go in so you can get a cupcake."

They both burst into laughter.

"I need one too," Lyla admitted. "Let's go."

They changed directions and walked toward the metal building. Everyone else was already inside. There were so many people that it was hard to navigate in the room. Everyone in town must have come to this wedding. Lyla was happy for Bailey. She deserved a lifetime of love and happiness. Her parents had turned their backs on her, but the town hadn't. Echo Cove was small but strong in its support of those it loved.

Lyla found herself looking for Travis as Allison led her through the cliques of people, stopping every now and then to hug someone's neck. He was nowhere to be found.

"Lyla! Allison!" Bailey hurried over to them and hugged them both, her white veil clinging to Lyla's hair momentarily.

"Oops." Nothing could bring Bailey's mood down today. She was visibly lit up with joy. "Thank you so much for coming! It means so much to me to have you both here."

"Of course. We wouldn't miss it." Allison glanced at Lyla and then back at Bailey. "Where's your brother?"

Lyla wanted to bury her face in her hands out of embarrassment. It was obvious that Allison was asking on her behalf.

Bailey's smile faded. "He could only stay long enough to walk me down the aisle, which I appreciate. He left already."

"*Left?*" The word punched Lyla in the gut. "What? Why?"

"He had a job. My wedding was delayed, so he should have already left by now. He postponed as long as he could, but now he's gone." Bailey narrowed her eyes at Lyla. "He didn't say goodbye?"

Lyla wanted to run into the closest bathroom, hide inside a stall, and cry her eyes out.

Allison reached for her hand and squeezed it tightly, a gentle show of her support.

"He didn't say anything," Lyla said, rolling her lips together.

Bailey reached for Lyla's other hand. Was her devastation that obvious?

"It's okay. This is your day," Lyla told Bailey, blinking her tears away. "You only need to be concerned with you and your new husband." She hugged Bailey again, careful not to get caught on Bailey's veil this time.

"I'll tell my brother what an idiot he is later," Bailey promised.

"No, don't do that. He's actually pretty smart. We're going to go grab a cupcake," Lyla told her, stepping away with Allison.

And then they were going to leave, because Lyla wasn't sure she could hold herself together for much longer.

Minutes feel like hours when you don't have a couch or TV, or anything to distract your brain when you need it most. Lyla had been home for barely two hours, and she was losing her mind. If she was going to live here for any length of time, she needed a few things.

Resolved, and still wearing the dress she'd worn to Bailey's wedding, Lyla got into her car and drove over to the thrift store. It didn't close until 6:00 p.m., which gave her a solid half hour to make her living situation a little homier.

"Here to drop off more things?" the thrift shop manager asked, remembering her face.

"Here to find a few things. Do you by chance have a TV?"

"Of course I do."

"And a coffeemaker?" she asked hopefully.

"You're in luck." The man loaded her cart with all her requests. Then she checked out and put them in her trunk. She told herself to drive home, but found herself driving in the opposite direction toward the empty lot where Travis had his camper. Maybe he was still there. The wedding was only a few hours earlier. It was possible that he hadn't left without saying goodbye.

As she slowed her car on the road where Travis had been living, her hopes draining out of her, leaving a painful ache in her chest. The lot was empty. His RV was gone. He was gone too.

Tears rolled down Lyla's cheeks. She wiped them away as quickly as they fell, but they kept coming, springing to her eyes until she had to pull over on the side of the road because she couldn't see. When she was done, she drove back to her parents' home and went inside and cried some more.

When the sun came up the next morning, Lyla felt hungover from all her crying the previous day. She used her new coffeemaker and prepared a cup of much-needed coffee. Then she sat on a lawn chair she'd purchased at the thrift store and reached for the old diary she'd found under her mattress the week before. She opened it to a page near the back, choosing it at random, and began to read.

Dear Diary,

I looked Travis square in the face and promised that we'd keep in touch on a daily basis. I promised, knowing that it was a lie. I can't be friends with a guy that I have feelings for, and I can't have feelings for someone who's six hours away. I have dreams to chase and a life to conquer. So, I told him that me going off to college wasn't goodbye, but I lied. I already know he won't forgive me for this and I probably won't forgive myself.

Goodbye, Travis.

Lyla rolled her eyes. What kind of logic was that? That she had to turn her back on the possibility of love to achieve her successes. Lyla sipped her coffee and then got to work, making the house feel a little more like home. When she stood, her eye caught on the bucket list, still on her kitchen counter—still with one unchecked item. Hurricane Bill had come and gone, wreaking havoc on her parents' home, but there was still a lot to lose. That last summer in Echo Cove, Lyla had lost her very best friend, all because she was too scared to keep him. To lose him. To be so weighed down that she never learned to fly.

Maybe jumping off the Pirate's Plank wouldn't make Travis forgive her, but she didn't want to run from fear anymore. She wanted to run toward it. There was that one item on the old bucket list she and Travis had made, and she didn't want to avoid it anymore. Instead, she felt compelled to check it off, and she wanted to do it now.

Her phone rang.

Lyla answered. "Hello?"

"What are you doing?" Allison asked. "Want to plan a Dinnerware Party with me?"

"I would love to, but first I have something important I have to do."

"Oh? What's that?" Allison asked.

Lyla started walking toward her bedroom to find her bathing suit. "I'm going for a swim."

"What? Now?"

Lyla was well aware that she was making a rash, possibly irrational decision. "Yes. Now." There was no time like the present, and if she waited, she might back out.

"Fine. Then I'm going with you," Allison said immediately.

"I didn't ask you to come." Although it wasn't a bad idea. If Lyla was even considering getting into the lake, she should have someone with her. Never swim alone was a rule for good reason.

"If you go under, I go under too," Allison added. "Because that's what friends do."

Lyla felt her brow line bunch up. "I thought friends were there to make sure you didn't go under. Shouldn't you be offering to save me if I go under?"

"I would, but I can't swim," Allison said. "But I'll at least call nine-one-one."

Lyla laughed quietly into the phone. "You should learn to swim. I'll teach you next summer."

"You're coming back to town?" Allison asked. "For what?"

"For you. Among other things."

"Or people." Allison squealed happily. "Let me get my swimsuit on. I'll meet you at the lake."

Lyla disconnected the call and blew out a breath. Then she pulled open her dresser drawer and grabbed her favorite one-piece swimsuit. After stripping down, she stepped into the bathing suit and pulled it up her body, hooking the straps over her shoulders. She was doing this. Sink or swim. And a little added motivation to stay afloat was that if she sank, she was taking Allison down with her. Allison didn't deserve that. She deserved the world, and so did Lyla.

August 31

Dear Diary,

I'm about to leave home for the first time in my life, and my mind feels suddenly very quiet. My mind is never quiet. It's always racing, chasing new ideas and thoughts. I don't like the silence. It's lonely and I haven't even left yet.

I dug a hole in my parents' backyard and it felt like I was burying our friendship. In reality, I was burying my time capsule with a dozen things inside that remind me of this awful summer. The bucket list is in there too. For the first time, it's unfinished. According to Travis, that means bad luck. I'm not sure my luck can get any worse though.

In ten years or whatever, I'll dig this time capsule back up and look at the items inside. Hopefully the woman I am on the other side is a better version of me. I can't wait to meet her. I hope she's cool and has amazing hair. I've always wanted to be a redhead. Maybe she'll have red hair. Maybe she'll have a cool job where she gets to write all the time. Hopefully she's kissed a boy by then. Hopefully she's gone through all the bases and has done more than that.

Anyway, Travis is gone, the time capsule is buried, and my bags are packed. Unfortunately, dear diary, this is goodbye for us too. I'm going to slip you under my mattress and see you later. You aren't meant to go to college, but I am.

Yours Truly,

Lyla Dune, a woman destined for greatness

Chapter 29

Opinion: If it scares you,
that means you're doing something right.
—Lyla Dune, aspiring author

Memory Lake was empty. People in town were still cleaning up after Hurricane Bill. After such a big storm, one would think the water would be murky and full of debris. It wasn't, though. The lake was crystal clear. The reflection showed nothing but blue sky that went on for miles. It was as if there'd been no storm at all.

She kept walking, ignoring the slight tremble in her body. It felt like it was now or never—like the rest of her life hinged on gathering her courage, being brave, and jumping off that stupid Pirate's Plank.

Sink. Or swim.

"You can do it!" Allison called out in her best cheerleader voice from high school. She had stopped walking several feet back. Maybe it was all talk that she'd be going down too if Lyla sank like a piece of lead. "You got this! You are—!"

Lyla cast a glare over her shoulder, silencing Allison. Then she continued forward, one foot in front of the other. She left her towel on a large rock. The same rock she'd left it on that summer when she was fifteen. She climbed the wooden steps that led to the Pirate's Plank, a narrow strip of wood that had been the focal point of all her adult nightmares.

Slowly, she stepped onto the plank and felt a rush of adrenaline zip from the top of her scalp to the tips of her toes. No wonder she'd been scared that day. Being up here was indeed terrifying. Actually, it was a bad idea. So bad. If she drowned out here today, there was no one to jump in and save her. Allison said she would dial 911, but by the time any emergency crew got there, it'd be too late. Lyla would be dead, and what would be the point of that?

She took a step backward and her body lost balance momentarily. Her arms flew out by her sides.

Jump, Jump, Jump.

The sounds of the past haunted her. She was suddenly frozen, listening to the chant in her head, too scared to turn on the board and lose her balance again. But she couldn't move forward either.

As she stood there, trying to figure what her next move was, a light flashed in her peripheral vision. A firefly. It flashed again, a few feet forward, and this time she saw it plainly. It was so clear that she could make out its little wings and body. The light flashed as bright as a candle even though it was daytime.

Opinion: Magic isn't just for children with big imaginations. It's for everyone willing to believe.

Lyla closed her eyes, shutting everything out for just a moment. No more freeze mode. No more flight. This time she was going to fight.

Taking a breath, she opened her eyes, and stepped forward again. It was a silly bucket list. Not checking items off didn't give her bad luck, surely. The only thing left to repeat itself that summer was saying goodbye to Travis. He'd already said goodbye, though. Keeping him in Echo Cove wasn't the reason she needed to do this. She needed to do this because she was tired of letting her fear win.

"You can do it!" Allison called from far away.

Lyla didn't acknowledge her this time. She looked down into the depths of the clear lake water. The fear was still there, taunting her. The urge to turn back was so strong, but she was stronger. *I can do this.* If she didn't, some part of her would always regret it.

Sucking in a deep breath, she bent her knees, and canceling out the loud voices in her head, all telling her to turn around and go back, she propelled herself forward. The one-point-five seconds it took for her to hit the water felt like minutes. A million thoughts rushed through her mind as if her life was flashing before her eyes. Her most pressing thought was that she hadn't done anything in her life that she'd wanted to. She wasn't who she wanted to be—not yet. She was treading water in this life, surviving but not thriving. She hadn't succeeded in love, hadn't landed her dream job. Hadn't written that book and become the author her younger self had wanted to become.

The water swallowed her up and sucked her down before it spat her back out. She gasped as she broke through the lake's surface, flailing her arms and legs and thrashing wildly about. Then she laughed as she gathered her bearings, treading water while using her hands to wipe water from her eyes. "Yes! Yes! Yesssssss!" Her voice echoed off the surrounding trees.

She kicked and looked around, making sure she was only making a fool of herself in front of Allison. Then she yelled one more time. "Take that, fear! My professional opinion is that you're overrated!" Breathlessly, she swam to the shore and lay out on the ground, face up to the sun, soaking in its warmth and this moment. She felt amazing. A weight had been lifted off her, and she imagined that she could float away right now if she wanted to.

Tears rose in her throat, making their way to her eyes. She wasn't even sure what they were for. Happiness? Sadness? Both?

"I can't believe you actually did it." Allison lay back on the shore beside her. "You. Are. Amazing."

Lyla wiped at a tear that slipped down her cheek and turned her head to look at Allison. "So are you."

They lay there quietly for minutes that turned into half an hour.

"I wish Travis could have seen me," Lyla said when she finally sat up. "He won't believe that I actually jumped. He used to call me a scaredy-cat."

"Well, you have me as your witness. I saw it. Is this the thing that's always scared you most?" Allison asked.

Lyla was taken off guard by the question. She thought about her answer, wanting to say yes, but that wouldn't be the truth. "No," she finally said.

"No? There's something scarier than jumping off a piece of wood suspended over a large bottomless lake?"

Lyla's breath hitched as she realized that, yeah, there was something that had always scared her more. That last summer in Echo Cove had ended with leaving Travis without telling him how she felt. She'd been too terrified that he would laugh or reject her somehow. She was still harboring that same fear.

She could make a different choice this time, though. She could tell Travis how she felt, even if it was scary. Even though he still could leave and probably would. Their relationship didn't hinge on checking off the final item on their bucket list. It hinged on her taking another leap—a leap of faith.

"I need to go home and get dry," she told Allison, holding

a hand above her eyes to shield them from the sun. "And then I need a glass of wine and some time to think. I have a lot to think about."

Allison seemed to understand. "I know you do. Anything I can do to help?"

Instead of answering, Lyla leaned over and gave Allison a long, tight hug. "You are the best friend. Thanks for being here. I'll call you later."

"If you don't, I'll show up at your door," Allison threatened, pointing a finger in her direction.

"Counting on it." Lyla stood. "Are you coming?"

"No." Allison shook her head. "I have some things to think about too. I'm going to sit here a while."

Lyla nodded. "You're not jumping though?"

Allison laughed. "No way. I don't have any bucket list to take care of."

"We'll take care of that next summer," Lyla said.

Allison pulled back and tilted her head. "Sounds like a plan. Can we put hosting a few Dinnerware Parties on your next list?"

"We'll talk about it. Later." With a wave, Lyla headed back to her car as a million thoughts raced through her mind at once. She'd jumped off the Pirate's Plank, but deep down, she knew the only way to change fate for this last looming awful thing—Travis leaving forever—was for her to tell him how she felt.

Travis was upset with her, and she understood why. When she'd left for college, promising to keep in touch, she hadn't. Now they'd grown close again and her last opinion article had sent a clear message that she wasn't committed. In his mind, that probably meant that Lyla would ghost him again when she left this time.

Maybe that was true before this afternoon. Maybe she would have let the fear of exploring something real with

Travis scare her. Not now, though. Now she knew it was okay to be scared, but jump anyway. Always jump.

Before she put her car in motion, she stared at her phone debating whether to text Travis one more time. He wasn't responding to her, so she should have gotten the message by now. She should leave him alone. He had made his choice. It was clear. But unable to help herself, her finger began tapping along the screen to send one more text that he could ignore. Maybe not even read.

Lyla: *Hi. I was wondering if you knew a good handyman to help me with some damage on my home?*

She hit SEND and immediately regretted it. She'd already texted apologies. What more could she say? Nothing. And he was saying nothing as well. On a deep exhalation, she put the car in motion.

Once she got to her parents' house, she changed clothes and poured herself a red Solo cup of cheap Chardonnay. She had an opinion article to write. One she was pretty sure would be her last. She was tired of holding on so tightly to something she didn't love anymore. She loved writing, but she was tired of writing opinions that weren't necessarily hers. It was time to move on. Move forward. Dive into the unknown.

Sitting against her kitchen wall, her laptop laid across her thighs, she sipped and typed. Instead of writing her final article, however, she opened a new Word document and started working on a story. There was no outline. She had no idea what this story was about, but the characters showed up on the page as if they were real live people. Inspiration flowed in and through her, and the story poured out like it was writing itself. She was just the instrument. This is how writing had felt when she was young and had first fallen in love with the process. Writing was supposed to feel like magic, and in this moment, it did. It felt like fireflies and those little coincidences that were never coincidences at all. It felt like those first sparks between two people destined to fall in love.

Opinion: If it feels easy and effortless, it's probably right.

Being back in Echo Cove felt easy too. She loved this house. No, it was more than that. It was a home. She didn't mind that her parents were ready to leave. She wasn't. In fact, maybe she wanted to buy the house. The thought sprang up out of her as if it had come from some other source, just like the words of her story. There'd been some sort of wall blocking her from even considering the thought. But now the wall seemed to have crumbled, and there the thought was. The idea of staying no longer seemed like a death sentence. It felt like the golden ticket to the life of her dreams.

Dreams didn't have to be on such a grand scale. Dreams could be small, at least in others' eyes. A dream only needed to feed excitement. Contentment. Happiness.

Who was she, and where had the old Lyla gone? Maybe the old Lyla had been left at the bottom of Memory Lake this morning. She'd plunged into the chilly waters and had left her fear and reservations at the bottom, and she'd come back up taking the first breath of a new life.

As she sipped from her red Solo cup, she poured herself into her story. Time disappeared, which was exactly how it felt to be in "the zone." Once she was done for the day, she got up and stretched. The list was done, and all the events of that last summer had repeated, playing out in the same, but also different, ways.

All except . . .

Oh, no. A memory surfaced. There was one final disaster from that summer. Sonny. He'd chased a couple of kids on the street, being his watchful, guard dog self and no doubt trying to keep the children safe. And in return, he'd died.

Sonny was dead, but Ms. Hadley had another little dog that loved to chase and bark, as well. What if that was yet another event destined to reoccur?

Crap! Crap, crap, crap! She'd drunk an entire cup of wine. She couldn't drive. What was the likelihood that this new dog would have the same fate as Sonny? A sane person would say it was next to nothing, but she knew better. Nothing about this summer would make sense to a sane person.

Veering toward the garage, she grabbed her bike and pedaled as hard and fast as she could. Ms. Hadley's new little dog didn't come out to chase after her, which was a small confirmation that something horrible might happen. But not if she could stop it first.

Sweat rolled down her face and her breathing was labored. Sonny had been hit near the town square, right where the little memorial for him was these days. She'd just ride around the area and make sure the little dog was nowhere in sight.

As she drew closer to the town square, however, she heard tires screech—an unmistakable sound of a car slamming on brakes. She heard the screams of a child as well.

"No. No, no, no!" Lyla pedaled impossibly faster, nearly getting hit by a car herself. Poor Ms. Hadley couldn't lose another dog, and Lyla didn't want to lose this new little dog either. He reminded her so much of Sonny.

Rounding a corner, she saw a car and a blue truck were stopped diagonally in opposing lanes as if they'd hit each other head-on. Travis's truck.

Lyla got off the bike, threw it down, and raced toward the scene. Travis's truck and the car had T-boned. The impact was clear, but it didn't look like they'd hit at high speed. The indentation on both vehicles was minor. In a panic, Lyla searched until she spotted Travis sitting on Sonny's memorial bench with a little boy at his side. The child was obviously upset, but he didn't appear to be hurt.

Lyla stopped for a moment, wondering at the scene. As she stood there, a woman ran past her, screaming the boy's name.

"Jeremiah!"

The boy looked over and ran toward his mother, embracing her and crying harder.

"I was almost hit by a car!" the boy cried, loud enough for Lyla to overhear. His voice was shrill and upset. "If not for the truck, it would have hit me for sure!"

Lyla couldn't process what she was seeing. She'd come to save the little dog, but there was no dog. Just Travis sitting there, his shoulders rounded as if he was exhausted.

"Are you okay?" she asked, gaining his attention as she walked toward him.

He looked exhausted, like someone who'd been through an ordeal. Honestly, she felt the same. "I suppose so. I'm a hard man to break. At least physically."

Guilt bloomed in her stomach.

He watched her as she stood there in front of him, wringing her hands. "What are you doing here?"

"I could ask you the same. I thought you left already."

"I did. Then I remembered that Kevin was nearly hit on his bike that last summer here."

Lyla's mouth fell open. "I thought you didn't believe things were repeating."

"Maybe it's not that I believe that things are repeating as much as I believe in you." His brown eyes narrowed. "I was driving out of town, and I remembered how Ms. Hadley's little dog was hit chasing Kevin on his bike."

Kevin, who was now the town's mayor.

"I thought there was a slim possibility that another kid might find themselves in the same situation. It was nearly noon because the church bells were tolling. I looked at the time on my dash and turned around and came here to the town square."

"Where the bench for Ms. Hadley's dog Sonny is now,"

Lyla agreed. "That's why I was racing up here too. I worried another of these wild coincidences might happen." She looked around for the dog, suddenly worried. If the boy was okay, did that mean—? "Where is he?"

"Where's who?" Travis asked.

She thought they were on the same page, trying to stop fate one more time. "Ms. Hadley's dog."

Travis shook his head. "Ms. Hadley doesn't have a dog. I did a job for her a few weeks back. She told me she could never replace Sonny."

"No dog? There wasn't a little brown dog here?" she asked, her mind whirling.

"Just the boy on the bike, which is what I was looking for. I was parked across the street, waiting for noon to pass to ensure there wasn't a kid in danger somehow. Truth be told, I was about to leave when I saw the kid ride up on his bike. He was holding an ice cream cone and trying to steer with one hand. Then he veered into the oncoming lane as a car was coming fast. I honked my horn, but realized the driver wasn't going to see the boy before it was too late." Travis ran a hand through his hair, looking stressed as he relived the moment. "I hit the gas and just plowed between them."

"Saving the boy's life. The woman. Is she okay?" Lyla asked, taking in all the information.

"Yeah. She was texting and driving. She seemed a little shaken up about what nearly happened, but she's fine. Everyone is fine."

"Your truck," Lyla said.

"It can be fixed. As a handyman, it my firm belief that anything can be fixed." The way he was looking at Lyla suggested he was referring to so much more than just his truck. "Now that my truck is damaged, though, I guess I'll be staying in Echo Cove a little longer."

Well, that was new. The first time they'd parted, she'd kept her feelings hidden, and there hadn't been a second chance for her to say all the things built up inside of her. Maybe that meant fate was changing.

"Travis, I didn't mean what I wrote in my article. In fact, it was all a huge lie. A lie I told the entire country—and myself. All my opinions over the last year have been lies. They aren't real. They don't reflect my true values. My thoughts."

His brows lifted high on his forehead, but he remained silent, waiting for her to say more.

"I've only been writing those things out of fear of losing something I didn't even want. I only stayed with Joe out of fear of never finding what I truly want and need. Everything I've done since leaving town at eighteen has been out of fear."

"And now?"

"And now . . . Now, I'm still afraid," she admitted. "In fact, I was terrified when I jumped into Memory Lake this morning."

Surprise crinkled his forehead. "I thought you didn't believe it was bad luck not to finish the bucket list."

"And I thought you didn't believe things from that last summer together were repeating."

"Maybe not, but I believe in you, Ly. I always have."

It was hard to pull in a full breath with all the butterflies—*scratch that*—fireflies in her stomach. "That's why you always pushed me with those things on our lists." She reached out and laid a hand over his. "Travis, I'm sorry I hurt you. If this summer has taught me anything, it's that do-overs actually do exist. I'm not sure how it would look if we gave our relationship another chance, because I'll be here in Echo Cove, and you'll be roaming the world. I want to try, though."

"What do you mean you'll be here?" he asked. "Last I heard, you were in a hurry to get on with living your life."

"That's still true, but I've decided I'll be living my life here. I'm staying. In fact, I'm buying my parents' home." She couldn't contain the smile that stretched through her cheeks.

"I'm also writing the book of my heart, thanks to your encouragement."

"Yeah? That's great, Ly. I'm happy for you."

She laughed even though she was all nerves, knowing the next thing she was about to say. "And I'm hoping my best friend will forgive me and consider widening the friend zone." She raised a finger. "Because it's my true opinion that you don't have to step out of the friend zone to fall in love. In fact, love and friendship go hand in hand."

Travis's eyes bore into hers. "That doesn't sound so delusional to me," he said quietly.

"That's because it's not 'Delilah's Delusions' talking. It's Lyla Dune. Me."

His gaze roamed the town square. The commotion had died down, the boy and his mother were gone, and a tow truck was hooking up the woman's car. "The thing about being a traveling handyman is that I decide where I want to be. I've been looking for home since I left town." He returned his attention to her. "And I think I've realized that home has been here all along."

"Echo Cove?"

"No, Ly." He angled his body on the bench. "Opinion: Home isn't a place. It's a person. For me, home is you."

She wondered if she should say what she wanted to. The only reason not to was the fear that he might not say it back. But it didn't matter. When you felt this deeply about someone, you had to say it. No matter what. "I think I love you."

Travis didn't even blink. "You *think*?"

Her smile was shaky, like her legs while standing on the Pirate's Plank. She was facing something that terrified her to her core, but turning back wasn't an option. "I know, actually."

"This isn't one of your pranks, is it?" There was a teasing glint to his eyes.

She tilted her head. "You were always more the practical joker. And that would be one brutal prank, wouldn't it?"

"It would. Because I think I love you too. In fact, I know it."

The admission felt like nothing Lyla had ever experienced. Like every cell in her body was overflowing with joy. "That's a good thing."

"Yeah, it is. Look at the two of us. I wish I could rewind time and get back all the years we've lost."

Lyla shook her head quickly. "No, no—no time traveling, okay? How about we just leave time exactly how it is, shall we? I happen to like this point in time very much." She tilted her head, watching him. "I was thinking, maybe you need a home with roots to rest up in every now and then."

"And I might need a traveling partner every now and then too."

Seeing that she worked remotely, that sounded perfect. "The best of both worlds."

Something flashed in Lyla's peripheral vision. She turned to see a tiny firefly as it twinkled again, already knowing that Travis couldn't see it. She also instinctively understood that it was the last "magic" firefly she'd ever see in broad daylight or in places where fireflies shouldn't be.

She'd done what she hadn't even known she'd come home to do. She'd dug up the time capsule full of memories, which were never truly buried in the past, and with Travis, she had completed that old bucket list and faced her fears. Now it was time to move forward.

Opinion: Sometimes moving forward means staying exactly where you are.

Epilogue

*Opinion: Time shouldn't fly when you're having fun.
It should slow down, and you should remember to
enjoy it—every moment.*
—Lyla Dune, aspiring author

Lyla raced into the wind that kissed her cheeks and ran its fingers through her newly red hair as she sat on Sonny's memorial bench in the town square. She was trying something that she would have been too scared to try in her former life. Now, she laughed in the face of fears like that. Granted, the first time she'd dyed her hair, it had been more orange than fiery red, and she'd cried for an hour straight. The second box had done the trick though, and she loved who she saw looking back at her in the mirror.

"Hey, Sonny," she said, speaking softly. There was no dog there. The little dog she'd seen hadn't returned since the accident, and she suspected he wouldn't. Just like the magical fireflies and all the "coincidences" this past month and a half, he was part of whatever strange and mystical experience had taken place just for her. "I want you to know—heel-nipper, bike-chaser, or not—you were a good dog. I also want you to know that Ms. Hadley's okay. You could never be replaced, but Travis and I did convince her to try again. You'd like Ruby. She's as feisty as you, and she keeps Ms. Hadley company."

Lyla traced her fingers along the grooves of Sonny's name on the bench. After a moment, she stood and climbed back onto her old glittery purple beach cruiser. "See you later, Sonny," she called as she pushed off, pedaling fast, and soaking in the feeling of freedom as she made her way home.

Home. She'd put the offer in today, laughing in the face of that fear, as well. Deep down some part of her had been considering purchasing her childhood home since she'd arrived in Echo Cove in early summer. The house would be hers, and her parents could take the money to continue their trip around the world.

Opinion: Sometimes the road to nowhere is linear and the road to success is a full circle.

Lyla's phone buzzed in her pocket. She put her legs down and used her feet to stop her bike along the roadside, kicking up dirt as she skidded to a halt. She pulled her phone out and saw Bob's name on the screen. "Hey, Bob," she answered, as she admired the landscape ahead. The colors of fall were in full effect. Reds, oranges, yellows, and browns painted the blur of trees before her.

"You're quitting?" Bob practically yelled, getting straight to business. "You don't quit until I say you quit," he demanded, stressing every syllable.

"My contract is up, Bob," she said calmly. "I'm not signing the new one."

"And just what do you think you're going to do, huh?" Bob asked in an almost mocking tone. He sounded angry, but Lyla knew better. She recognized the screech of desperation that she heard. Bob was scared.

"Write a book. I'm going to write a novel."

Bob began to chuckle. "You're more delusional than I thought. Everyone and their mother wants to write a book, Lyla. Not everyone is cut out for it though."

"Maybe not, but I am." Lyla ran her opposite hand over the smooth cream-colored leather of her bicycle seat. "I appreciate the years we've worked together," she said, meaning it. If not for her column, she might not have realized how cynical and bitter life was making her. She could easily look back to all her opinion articles and see the progression from someone who was curious and excited to a woman dulled by life's blows. If not for this summer, she might have continued down a path that didn't lead to happiness.

"Yeah, well, good for you." There wasn't an ounce of sincerity in Bob's tone. "You aren't that special of a snowflake. I can find someone else to write those opinions for the column. Don't think I can't."

Lyla waited for the fear to grip her, but it didn't. There was no trace of anything other than peace with her decision. "Goodbye, Bob." She disconnected the call and shoved her phone back into her pocket, feeling freer than ever. Free as the wind that pressed against her back and lifted her fiery red hair along the sides of her face. Sliding back onto her bike's seat, she took hold of the handlebars. Then she pushed off with her feet on the pedals and coasted back home.

A dog barked in the distance, loud and high-pitched.

Opinion: As long as memories exist, there are no true goodbyes.

After rolling her bike into the garage, Lyla headed into the kitchen and grabbed a bottled water, taking long gulps. She set the bottle down when the doorbell rang and hurried to open the door. "Ms. Hadley. You're a little early," she said.

"I know, I know." Her older neighbor stepped inside, holding a tray of finger foods. "Where should I put these?"

"On the kitchen counter. The others will arrive soon." Lyla gestured down the hall. "Do you mind if I go change?"

"Of course not. I'll answer the door if anyone arrives," Ms. Hadley said.

"Thank you." Lyla headed back to her bedroom and pulled on a pair of jeans and a soft T-shirt. Then she stepped into the bathroom and splashed some water on her face. After running a brush through her hair, she pulled it into a smooth ponytail. Her reflection stopped her for a moment. There was something different about her face, and it wasn't because of her new dye job. It took her a moment to process. This was what satisfaction and contentment looked like.

Opinion: True happiness is the ultimate facelift.

She wasn't in the business of writing opinions anymore. All opinions were her own, and even if no one else in the world cared, she did. She heard the doorbell ring again and knew her friends were here. Tonight, they were having a Dinnerware Party. Her. Allison. Bernadette. Ms. Hadley. And Travis's sister, Bailey. Lyla had even invited her old teacher, Ms. Davis—Louise. Lyla was going to fill her cabinets with BPA-free Tupperware and her home with laughter. And lots of love.

Then tomorrow she'd wake up at 4:00 a.m. and continue writing the book she'd always dreamed of. She had to wake early before her shift at Bean Time Coffee. Sure, some might look at her new lifestyle as a downgrade. In her not-so-professional opinion, however, this new life of hers was an upgrade.

"Lyla-la-la-la!" Louise sang out, calling for her down the hall.

"Lyla, where are you?" Allison called as well. "Come on! The party can't start without you!"

Lyla gave herself another once-over in the mirror, then turned and headed toward the living room with a spring in her step. The couch and recliners she'd purchased at the second-hand store a couple weeks back were full. The countertop was also full, covered with delicious homemade dishes and sugary treats. A lot of moments had seemed to repeat this past summer, but never in her life had she hosted a house full of friends. In fact, she was sure that all the déjà-vu moments and coincidences were over. Now all she needed to do was focus on the future—which, from this viewpoint, looked brighter than ever.

Lyla looked at Allison. "So, how do we start this Dinnerware Party?"

Allison sat on the couch and crossed her legs. "It's your party, Ly. How do you want to start it?"

"With drinks?" Bernadette suggested. "That's always a good place to begin."

Lyla laughed and gestured to her kitchen counter. "Be my guest. We can all pour a drink and have a toast to get us started. How about that?"

"Great suggestion," Ms. Hadley agreed.

Once everyone had a red Solo cup in hand, Lyla raised her drink, prompting everyone else to do so as well.

"A toast to new friends and new beginnings." Lyla tapped her cup to those around her.

"A toast to new neighbors," Ms. Hadley added.

The cups remained in the air.

"A toast to old friends, as well." Bernadette scanned the group, her gaze landing on Lyla. "And old enemies turned friends."

"Hear, hear." Lyla looked at Allison, who hadn't said anything yet.

"A toast to . . ." Allison seemed to ponder what she wanted to say. It was rare that Allison was ever at a loss for words. "A toast to memories, new and old, good and bad."

Lyla thought she saw her friend put on an invisible mask for a moment, forcing a wobbly smile. It only lasted a second before Allison exhaled and seemed to relax. She didn't need to mask with the folks in this room. She didn't need to pretend that everything was perfect, because it wasn't. That didn't mean it wasn't full, though.

"A toast to loved ones who may not be here physically with us," Allison said, "but who are always here in our hearts."

Lyla held her cup up in the air with one hand and reached for Allison with her other hand. Everyone else reached for Allison as well, holding her until the invisible mask slid away and Allison's eyes filled with tears. "I'm not crying because I'm sad," she said through shallow breaths. "These tears are because I'm so overwhelmed by the amazingness in this room."

With a serious face, Louise began, "*Amazingness* is not a word," then interrupted herself. "Sorry! Once an English teacher, always an English teacher."

The group laughed.

"Are we done with the toasting?" Lyla looked around.

"One more," Allison said, sniffling softly. "A toast to good Dinnerware. Like friends, a woman can never have enough."

They tapped their cups and drank their wine. Afterward, they all sat back and laughed until they cried, and cried until they laughed.

Lyla awoke with a start the next morning, lifting her head to see that Allison was in the bed beside her. Allison was a lightweight and had drunk too much last evening, and she'd fallen asleep on Travis's side of the bed.

Quietly, Lyla climbed out of bed. Peeking in the living room, she soaked in the sight of Travis sleeping on her couch. Making as little noise as possible, she poured ground coffee into a filter and turned on her coffeemaker. As she waited for her coffee to brew, she looked at her back window. The cypress tree had been dragged away by Travis, but the stump remained. Travis had sanded it down and used some of the wood to create a bench top that sat on the old stump. She looked at a Dr Pepper bottle on the kitchen counter now. It no longer held soda, but it wasn't exactly empty. Inside, she'd dropped ten items to remind her of the last couple months, which had been life-altering, to say the least.

Stepping over to the new time capsule, she began to pull the items out one by one. A bottle cork from The Sippy Cup. This exact cork was the one from the first bottle she'd shared with Allison when she'd first arrived this summer. Next, she pulled out a business card for The Handyman and laughed quietly. Travis was and forever would be her handyman. Reaching into the bottle again, she pulled out a receipt for the shovel she'd purchased from Mr. Tibbs and then a party favor from Bailey's wedding. All these were memories from one of the most amazing summers she'd had, full of highs and lows, but no regrets.

Reaching into the bottle another time, her fingers brushed up against a folded piece of paper. She and Travis had been working on a new bucket list all week, but they only had one to-do on it. The item was written in Travis's handwriting.

Travis and Lyla's Forever Bucket List
- Get married and live happily ever after.

When he'd written the lines a few days earlier, she'd immediately started crying.

"Bad luck if you don't check that item off, Ly."

"Well, I don't want any more of that." She'd stared at him for a long moment, her thoughts racing. She was almost scared to believe it was true, because bringing her hopes up that high would surely bring a painful crash if it wasn't. "Not a prank?"

"Not a prank." There was something vulnerable in his expression as he waited for her answer. He hadn't even asked a question, though.

Finally, she'd taken the pen from his hand and checked the hand-drawn box on the paper.

"Is that a yes?" he'd asked.

She put the pen down and leaned into him, pressing a kiss to his lips. "Yes."

It was a simple proposal, but that's all they needed.

With a sigh, she reached into the bottle now and pulled out one last item—a page from the diary she'd written in the summer that she was eighteen. Last week, she'd added a final entry. Then she tore it out, folded it neatly, and placed it inside. Because this wasn't about the past, as journal entries usually are. It was more about the future.

Dear Diary,

I was wrong. I never needed to go off to find myself. Actually, I left Echo Cove and got lost. Now I'm back and I'm grateful for all the mistakes and the journey because they led me exactly where I want to be. Ten years from now when I dig up this new time capsule and open you, dearest diary, I hope there will have been many more mistakes because they create change for the better. I also hope there will be many more friends, laughs, and the little moments in between that make life full.

Opinion: Bottle up the ordinary moments. It's the ordinary that leads to the extraordinary memories of a lifetime.

See you in the next ten years, Diary.

Yours Truly,
Lyla, aspiring author, best friend, daughter, and future Mrs. Handyman

Acknowledgments

As I reflect on the journey of bringing this nugget of an idea to life in a novel, I'm overwhelmed with gratitude for the many individuals who donated their time, talent, and support to make this book a reality.

First and foremost, I owe an immense debt of gratitude to my incredible editors, Elizabeth Trout and Shannon Plackis. Your collaborative efforts and keen insights shaped this story in ways I never could have imagined. Shannon, your ability to share my vision for this book and expand on it was invaluable. Elizabeth, your fresh perspective and thoughtful suggestions breathed new life into scenes that I thought were already finished. Together, you were my "dream team." You both pushed me to dig deeper, to find the heart of this story, and to bring out the best in my writing.

To the entire team at Kensington Publishing, I extend my heartfelt thanks. Your collective efforts transformed my manuscript into the book that readers now hold in their hands. Jane, my publicist extraordinaire, your enthusiasm and creative strategies are instrumental in connecting this story with its audience. To the meticulous copy editor and proofreader, I extend my appreciation for your attention to detail. You've caught the things I've missed and polished the scenes and chapters until they shine. And to the talented cover artist who has created such a beautiful and inspired cover—thank you so very much for capturing the essence of this story.

Sarah Younger, my literary agent extraordinaire, where would I be without your unwavering support and guidance? Thank you for believing in me and for always being in my corner. I'm deeply grateful for your partnership.

To my longtime critique partner, Rachel: As one of my first readers, you've seen this story in its rawest form and helped

314 Acknowledgments

shape it from the very beginning. Your honest feedback and insightful suggestions were crucial to this project.

And Laura, your role as one of my early readers for this project has been equally vital. Your fresh eyes and perceptive comments were extremely helpful. Thank you for your time, your honesty, and your enthusiasm for this story. I appreciate all your expertise and help.

To Kimberly, my author assistant, your behind-the-scenes support has been essential in allowing me to focus on the creative aspects of this project. You keep me organized and on track, and I'm so grateful to have you on my team.

To my readers, especially my longtime and loyal fans like DeeAnn, thank you! Your support, enthusiasm, and willingness to embark on new literary journeys with me are what make this author's journey worthwhile. Thank you so much for your letters, your messages, and for sharing how my stories have touched your lives. You inspire me to keep writing, keep exploring, and keep pushing the boundaries of my craft.

Finally, to my family—words cannot express how much you all mean to me. Thank you for respecting my writing time, bearing with me through the deadline crunches, and for understanding when I'm lost in my fictional world (which may include my talking to myself).

To everyone mentioned here, and to those whose names I may have missed, please know that I could not do this without you—and I wouldn't want to. This book is as much a product of your efforts as it is mine.